Mr Vitriol

Paul Burns

Published in 2012 by FeedARead.com Publishing
– Arts Council funded

Copyright © Paul Burns

First Edition

The author has asserted their moral right under the Copyright, Designs and Patents Act, 1988, to be identified
as the author of this work.

All Rights reserved. No part of this publication may be reproduced, copied, stored in a retrieval system, or transmitted, in any form or by any means, without the prior written consent of the copyright holder, nor be otherwise circulated in any form of binding or cover other than that in which it is published and without a similar condition being imposed on the subsequent purchaser.

A CIP catalogue record for this title is available from the British Library.

All characters and names in Mr Vitriol, with the exception of the passing references to David Kelly and Bill Wyman, are fictional. Fort Gatgash has never existed. The business names used are also invented.

In memory of:

My mother and her many acts of kindness

Julia Burns (née Demunnik)

1919 – 2008

who was known as Julie to her friends

&

Baha Mousa

1977 – 2003

Who died as the result of prolonged torture

committed by British soldiers.

From the Report of the 2011 Baha Mousa Inquiry:

"My findings raise a significant concern about the loss of discipline and lack of moral courage to report abuse within 1st Battalion the Queen's Lancashire Regiment (1 QLR). A large number of soldiers, including senior NCOs, assaulted the Detainees in a facility in the middle of the 1 QLR camp which had no doors, seemingly unconcerned at being caught doing so. Several officers must have been aware of at least some of the abuse. A large number of soldiers, including
all those who took part in guard duty, also failed to intervene to stop the abuse or report it up the chain of command."

Inquiry witnesses described a culture of bullying within 1 QLR before the death of Baha Mousa and following it to deter the giving of evidence and punish those who had given a statement.

Chapter 1: Norman ~ Decoding Perry Gray

Before I had decoded Perry Gray's account of his life, I loathed Mr Vitriol, as the media had dubbed him before his unmasking. Now he abides with me the way some authors do even though one has never met them other than through their writing. Had someone a year ago foretold the looping path of my feelings towards Perry, I would have thought the prophet deranged. As such, I understand how others who learn what overtook me might question my grip on reality. All I ask is that you judge me in the round. The pages that follow dwell on a late flowering of quirkiness that is a small and untypical part of my life. Give some weight to my strait-laced decades defending national security, the family life I contributed to and other everyday activities.

My reaction to the news of Perry's death illustrates how much I used to detest him. A lunchtime forecast mentioned the possibility of thunderstorms, my oldest and most intractable phobia. I replaced plans for weeding with cleaning a jumble of plant pots in the large shed situated near Foxenearth's back fence. The morning's sunlight had filled the shed with a dry heat that, along with the scent of resin from the walls, evoked soporific memories of saunas until a chill gust slammed the door. The distracting sound of wind grew. By the time I had dealt with the last of the pots, stout branches swayed and patches of shadow zipped over the land. My chest tightened just as it had in childhood when there was the possibility of lightning.

Telling myself to buck up, I looked for another task to take my mind off the weather. Sharpening the lawnmower's helical blades within their confined housing requires concentration to avoid scraped knuckles. I angled the machine on the bench to catch the diminished daylight and clamped the cylinder with locking pliers before filing a third of each blade at a time. To counter the rasping, which had the same effect as nails on a blackboard, I turned on the paint-splattered radio hanging just above the window. Although the batteries were too flat for FM, medium wave brought a moan-a-minute talkback show hosted by a sharp-tongued woman bent on provoking reactions. Despite seldom agreeing with her or the callers, I admired their willingness to speak to an audience of thousands when sharing my opinions one-to-one was a rare event.

Radio interference heralded that electricity was in the air and dispelled the pretence of rationality that had allowed ignoring other storm signs. I longed to be curled up under a duvet with a pillow covering both ears and curtains drawn, but an exaggerated fear of attracting a bolt while crossing the garden made going the twenty yards to the house impossible. And Rose, my wife, would not collect me as she often did because she was out for the day. I inhaled as slowly and deeply as my jitters allowed, adjusting the filing to the new rhythm until the first thunderclap caused my hands to jolt as they pushed and angled the file. Little scallops of flesh were left hanging on the backs of two fingers. I leapt to the centre of the shed and squatted to ensure the maximum distance from anything metal. Just after wrapping a handkerchief around the bleeding, a very bright flash turned the panes purple for the blink of an eye. The lurid green wash that followed made the landscape appear alien. From habit, I counted out loud the seconds between lightning and thunderclap; the discharge was just over three miles away.

More like a six-year old than a man in his sixties, I chanted, "I'm insulated by wood and glass. The house and trees are taller. The ridges along the vale are higher still."

Then a great darkness, no doubt the shadow of an enormous anvil cloud, descended. Fear of the fizzing heavens stopped me switching on the light and I wanted to turn off the radio before the paltry current left in its batteries attracted the next strike. But what if the lightning arrived as I reached above the window for the knob? Before I could decide, breaking news distracted me.

"Mr Vitriol has been identified as Perry Gray, a computing consultant with no previous convictions. The police believe that Mr Gray took his own life shortly after sending them a letter admitting his guilt. More details in our next ..."

Static crackled. The sky dazzled. A boom rattled the shed before the glare had ended. I crouched lower with trembling hands shielding my ears, eyes shut tight and wondering if a flowerpot over my head would offer any protection. Probably not, because of the holes in the base. How about placing a saucer on top?

I smile now at my desperation. Back then there was not as much as an hysterical giggle; all I could manage was forcing my eyes to open and fighting the urge to soil my trousers.

The talkback host sought to enliven the show. "All those secrets taken to the grave by Mr Vitriol topping himself! If you could've asked this Perry Gray anything, what would you want to know? Or what would you want to say to him?"

Perspiration oozed despite the grisly chill penetrating the shed. Hail and several downpours came and went. Leaves swirled upwards as if summoned back to branches. And while I crouched through all this, the callers, rather than berate Perry Gray, continued with earlier topics, the pettiness of which compared to his crimes incensed me. Surely it was not too much to expect one of the Jeremiahs to express sentiments about the poison penman similar to mine? An urge to rant over the airwaves about Mr Vitriol took hold. How dare he evade justice and deprive his victims of the satisfaction of watching him squirm in court. Death was not punishment enough if he preferred it to imprisonment.

The squall passed leaving cracks of blue sky. Clouds lost first their black edges and then their dark hearts. After it felt safe enough to return to the workbench – though not to go outside – I switched off the radio and filed the mower blades like a man possessed. Sparks flew and metal scuffed skin. My rage had its roots in a mining village where bullying, especially the slanderous taunts about my father, had left me with an abhorrence of all who harass and defame. Mr Vitriol's hate mail had done both and perhaps worse.

In addition to detesting this criminal, I loathed the stupidity of my phobia and the wimpishness that inhibited voicing an opinion. Could I marshal arguments for a radio audience and appear credible rather than crackpot? Would the listeners wrongly assume from my vehemence that I was one of Mr Vitriol's victims? This emotional tempest swamped the reason that was ready to reassert itself with the passing of the cumulonimbus. At one point,

I considered using a fictitious name and a disguised voice to rail on the talk show against Perry for sending anonymous letters. Mercifully, I had not taken a phone to the shed, and by the time I ventured out the glut of adrenaline had exhausted me.

The British Intelligence community in the 1960s, and especially CARE, The Centre for Advanced Research and Evaluation, which I joined after National Service, retained a smattering of eccentrics recruited during the war from mathematics, chess, and philology. Other queer fish had been recruited via a fiendish cryptic crossword competition held to identify particularly divergent thinkers for Bletchley Park. One of the cruciverbalists was Iphigenia, a blue-blooded bluestocking who would hold in a cold stare anyone abbreviating her name to *Iffy* or *Genie*. Fortunately, a boffin had dubbed her Posy because of her fascination with Edgar Allan Poe and she liked this nickname the way she liked anything to do with this author. Posy would talk about Poe, lecture even, at the hint of an invitation and lampoon his fruity Gothic style, such as the time she heard the rattle of the tea trolley.

"Hark! What is this tintinnabulation? Could it be the blessed chariot that carries along with its cheering cups a selection of viands? The sylph of a driver enters our corridor with a countenance pale even to ghastliness and her deep-set eyes glaring with unnatural lustre. As if plutonian demons nipped at her heels, she has raced the vehicle to ensure our tea is at least lukewarm and the sandwiches no more curlicued than befits bread baked only last week. Let us partake of a gobletful and a morsel before the gliding feast escapes."

I assumed that she prepared these parodies in writing and rehearsed them at home. That is until the day she drove me to a meeting and we got caught in traffic behind an accident. While we waited for the police to sort out the jam, Posy provided an effortless running commentary in the style of Poe.

"How did you learn to do that?" I asked.

"It's nothing special. Many people who have immersed themselves in an author find they can simulate him. There are works by people who claim they penned literature that Poe and others dictated from beyond the grave. I doubt if any of these spirit writers could act as an amanuensis without having first read the author. Everyone who reads enough will find eventually an author who communicates more than is on the page."

"So what do you make of Harding?"

This was a question I had been waiting to ask. Harding was a fifty-something bachelor statistician who only spoke to colleagues about work or Blaise Pascal, whom he regarded as his friend and mentor. Staff did no more than smile wryly after Harding had updated us on Pascal's latest communications to him. I felt very odd because others acted as if there was no question of Harding being unhinged or a security risk and they were unperturbed by the other eccentrics, including Posy, whereas I was uneasy with oddballs.

"How do you mean?" She said it as if Harding was as conventional as me.

"He gives the impression of literally hearing the voice of Pascal."

"Oh, he does. And when he writes what Pascal has dictated, the seventeenth century French is most convincing. But you needn't worry. The dear man has been like that for years and it hasn't stopped him being highly productive or quite content as far one can tell. Mind you, when he was nominated for an MBE and asked for a second gong for Pascal it raised a few eyebrows at the Ministry."

Perhaps she found me rather dull and invented the second MBE to enliven the trip or simply to tease. I did not check with colleagues in case they laughed at my gullibility.

Perry Gray had communicated to me more than is on his pages and he became my friend. But not a mentor, because who in their right mind would want to be guided by a devious criminal? However, I have acquired compassion for him and a curious intimacy has grown between us, though not a relationship that has reduced my sympathy for the targets of his snooping and noxious letters. This change of heart brought about an unrivalled ability to understand Perry. Abhorrence, however much deserved, had blinkered me and still blinkers others, not least journalists and those expressing professional opinions about Mr Vitriol and his motives.

Perry became the senescent equivalent of a childhood imaginary friend. I had no pretend companion during my early years, at least not one who answered back. The God and guardian angel I then believed in were as mute as clams despite a dearth of earthly pals in the village. The faith instilled by my parents encompassed saints experiencing visions and hearing voices, and the fairy stories read to me featured preternatural beings, some of whom befriended unhappy children. Yet Christian superstitions and legends failed to inspire me then to invent a playmate. Is it not rich that after half a century of being a rationalist and sceptic I communicate with an entity hovering between illusion and delusion?

On the day after the announcement of Perry's death, newspapers revealed we were both born in 1940 and shared the same meagre height. In his most recent picture, taken only eight weeks before his death, Perry looked a decade younger than me. I am bald apart from a horseshoe of white hair; he sported a full grey mop. His brow had a few wrinkles, but the cheeks were childishly pink and smooth rather than the grooved brown leather of my face. And Perry's proportions were consistent if elfin, whereas trophy-handle ears on a large head, a stocky body and paunch give me a dwarfish appearance.

A gospel hall with walls of corrugated iron hosted his funeral service. Television showed a stuttering pastor outside the drab chapel attempting to explain what had prompted him to officiate for such a sinner while bystanders jeered at his charity and waved placards for the camera. One read, "Rot with Satan, Perry Gray."

I watched this in a pub where some of the rowdier youths raised their glasses to the slogan. Most who had trailed Mr Vitriol via the media's outpourings continued to bay at the slain monster. Inwardly, I was no different. My drinking companions, fellow choristers after our weekly practice, disliked the barracking of a reverend, but debated with much laughter which of Dante's circles was most appropriate for Mr Vitriol. Should he suffer alongside the wrathful, falsifiers, murderers, or those who had committed suicide? Behind the fanciful repartee were alliances and point scoring that meant I contributed no more than a chuckle when the majority laughed.

Leaving banter to others is another fruit of the bullying during my childhood. I have sat on the fence unless notions of duty required the stating of my views. If I did express an opinion, I breathed far more quickly and the endpoint of my intake climbed from belly to upper chest. It always came as a surprise when people claimed they were unaware of the nervousness that had me panting like a sun-broiled dog. My reticence has misled many, including the people at the church where I sang. I let the vicar and parishioners assume that I had retained my Anglican faith rather than admit the quality of the choir was the attraction. In fact, few know of the atheism that has never wavered in me since secondary school. Before today, tight-lipped discretion characterised my life. That I record so openly here is due to Perry.

He wrote to the constabulary acknowledging that he was Mr Vitriol and said they would find him dead in his house, for which he provided keys and the alarm code. Detectives discovered in his cellar a lever-arch file full of handwritten symbols that no one in the police recognised apart from page numbers. Forensics reported the fountain pen ink was recent and that the only fingerprints on the folder belonged to Perry. Deciphering his manuscript was my first and last police assignment. I discovered an unrepentant autobiography, the reading of which stopped me howling for Mr Vitriol's blood.

Soon after Perry's death, three videos surfaced that featured him talking. Broadcasters played them repeatedly, as if a surfeit of his innocuous voice might explain the waspish letters. His dialect, like mine, occupied that plateau between Estuary English and the pinnacle of Received Pronunciation. My tongue carries traces of East Kent and Surrey and he spent much of his first forty years in a two-up two-down cottage in Harrow. Yet our voices were close enough for speech recognition software to produce accurate text from my imitation of him.

An admired colleague, another eccentric during my early CARE years, had persuaded me that it helped to picture the creator of a code, think in his language, imagine the personality and pretend to be the person. Thus, after cracking Perry's symbols, I mimicked his speech. By the time I had transcribed the third chapter, I could read fluently much of the coded text and began to dictate via my PC. I thought nothing at first of simulating his voice and, had anyone suggested this might lead to Perry squatting in my skull, I would have dismissed the idea as preposterous. The first inkling of something strange happened as I was about to start dictating another paragraph.

My lips moved, but not with the text that held my gaze.

I heard his accent saying, "Hold on, Norm. Go back and look again. It's *invisible*, not *invincible*."

This was bizarre, but it helped and what he had written was engrossing. In the next hour, Perry's voice pushed past my lips four more times with corrections. Then I encountered another of his occasional flurries of poor handwriting and switched off the microphone to experiment with different phrasings.

After struggling in vain, I vented my frustration by typing: What does it mean?

My fingers immediately keyed a sentence that made perfect sense.

I added: Thank you, Perry.

Before I could delete this from the screen, my fingers tapped: My pleasure, Norm. I appreciate your efforts to get it right.

One hand squeezed my gaping mouth while the other typed with one finger: what the hell.

In a flash, both hands typed: It's just Perry wanting to help you be accurate.

This fingertip exchange so spooked me that I raced to Rose who was reading in bed. She got me to breathe more slowly and then listened. The day before, seeing how information about Perry obtained from a detective had agitated me, she had urged giving up the decoding. After Perry had alarmed me, I was all set to quit until her flabbergasting advice.

"I'm tempted to use this as an excuse to get you to stop working on the assignment, but if I did that, it would be dishonest. I think that what you've described simply means you've made good use of imagination. It's no less creative and no weirder than an actor who steps into another personality to add to his performance. If you're still determined to complete the decoding, your gift will speed up the work and I would rather you finished it sooner. Why don't you come to bed and sleep on it?"

In the morning, her interpretation of what had happened, along with my curiosity about the remaining chapters, led to a return to dictating the manuscript and querying Perry with increasing frequency. Because alternating voices out loud sounded too close to lunacy, I preferred to type our discussions. Sometimes these were lengthy and to make them easier to follow, I started his thoughts with *P* and mine with *N*.

Although we readily agreed on the decoding, we disputed many other things. Here is an example.

N I don't like the way you celebrate vengeance.
P Have you ever considered that revenge is a quality that defines humans as much as cooking or humour? Apart from an animal patrolling its territory to hunt or keep out competitors, its attacks happen in the moment. And if during a clash it comes off worse, an animal does not retreat to plan how to get even. To do so would require dealing with the past, future and other abstract ideas. Only our species has the capacity to hold a grudge, plot revenge and strike in a calculated manner.
N Homo sapiens also make weapons of mass destruction and has used them on a number of occasions. Just because we have the capacity does not make something desirable. It seems to me that many people have a level of technical ability without the emotional inhibitions needed to avoid bloodletting, wilful mass extinction, or vindictive vigilantism.
P I disagree with vigilantism that is too hasty or brutal, but I'm not against deterring assault or robbery or dealing with offenders when the police aren't available. But going back to what you said about human abilities, have you ever considered that the brain is hugely over-engineered?
N I don't think we're too intelligent so much as short on the compassion, tolerance and generosity needed for rubbing along together on an overcrowded planet. Think how much better off everyone would be if the ingenuity

that went into displaying aggression and making armaments was applied to promoting peace.

P Let me explain what I mean by over-engineered. You know the way programs have got more sophisticated? With what we know now, you could write code that would make a 1950s computer much more efficient with no new hardware.

N And?

P Hominid brains became more powerful because greater size increased the chances of survival. At some relatively recent point, language flowered allowing brains to do so much more with the same cubic capacity. Evolution usually dictates that as an organ becomes more efficient, it shrinks to allow the transfer of resources to where they will make a bigger contribution to the transmission of genes. But the acquisition of language did not reduce our brain size because groups began to compete with each other not just for resources but also to impose ideas, such as our tribe is better than your tribe and our god is the most powerful. We needed the extra intelligence to organise and invent better defences and ways of attacking.

N I don't see how any of this justifies vengeance. If you can reflect in this way, how come you didn't make better choices? Feeling the way you do about prisons and further humiliations, the consequences of being caught must have included suicide. Yet you persisted, driven to self-destruction no less than some male beast with a herd of females who exhausts himself rutting and fighting until a rival dispatches him.

P And what about in your life? You were driven to recklessness at times.

N Setting aside my phobias, I can think of only two occasions. One was meeting Rose and that was the best risk I ever took. The other was a madness I soon regretted.

N What was it?

P It seems strange telling you when Rose does not know. I was unfaithful once. I much regret it now.

P Regret often comes later. The truth is, the satisfactions of our vices appear adequate recompense for the risks until events catch up with us.

Neither of us liked to give ground. The debating did not change my condemnation of his crimes and our frequent intellectual stalemates assuaged my concern about his presence. Moreover, it was liberating after a lifetime of self-suppression to argue no holds barred without feeling physical discomfort.

His ideas continued to pop into awareness after the completion of the decoding. At this point, I stopped all imitation of his speech because he had gained entry in this way and what if further vocalisation allowed him to occupy more of my mind?

Rose heard me gripe about his continuing presence and asked, "Apart from being unusual, how's Perry a problem?"

She drew from me that my main concern was what people less wise and tolerant than her would make of my muse, as she called him. As soon as I realised there was no need to tell others, I focused on the benefit of having access to Perry's different perspective and the delight of being outspoken with him. Disapproval of his spiteful actions meant that, while generally courteous, I kept him at a distance, responding and drawing on his knowledge as it suited me. Only after my life fell apart did I warm to Perry.

Earlier today when he sought a favour, he did not exploit my misery. Indeed, the project he suggested, which you are reading, provides solace when little else has helped.

Chapter 2: Perry ~ More Sinned Against

The public think they know me from police and media spoutings about Mr Vitriol, a name created by the press in much the same way that they invented my notoriety. Bugging devices and computer snooping have enabled hearing and reading what people who know me as Perry Gray have to say about him. Not one had any reason to suggest I was a monster. Yet without a turn in the tide of events, raucous opprobrium will supplant my quiet anonymity.

I predict three sorts of responses when people who met me in the flesh discover my covert activities. Honest souls will admit to being gobsmacked because they thought Perry Gray too meek to take such risks. Shiftier folk will be wise after the revelation and claim that they always thought me a weirdo. A third group, the smallest, will not speak ill of the dead. But who would be brave enough to sing my praises when the tabloids have whipped up so much hatred of Mr Vitriol?

Their reporters have poisoned the well of scrutiny and I want this account to be an antidote. My hopes are more with historians because editors are obsessed with circulation and ratings more than accuracy and fairness. The stock of legends can go up as well as down over time. I don't expect to receive the same scrutiny as the great shapers of society or to be seen as anything more than a minor character, but I hope that a scholar or two in decades to come will be more interested in facts than sensationalism.

I would not complain if someone summed me up with, "He was more sinned against than sinning."

Do I have the courage to disclose for the first time the greatest sin done unto me, an event that is literally the stuff of nightmares? If I cannot share here my most terrifying and shameful experience, what happened towards the end of my National Service basic training, there is little point in writing about the rest of my life.

In the early hours of that morning, someone shook my shoulder and roused me from a deep slumber, the kind that follows weeks of gruelling activity without enough time to catch up on sleep. The rays of a torch stung my eyes. Why was no one speaking? I wondered for a moment if I had gone deaf from weeks of NCO lips pressed to my ears and screaming abuse.

The cold in the hut made visible the breath of the two men above. Corporals Stace and Payner smelt of gin, beer and cigarettes. My squad called them the Owls because they came to harry us at night. Never before had the Owls been so quiet. They gestured for me to dress and the bodies in the other bunks slept or pretended to be asleep.

We trudged through the sleet blowing from the North Sea and falling on Fort Gatgash. Lamps attached to buildings cast our shadows; mine swayed less and was always far shorter than the other two. To ask what this was about would only invite invective. We arrived at a part of Fort Gatgash that I was less familiar with and stopped at a brick building. Payner took a key from his parka pocket, fumbled and dropped it. I picked it up without thinking.

Payner barked, "Open the fucker."

He made his West Country accent sound menacing even on the few occasions one of his sentences didn't contain a swearword.

The Owls were blocking what little light fell on the door and they didn't use the torch. I patted with my fingers to find the metal of the lock.

Stace said, "Would it help you find the cunting hole if it had hairs around it?"

He had long, flat Lancashire vowels. As far as I could tell, his postings in Korea, Cyprus and Germany had not altered his speech. Payner sniggered. I turned the key and was ready to stand aside, but they pushed me into the black interior, which was strangely warm and had a smell that resembled a gasworks. The torch came on and lit the polished brass knob of an interior door.

The next room oozed dry heat. There was a roaring sound and a fainter engine-like noise. Payner switched on a single meagre bulb to reveal a furnace and lines of lagged pipes. The Owls hung their coats and berets on valves and told me to do the same. My cold-stiffened fingers struggled with a caught zip while my eyes scanned. There were no windows, only two grills almost at floor level and a square hatch with a green metal door above a pile of coke. Every surface was free of dust, which would have been strange in most other coke-fired boiler rooms, but not at a National Service induction centre. The Army was awash with conscripts and the NCOs competed with each other to devise time-consuming punishments. The summer intakes were reputed to have whitewashed mounds of coal.

Images from that dim boiler-house have haunted me with an invented brightness that leaves nothing hidden. When most afflicted, I relived the events and felt the pain and terror as if for the first time. These were not memories in the usual sense because often I was back in that room re-experiencing everything with the exception of the level of lighting.

The images have also appeared like floodlit scenes from a horror film; then I am both audience and the unfortunate on the screen. On these occasions, understanding that the movie was the regurgitation of a past episode did little to reduce the distress. To deliberately focus now on what used to arrive unbidden is spine-chilling and writing the next part in the third person may make the task slightly easier.

The Owls take off their blousons. He does the same. At first, he thinks they will make him shovel coke; at least he will be warm. Stace yells to take off his boots. He does not understand, but he knows not to question. Suspicion begins when Stace orders him to remove his trousers while Payner is spreading sacks on the floor. But what can he do?

When they want the longjohns off as well, panic freezes him. He thinks they want to blacken his genitals with boot polish, a practice he has heard of in the Army. Something inside him snaps; in the last two months, he has had a gutful of insults about the size of his penis. He does not move.

The Owls exchange a look. They understand that commands will no longer work.

Stace tosses something to Payner and says, "Catch, Harry".

The wide eyes of the half-dressed man follow a jar of Vaseline arcing through the air. He is such an innocent that he thinks they have it to prevent chilblains. A kick from Stace takes him by surprise. As he winces and hops, Payner punches the wind from his belly and trips him. He lands front down. The rough sacking reeks of coke and it's not dust free. A knee traps one arm. As much force and hurt comes from fingers digging into his other shoulder.

He feels as helpless as a butterfly pinned by a talon. One wing flapping does not lead to flight. Cold, scratchy fingers pull off his longjohns. He begins to scream. A hand forces his lips into the sacking. Acrid particles combine with ropes of snot to clog his nostrils, making breathing difficult.

The Owls curse and threaten the butterfly for crying. He has no choice; the pain is intense. Were all the other hurt and indignities of his life combined into a single injury, it would not match one of these vile intrusions. After the second invasion ends, he hears Payner complaining.

"Carried on like a fucking girl. I'll give you something to cry about."

The butterfly dares not look. He hears the snap of wood followed by a thwack. He has never seen a cudgel, but he thinks one just hit his left buttock. It stings, but that pain is negligible compared to what went before and what follows. The cudgel pins the butterfly. He fears that it will exit his body through his stomach.

He sobs violently. Each spasm sends a further jolt of excruciating pain through his body, which is confusing. Why is his body adding to his pain? But the crying and jerking it brings are beyond his control.

He hears an Owl hoiking. The gob lands on the butterfly's neck. Such contamination now hardly matters.

The last abuse by the Owls is a hefty kick. He barely feels the pain in his left knee because the movement of his leg magnifies the agony of the cudgel even more than the sobbing.

Sometime after he hears the door closing, the butterfly reaches behind his back and gets a splinter in his hand. He uses his left hand and finds where the wood is smoother. Despite the agony of manipulating the cudgel, he finally extracts it. One watery eye sees that it's the end of a broom handle. The shattered wood looks pale against the polished dirt left by hundreds of sooty hands. At the other end, shit, blood, Vaseline and alien secretions glisten.

The relief that he expected from removing the wood does not happen. It's as if a reservoir of pain has filled the space vacated. He is vaguely aware that the reservoir does not distinguish between mental and physical hurt.

Did the butterfly black out to escape the pain and revulsion, succumb to the heat and fumes of the furnace, or fall asleep from weeks of fatigue? He does not know; only that when he wakes, two young soldiers look at him with horror. He cannot answer them except by crying. One man covers the butterfly's buttocks with the discarded long johns and the parka warm from the pipes. The other says he will get help.

The butterfly thinks that he is beyond succour and continues to weep.

Chapter 3: Norman ~ The Dream

Lower Lychinclay sits in a hollow that brings many an unseasonal ending. Three decades of living here had made me philosophical about ice-nipped blossoms, lush growth perishing in summer and the cells of September fruit pulped by freezing. But nothing had prepared me for the untimely blasting of the human life dearest to me.

The climate is much milder three crow miles from my garden. In Upper Lychinclay's cemetery, I saw rose bushes in bloom on Christmas Day and each petal stabbed like a thorn because I had expected my Rose to live at least until she was eighty.

Death's cold fingers had sowed a pernicious weed in me before dispatching my wife. She went soon after steeling herself for my demise from cancer, as if the Grim Reaper mocked our acceptance of the order of scything. Rose was her usual healthy self until, on the day after I had shared the oncologist's black-capped verdict, her stomach became upset. Gastric discomfort turned to agony with no obvious cause. She had an allergic reaction to an anaesthetic administered for an exploratory operation and never regained consciousness.

Until Perry's proposal before sunrise this morning, an encounter four days after Rose's interment had provided my greatest consolation. I was the only visitor to the cemetery until a stocky flaxen-haired woman in her late twenties arrived with magenta zinnias. She noticed me staring at the latest mound. While squatting to place her flowers at the third most recent grave, she looked up and towards me with a hint of a smile. I nodded an acknowledgment. She raised herself in one slow movement without any sign of effort and slowly approached. Her blue eyes studied me for signs of diffidence while ignoring the worm casts that threatened her gleaming white trainers and the denim hems that flapped around them.

She stood alongside, looked back to where she had been and said with a Polish accent, "He is my husband. He was dead twenty-three days ago."

"And this is my wife."

With a slight turn of her head, she caught my eye, took a bare hand from her yellow puffer jacket and did not flinch at my chilled flesh. We said little else. Mostly we cried together, squeezing fingers to show support. I did not share that I knew her language in case this made her want to keep in touch. The last thing she needed was a new friend soon to die.

Her reaching out reminded me of Rose's compassion for outcasts and her ability to connect with awkward strangers. Although the resemblance inserted another shard of grief, I drew comfort from the widow's kindness and from my having shared so many more years of marriage than the Polish couple had known.

Nothing intimated last night that Perry was about to offer solace of a different kind. Each time I left my bed I lifted a curtain and, as is my habit, scanned the land behind the house. The first time my bladder woke me, moonlight and cool air made everything sharp. Near one o'clock, mist lapped over the lawn and around the bushes while frost glinted above the hazy waves. By three, trees without trunks and houseless chimneys floated on the fog. The fourth time I got up, an immense dense cloud was whitewashing every pane. I had just dreamed of Perry speaking with me in his house and parts of this fantasy are still curiously memorable.

I cannot say how or why I arrived at night. Whatever the circumstances, he made me most welcome. A great flaming log warmed his living room, unlike the chill of Perry's house two weeks after his death when the police had arranged for me to visit. He fetched vintage bottles from the cellar and served food from his enviable garden. Because I have never seen pomegranates grown in England, I recall them, but not the other produce.

Convinced that I was seeing Perry in the flesh for the first time, I studied him. His pale eyes flitted. An occasional tremble crept into his tenor voice. Nor was his body at ease in the well-upholstered chair. I sat on a matching one, again noticing how well his furniture suited short legs; the dimensions let our feet rest easy on the carpet while fully supporting our backs.

Four arum lilies, which so easily freeze to mush in Lower Lychinclay, graced an inscribed canopic jar that in reality did not exist in Perry's house. Next to the flowers was the jar's cap with the erect ears and piercing eyes of

Anubis, as if he was waiting for the chance to snatch food or a soul.

"Perry, the hieroglyphs, do you know what they say?"

"Why do you ask?"

"They might be the name of the person whose viscera once filled the jar."

"It's a replica. Perhaps this ancient Egyptian is now better known because tourists take home copies."

"But if tourists can't read the name?"

"Then, like my writing until you arrived, Norm, he awaits an interpreter. Do eat something."

The meaning of the ancient symbols continued to fascinate, but Perry kept my taste buds busy so that he could talk.

"Despite your faithful deciphering, my story was not enough to counter the media frenzy and yet more invention has followed. How can history do me justice when every other source is hostile?"

In the dream, Perry poured out his heart as freely as the wine and I felt honoured because he had trusted so few. However, the request that followed surprised me.

"Please add to my account. Flesh it out with chapters about your own experiences so that future researchers will appreciate the extent to which bullying blighted you and me. Add your credibility to counteract the second wave of hysteria and distortion."

"It's kind of you to invite me." My demeanour conveyed reluctance more than gratitude.

"May I speak frankly?"

He did not wait for consent.

"I'll be remembered one way or the other. But what of you? The masses who read my account don't know that you cracked the code, let alone how the police played ducks and drakes with your rendering. And it's not just you, Norm. How would you like Rose's grandchildren to regard her?"

He paused for effect. I knew what was coming.

"Your feckless stepson doesn't honour his mother. Despite your generosity to Colin's children, they'll assume that Rose and Norm screwed up their dad."

Perry pretended to brush some crumbs off his maroon sweater to give me time to dwell on Colin's estrangement and the fact that Rose had never laid eyes on the grandchildren favoured in our wills.

"You could write your heart out about the perversity of Colin and who would look at it? But grab hold of my coat-tails, slant your story to comment on me and you'll get readers. Rose is part of your life. Interweave our chapters and she will not just be known, but also admired."

His spiel was as subtle as an ice storm, yet I was about to agree until fear gripped my chest. My mouth hanging open prompted him to frown, gulp wine and flail his limbs, lending that moment a cartoon quality at odds with the rest of the dream.

"I'm sorry if I sounded disrespectful," he said.

I felt relief that he did not know why I dithered; it meant he could not read every part of my mind.

"My problem isn't the way you pitched it, Perry. You wrote that you hesitated to recount what you called the stuff of nightmares. Like you, I'm afraid to write about my worst experience."

He smiled and sighed. "Gatgash, eh? Have you ever wondered how many other soldiers acquired their worst nightmares there? I wish I'd put the boiler house incident on paper sooner. Not only did it help, but having let go of the biggest secret, smaller ones dribbled from the pen without strain. You need to piss again, Norm. Why don't you relieve yourself and then sleep on the idea of those grandchildren and future historians knowing the real Rose."

After peeing, slumber was deep and restful. Moreover, when my dog roused me for his overdue breakfast, the pain from my cancer was more tolerable. There was no recollection of any further dream, as if the vivid fragments of the exchange with Perry had dimmed other drowsy memories. By the time I had reached the kitchen, I knew that dredging my silt of bitter events would be worthwhile if it encouraged others to read about Rose and appreciate her qualities. And recording the facts of our relationship and my adultery would make some amends for what I had not spoken of. Besides, what distant memory could be worse than the current pain of her loss?

The one regret following the dream was longing to know what Rose would have made of such a memorable encounter with Perry who, as far as I knew, had never before visited my sleep. But she does not communicate like him. Sometimes I catch a whiff of Rose, a mixture of makeup, perfume and the inherent sweetness of her skin and hair. I go from room to room without finding the source. It is not her clothes. I have sniffed every sweater, cardigan and scarf; all lack the freshness that prompted my searching.

When I question Rose, no answers come, not even when I tempted her by offering to share the national secrets that work had made me privy to and we had never discussed. I constantly remember things that she said, her loving looks and tender touch, yet I experience none of these anew. The perversity of my gentle soulmate remaining incommunicado while a criminal I never met in the flesh converses at the drop of a hat can stir up bitterness.

She was not one to give up easily or to let me surrender too quickly and I have sought, without success, to provoke a response by shouting, "Rose, what's the point of last-chance chemo without at least your voice to will me on?"

Sometimes I think that she might speak if Perry left, but how to evict him? At other times, forgetting my atheism, I fear that karma is taking its course. For when Rose was alive, I missed so many opportunities to talk with her, such as the time she asked about my nightmares and I pretended they were about lightning. Through a combination of exhausting work and her love, it seemed that my bedtime screams, violent movements and sweating had ended. Then after my nightmares began to gallop again, she got me talking like never before about my terrors and the link between them and being retired. I started to understand how the challenges and urgencies of my role in Intelligence had acted like levees against a raging river. Office hours could be long and although no classified documents came home in my briefcase, the confidential conundrums that filled my head made me poor company at times. On vacation, I would look up and be surprised to see a pool surrounded by tourists; my eyes had scanned a novel yet the plot was vague because the larger part of my brain was wrestling with a Gordian cipher.

In response to the tailspin that followed my retirement, Rose developed a restorative routine that meant giving up her activities in the morning and foregoing days out. We took the last of the breakfast *cafetière* to the easy chairs in the dining room, shut the door to bar the dog and kept our backs to the French windows to avoid the distractions of the garden. She listened and soothed my latest spectres for as long as it took. Then I did simple chores, such as ironing or cleaning, for sixty minutes. To encourage reflection, Rose kept out of my way and suggested that I work without radio or music.

The next hour of my rehabilitation coincided with walking the dog. Over two months, we always followed the downhill path from the village. Rose held my hand as I took steps, a little nearer each day, towards the end of the stream and the phobia there that I had avoided. Another part of her healing was drawing attention to horticultural metaphors of renewal. The alchemical compost heap transmutes base detritus into noble fertility. A cold-damaged plant could recover under glass and harden in stages to cope with frost. My favourite flower, the black hellebore, needs freezing weather to geminate and blossoms in the snow.

We discussed the matters that most worried me only before lunch to allow time for muddied waters to clear before bed; alarming dreams were less likely when we held to this. Our afternoon and evening conversations often led to belly laughs and not least about the district, which is rich in human and architectural folly. I shared gossip from my choir, the Horticultural Society and the Lychinclay Lions while Rose reported on the Planning Committee and other meetings she attended as a District Councillor, her voluntary work with prisoners, Pilates classes and Mahjong Club. And we mocked our own foibles, such as the frequency with which we mislaid our spectacles, failed to remember a name, the results of her impulse purchases and my reluctance to discard old clothes.

After the nightmares had retreated, retirement was rewarding. I grew to love our habits, increased intimacy, the abundance of leisure that allowed reading a good chapter twice and reserving books whose names merely took my fancy. Rose once suggested volunteering, but I never shared her inclination to help others beyond what being a tolerable Lion required. Talking with yet more people would have been a chore because, before Perry, only with her did I feel fully at ease.

I often speak aloud and indiscreetly to my silent Rose. Despite years in Intelligence and Perry's accounts of bugging houses increasing my awareness of listening devices, I prattle in every room and disclose musings such as these into the microphone linked to my desktop. Sounds become black letters on a white screen to be saved in files that have no encryption, not even a password. I have dispensed with security other than the automatic updates of antiviral software, print without hesitation and the shredder remains idle. Until recently, the habits that come from classified work were ingrained and my commitment to secrecy as profound as Perry's. Like him, my time for concealment is over.

Following the oncologist's prognosis and Rose's death, mortality has preoccupied me. As Colin was a stepson and I have neither niece nor nephew, no meaningful fraction of my DNA goes forward. Rose and I never used contraception after our wedding and hoped for a child. Because she had conceived Colin within a month of her first marriage, I concluded that I shot blanks and suspected a genetic link between my infertility and flawed proportions. This, along with a stubborn pride, prevented seeking the expert advice suggested by Rose. What if the consultant concluded that it would be better for someone with my physique not to father children?

The fact that the Perry in my skull will die with me has increased my awareness of death erasing all mental impressions. Yet when my brain has long been decomposed, written testimonies, electronic files and optical discs could still communicate my thoughts, provided others care to access and can locate the files. But it is not just me I want others to remember. Along with Colin's children understanding how much their grandmother cared for him and longed to meet them, I also want people yet to be born to know Rose. So many people become little more than a name on a tombstone.

Once the people who tended the grave stop visiting, lichens and erosion hide the name of the deceased and any chiselled declarations of love. The reach of my ambition is less than the fool's gold of immortality; just a handful of intelligent people a hundred years hence appreciating something of our lives would suffice.

If keyword searches still serve some purpose for academics whose grandparents are yet to be born, my guess is that *Perry Gray* or *poison pen* will lead to this document. Well, researcher, why persevere with the Midlins when your interest is, I suspect, Mr Vitriol?

Through my chapters you will appreciate more fully the era that formed him. I reflect on what stopped me from acting as he did when we had shared many similar experiences. Compare and contrast, a technique used to find meaning in codes, is applicable to us. For example, what if Rose had spurned my proposal or someone like her had taken Perry in hand before he retreated into celibacy and a life of vindictiveness?

Others claim to understand Perry. Programmes, books and articles about him keep appearing. He has the same attraction for the Sunday papers as Myra Hindley and Fred West, despite never resorting to their kind of violence. The commentators and writers to date have lacked first-hand knowledge of the Austerity Britain that Perry and I grew up in. Our devout parents were closer in their morality to the Victorians than the liberal outlook that took hold after 1960; they went to great lengths to limit what we read, listened to and watched. Nor has any writer yet disclosed personal experiences of horrendous bullying at school and in the Army; key events in Perry's life and mine.

Someone in the police was careless with my decoding or, worse still, sold it. Suspicions were raised because almost as soon as a Moldavian-registered website carried the document, a tabloid ran a five-page spread that included photographs of people targeted by Perry whose names had never been made public before. Millions became aware of what he alleged, making the leak worse than the original poison pen letters with their minute audiences. And while the paper's initial treatment emphasised the vileness of Mr Vitriol and the virtues of his victims, reporters later dug for dirt on those named. Given all the exposure, there is no point in disguising here the identities of those named by Perry.

Unfavourable references to the police are missing from the leaked decoding. This came as no surprise to me because the constabulary had asked me to lend my name to such a version. Summoning up my courage, I refused, but took no further action despite the unmistakable bribe offered. Now my impending death allows me to overcome a lifetime of deference and make amends by using the full decoding and describing the dishonesty, mine included, that surrounded the decoding.

But, you may ask, why trust an author who admits to past dishonesty?

You should not trust me. Perry's anonymous letters demonstrate *par excellence* how guile can use a few facts to make an accompanying parcel of lies appear credible. Our only defence against such dissembling is to treat all allegations as suspect. Accept nothing as factual from Perry, me or any other pundit on Mr Vitriol without sound corroboration. Be on your guard all the more when sentiments expressed resonate with your prejudices or excite fear. And even when descriptions and details suggest accuracy, it is not just Perry who may be unreliable.

N Is there anything you want to add here, Perry?
P What can I say? You've just stitched me up like a kipper.
N But is there anything specific you want to comment on?
P I feel like a Cretan introduced with, 'The Cretans are always liars'.
N If that's all, readers should continue your story and judge for themselves.

Chapter 4: Perry ~ Endgame

The media accuse Mr Vitriol of cowardice for operating anonymously, as if guerrilla campaigns did not rely on evasion and camouflage. Why risk overwhelming firepower rather than wage the war of the flea? For the record, many of my actions required ignoring the consequences of being discovered, in particular the dread of sexual assault while in a prison. I could never decide whether being in solitary confinement would offer some protection or make me more vulnerable to molestation. The fewer people and the more remote the cell, the greater the chance of an attack going undetected. In addition, many prison officers are ex-military. I imagined two or more of them behaving like the Owls. And it's not unknown for prison staff to take bribes or succumb to blackmail. What if some sex fiends paid to have access to me when no one else was about? But even if such an assault was not part of incarceration, that still leaves the prospect of endless humiliation and intimidation from inmates and their gaolers.

No one is born destined for a lifetime of timidity or courage. Rather, much of a person's level of nervousness or confidence stems from early experiences. My start in life included a degree of maternal over-protectiveness, yet this did little more than frustrate me. It was the ridicule and bullying that began at infant school that caused the real damage and taught me, as it has taught millions of others, to keep a low profile and avoid cruel people and uncertain situations as much as feasible.

The boiler house incident and the whitewash that followed led to a very sweet tooth when it came to revenge. I had enjoyed covert retaliation before then. The difference after Gatgash was a determination to hit back harder and take greater risks. As well as imagining all the horrors of getting caught, I was adept at picturing the distress of those upon whom I wanted to wreak vengeance. Thus, writing an anonymous letter not only triggered palpitations from thinking about my arrest and the abasement that would follow, it also enabled envisioning the anguish visited on the target. The latter helped maintain my motivation and could provide some relief from obsessing about things going wrong.

One of the chances I took was searching databases at the many computer centres that employed me. More and foxier measures to prevent and detect unauthorised trawling have appeared year after year, yet neither these nor the penalties laid down by the Computer Misuse Act stopped me scouring for information to use against the people on my hit list. I took what precautions were feasible and lived with the fear of being caught. Sneaking into homes to snoop, plant evidence or install listening devices were my most nerve-wracking illicit activities. Despite entering over a score of properties, my trepidation never diminished. The statistical chances of being disturbed that grew with each intrusion countered any habituation of the fear response.

I persevered in my pursuit of retribution with one exception linked to the boiler-house incident. I had searched in vain over decades for Bert, the Army sergeant who had persecuted me, commanded the Owls and destroyed evidence of their outrage. Eight years ago, I had just returned home from three days of frantic work to ensure hackers could not return to a government database. After the junk meals, salty snacks and bear's piss and mud masquerading as coffee – the fare that goes with a crisis at a computer centre – I craved wholesome food, a decent drink and an early night. I was preparing crudités, sipping a delectable Brunello di Montalcino and half-listening to the early evening TV news in the next room. My mind was grappling still with the hackers' ingenuity and its implications for other centres until I heard Bert's unusual surname for the first time in over thirty years. That was shocking enough, but then it became clear that someone with this name was working for my local Constabulary. I sliced a fingertip. Blood stained the white chopping board.

I put the cut finger into my mouth, pressed my tongue over the wound and ran to the lounge. A reporter in the studio gave way to a recording of a man outside a court denouncing someone sentenced that day for grievous bodily harm and intimidating witnesses. Although age had bloated the face and greyed his hair, the deep Brummie bray left no doubt; this was Bert. A caption appeared – Detective Inspector Robert Knattmaw. No wonder he had escaped me!

A fellow conscript at Gatgash had used his bayonet to trace something in the mud during a break on a route march. His leering grin made me curious. He had scrawled *Natmor fucks spyders.* The youth spat at the marks before erasing them with hefty kicks.

   A lad who could not spell spiders was likely to have the surname wrong and I had looked for variations beginning with *Gnat* as well as *Nat* and ending with *more*, *moor* and *moore*, but not *Knat* or *maw*. And with the first name, I had covered possibilities like Albert, Bertram, Bertrand, Gilbert, Herbert and Hubert and even searched for Engelbert after hearing of the singer with that name. But the possibility of Bert being a contraction of Robert had not occurred to me.

I returned to the kitchen and spat blood into the sink, splattering its surfaces and triggering nausea. Not even the sight of my own blood is tolerable. Regurgitated celery stained red by the wine followed. To avoid seeing the vomit, I closed my eyes and fumbled for the tap. The spurt of water wafted the puky smell making me retch again. I rinsed my mouth in the bathroom, but dared not drink with guts in such turmoil.

   Releasing my left index fingertip from the palm it was pressed against allowed more blood to flow. Layers of toilet tissue around the cut turned red and soggy, the sight of which brought dizziness. I replaced the paper with a white towel and held the turbaned hand aloft as I wandered around the house in shock and disbelief.

After the Knattmaw clip reappeared on the late evening news, stupor and exhaustion gave way to molten rage at his months of abuse at Fort Gatgash and the conspiracy that he had launched to conceal the Owls' hideous crime. His hypocrisy on television, condemning acts of violence and the perversion of justice, added to the urge to lash out. In addition to the angry heat, I felt a chill that was not simply an echo of past terrors; Knattmaw still held power and because he had worked in the county unbeknown to me did not mean that he was unaware of the former Private Gray. Had he seen me? Had he kept tabs on me? How was he to know that for me our last encounter was unspeakable? He would fear for his reputation from revelations about his bullying and wilful destruction of evidence.

Being so overwrought meant that I could not dwell on the prospect of making his life difficult. The Hollywood in my head churned out movies of again being powerless in the hands of Knattmaw. The scenes of future beatings and taunts were so convincing that I forgot for minutes at a time that these were only possibilities. Even after pinching myself, the images and sounds of him being abusive still retained an aura of inevitability.

I had assisted police forces around the country with their fight against cyber-crime. All of the detectives encountered were far more intelligent and observant than Knattmaw. Yet I did not think even the brightest of them would have been able to recognise me in the street after thirty years the way I feared he would. Less irrational was the dread that if Knattmaw was to see or hear my name he would link it to Gatgash. And if he saw me at the same time Perry Gray was mentioned, how could he not recognise me as the person he had so wronged?

Some consolation came from the way Constabulary resources, especially the detectives, were focused on the larger urban centres. With this and several brandies, I began to accept that living in the same shire as Knattmaw was not particularly significant provided I went to another county for anything that required a visit to a city and kept my head down in other ways. This conclusion and another large globe of brandy finally enabled me to start considering revenge.

It was inconceivable that Knattmaw would have become a better person. If one could probe deep and wide enough his more recent misconduct would turn up. I expected that he abused not just criminals and suspects but also others he encountered who had significantly less power, including junior police officers. And it would not have surprised me if a bug or some other form of snooping revealed that he was on the take and fitted up suspects to boost his success rate.

But every time I contemplated making enquiries about him or bugging his car, office or home I bottled out. Should Knattmaw become aware of me after an attempt to sully his name, he would conclude that the former Private Gray was after revenge. And Knattmaw would have the choice of acting via official channels or through pure thuggery. Murdering me might seem the easiest option to him. Or if he left it to other officers, they would hate me for attacking one of their own and his less scrupulous colleagues might be no less violent than him. And what if a detective pressured me into revealing what lay behind my grudge? I did not want more people knowing what had happened in the boiler room and least of all coppers likely to assume the story was merely an excuse for my behaviour.

I had another brandy in the hope of escaping the escalating tension between wanting to lash out and fear of the consequences. Drinking on an empty stomach when exhausted and eager to end indecision proved to be disastrous. Frustrated by my cowardice, I started a letter. Unusually for my anonymous mail, I made no rough draft; my only plan was to send multiple copies. This meant that I used a PC rather than the typewriter favoured for such writing. Seeing accusing words on the screen helped me to imagine the distress they could cause Knattmaw and, without thinking through the pros and cons, I printed copies.

Dear Chief Constable Catchpole,
I am no saint but my conscience has its limits. I recently heard a man say that that DI Robert Knattmaw had

punched him to the ground and then kicked him during an unresisted arrest. The victim would be horrified to learn I was reporting this as he is the sort who believes one should never grass, not even when a senior policeman did the deed.

What he said struck a chord because Knattmaw arrested me years ago on suspicion of handling stolen property. There was menace about him from the start. I expect cops to be tough, but Knattmaw is sick and evil. He wanted money that he knew I had and made it clear that a beating would follow if I did not hand over £1000 in used notes. His boots and fists were not the only threat. He said how it easy it was to keep enough heroin from a drugs raid to fit up people like me for dealing, an activity I have never been involved in. I paid up rather than risk a long prison sentence.

Now here's the rub. I was guilty of what he threatened to charge me with in the first place, but he had no proof. The way he put it, he needed a result and it did not worry him who got sent to prison and not least someone like me who had been inside before.

Because I paid him off, he fitted up another man for receiving the stolen goods. I have always regretted someone else did my time, but the bottom line is he was put there by a bent copper who knew he was innocent.

There are other stories about Knattmaw that involve him assaulting passive prisoners, selling seized drugs, backhanders for information about police operations, and charges dropped in return for payment. I can't provide proof for any of them, but why does Knattmaw feature in such talk far more often than others coppers from your force?

It's time that someone reviewed his work and personal finances. To give the police an added incentive, I am sending copies of this letter to two local papers.

My befuddled brain did not appreciate that these insinuations were well short of my usual standards and the urge to hit back drove me to make three further mistakes before I went to bed. The first, which should have been obvious even then, was adding to the letters *Mr Vitallium*, a pen name I had often used. The second followed the printer jamming. I ended up with four copies of the letter and it seemed a shame not to use all. An Internet search threw up a Mrs Gladys Knattmaw, a primary school head teacher in the east of the county. It had to be his wife. I hesitated before making her a recipient because she must have suffered greatly living with such a vile man. Then I overcame these reservations by saying that either she must have left him by now or the letter could help persuade her to leave.

After sealing the four envelopes, I could not wait to send them and drove eighteen miles rather than waiting two days to post them on my way to an assignment in Cardiff. With the contents already suggesting the author came from the county, the postmark added to the suspicion that he still lived locally. It was also rash to have got behind the wheel when I was not just drunk but also exhausted and perturbed enough to drive at speed.

After sleep of sorts and showering away the stickiness left by nervous sweating it was almost noon. Too tired to dress, I sat with a mug of espresso wondering why no road accident had occurred and reviewing my actions. Using Mr Vitallium was bizarre when every previous letter containing this name had always suggested a law-abiding man. And it made no sense that the letter purported to come from a self-confessed criminal. Why would anyone heed anonymous allegations from a crook?

With no facts to lend a modicum of credibility to the letter's scandal mongering, Knattmaw would be able to turn the accusations to his advantage by saying, "Look what a great job I'm doing. I've got villains so angry they send bollocks like this."

The smart thing would have been to check databases for his bank accounts or details of a home Internet connection to help covert gathering of information from his computer. I hated my stupidity and the way I had bottled out at the prospect of more active snooping on Knattmaw. But by this time I accepted that the level of fear, which derived from the combination of his actions at Gatgash and his police rank, was unlikely to change.

Waiting for a database to yield information that I could use against him was unbearable. And each action against a target I hated less that Knattmaw reminded me of how ineffectual my initial response to his discovery had been. Five months after sending the letters, during which time no useful data on Knattmaw had turned up, the two newspapers that had received copies of the letter printed a joint exclusive that was little more than a Constabulary press release. It spoke of how the Chief Constable had met with the wife of an officer to reassure her after she had received a letter in which a man using Mr Vitallium as a *nom de plume* had alleged her husband abused his powers. There was no mention of rank, role or location and the types of abuse went unspecified. Catchpole said that the most diligent officers often attracted allegations and normally he would not act on an unsupported and anonymous complaint. However, because the press had also received copies he had invited another force to investigate and was happy to report that the two editors, having studied the independent review, accepted that the accusations were malicious and without any foundation.

Of course, the editors knew nothing because neither paper had a crime correspondent and they had barely enough staff to do more than reprint corporate bumf tarted up as news. In fact, it was surprising that they had convinced the police to do anything about the anonymous letter.

I was left so angry, not least with myself for blowing my chances with Knattmaw, that the idea of shooting him crossed my mind. There was a rifle with a telescopic sight in a house where my visits to plant and then to retrieve a bug had gone unnoticed. Provided that Knattmaw could not see me and I had time to steady my breathing, I would not have missed him from fifty yards. And what poetic justice, seeing as Sergeant Knattmaw had abused me for my clumsiness with firearms. But, regardless of what the media have concocted, I have never resorted to violence and let the idea go.

The owner of the rifle also had a Luger that was probably an illicit souvenir from his RAF service in Germany. Since I had last visited him, all handguns had been made illegal, but a man ignoring the law in the first place would be unlikely to comply with the ban. I returned to his home for a third time and took the pistol. Then I packaged it, taking care to use several of the features associated with a suspicious package right down to fragments of fine copper wire under the loops of transparent tape. I posted it to Knattmaw at work so there was a chance that another copper would spot it, just in case the parcel failed to rouse suspicions during its time with the Royal Mail. Inside the package was a typewritten letter with spelling mistakes to suggest it was not from Mr Vitallium.

Bert, Couldn't make rondyvous. Things have got very hot and I need to go abroad. You said not to call so posting is all I can do as I have spent your money and you will want to have what you payed for. Sorry to send it to you via work but you aren't listed in the phone book and time is short.

I fantasised about the ploy working for some weeks after sending, but nothing so much as hinted at any impact. After two months, I rang the Constabulary from a call box in Cardiff and asked to speak to Knattmaw. He was not in till the next day, which confirmed that he was still on duty. Had someone in the Royal Mail stolen the package? That was the best I could hope for. If the police knew of a second attempt to discredit Knattmaw they would be on their guard for someone trying to raise suspicions about him. Post-Luger, my hopes of settling the score rested with data mining hitting pay dirt.

As much as I hated waiting, haste had weakened my hand. The idea of snooping on Knattmaw had been scary enough before the letters and gun. After them, my fear was higher than ever because he and others would be vigilant and show no quarter to anyone suspected of sending the items. I had begun to look for an innovative way of getting at Knattmaw with less risk and less chance of being linked to the letter and the Luger when life bowled me the first of a number of googlies.

I was reading at a window seat on a jet about to fly from Luton to Aberdeen when a very tall man in his late-twenties stowed his knapsack and a briefcase belonging to a woman old enough to be his mother. As they sat alongside, I nodded an acknowledgement and returned to my book. When the man spread his thighs to create a space between his knees and the seat in front, I glanced up and guessed from his large pupils and pale damp face that he was nervous. He was soon talking compulsively, saying his name, how much he disliked flying, rambling on about his post-doctoral research in Ottawa on the spleen and how his companion was a professor of medicine from Baltimore.

"We only just met in the terminal and we're going to the same conference in Scotland. Isn't that fluky? She's an expert on splenic diseases and I've been reading her papers for years. Isn't that incredible?"

I feigned amazement and decided not to look up from my copy of *The Hacker Quarterly* after the engines had boomed. Besides, my neck would have hurt from looking up to such a giant for more than a few minutes. The professor had remained silent and when she did peek at the window for a moment, as the plane taxied, her wry expression conveyed that she also found his blathering irksome. After the jet had climbed and the roar dropped, he spoke with her. From what I overheard, he was a biologist rather than a medic and seemed to be trying to impress with technical talk and gossip from academia.

Just as the descent reduced the engine noise he asked the professor, "Do you know about the paediatrician who sent hate mail to a colleague at the University of Toronto?"

"No. What happened?" She sounded interested.

"It was in *Nature Medicine*. Dr Koren's DNA was found on the correspondence. He had to admit to being the author after he'd already denied sending the letters. Can you imagine his face when they told him – a scientist undone by science?"

My spine quivered at the idea that my very essence could be my undoing. Guarding against conventional fingerprints clearly was not enough when DNA could be recovered from mail.

I stopped all revenge mail until I understood how the police used genetic science. The more I delved, the shakier I felt about items posted over the years. When did I last lick a gummed envelope? Had I absent-mindedly licked a self-adhesive one? What about a fragment of skin, a sweat mark or dandruff posted along with the letter? Gooseflesh and jitters followed every story of long-stored criminal evidence yielding to DNA scrutiny.

My fears proved to be well founded for once. Seven months after the flight, the Constabulary announced finding a fragment of hair in a letter signed by Mr Vitallium. I scared myself witless with movies of my arrest and humiliation. Acquaintances who observed bouts of laboured breathing and perspiration-drenched clothes urged me to see a doctor. When one asked if I was having a panic attack, I pretended it was a virus.

Reason gradually reduced my nerves to a more manageable state. What could the police do with this hair? Adding its DNA profile to their collection brought them no closer to me provided they never obtained a genetic sample from me as Perry Gray. I started to observe every speed limit and ignored the other drivers tailgating or honking their horns. If drinkers began to argue too fiercely, I left the pub. When I encountered a gaggle of football fans, no matter how agreeable they seemed, I went the other way.

But I had not reckoned on the tenacity of my former sergeant. The media later revealed how Knattmaw asked police around the country about Mr Vitallium and unsolved cases of anonymous letters. After he retired, he continued to pursue me with a doggedness that rivalled my former search for him. Through calling in favours and using his clout, he ensured that forensic testing took place as if his hunt was for a mass murderer. Scientists found a partial DNA match between Mr Vitallium's hair and a deceased armed robber from Luton. The Constabulary announced they were searching for a man with a criminal record related to the robber, someone who probably had Bedfordshire connections. Fortunately for me, they expected to find someone Knattmaw had helped to convict, and my mother, although born near Bedford, had moved to Hertfordshire while still very young. And by the time Mum moved to Harrow as a young wife, she had broken with her family.

News about the hunt for Mr Vitallium featured so often on the local radio station and in the county newspapers that I suspected Knattmaw wanted me to squirm. If he had, he succeeded. Just when I thought the hassle could get no worse, his funeral notice appeared. I went to my cellar for a bottle to celebrate the fatal heart attack and chose a good rather than a great wine. Why? Because I had failed to make him suffer. Any irritation my letter and the gun had caused him was piddling compared to his brutality at Gatgash.

Then six weeks after his funeral, the local press said that Mrs Gladys Knattmaw would be appearing on national television with the Chief Constable to speak about anonymous allegations. I could hardly wait for the programme.

Tears rolled down the widow's plump cheeks while she claimed that Mr Vitallium's letter was the most significant factor in the coronary that ended hubby's heroic life. She claimed that what had most upset him was the copy sent to her and how she wished she had never told him about receiving it.

"The letter to me made it personal for him. After that, Bert was determined to see Mr Vitallium caught. He could not even enjoy retirement knowing that the person who caused me distress was still at large. As far as I'm concerned, the poison pen author murdered my husband and stole his retirement from him. And that's why I'm going public in spite of the advice some have given."

She glanced away from the camera to where the group shot had shown the Chief Constable was sitting. The old battle-axe had twisted Catchpole's arm up his back. I was admiring the way her decades with Knattmaw had toughened rather than squashed her spirit when she trotted out the accusation about me that is so undeserved.

"I want to see this coward who hides behind a made-up name brought to justice."

Despite this, I felt sorry for someone who after almost forty years could not admit what kind of monster she had married. In her heart, she must have known that Bert got so worked up about the letter because the cap fitted.

There followed several video clips from civilian and police worthies seeking to convince the public that Knattmaw was the salt of the earth. Then the programme showed three Mr Vitallium letters with the addressees' name and pillorying phrases blanked out because, according to the presenter, "The accusations are so vile and ill-founded."

I knew the recipients from the text still visible and, although my Knattmaw allegations were speculative, the accusations against the other two were factual.

Catchpole was enjoying the spotlight despite his earlier reservations about letting the public know that Knattmaw had attracted anonymous allegations.

The Chief appealed to recipients of any similar mail. "You can be sure of a sympathetic response and that the information will be treated with the utmost confidence. Even if you haven't kept a letter, just knowing other victims will help to unmask Mr Vitallium and bring him to justice. If you're still hesitating about coming forwards, consider this. We've recovered an automatic pistol that we know was smuggled into this country and is linked to Mr Vitallium. Sending hate mail is bad enough, but criminals who own guns have a tendency to use them and clearly this man is particularly vicious."

I opened a fine bottle to celebrate the news that I had got under Knattmaw's skin enough for him to obsess about Mr Vitallium. Although not the public disgrace I had wanted for him, it was enough after thinking for so long that he had enjoyed the last laugh. If you ever want a magnificent wine to go with sweet revenge, try a Château Suduiraut Sauternes, 1976 if you can afford it.

As for the pistol and the accusations made by Catchpole, I admit to a sneaking admiration for the way he created so much from limited facts; he is an artist with weasel words after my own heart. The fact of the matter is, though, it was my actions that removed the illegally owned weapon from a brute and made it available to the police.

National newspapers followed up the broadcast for several days, competing to be the most hysterical in their admiration of Gladys, congratulating the police for taking up her cause and vilifying Mr Vitallium.

A national redtop reproduced the blanked-out letters and highlighted features to look for, "... if you think you might also be a victim of this sicko."

"Help catch this dripper of poison ink before he kills again," said another.

In the childish way that tabloids play with words, a third title morphed Vitallium to Vitriol. A reluctant star was born. The brouhaha threatened to remove the veil that had allowed me to live without the glare of publicity.

Had every school in the shire received an envelope of anthrax spores, the media could not have been more attentive or outraged and I am sure others grew sick of Gladys's fatuous smile and Catchpole relishing his extended exposure to national publicity.

I thought the editors had followed police requests designed to panic me into providing an extra clue until the sheer amount of nonsense made it obvious that boosting circulation and viewers underpinned their sensationalism. Dastardly villains attract audiences, whereas shades of grey and complex motives spoil the news pantomime and deter sales. I wished for a supply of anthrax to send to news- rooms. Then my hatred subsided after realising the hacks were only doing their jobs. How many rags had I bought because the headline titillated? Which channels had I turned off because the news coverage was too sensational? And when had I ever written to object that a report unfairly crucified another?

The Constabulary thanked members of the public for providing them with a further twenty-three anonymous letters. From their total of twenty-six, four featured Mr Vitallium and another two came from a typewriter that matched an item carrying this name. A forensic linguist compared the language of the linked and unlinked letters and concluded another one was likely to be the work of Mr Vitallium and four more were possibly by him.

Dispersed addressees and postmarks frustrated the detectives. At first, the police insisted that I knew my victims, described by Catchpole as "model citizens" whom I sought to besmirch because I loathed their good standing.

When lack of progress led to criticism, the Chief Constable became shy of press conferences and interviews. The head of the investigation, Chief Superintendent Ann Grove, was left to answer the ravening media. Yet on one occasion Catchpole was ambushed by a reporter who, after asking him about the Constabulary's budget, turned to the topic of Mr Vitriol.

"Why with so many letters and so much public support haven't you arrested anyone yet?"

There was gulp and a less than confident voice said, "What makes the case so difficult is the randomness of the letters. They're sent from all over the country to people across the United Kingdom. A psychological profiler tells us that Mr Vitriol seeks sexual gratification through causing distress to complete strangers. That is what's making the job so much more difficult. But we haven't cut back on the resources dedicated to finding him. He's made mistakes before and we'll find him through one of these if more members of the public share what they receive from him."

Catchpole's lame answer prompted another frenzy of drivel with broadsheets featuring articles by psychiatrists and terms such as *scribo-eroticism* and *pornographomaniac*, while the tabloids screamed *Pervy Penman* and *Vitriol's Randy Ink*. The dust kicked up by the police and media prompted the disposal of my typewriter into a reservoir. I missed pounding its keys and typing envelopes was quicker than making one-off labels, but having the older technology might have aroused suspicion and a laser printer has fewer distinguishing marks.

Letters signed Mr Vitallium sent to people whom I had encountered only briefly, such as one sent to an oaf I had witnessed humiliating a hotel waitress each time she came to his table, had mystified the detectives and must have started many a fruitless search. It made sense to send more letters to those who barely knew me. In addition, to add a further red herring, I posted most of this type of letter from the Gloucester area, a city where work never took me, but was on route to three that did. And after Catchpole had spouted his nonsense about perversion, I enjoyed all the more baiting his force with arbitrary targets for my letters and misleading postmarks.

The Internet revealed details of the shenanigans in Toronto that had alerted me to the threat posed by my DNA. Dr Gideon Koren, the cornered author of five anonymous letters to colleagues not only avoided prison but also continued to work at his university and a children's hospital. The leniency with which he was treated might have been encouraging before Mrs Knattmaw started her campaign, but any flights of fancy I had about a low-key trial or a non-custodial sentence crashed following the hype surrounding Mr Vitriol. And just when I thought it had died down, Mrs Knattmaw's death and her friends saying they would continue her campaign reignited the media's interest. Let them rant, I thought, a further rehash of the old vilification will be no threat to me.

The Constabulary jolted my smugness two months ago after the discovery of a third woman's body in Ryego Forest not far from my home. The murderer was also a rapist and the best clue the police have is his sperm. With other leads exhausted, local men are volunteering DNA. My one slim hope is that the psychopath is identified before others notice my aversion to providing a sample.

Meanwhile, I must assume that my time is almost up. Fleeing would accelerate arrest. The Luton genetic link should have prompted my preparation of Plan B – acquiring another identity, learning a language and setting up a secret bank account abroad. Now it's too late.

Wine sometimes amplifies my jitters rather than dulling them. In a boozy funk last week I shredded the index cards that record the names of my targets and what I had done to those I had located. As the smoke rose from my garden incinerator I was full of regrets. Imagine how a train spotter who logged every sighting would feel if he saw forty years of data go up in smoke. Some details of letters sent are now hazy, but I recall more than enough to illustrate what stung me and to what kinds of action. In any case, the time remaining would not allow a comprehensive listing of my targets.

Two nights ago, the knots in my stomach kept me awake longer than usual. When I asked what was most terrifying, death though unwelcome was way down the list. More than loss of life, I dread facing detectives bent on belittlement, a hectoring QC, a judge ranting with righteousness, and seeing quackery in the papers about Perry Gray's defective personality. The quiet jail I might cope with does not exist. Has anyone ever been so naive as to buy the notion of incarceration as a holiday camp? And in the implausible event of a prison resembling Butlins and screws as jolly as Redcoats, what about the other campers with their predilections for violence, theft, abusive language, bullying and sexual exploitation?

I fell asleep considering ways of committing suicide; the many possible exit routes worked as well as counting sheep. I woke refreshed and began recording my story in code because, in the unlikely event of remaining undetected, I have no wish to provide blackmailers with easy opportunities. A downside of spying on others is fretting about my privacy. The odds of having a skilled snooper among my circle of acquaintances are remote, but unearthing the secrets of so many people fills me with suspicions that approach paranoia.

So here is an account of my life, a reward for the person who persists and finds meaning in these symbols. Not that I imagine a professional in ciphers would be impressed by a code developed to fox my little-educated parents, but it may flummox amateurs such as Catchpole's provincial plods.

If you are a professional code breaker, I hope the dirty washing of a fellow Brit will be a welcome change from ranting Jihadists or news of consignments from Colombia.

Chapter 5: Norman ~ Ann Grove

The remarks at the end of my last chapter upset Perry. I have not felt his presence since writing them and my questions to him have gone unanswered. I hope today that he is willing to communicate.

N Have you withdrawn?
P I'm here now.
N When I can't sense you, where are you?
P Sometimes I prefer to be quiet.
N Were you angry with me?
P Did you really need to warn people about me at such an early point? It felt like you were damning any chance of a sympathetic reading.
N I want readers, or at least those who do not jump to the conclusion that I am possessed or barking mad, to sense that I am informed by you without being unduly swayed.
P Surely there's a way of skinning and stuffing the beast without making it look like a fiend?
N You can always change your mind. If you prefer, I will write only about Rose and myself.
P You have me over a barrel. Who else could I turn to?
N Is there anything you want to say before I continue?
P No.
N Then I have a question for you. How could you be so sure that Knattmaw mistreated his wife?
P Can a leopard change his spots?
N People change all the time. I have known adults turn major corners after a crisis, or getting religion, or because an illness gave them time to reflect.
P Were any of them utter bastards to start with?
N No, but neither were they saints.
P Imagine meeting now the worst bullies you met in the Army and they still have the power to put your life at risk on a whim. How much would your trust them if one ordered you to cross a raging torrent?
N That's hitting below the belt.
P Only because you put off writing about what left you phobic of moving water.

Chief Superintendent Ann Grove's call came out of the blue. David Stancher, a mutual friend and former Commander in the Metropolitan Police, had recommended me. Ann's voice had an urgency that meant we soon got down to business. After seeking assurances of confidentiality, she said it concerned Mr Vitriol. It was the only time she said the name.

"V left almost four hundred pages in code. I want you to crack his text at the Constabulary's headquarters."

"I'd rather work at home."

"The thing is, he worked for a number of government departments and important people are concerned about what he might have to say. Given the media interest in V, we have to very careful."

"My home security is more than adequate and if I'm not working on the material, it'll be in a safe. And then there's my library and specialist software here that might be needed."

In truth, a code devised by a solitary criminal was unlikely to need anything from a book and my collection of programs fitted onto a few discs. I simply did not want nights in a hotel without Rose. This fib launched my second most significant episode of adult dishonesty.

"We need the decoding as soon as possible, so I won't insist on you working here."

Ann then mentioned what the police would pay, which was way below CARE's rate for the contract work I had undertaken after my retirement. Nevertheless, I accepted without bargaining. Just then, the sound of someone knocking on a door came down the line.

Ann put me on hold and before saying, "I have to go now. I'm sure you're perfect for the job. Can you be at home tomorrow at zero eight hundred?"

I rang David a few hours later to thank him and mentioned the rate in passing.

He harrumphed and said, "The police pay a good deal more to many specialists of your calibre employed as intellectual day labourers. Ann's probably worried about accusations of nepotism because she recruited by word of mouth."

His insight irked me because of the impracticability of advertising for a code breaker for an urgent and confidential assignment. Why hadn't I told Ann what CARE had paid?

"I'll know better next time. And I'm still grateful for the recommendation. As soon as the work is finished, I'll treat you to a good lunch in London."

Not long after this call, Rose returned from a fractious district council meeting. She was downcast; an unusual mood for her.

Even more unusual, she said, "I'd rather not talk about it now."

Because she had so often lifted my spirits, I wanted to return the favour. After swearing her to secrecy – though this was hardly necessary with Rose – I mentioned Mr Vitriol's pages and how I expected a call in the morning to confirm a contract to break the code. I saw no harm in revealing this when only a provincial police force and a poison pen author were involved. Rose was thrilled not only with the novelty of my openness about work but also that it involved Mr Vitriol. Like most people, all the reporting had made her curious. Unlike most, she questioned the motives of much of the coverage and, as with other criminals, disapproved of the offences rather than raging against the perpetrator. Her being so unruffled by Mr Vitriol had led me not to share the embarrassment of my reaction to hearing of Perry's death.

Rose's improved mood made the fee to be paid by the constabulary less of an issue. In any case, my pension was adequate and a generous bequest from my uncle had boosted our savings.

She said, "After you've finished the assignment, we could visit Perry's town, which by all accounts is unspoiled, and see his house."

"And stand outside like rubbernecking ghouls?"

"I don't think the police found any bodies there other than Perry's. Come on. It will do us good to go a bit further afield than usual. And it's a county we've hardly been too other than racing through on the motorway."

Just before eight the next morning, tyres crunched the gravel on Foxenearth's drive. A lanky man of about thirty-five wearing a dark grey suit and white shirt emerged from a black saloon. He retrieved a taped cardboard box from the boot before using remote locking. The indicators flashed, yet he tested a door handle as if he was in some rough city area. This and the two rear view mirrors inside the car prompted me to look for and spot a blue strobe light behind the front grill.

During his shoulders-back march to the front door he scanned the house. Detective-Sergeant Thorsen presented his identification as if he wanted it to be studied. There was something of a gingerish, if short-haired and beardless, Viking about him. A Royal Military Police tie completed the sober image. Television dramas lead you to expect plain clothes officers of his age and rank to dress down. I wondered whether he was giving evidence in court later that day.

After declining refreshments, he said, "I need to check your safe, burglar alarm, locks on windows and doors and computer security."

His methodical manner, clipped delivery, a Norfolk accent that I expected his Army service has speeded up and added grit to, suggested that he equated casual with scruffy: one of those men made forever formal and fastidious by military service.

"You're not taking any chances then?"

He smiled grimly. "The Chief Superintendant insists on thoroughness. Especially when a minister might be embarrassed, she takes no prisoners."

Though I knew what he meant, I fished. "Cabinet ministers or vicars?"

"I'm sure she prays for both sorts."

Thorsen carried the box under one arm while he inspected. I saw something of myself before retirement in him; he felt more comfortable with work than relationships and preferred following rules to risk taking. After home security had met with his approval, he had me check the contents of the box against a list. As well as photocopies of the pages in code, it held an analysis of Perry's linguistic style, a list of government departments and companies that had been his clients, four of Perry's reports on computer security written for private companies, and the names and locations of Mr Vitriol's known targets. Although I only glanced at the latter, Knattmaw stood out and brought to mind his distraught widow on television.

"Now, Mr Midlin, if you'll just sign and date the two copies."

The forms included my date of birth and middle name, George. I had not given these to Ann and only had used George when legally required to do so. While I know better than most how easy it is to locate such information, still a shiver rattled my spine. The form required the safekeeping of the documents but, curiously, there was no mention of confidentiality or making copies. These lapses, two spelling mistakes and a misplaced comma suggested hurried drafting. I suspected that the author of the form was not my meticulous visitor.

As I saw Thorsen out, he said, "You do understand, sir, even though Gray is dead, this is still very important for us."

"I appreciate that Knattmaw was very popular."

He puffed his cheeks as if to indicate that I was wet behind the ears and appeared to be about to contradict before saying, "A force like ours doesn't often take the lead in something high profile. You could find well-known names in the coded pages."

"So the code might reveal some ministerial cock-ups?"

Rather than denying or confirming, he looked around and said in cod Cockney, "Very nice house, Mr Midlin. And the garden too. Very picturesque. Shame about the frost pocket. It could do a lot of damage."

His imitation of an East End racketeer demanding protection money was amusing rather than worrying because someone who rigidly sticks to the rules is not that menacing. His sense of humour was also unexpected. Odder still was the way he knew about the frost pocket when there was no mist or ice that morning.

"How do you know about our micro-climate?"

"I looked up Lychinclay on the Internet. It's surprising the difference that a few miles up the lane can make to the temperature."

I worked in my study, the one Foxenearth room not made over by Rose and still with furniture from our first shared home. The overloaded open shelves were made messier with layers of papers and cuttings on top of the books. An Afghan rug with one fringed end coming undone covered much of the stained and worn fitted carpet. One reason it remained was that fifteen years earlier lifting the safe had required four very strong men. Cables climbed from sockets, trailed from devices and tangled like lianas. Knick-knacks that Rose no longer wanted and I valued, such as three sea-polished coprolites, gathered dust on the mantelpiece and windowsill. Only the filing cabinet maintained by Rose with its papers that concerned both of us was tidy and systematic.

The forensic linguist noted that the code consisted of sixty-one symbols taken from fourteen exotic alphabets, a fact she found curious as there was no reason to believe Perry knew any foreign languages. My perusal of the manuscript suggested cracking would take no more than three days. To get a feel for the man and his writing style, I studied his reports. They showed that he had been a world class expert on the security of large information systems. His list of clients explained why the constabulary had not been able to get Intelligence to do the decoding; none of the government work was for the Ministry of Defence, Foreign Office or Treasury and the businesses listed did not include any directly involved in military matters. Most of Perry's consulting was for utilities, insurance and financial companies, the sort of firms that would have millions of customers.

Over lunch, Rose lapped up the new details. She was so happy and curious that I offered to let her read the documents brought by the police.

"Wouldn't we be breaking the law?"

"The contract is deficient and what people fear is being embarrassed, not a threat to national security. In any case, you'd never tell anyone."

"You don't sound completely sure."

Although I won her round by fetching the contract, sharing the material felt disloyal after the assurance given to Ann about confidentiality; it also went against the grain of everything my career had instilled.

Yet rather than speak of these misgivings, I said, "Thorsen had looked up Lychinclay on the Internet and knew about the frost pocket."

"I'm glad the web didn't exist when we first saw Foxenearth. If we'd known about the frost, we wouldn't have bought the house."

Her mobile rang just then and I stepped into the back garden. The sun shone through gaps in the clouds making the autumn crocuses, purple cyclamen, speckled toad lilies and red leaved heucheras all the more stunning. Rose was right. While our setting was not as perfect as we first imagined, we were very fortunate and I was a lucky man to share this place and my life with her. How I wish I had said this to Rose when she joined me on the patio. Death seemed so distant then that I took for granted the sharing of many more years.

"It was the organiser of my course in London tomorrow," she said. "Two councillors have pulled out and they want the other participants to go next month."

She sounded disappointed and I understood why. Before her mother had died in 1991, Rose had travelled to London at least once a month. She still enjoyed going back to where she had grown up, doing some shopping and taking in an exhibition. When the visit was linked to her role in local government and meant leaving home extra early and getting back late, she would skip lunch in order to walk a few streets of the capital. It was a pity that my work meant I could not offer the consolation of a jaunt with her the next day.

When we resumed our discussion of my assignment, Rose's questions made clear that Ann had not agreed the scope of the contract. Just providing the key to the code would not earn very much but, more than that, I wanted to transcribe the whole document to satisfy our curiosity. I left a message for Ann and, before she called back, a way of wangling more from the police occurred to me.

As Ann still had a note of urgency in her voice, I was equally brisk. "It may help me to get inside Perry's head if I see where he wrote and hid his notes."

"Is the code difficult?" Disquiet had crept into her voice.

"I'll crack it within a fortnight at the very most, but I think having more of an instinct for the man would speed up the process. And once I have the key, knowing Perry better will accelerate my transcribing." I emphasised *my*.

"Well, speed is important to us. Could you be at Perry's house tomorrow for ten hundred hours? I'll arrange for someone to show you round."

Two things were hard to believe; that I could so easily lie to a senior police officer and that she so readily obliged me.

Exploiting Ann's trust made me squirm as I said, "Yes, no problem. And you have my assurance that I'll work on nothing else until you have a complete transcription."

"Will you send instalments?"

"Of course. And I can work more than eight hours a day, provided you let me charge pro-rata."

"That's only fair."

She sounded so reasonable that I wondered how I could make amends before I asked for another perk.

"Tomorrow I'll give your man a decryption disc and email each day's output care of him. Without the CD, my attachments will be gobbledegook."

"That's great. Anything else?"

"I'll ask my wife to drive me tomorrow. If she can spare the time, it will leave me free to work on the journey. Should your man need to say anything sensitive, Rose will understand and retire."

"You're not planning to take your copy of the manuscript?"

I cursed inwardly for not anticipating this concern and said, "Certainly not. At this stage, all that's needed is a list of the symbols and more common combinations in order to crack individual words."

"Good. But do keep that list on you at all times."

My qualms about taking advantage of Ann's trust faded when Rose clapped her hands at the news that we would enter Raventulle, Perry's house. I did not explain to her how I had finagled her treat other than saying it was to help the work. Nor did I mention how this unnecessary trip would delay what others, probably departmental heads and ministers worried about their reputations, regarded as urgent.

Chapter 6: Perry ~ Rayners Lane

The secrets from my parents' childhoods and their black market trading, which continued until sugar rationing ended in 1953, meant that they ceased talking when I entered a room. If I asked about the fragment overheard, they frowned or said something like, "Little jugs have big ears." An innocent topic made no difference to them; nor did their habits change after I became an adult. This shared reticence always annoyed me despite the other things they did that conveyed their love and care. Dad went to his grave having told me almost nothing about his childhood and family of origin, of which he was the sole survivor by 1943.

Had Mum met with an untimely accident, she would have been equally uninformative. She even led me to believe that she had no living relatives until one knocked on our door. He never came again and she deterred my questions about him. Only strong medication, given to Mum during the last months of a painful cancer, lowered her guard. What she revealed during my hospital visits allows me to write with some authority about events that I did not witness. Where I use speech marks for words I never heard directly, it is because I believe Mum spoke the truth toward the end.

Gordon Gray and Maud Owens grew up in Watford and married there in 1938. Instead of a honeymoon, they moved nine miles south to a rented and dilapidated end-of-terrace cottage, one of a row of four, in a suburb of outer London called Rayners Lane. Their new location lent a respectability my parents had not had before because most of the area was recently built and affluent. Sadly, the terrace of cottages looked like slums compared to rest of the street, where every other property was a 1920s-built semi-detached house. The cottages dated from the time when much of Harrow grew hay for the horses of London and before the railways had begun to turn the meadows into suburbs for the middle-class. My parents were at the bottom of the street's social hierarchy when they arrived, but at least no locals knew about their origins. And while some in our street claimed to live in Pinner, because houses in that adjoining suburb tended to be bigger, Rayners Lane was achievement enough for Gordon and Maud.

Dad's father had laboured in a lime kiln until the Great War prompted him to join the Royal Navy. He was convicted of mutiny in 1916 for signing a petition against an officer regarded by ratings as brutal and incompetent. Many people regarded mutiny as unpatriotic and attitudes towards bolshie servicemen hardened further after sailors killed their officers in St. Petersburg. My grandfather felt deep shame for the conviction, a shame shared by his children because the gossip had spread around Watford. The lime kiln refused to re-employ him and he laboured where he could until, overcome by tiredness and a hacking cough, he could work no more. My grandmother then had to fend for five children as well as a husband dying of TB.

A twist of fate – more of which later – enabled Gordon, the youngest, to become an apprentice toolmaker. The lad had a talent for engineering and looked set to break out of poverty until the Depression closed the factory that had employed him. He was only five months from getting his certificate, but no one was prepared to help him finish serving his time. Unable to work at his trade where shop stewards held sway, he sought out non-unionised firms until one took him on as a toolmaker's assistant. The factory's design engineer, Sidney Beaufort, got Dad to make his prototypes, but was unable to persuade the works manager to pay the journeyman rate. Dad blamed communists in the unions more than employers for his unfair wage because, although never the owner of a black shirt, his sympathies lay with Mosley until the prospect of Britain and Germany again going to war. The same international tensions created a munitions-led demand for skilled workers. Mr Beaufort joined a firm in Harrow Weald as Production Manager and recruited Dad as a journeyman toolmaker. His new wage allowed my parents to rent the cottage.

In addition to his work realising designs and preparing workshops for mass production, Dad trained others to set up machine tools and supervised their work until he judged them reliable. There was dismay in the company when, towards the end of 1939, he spoke of volunteering for the Army. Dad agreed to remain after being persuaded that disrupting vital military production would be unpatriotic. The company, fearing another munitions plant might seek to poach such a valuable worker, promoted him from leading hand to foreman, designated him Master Tool Maker and paid enhancements to his hourly rate for both roles. None of this was necessary because Dad would never have left once he accepted his role was vital to production. He dreaded the idea of anyone doubting his patriotism the way they had doubted his father's loyalty to the crown.

Maud's father worked in a brewery and relied on the beer made available to employees to cope with his memories of the Western Front. Her stepmother, who had no children of her own, was a binge drinker. Four or five times a year the neighbours would know from her loud swearing or falling over in the street that she had hit the bottle. With such parents and living in a disease-prone slum, it is little wonder that only two out of six children reached their seventh birthday. From about the age of twelve, Maud shared a tiny attic room with her older brother until, just after she had left school at the age of fourteen, he went to prison for theft. My grandparents let the empty bed to a male lodger, an arrangement that alarmed a welfare worker who spoke to her minister, the Rev. Newelm, of her fears for the girl.

As a result of this, Maud skivvied for eight years in the parsonage attached to the Congregation of the Upper and Lower Tables, an independent church founded by Peregrine Newelm to combine his dour Christianity and talent for sermons with spiritualism. He and his wife saw themselves as channels between the living at the lower table and the dead at the higher.

The employers saw it as their Christian duty to deter further contact between Maud and her family and encouraged forgetting the past in favour of the standing that would come from piety and honest work. Mrs Newelm expected much from her domestics in terms of hours and standards and there was little by way of amusement in the puritanical house. On the plus side, Maud had three square meals a day for the first time in her life and the cook took pride in putting flesh on a bag of bones, so much so that the gaunt adolescent became a curvy young woman. But what Maud relished above all about her years in service were the comforting messages from her mother, whom she could barely remember, relayed by Mr and Mrs Newelm. Gordon also found consolation in spiritualism and became a regular at the Congregation's services and séances.

Mum did not seek employment after leaving the parsonage to marry until the war effort required women. Then she worked at the Kodak complex, a bus ride from our cottage until advanced pregnancy allowed her to return, at first happily, to being a fulltime housewife.

Before I was born in December 1940, the Newelms had agreed to be godparents. After the midwife had left the cottage, my parents discussed what to christen me.

"How about Peregrine Newelm," said Mum.

"The thing is, the Reverend's got a bad name for all those letters he used to write to the Times in support of Mosley, Mussolini and Hitler. No one round here knows we're linked to his church and I'd rather keep it that way."

"I suppose you're right. It wouldn't do having people wondering if we can be trusted, especially with your factory doing work for the Air Ministry."

"Tell you what, there's a Rolls Royce engine called the Peregrine. We could name him after that and not let on to the Newelms. They'll just assume it's in honour of him."

"What about the second name?"

"How about Sidney?"

"If that's what you'd like, I understand."

The way Mum in hospital described my naming rang true. She usually had given way when there was a difference of opinion between my parents. Her account left the impression that, were it not for Rolls Royce, a different first name was a distinct possibility. I wish they had chosen another because Peregrine prompted much teasing. Whenever a group heard it for the first time, such as at the start of the school year, sniggering and baiting followed. And sometimes snide comments came from adults, such as the PE teacher who said, "I can see birdlike legs, but they're more wren than falcon."

Even Perry, being unusual, invited comments. I longed for an everyday name and as a youngster had dreams in which others called me Ted or something equally unremarkable. But the only change came after Mum understood I winced to hear Peregrine. Then, apart from rebukes, she followed Dad in calling me Perry.

With Dad working colossal amounts of overtime, Mum found herself isolated in the cottage with just a baby for company. The working class housewives that she was close enough to feel at ease with had wartime jobs in addition to housework. Despite being desperate for an adult to talk to, Mum usually responded to better-off neighbours by saying the minimum before edging away. Yet one day her need for company was so great that when a well-dressed woman with a middle-class accent commented on me asleep in the pram, Mum poured out her worries about my size and her not having enough of the right kind of food for me to thrive. Not to mention her husband who worked all hours at a demanding job, but got the same rations as someone who worked half the hours sitting down.

The stranger, Mrs Holden, invited Mum to her house in a neighbouring street for tea. The leaves were fresh, the sugar bowl was full and there was a sponge cake made to pre-war standards. Urged on by Mrs Holden, Mum had another cup with two sugars and a second slice. She could not stop herself asking how her hostess could be so generous.

"I would like to tell you, but you have to swear not to tell anyone else."

"On the Bible, I won't."

"Mr Holden has contacts. The way we look at it, the upper classes don't worry about rations, so why should we? I was a governess in Belgravia during the last war for a family with an estate in Scotland that sent meat, game, fish and vegetables to King's Cross Station. There was far more than the house needed. The surplus was traded for things like flour and sugar and her ladyship had a horde that would have fed three large families for a year. You can bet the same sort of thing is happening in this war. Well, if the government stops the privileged being greedy, Mr Holden and I will live on our rations. He doesn't want to be made a mug of twice."

"How do you mean?"

"He was the butler where I worked. He collected the hampers from the station, took all the risks trading the surplus and keeping the bulk of the horde hidden from the other servants. Had the police come, the family would have expected him to claim sole responsibility. And, of course, with the war on, there were fewer servants and both he and I had many extra duties trying to keep up standards. That's how we got to know each other. But come the slump, the family sold their London house and Mr Holden was out of a job. We had a very hard time until he went into business for himself."

I have no way of knowing the truth of the story, but it was enough for my god-fearing parents to spend part of Dad's overtime-boosted pay on black market food. At first, it was about improving Mum's breast milk and Dad having sufficient fuel for the hours he worked, but, as children who have known hunger often do, my parents found great comfort in eating heartily. Then as I progressed to solids, they were determined to increase height and weight by boosting my protein intake.

It's not easy for someone raised in poverty to pay over the odds and Mum's solution was to buy extra and resell it to women she knew, which had the added benefit of bringing company to the cottage. The Holdens acted as wholesalers for dry goods and Mum, instead of bribing a butcher with two bob for a pound of meat, gave five bob and another desirable item, such as a bar of soap, in exchange for a larger amount, most of which she sold on. She swore her customers to secrecy in the hope that none of them would realise the extent of her trading.

Dad left the black market business to Mum apart from supplying the Holdens with devices for pilfering sugar from sealed jute sacks. After a metal spike had pushed back the woven strands, a fine tapering tube allowed the grains to be harvested. The probe needed to be completely smooth and made of a metal that resisted denting and tarnishing to allow the sugar to flow quickly.

Needless to say, I was not meant to know about such things. After the age of three, customers arriving when I was at home meant being sent to my room, where I was expected to remain behind the shut door until called. Yet somehow I understood almost as soon as I could talk never to boast about how much food was on our table or the store of goods kept under my parents' bed. And later, as much as I wanted to know how being a ration cheat could be squared with the Bible, it was prudent not to ask.

My family spent many nights in an Anderson shelter at the bottom of the cottage's garden. The Luftwaffe dropped most of their bombs miles to the south, but there were air crews that either through disorientation or panic rained death at random. Mum knew from her time at Kodak that the plant sent most of its output to the military. She came to believe the complex would attract a massive raid that would flatten much of Harrow. Desperate to allay her anxieties, she travelled to Watford to consult the Newelms.

The minister, after praying with Maud and contacting the other side, said, "Your mother is concerned for you and her grandson."

"Will we be safe in the Anderson shelter?"

"She prays for you, but wants you to know that the German war machine is very powerful. Your mother seeks the support of other spirits to help you, yet all of us, living and passed on, must bow to the will of God and his greater wisdom."

"But should we move from the area?"

"Your mother thinks that would be wise, yet it may not be possible for Gordon to quit his job."

The séance made Mum so nervous that she begged Dad to flee with her to the country. While the spirit message bothered him, how could he shirk his duty at the factory when other men risked their lives in battle? As a compromise, he arranged for Mum and me to live in Vaulting Ryego.

One of his factory's workers, Joan Plasholl, came from the town. She returned from a visit there with an invitation for Mum and me to lodge with the Hoggsons in return for domestic duties and a small wage. Mr Hoggson was a magistrate and his wife a driving force in the Women's Voluntary Service. Both chaired several wartime committees that brought to their large home a constant stream of visitors, for whom they received extra rations. Mum made tea and food for the guests as well as her employers. She found that she could talk with many of the people who came to sit in her kitchen once they had praised the refreshments she provided.

Years after the war, Mum's eyes gleamed as she recounted the stew prepared most days from six or more rabbits and vegetables. "The Hoggsons were always telling people to grab a bite. The vicar, the policeman, Red Cross people, the squire and his wife – they all followed their noses, had a bowl and said they didn't know how I made it taste so good. And you loved it too, Perry, once I had taken out all the bones."

After German bombers over London became less frequent and numerous, a much-restored Mum returned to Rayners Lane. My first memory involves the keys for the cottage clinking. I reached out with both hands for the glinting bunch. Tiny fingertips explored the cold metal's curious indentations and the way the keys travelled endlessly around a gleaming ring and jangled when shook. I scraped one across the kitchen flagstones making an unpleasant noise and leaving a faint mark. It must have been a Sunday because Dad was home in the afternoon. My parents smiled until Mum slapped my wrist without warning for putting a key into my mouth.

When I would not stop crying, she walked the two largest keys across the floor while lending the curious puppet a squeaky sing-song voice.

"I want to play with Peregrine, but not if he eats me. He can hold me, rattle me or put me in the door, but he must not put me in his mouth."

Then speaking normally, "Do you agree? Mr Keys will let you play, if you don't bite him."

Mr Keys was so fascinating that Mum came to rely on the curious voice and bunch to soothe me. Because I sometimes mislaid the house keys, Dad collected rusty old ones and added them to parts being dipped in acid and electro-plated. That they opened nothing did not spoil the pleasure of having my own gleaming set. His next present was even better, a petty cashbox someone had thrown away for lack of a key. Dad had cleaned and painted the box green; the inside still smelt of paint. Then he asked for my bunch of keys, took the smallest one and led me to his shed. With the key in a vice and me sitting alongside it, he used a variety of files until it turned the lock, something that struck me as quite magical. Mum put the modified key on what had been the string of an apron and placed it around my neck.

My happiest early memory comes from that afternoon when both parents contributed to something I treasured. Hours were spent putting my bunch of keys inside the box, locking it, hiding the key down my chest, walking away for a minute and then reversing the actions before starting again. After that, I would cry if separated from the key on the string. It went to bed with me and got wet during my weekly dip in our tin bath.

Mum's return to Rayners Lane led to a resumption of her black market activities. She took me at least once a week by pram to Mrs Holden's house. I saw more of the world on the way back riding high on the goods stacked beneath the mattress.

Among Mum's regular customers was Mrs Amberton, who usually came to the cottage after a night shift at Kodak with her hair hidden by a scarf tied at the front. One morning as she sat at the kitchen table, she slid off her shoes. I crawled under and emerged holding one.

She ruffled my hair and called me, "Pet."

I held her shoe to my nose and down came one of Mum's gentle smacks, the sort delivered when others watched.

In her attempt at a genteel voice she said, "No Peregrine. Nice boys do not do that. I'm sure Mrs Amberton's shoes smell as fresh as a daisy, but it's just not done."

The visitor stifled a smile. "I don't know about fresh, Maud, not after ten hours on the line."

I sulked, pushed the shoe away and retreated under the table. Cups clinking on saucers accompanied their talk about other women at Kodak. Mum expressed surprise that one former workmate was getting married and shock on hearing another had a son who had almost died at sea. I resented being ignored. Then it dawned on me, just because Mum was only inches away did not mean she knew what I was doing. I lifted the other shoe to take a slow deep sniff despite knowing that the smell was unpleasant. The attraction was being invisible and defiant.

With the women still engrossed in their conversation, I edged towards the stairs at the other side of the kitchen, climbed and ignored the prohibition not to enter alone my parents' bedroom. Mum found me by the wardrobe with my nose in one of her shoes, threw me over the bed, rained blows with Dad's slipper, took away the key on the apron string and shut me under the stairs. Once my wailing had turned to snivelling, I could hear the women.

"Peregrine's never defied me like that before. I don't know what got into him."

"He's just curious, Maud. And a boy's got to have pluck to get on in this world."

"He can have all the pluck he likes, so long as he does what he's told. I'm not raising a child to bring shame on the family."

"Isn't it a bit soon to be talking like that?"

Defensiveness speeded up the reply. "As the twig's bent, so grows the tree. Nip it in the bud, that's what I say. He won't be in any hurry to disobey me again, that's for sure."

I felt so angry that I wanted to defy her prediction. A combination of the desire to prove Mum wrong, fearing another beating and wanting my own way launched me down the slipway of slyness.

There were some hard lessons, such as burning fingers on a poker that had been left in the fire and eyes stung by pepper. Occasionally, the pain came from a thrashing, but punishment only taught more cunning in my campaign to avoid constraint. For all that I loved Mum, some instinct warned that her affection would suffocate if not checked.

Chapter 7: Norman ~ Raventulle

I cracked the first seven symbols of the code within two hours of Ann Grove's second call. The lack of challenge – imagine a seasoned chess player facing a novice – limited the satisfaction. And Ann's sense of urgency was not compelling; finishing the decoding a week later would not have disadvantaged the national interest one iota. Ministers and mandarins waiting to hear whether the text embarrassed them was not enough to keep me working after my usual bedtime.

Rose drove us to Vaulting Ryego the next morning. Four more symbols yielded their meaning between bouts of conversation on route. I could have asked to work without interruption, but going that distance without speaking would have taken the shine off her day out. Each breakthrough acted as a reminder that the reason for the trip sold to Ann was bogus. If people at CARE had heard about needing to visit Perry's house to help crack the code, they would have laughed out loud; the age of tolerating eccentrics in Intelligence had long gone. And they would have roared louder still at the estimate of a fortnight to break the kind of code a schoolboy might have cobbled together after consulting a children's library.

When Rose announced we were on the outskirts of Vaulting Ryego, I looked up from the pad on my knees. The road followed a broad sluggish river towards a town with nothing taller than the roof of a church other than its Norman tower.

"We're early," she said. "Mind if I scout around?"

"Not at all. Let me know what you think."

She cast her eye over a hundred or more large modern houses on an oxbow. "Look at that estate built on water meadow. One of these days there'll be a flood and the residents will demand defences. The developer should never have got permission without agreeing to fund anti-flood measures."

Sitting on our local Planning Committee had opened Rose's eyes to such matters and in turn I had begun to take an interest in the deals, if not outright sleaze, that surrounded changes in land use and approval of designs. Before we got to the old core of Vaulting Ryego, there were more new houses, some developed in groups and others squeezed between existing buildings. As well you can from a moving car, we admired the ancient church, half-timbered buildings, the square containing most of the shops, a terrace of Georgian almshouses, a green with a cricket pavilion and a fowl-filled pond with a sizable wooded island. Rose found the road to Raventulle, but rather than take it she circled the town until we returned to where we had entered. She took a different route towards the centre, pulled up at a bus stop, got out to read the timetable and returned looking peeved.

"Six buses a day and the first at nine-thirty. If you don't have a car and can't find work within cycling distance, you've had it."

"Surely they need more buses with all the new residents?"

"We haven't seen any new housing for people on low incomes. The recent properties are too expensive for families that haven't got at least one well paid job. And I haven't seen a business park or anything else recently created to provide employment for locals."

She parked our maroon Volvo in front of the Ryego Museum, based in the old Corn Exchange that made up half of one side of the commercial square. As the museum was not yet open, we inspected its window display of local family histories prepared by secondary school students. Pride of place went to the descendants of Ralph de Raventulle, to whom William the Conqueror had awarded the local earldom. We read that the Raventulles had prospered until the Wars of the Roses and then one generation after another had backed losing sides until the surname in England had died out. Meanwhile, other local inhabitants had flourished and several grand old houses, though none matching the scale of Raventulle Castle before it had become a ruin, had belonged to the same families for centuries.

We zigzagged slowly through short and sometimes winding streets of old and small houses, many of which needed refurbishment, especially the roofs. It had yet to emerge that Perry had lived in Vaulting Ryego during his childhood and journalists were speculating on his reasons for buying a house there. Most assumed his motives were malign.

"I don't see any advantages for Mr Vitriol living here," Rose said. "When we moved from London we stood out like punks at a Puritan's funeral."

"Lots of city-dwellers would jump at the chance to live in one of the nicer houses here, if they had a local job or could afford to commute."

"I suspect people move here and then find it's not quite what they thought."

"How do you mean?"

"Rather like Lychinclay in terms of old money and the depth of your roots in the area. People buy a house and then find their faces don't fit because they're *nouveau riche* or their home is too modern, or just because they're new to the area."

"We were Johnny-come-latelies and you still got elected."

"Being a newcomer isn't the only distinction. And I try to avoid confronting the other divides if I can do it in good conscience."

I knew what she meant. Tensions existed between young couples born in our valley and holiday-home owners who inflated the cost of accommodation; between those who did and did not own land; farmers and non-farmers; posher and cheaper housing areas; the local unskilled and migrant workers; and, of course, the hunt and anti-hunt factions. Rose had stood as an independent after a clique of sitting councillors, mostly from leading local families, had pushed through a supermarket development that had the whiff of corruption. She had led a campaign to review how the decision was made and then a protest vote had elected her as an independent councillor. Her re-election was due to the help she had given residents, especially the ones who could not afford solicitors or other expert advice.

And then it struck me, had Perry lived in Lychinclay a bit of eavesdropping and talking to gossips could have supplied a wealth of canards for his poison-pen letters. What use had he made of rivalries where he lived and the tittle-tattle that goes with them?

We drove north from Vaulting Ryego on the meandering sort of road Chesterton attributed to rolling

English drunkards. The pavements on either side gave way to a single footpath overshadowed for thirty yards by an unchecked leylandii hedge, another source of discord in the Lychinclay district. Then three terraced houses with very long front gardens marked the end of the restricted speed zone and the point after which pedestrians choose between walking on the grass verge or the road. Perry's house appeared after the next bend; little more than a mile and a half from the centre of the town yet without close neighbours.

Carved into the lintel over the porch in characters large enough to read from the road was *Raventulle 1867*.

"Not a castle," Rose said, "But every window top and bottom has sliding grills."

The well maintained house occupied a modest level footprint about six feet higher than the road and thirty feet back from the verge. Its orange-tinted local limestone, slate roof and tall proportions were all attractive. Less charming were the slim windows that appeared even narrower because of the double glazing with leadlight diamonds that repeated the cage-like pattern of the grills. Although no one had tended the garden for several weeks, the work to establish it was obvious. I envied the range of plants and remarked that unseasonal frost had not been an issue for Mr Vitriol.

A tall sliding gate barred entry to the drive and as we waited by it cars slowed. Some of those passing stared at the notorious house and a few, presumably people from the area, were more interested in who was in the Volvo. I waved because I fancied speaking later with a few locals about Perry to satisfy my curiosity. Someone recalling us outside Raventulle might help to start a conversation.

An unmarked police car that might have been the one Thorsen drove to Foxenearth arrived at two minutes to ten. The single occupant was a brown skinned woman. I assumed she was of Indian descent until she got out and stood as tall as Thorsen. Despite an unremarkable business suit, close cropped hair, scant make-up and being near enough to forty, she had the sort of western glamour more often associated with young models dressed to kill.

She offered her hand and said, "Hello Mr and Mrs Midlin," with a confidence that suggested Thorsen had provided at least one description. "I'm Daya Shaksena. Call me Daya. I hope you haven't been waiting long. I allowed enough time to get here for nine-forty-five, but then the guvnor wanted to talk and I didn't have a hands-free."

"Is Detective Sergeant Thorsen your guvnor?"

The smile wavered and recovered. "Actually he reports to me. I meant Chief Superintendant Groves."

Had Ann chosen this woman as a rebuke? If so, *touché*. I had not only spoken about meeting a male at Raventulle but also had expected one of European descent. Daya did not surprise Rose, but then she mixed much more widely than me and had been on diversity courses.

"I'm sorry I misjudged your rank," I said, "What is it?"

"Detective Inspector. Perhaps I should have mentioned it sooner."

I felt awkward and was relieved to hear Rose say, "I liked the way you introduced yourself. And please call us Norman and Rose."

My abhorrence of persecution includes racial intolerance. At the same time, nothing has equipped me to understand what it is like to be part of a racial minority. My fellow pupils at schools were all European and mostly English. I met all classes and inhabitants from every part of the UK during National Service, but the few soldiers with darker skins were never around long enough to become friends. And until quite recently, CARE was almost exclusively white, rather like Lychinclay which has little more to show beyond two ethnic restaurants and two GPs, a married couple born in Sri Lanka. My unease with less familiar cultures stems from a fear of giving unwitting offence and not from any dislike of difference. I wanted to say as much to Daya, but it seemed unreasonable to burden her with my ignorance when, no doubt, she already had the hostility of bigots to deal with. Just the idea of asking if her name was Iranian – she reminded me of a tall woman physicist from Tehran met at a conference – felt fraught.

Daya's accent and articulation suggested she was raised in the Midlands by a professional family and had gone to university. I wondered where and what her father had studied until I realised I was making far too many assumptions. Unfortunately, worrying about saying the wrong thing clogs my thinking with such unwarranted speculation and makes gaffes more likely.

Daya pointed a small gadget at the house and the tall gate slid behind the fence. Rose drove in behind the police car and as we were getting out the gate closed. If you discounted the Friesians on a rise behind the back fence topped with *Rosa Rugosa,* no neighbours overlooked the windows of the house. Thanks to my Rose, we enjoyed good relations with those who live nearest to Foxenearth, but how much I would have liked to work in the garden unseen and unheard, or to leave curtains open knowing that no one could see in.

At the front door, Daya said, "I'll show you the outbuildings first, but they're all linked to the security system. Perry sent us the code along with his keys and suicide note. Perhaps he didn't want his house vandalised by the police trying to gain entry."

While she was inside, Rose and I sniggered at the idea of police vandalism. Then the tour started in the most modern of the structures, a workshop of recycled red brick hidden from the road by the house. The windows were barred and we passed through a very solid door with two Banham locks. Inside were walls of white-painted breeze-blocks, a workbench with a vice, pegboards and cupboards stocked with tools, and racks of tidily stored odds and ends. A shelf of garden chemicals indicated that Perry had no interest in organic horticulture.

Yet one red-top columnist had assumed Perry's garden was chemical-free and wrote of "… an organic gardener who gave free range to his own toxic hatred".

On the same day, a broadsheet columnist had speculated that Perry was up to no good with so many deadly garden compounds. The opposing claims had suggested, and not for the first time, that Mr Vitriol provided hooks on which to hang different prejudices.

Daya opened a drawer with a collection of tools and seeing that the contents puzzled us said, "They're lock picks. Perry did many odd jobs for locals, but no one knew that he had these tools. When a woman asked him for help after she locked herself out of her house, he said that he wouldn't know where to begin. We think he bought the tools new, as some are unused. But we've no idea what he did with the ones that have scratches on them."

There was a neat pile of folded local newspapers. A headline about objections to social housing caught Rose's eye and we left her to read the article. Another solid door, this time with three stout bolts, connected the inside of the workshop to a glasshouse added to the long south-facing wall. The desiccated seedlings and brown-leaved plants contrasted with the lushness of the garden, which was green with one exception. I asked about the line of withered shrubs that had been dug up and laid on their sides.

"Perry's letter said we'd find morphine buried under lavender bushes. He said he didn't want some kid digging over the garden and stumbling on them. We found two containers with military-issue syrettes, quite old. He never told us why he had them. The post mortem discovered a cocktail of sedatives and alcohol, but no trace of opiates or anything to suggest a history of injecting."

Rose joined us and said, "Have I missed something?"

Perhaps the police did not want her to know about the morphine. After all, they had not told the press. I decided to tell her later and changed the subject.

"It's interesting how different newspapers deal with the story. Like suggesting his garden chemicals were for other purposes when all he had was similar to what you would find in many sheds."

Daya's smile hinted that my discretion about the drugs pleased her. "The press have been very helpful at times but, they also can be, erm, fanciful."

She next unlocked the former stable built from the same stone as the house. Though beautifully restored, it held only a tree-stump chopping block and firewood. One of the three horse stalls was filled with a stack of two-foot logs reeking of resin and another stall had a stock of kindling and pine cones. In the adjoining coach house with double doors that faced the sliding gate was Perry's car, a grey Peugeot 206. Commentators had concluded that he drove a modest and common model to go unnoticed.

"He had money so why do you think he drove that?" Rose asked. "Was it to be less conspicuous?"

"Perhaps," said Daya. "But if he wanted to be less noticed just for some of the time, he had room to park a second vehicle here. Or he could have rented popular models when he preferred not draw attention."

"Do you know if he ever had an expensive car that someone stole?" asked Rose.

"I thought that might explain it, but he always bought inexpensive cars. Curiously, he kitted them out with the kind of security you might find in a luxury car. Not just a top of the range alarm and immobilising system, but also modifications to the locks and a hidden tracking device."

"What do you make of him?" I asked.

"I met him once. After the second Ryego Forest murder he was one of the hundreds of locals we spoke to. I never suspected that he had any great secrets. He seemed unremarkable, apart from being anxious. I thought he was nervous of the police, the way some quite innocent people are, or shy of women. And some people still find it strange when a detective is not only a woman but also from a family of Indian descent."

Thank goodness I had not asked if she was Iranian. But was she Hindu, Muslim or Sikh? I plumped for the latter because of her athletic build.

Rose asked, "Were you the only police officer to interview him?"

"I'm afraid so. You can imagine the stick I've taken. If he hadn't deceived so many other people, I'd be questioning my choice of career. I still can't square the way he was that day and what his death revealed."

Rose went to the hedge and studied the cows approaching, as if they were eager to commune with humans. Daya and I continued to the front of the house.

"While Rose isn't here, there's something else not made public. Perry had a collection of bugging and recording devices, but like the lock picks, we don't know what use he made of them."

"Was he a psychopath?" I noticed it was another assumption, but at least it was not about Daya.

"He was anti-social and abusive, but empathised with people to some extent. Look at the way he worried about kids digging up the drugs. And as far as we know, he did not physically hurt anyone. He sent a package to someone. We think it was meant to look as if there was a bomb inside. Given his skills, he could easily have made a letter bomb, had he wanted to."

We stopped to wipe our feet on a large mat between the main door and the hall. Printed on the coir fibres was the outline of two stem glasses in black with red filling the upper part. They bracketed a slogan: *Only good wine served here*. Although the building's interior was no colder than the breeze outside, the house had that damp chill that follows lack of habitation.

"Something else makes me think Perry wasn't a psychopath. They can be charming when it suits them, but if you write anonymously, there's no need for restraint. Perry was devious and accused people of all sorts of things, but he never abused women just for being female, and for targets from ethnic minorities he never used racist language."

Rose appeared as Daya opened the door to the living room. After the immaculate exterior and hallway, the patches of ripped wallpaper and carpet edges lifted from their gripper strips came as a shock. Daya said the damage was due to police searches.

Rose was looking at me, as if to say, she wasn't joking about the police vandalism.

"What were you looking for?" I asked.

"Cables more than anything else. You'll see why in a minute."

"Do you have *any* idea what made him tick?"

"Our psychologist is reluctant to commit himself again until he sees your decoding, so offering my amateur views would be pretty rash."

"No disrespect to your expert," said Rose, "But you're an experienced detective and a woman's intuition should count for something."

Daya beamed and I admired Rose's ability to get people to talk.

"Sometimes categories are too limited for a complicated person. It's better to build on what we know rather than grab at labels. Perry was intelligent, clever with his hands and able to learn new skills quickly."

When she hesitated, Rose, who by now was perched on a windowsill to catch the warmth of the sun, said, "Go on."

"Being seen as wealthy probably wasn't that important, look at the car. A data centre manager said she admired Perry because even though he was uncomfortable criticising others, he still did it when the issue was serious. Around here, people saw him as inoffensive. Perhaps that relates to how he responded to offence and fearing that others might deal out retribution the way he did?"

Her insights confirmed my favourable impression. She was like Rose. Along with a pleasant manner, there was depth and a talent for reasoning. Then I realised that comparing her was like grabbing a label. Daya was another individual. To start with, she had grown up in a family that probably had its roots in a different culture and I had no idea what that might involve.

She led us across the hall and through a dining room dominated by a round table surrounded by eight upholstered chairs.

"From what we can gather the table was used mainly for poker. There's a group in the town who've met for years and it was the nearest Perry came to joining a club. But no one thinks that Perry had any particular friend among the players."

"What do local people tell the police about him?" I asked.

"The most striking thing is no one thought he was opposed to their views. For example, supporters of blood sports and those against both thought he was sympathetic to their cause. In reality, he never said and no one knows where he stood on religion or politics. He seems to have been a human chameleon."

She sounded mystified by the guardedness that made perfect sense to me. It was the first hint that parts of Perry's personality overlapped with mine.

"What about relationships?" asked Rose.

"For all we know, he might have died a virgin because none of the women who went out with him speak of much more physical contact than a peck on the cheek. He took them out for meals and to the cinema or they went for a walk. He liked pubs and he readily spoke to women in them, but he didn't seem to take any of his girlfriends to a pub just for a drink. And when he cooked the odd meal for his women friends from around here, it was always lunch with lots of good wine and no hanky-panky, if the ladies are telling the truth. One says she invited him in for a coffee at the end of an evening and Perry declined. Her reading was he knew she was offering more than a hot drink."

Rose, who had looked in several cupboards, said, "It's a well equipped kitchen, especially for a man living alone. He seemed to like buying gadgets, but at least they look used. The décor suggests a couple with different tastes and at least one of them very house proud."

I asked, "Do you think he was gay?"

She tutted. "Men don't have to be gay to be in touch with their feminine side."

"But turning down women and pictures of Bugattis in a kitchen that is largely pink?"

Daya watched us while giving nothing away.

Rose did what she was so good at, making me laugh at myself. "Turning down a woman doesn't make a man gay anymore than a woman rebuffing a man makes her a lesbian. And it's to Perry's credit that he could encompass differences in his tastes. He was the one living here so why shouldn't he furnish it to meet his needs? If you're trying to say Perry's tastes are part of his malady, God knows what the fashion pathologists would say about your study. But I'm sure you would pooh-pooh such experts for linking it to the state of your soul. What do you think of Perry's décor, Daya?"

"My parents think my flat is so plain that I must have renounced the world. I think their tastes are over-the-top and make anything here look restrained."

We all laughed.

Daya led the way to the staircase. On the way up, Rose and I exchanged glances as if to say that we had not expected to find such merriment at Raventulle. The smallest of three upstairs rooms was a carpeted office. All the furniture, apart from an Aeron chair and the filing cabinets, was solid oak that might have passed for antique had Chippendale and his contemporaries cut holes in surfaces for cables. The desk, which was shorter than most made for adults, overlooked the road and had the monitor to one side of the window.

"This was where Perry did his legitimate work. We went through every paper and file and found nothing out of the ordinary, apart from his level of computer security."

Next door was an *en suite* bedroom, which the police had no reason to believe anyone had ever used.

"But it's such a beautiful guest room," Rose said. "Why go to the trouble of fitting a shower and toilet if no one is going to use it?"

"It's just one of the lesser mysteries we're working on."

In the main bedroom, I looked at Perry's clothes. His sloppier sweaters might have fitted me thirty years ago. The tweedier items reminded me of my tastes. I examined some of the labels and showed Rose a jacket and a cap sold by Dunn & Co.

She chortled. "Once Dunn's disappeared from the high street, Norman lost interest in buying clothes. It was the only menswear shop he was ever comfortable in."

"I do miss them. They knew how to be of service and their stuff lasts."

"Take no notice of him, Daya. Sometimes Norman thinks that everything that came after penny-farthings is too modern."

Though Rose's mockery was affectionate, Daya hesitated to laugh until I chuckled.

We returned to the hall and walked towards the rear where side-by-side open doors led to a laundry and a toilet. Opposite these and under the landing was a long modern tapestry reminiscent of a Chagall painting. It was odd that such a striking feature would be seen most readily by guests coming from the toilet. Daya pushed the tapestry along the brass rail that suspended it to reveal a steel door and architrave. Both were painted oxide red as if to make clear they were not mere wood. She unlocked the door, pulled it open and turned the key again to demonstrate how it moved five bolts.

Rose said, "It's the sort of security you expect to find in a bank. I thought the papers were exaggerating."

"They got carried away with a few things," Daya said as she switched on lights. "But Perry's investment in security was huge and the cellar was his citadel. Look at how the area of wall that could be broken into from the hall is reinforced with bars."

We descended onto a shiny concrete floor with tall wine racks on three sides, including one tapered to fit under the steps. Hundreds of bottles remained.

"One of the detectives who worked here is a wine buff. He reckons about ten percent of the bottles are the sort that could go to *connoisseur* auctions and the others would all very drinkable."

A pine bookcase obscured most of the cellar wall at the back of the house. It was rather large for its two dozen or so books about wine, three decanters, decanting cradle, large torch and a smattering of corkscrews and sommelier knives. Daya pointed the device that had opened the gate towards the back wall and a click echoed.

One side of the bookcase had three stout brass coat hooks at different heights. When she pulled on one, the bookcase glided over the floor in an arc to reveal a door with a rope handle that sat in a recess chiselled into wood . There was no obvious gap underneath the shelves despite the rollers required to allow such effortless movement.

"If Perry hadn't left the hidden door exposed, we might have smashed our way in from the outside after we found ventilation ducts behind some bushes."

Alongside the door and cut into the brickwork was a metal fitting the size of tin of corned beef. Daya shone the torch towards it to reveal a sturdy tapered pin. Then she pointed the gate gadget in the same direction. The steel pin moved up making the clicking noise we had heard.

"It's simple and effective," said Daya as she illuminated three hinges attached to the far side of the bookcase and then an eyehook screwed into the back at the other end. "The pin is mains-powered and slightly angled. It pulls the hook so that the timber is flush against the wall. And the hinges can't be seen when the bookcase is returned."

"Is it Perry's own design?" Rose asked.

"We're pretty sure he put in the wall and door for the hidden room without help. Builders had expanded the cellar for him, but they left it as an undivided area.

As Daya entered the hidden room, I whispered to Rose, "After years in Intelligence, I finally see something worthy of a James Bond film."

The concealed part of the cellar had prompted reporters to use terms such as *command centre for evil* and *the psycho's bunker*. I saw the windowless room as a prison-like lair where Perry retreated to lick his wounds. The starkness of the walls in flat white paint, fluorescent tubes overhead, grey metal bookcase and filing cabinet, and grey linoleum underfoot resembled the nuclear shelter beneath the first CARE building I had worked in. Apart from the padding on the black office chair, only the built-in work surface and monitor shelf contained a hint of comfort because their height would have suited Perry.

I pointed to cables that indicated a missing computer. "What did you find there?"

"Our experts say that Perry deleted a lot from the PC in here shortly before he died. However, on an obsolete backup device that was on that shelf we found a copy of a local person's hard drive. That's not public information, by the way. We're waiting to see what's in the manuscript. Perry helped a lot of villagers with computing problems and we wonder how many other hard drives he copied."

"And he might have copied from PCs and databases in large organisations," I said.

"We just don't know. All his clients have been checking, but we expect Perry was skilled at covering his tracks. For all we know, he might have created gaps in defences so that he could hack in whenever he wanted."

"No wonder Whitehall is so twitchy. If he's left holes in the fence, others might exploit them and the public get rather cross when their privacy is compromised."

At the mention of Whitehall, Daya opened her mouth in surprise and Rose looked intrigued. I enjoyed their reactions. Daya did not expect me to know that cabinet ministers were concerned and I had not mentioned Ann's and Thorsen's comments to Rose.

I could not resist appearing better connected than I was. "A contact advised me that ministers were on tenterhooks. He suspected, rightly, that the police would not tell me as much."

Daya looked uneasy, so I added, "You don't have to worry about Rose. She's the soul of discretion."

I picked up a brown mug full of pens and pencils, many of which had chewed ends. I fancied Perry sucked these while he scanned the secrets of others and bit them as his hatred mounted.

Daya showed how the wall-mounted television in the concealed room, rather than connecting to Raventulle's aerial, displayed on a split screen views from external cameras.

"The firm that fitted the system ran the cables to the monitor in the living room. Perry extended the wiring to here once he had paid them off. He also added two microphones that link to here. We searched in case there were others. One mike is on the gate intercom, but works all the time, not just when you press the buzzer. He hid the other mike above the front door. Both mikes were linked to a voice-activated recorder. If he saw anyone coming, he could start the tape and not miss anything while he went to the door."

"I don't remember reading about the microphones in any of the coverage of the house," said Rose.

Daya grinned. "We invited journalists to the house and the first to arrive were so indiscreet while outside that I thought it better not to mention the microphones."

The cellar was cold. I switched on the electric wall panel in the concealed area and we returned to the living room. I studied the large handsome stove and regretted no logs burned in it.

"When we spoke to suppliers," said Daya, "everything at Raventulle turned out to be legitimate and he paid bills promptly. After moving in, he insisted on being here when workmen came into the house. He effectively and pleasantly negotiated discounts for cash, but insisted on invoices and he didn't want anything cheap in the sense of unreliable."

"Yet his car isn't the most reliable model." I said.

"Yes, that's odd. And apart from the hidden room, the house is so well finished. He also had bespoke clothes. So why not make a statement with what he drove?"

After soaking up some sun at a window, I asked to be alone in the cellar with the multipoint door closed. My instinct was that Perry sealed off the outer world before he set to work on his poison letters or the coded pages. Although the heater had made little difference to the room's temperature, I endured the chill for ten minutes so that Ann might hear that I had made an effort to put myself in Perry's shoes. Despite Rose being upstairs with a very amenable police officer, I could not eliminate the fear that somehow the steel door would stay shut.

When I rejoined them, Rose saw me shiver and suggested coffee in the village. I invited Daya to join us and, when she hesitated, I said that I still had some questions.
"Like what?"
"Like where can we get the best coffee in Vaulting Ryego?"
She flashed teeth as pretty and white as gardenias and said, "Follow me."
Did she guess that I wanted people in the village to see me with someone they knew was a senior detective? It would not surprise me if she had suspected this. Her brain was as bright as her teeth and I did not expect to match Perry in hoodwinking her.
While Rose followed the police car, I asked, "What did you and Daya talk about?"
"I told her about my prison work and being a councillor. She told me her family are Jains, but she's not really religious; just goes along with it now and again to please her parents. Their three great disappointments are her lack of faith, being unmarried and Daya not going to university. Her father's a jeweller and after finishing school she worked in his shop until she decided to join the police. She had come into contact with them as an interpreter; she speaks five Asian languages. Her family have never really approved, partly because Jains oppose the use of violence and coppers sometimes have to use force."
I wanted to ask Rose how she had gleaned so much information in such a short time. I could not imagine me getting so many details from even a white male detective without sounding intrusive. However, the drive was short and the moment for asking passed while I contemplated my full hand of prejudices. I had assumed incorrectly Daya's rank, race, gender, religion, higher education and

the occupation of her father. I also had counted on such a beauty being married and was about to consider whether she was a lesbian when I recalled how Rose had scoffed at similar speculation about Perry.

Chapter 8: Perry ~ Return to Vaulting Ryego

Mum's revelations began when, mellowed by a shot of painkiller and holding my hand, she recalled the incident that had started with Mrs Amberton's shoes. "You don't know the grief catching you in the bedroom caused me. I'd never hit you like that before."

I hated her fretting about the past when she had so little of her future left. "Don't worry. That was all a long time ago and I'd disobeyed you."

Her eyes closed and the face relaxed, much to my relief. I rested my hand on her fingers.

She spoke without opening her eyes. "I used to worry about you so much. Not just your size and health, but how you would turn out."

Instead of changing the subject or offering more words to soothe, curiosity got the better of me. "How do you mean?"

"Your Dad upset me when he got home. He said sniffing women's shoes wasn't natural and we'd have to watch you didn't grow up funny. But you weren't in the least like that. You really were a good lad after all. I'm so proud of you."

Her hand relaxed and she smiled as if without a care. I suppressed the urge to correct her.

After a while she said, "Bless Mrs Amberton. She was a good soul. Do you remember your walking harness?"

I remembered well the frustration at being tethered and unable to take a step without the bells on a once-white strip of leather across my chest tinkling. In fact, the reins had become a symbol of Mum's smothering care.

"I remember wearing them. What's the connection with Mrs Amberton?"

"I needed to take you on the bus to Watford and the pram was too big. When I told her how bending sideways to hold your hand hurt my back she gave me the harness."

I felt ashamed for not understanding Mum's reasons for the reins. But if you keep things hidden from your children, misapprehensions are inevitable.

A man that Mum had met at Kodak was killed in June 1944 when a doodlebug fell in the south of Harrow. Her nervousness returned and no matter how many times people pointed out most V1s never got more than a few miles past the Thames, her agitation grew. Dad suggested going back to Vaulting Ryego, but she worried that the weapons would find us there.

On a cold September morning she scrubbed me like never before, put on my tiny overcoat and buckled up the harness. We caught a double-decker and sat downstairs in the middle.

"Where are we going?"

"You'll see. Just remember to be on your best behaviour."

On a second bus with no upper tier, Mum took a front seat to avoid as far as possible the cigarette smoke from soldiers at the back. The driver had a wrinkled face and puckered mouth that made him look ancient. In the first mile he had a near miss with an RAF truck that led Mum to sit me on her knee with an arm around my waist. The improved view was thrilling and not having to hold Mum's hand meant that I could imitate the driver's steering and other actions. By the time we got off, I was so excited that I insisted on walking when Mum offered to carry me. My legs ached well before we arrived at a large house in a street dotted with mature trees. The woman who answered the door looked so stern that I backed away as far as the harness allowed.

Before offering any greeting, Mum said, "Is something wrong, Mrs Newelm?"

"Oh, Maud. Calvin didn't come back from a mission. The other planes heard him say everyone else had parachuted and that he was about to do the same."

The two women cried and hugged each other.

"I know he's alive. The spirits have told us he's well and in hiding. The quicker this war is won, the sooner he will come home."

They left me in the conservatory where I amused myself sniffing, touching and tasting different leaves. Then I followed their voices to a door. As I could not reach the keyhole to see, I listened.

"Maud, your mother says your son should go to safety, but not you. Now it's your patriotic and Christian duty to return to work and help the war effort."

"What about my baby?"

"We live in dangerous times, but your son will be safe from flying bombs if he goes well to the north of London."

"But Perry's not strong. He needs me."

"Maud, your mother is quite clear. Peregrine should go and not just for safety but also to allow you to contribute to a speedier victory."

I heard them stirring and tiptoed back to the conservatory, where they found me with my eyes closed. Despite pretending that a nap had refreshed me, Mum insisted on carrying me to the bus stop. She again sat at the front only this time I was on her lap with both of her arms pinning mine as she hugged me. Although I wanted to play at driving, I did not struggle because her breathing and creased brow reminded me of when she had lost her temper. I learned years later that Calvin, the only child of the Newelms, was two years younger than Mum and she had grown fond of him during her time as a maid. That alone would have upset her, but she also dreaded evacuating while she stayed in the cottage.

Dad told Joan Plasholl that Mum wanted me away from the flying bombs. Joan said Mrs Kyte, who lived just outside Vaulting Ryego, might be able to help because her two evacuees had returned to Sellyoak. Mum had met Mrs Kyte and her three young girls in the Hoggsons' kitchen. Despite Mum not approving of the family never attending church, the two women had bonded over their shared experience of London, which the Kytes had left in 1937. Mum also recalled the glowing health of the three young Kytes, all tall for their age, and the two teenage evacuees who had stayed at Raventulle, the family's home. From the chatter of other locals in the kitchen, Mum understood that Mrs Kyte, despite her city origins, was doing well with her milking goats, laying hens and large garden. And whereas the Hoggsons paid for snared rabbits, Mrs Kyte bartered for them with surplus produce.

She offered to take me for £1 a week, far more than the official rate for an evacuee. Her letter explained that she had just got used to having her own room again, having allowed the evacuee sisters to share the double bed there. But I could have my own bed in her daughters' bedroom. The fee was no barrier because of Dad's overtime and the prospect of abundant fresh protein to build me up.

Mum explained several times that I would stay with another family because it would be safer and she had to work at Kodak. I was not to worry. She would visit from time to time and take me back with her as soon as Harrow was safe. I understood on first hearing and resented being told the same thing day after day and sometimes twice a day. Perhaps she thought my frown was due to being puzzled rather than exasperated at the way she interrupted my play.

At Harrow & Wealdstone Station she briefly let go of the reins while buying tickets. I took a step towards the door to the platform, but the bells on my harness alerted her.

"No, Peregrine," she shouted and stood on the reins, causing me to fall.

I was not hurt, just furious, and resisted her fussing as best I could. A little later, I was beside myself with excitement when a steam engine arrived. I wanted to jump off the bench and clap with joy at the racket, vapour and sooty smell, but Mum's arm clamped me to her side so that only one of my hands was free. She kept me seated until other passengers had come and gone and then carried me under one arm while the other lugged a suitcase. I did not mind sitting on her lap, as that allowed me to see more, but she held me far too tight. I fell asleep and woke up to find we were on a small bus travelling through woods. The woman driver chatted with Mum until we reached Raventulle, which was not on the bus's route.

Mrs Kyte, fair haired and wearing high-waisted trousers that made her look even taller than she was, came to greet us. Seconds later, leggy young girls, all blond and with tanned faces, came running. Mrs Kyte suggested they take me to see the goats and hens. I soon lost my shyness because the Kytes were so friendly.

Lucy, who was six, took off my harness and said, "You won't need that."

After the hens, they took me into the orchard where two goats were tethered. Grace, aged four, showed me how to make friends with them by offering handfuls of weeds.

On the way back to the house, Tilda, who was my age but more than a head taller, offered her hand. Because she did not grab me, I took it. Then Lucy and Grace squabbled over who would hold my other hand until they agreed to take turns.

Mum and Mrs Kyte were talking in the parlour over a pot of tea made with leaves brought in the suitcase along with other black market gifts. The girls and I sat at the kitchen table where we could hear the adults without seeing them. Lucy cut into a large Spanish omelette with a sharp knife and then used the flat of the blade to put slices onto plates. Grace poured milk from a jug into enamelled mugs. I quickly finished my slice and milk. Lucy pushed the rest of the omelette and jug towards me. I had never been allowed to hold a sharp knife before, let alone cut food with one. Even pouring milk was novel.

Next the girls showed me upstairs. There were three bedrooms, but the one in the middle of the house was padlocked because the floor was unsafe. Mum's open suitcase was on the double bed in the main room and across the landing was a smaller room.

"But there's only two beds," I said.

"This one is yours," said Tilda, "But if you like, I'll share with you."

The other sisters objected to Tilda being the one to share. They agreed eventually that they would take turns. I was so thrilled with their bickering over me that I did not notice that they had dropped the question of whether I preferred to sleep alone. After a night of giggling and the comfort of snuggling up with a friend in bed, I had no reservations about sharing. The girls sometimes held me close, but their arms were never as restraining as Mum's.

She stayed two nights to settle me. Much of the time she sat drinking tea and chatting with Mrs Kyte and women who came to Raventulle. The girls were keen to show me everything within a mile radius of the house and I much preferred their company outdoors to the constraining maternal hugs and warnings inside the house. I do not remember crying at Mum's going or ever fretting when she was not there. Her visits pleased me, not least because she brought treats such as chocolate and did not interfere too much with my play. A constant stream of women she had met at the Hoggsons visiting Raventulle kept Mum busy. Dad came with her once and spent most of his only wartime holiday, all of four days away from the factory, fixing some of Raventulle's many defects. Lucy said her dad had only been able to afford the property because one bedroom was unusable and many other things needed fixing.

Mr Kyte was with the RAF in Calcutta training Indians to service aero-engines. He had left behind not just his wife and daughters but also six wall-mounted cases of butterflies he had caught. Sometimes I stood on a chair to admire the colourful details in the wings and the delicacy of the antennae until the pins that held the butterflies began to interfere with my enjoyment. I assumed the creatures had been stabbed when alive.

If it was not raining or too cold, I went with the girls after breakfast to play in the two-acre orchard to one side of the house or we rambled. We might be outside for four hours at a time, only returning when hungry. Provided it was light and we could see Raventulle's chimneys, Mrs Kyte allowed us to roam. When no adults were about, we left the footpaths provided we could do so without damaging crops or scaring animals. The girls said that only bad people and witches would do such things.

My parents had never hinted at a world of enchantment that existed alongside what we saw and heard every day, whereas the girls were full of country lore, ideas for spells and had several books that featured magical creatures. Sometimes we looked for fairies in a nearby copse, where Grace claimed to have caught a glimpse of one almost identical to an illustration in *The Charmed Foxglove*, our favourite bedtime story. Before long, Lucy and then Grace could read it. Perhaps they merely knew the words by heart because Tilda and I came to remember large portions of it.

After Mrs Kyte had read our bedtime story, she insisted that she needed time to herself and more than once said, "I only want to be disturbed if it's something very serious. If you need me, knock on your door without opening it."

A torch was suspended on a cord over the corner with the chamber pot. The blackout curtains meant we had to fumble to switch on its meagre light. After a while, I learned to find the chamber pot without the torch, encouraged by Lucy who declared it was unpatriotic to waste batteries.

Mrs Kyte's night-time rule did not trouble me other than curiosity about muffled voices and noises sometimes heard when I woke to pee. I asked the girls, but they had heard nothing. Mrs Kyte said I was probably dreaming and it might be a good idea if I had my warm goat's milk earlier, rather than with the girls before we went upstairs.

As soon as the sun was up, we were free to leave not just the bedroom but also the house if we wanted to. On some fine days, Lucy got us up early to go for a walk before breakfast or to collect eggs that Mrs Kyte would serve with porridge or fried slices of boiled potato. In poor weather, we stayed in bed longer and then played happily enough in the house or the old stables at games chosen by the girls. The only areas out of bounds were the unsafe bedroom and the coal cellar with its steep steps and missing handrail.

Towards the end of my stay, Tilda was my only playmate until her sisters returned from school. She persuaded them that, as she was my companion during the day, she alone should share my bed at night. Lucy and

Grace accepted this arrangement, which I welcomed because Tilda had become my favourite.

One cold day, Tilda and I came inside while her mother was sawing old branches in the orchard to supplement the coal. The sun filled the laundry and we played for a time pretending to light a fire under the copper, stirring the imaginary washing and turning the mangle. Tilda, having grown tired of the game, wandered towards the cellar door, opened it and peered down the steps.

"I can see shiny coal," she said before disappearing six jolting inches at a time. She did not beckon. The desire to be with her made me set aside the fear of falling and of the goblins that might dwell in the darkness. My palm ran against the rough cool masonry until I reached the cellar floor. Tilda took the other hand and turned me round. The light forced a scrunching of my face and a myriad of exquisite colours and patterns danced on the inside of my eyelids.

"There are patterns made by fairies inside my eyes," I said.

"Me too." She led me by the hand to the other end of the cellar and said, "Now it's even darker. That's what happens if you turn from the light after the fairies."

I nodded and she gently kissed my cheek. The girls often kissed me not only to say goodnight but also when I had a hurt that needed soothing or I was the baby in one their games. That kiss in the cellar was different. It was not play, I was not smarting and bedtime was hours away. Nor was it sexual, a word that had no meaning for us at that age. The kiss was pure affection and a reward for following Tilda into the darkness.

I have never felt so loved or happy as during those few seconds in the cellar. How to explain this? One element is the general happiness at Raventulle that came from good company, far more freedom than Mum allowed and Mrs Kyte never fussing or smacking. Then there was defying adult rules by entering the cellar, overcoming my fear to follow Tilda down the steps, our acceptance of being blessed by magic, and the way her words had sounded so profound.

Perhaps another element relates to what happened the next day and a desperate need to return to a state of innocence. After breakfast, Tilda and I went to the orchard. Lorries lumbered up the road and a convoy soldiers waved back at us.

"Lucy says they go to Ryego Forest. Let's follow them."

Assuming that Tilda knew the way, I followed her over the fence. The lorries were soon out of sight and before long we could not hear them, only the sounds of birds and insects. After much walking, I complained that I was tired and thirsty. Tilda urged me on until I insisted on going back. She pointed to an isolated farmhouse not far from the road with cows milling around a gate and lowing.

"Let's ask over there for a cup of milk and then we'll go back."

Cows' milk was a novelty because all we had at Raventulle was what Mrs Kyte squeezed from the goats. We expected the kind of welcome received at other farms that Lucy had led us to. Neither of us appreciated that the cows were in distress because no one had milked them that morning.

No one answered at the house. We went to the outbuildings. I saw the farmer first in the half-light of the barn and thought he was a suspended scarecrow. He had an open mouth as if about to say something, a face that was both pale and bluish, and a folded sheet of paper tucked into his belt. I stopped walking and blinked in the hope that this would help my eyes adjust to the gloom in the rest of the barn. After a while, the outline of a grey tractor appeared in a corner. Then on the opposite side were two bloodstained women lying on the ground, a dog with its brains exposed and a shotgun.

Tilda grabbed my hand, pulled me backwards and then sideways until my eyes could no longer see inside the barn. But the images did not leave me.

"We shouldn't be here, Perry. Let's go home."

I was beyond being tired as we walked back. All I knew was that I wanted the safety of Raventulle and nothing more to do with what we had stumbled on. When we reached the road, Tilda let go of my hand and walked in front, forcing me to run at intervals to keep up. By the orchard, she started to climb the fence separating the verge from the trees.

"But we can go through the gate to the house," I said.

"No. This way so Mum will think we've been in the orchard."

After we had climbed the fence, I asked, "Will we tell Lucy and Grace?"

Tilda looked uncertain, then shook her head and took my hand.

We never mentioned the barn again, not even two days later in a neighbour's field where Lucy reported the rumours circulating at her school.

"Mr Gilby went mad and shot his wife and daughter. Then he jumped with a rope around his neck. He left a note saying it was because his two sons had died."

I cannot remember how I coped with what I saw at the farm. Although the images are still vivid, I recall no nightmares. When I have chosen to think about the scene, the pictures were always still, but then I had never seen a film at that age and nothing moved in the barn. My memories are a series of snaps, as if taken from different turns of the head and from each step backwards.

The lasting effect of the incident was to turn me against violence. I am no pacifist in as much as I would have killed had the Army ordered me to shoot at enemy soldiers. And I can tolerate gory scenes in films by reminding myself the red comes from tomato sauce and the like. But the sight of actual blood and especially the idea of gratuitously drawing it has sickened me from the day of that horrible discovery.

After I bought Raventulle, an old timer in the Anvil and Shoe spoke of how Gilby had suffered from depression after serving in Flanders. He wanted his children to have nothing to do with war, yet both sons volunteered in 1939. The older became a pilot and died in 1940, a loss the father barely coped with. The massacre and suicide in the barn had followed the news that the younger son had died during a jungle skirmish in Burma. His suicide note insisted that his wife, daughter and dog deserved more peace than this life could provide.

He must have been deranged to kill others, but it is not madness to look at what the rest of your life has to offer and decide against living. I see more madness in those who have no reason to expect their lot to improve and choose not to avoid overwhelming disappointment and pain. Thank goodness that the notion of only God and those authorised by the state have the right to end a human life has lost its ascendancy.

Chapter 9: Norman ~ Rose

Yesterday's decision to work next on Rose's story meant that last night's sleep resembled the fitfulness immediately after her death. The mental preparation for the chapter made obvious how little I knew about her. Had Rose been writing about me, her attentiveness and skills in getting others to talk would have provided so much more material. Moreover, she held little back when invited to speak about herself; I had no need to prise or persist to hear what she knew or what was on her mind.

My self-reproach for not questioning and listening more was bad enough. Then as I lay awake after midnight, I reflected on how Rose and Perry, despite their intelligence, had ended up at secondary modern schools that limited their opportunities. Both endured terrible abuse in their late teenage years, yet he spent the rest of his life lambasting the people on his hate list while she went on to help and heal others. This comparison annoyed Perry, who argued few people would come out well with Rose as the yardstick. He insisted that I preface the chapter with this observation. I was so tired and low that I agreed. Looking back, I feel that he bullied me into this, but I will not go back on my word.

P Bullying is a terrible thing to accuse me of.
N You were very insistent. I found you insensitive to my mood, my inability to sleep and the misgivings I already had about the chapter. You may not have meant to bully, but that is what it felt like.
P I'm sorry for being so robust and not making allowances for the state you were in.
N I accept your intention was not to bully, but without good sleep I feel more pain and then the tablets needed to dampen it make me wearier. Please, let's avoid further debates when I'm in bed or winding down for the evening.
P Of course.

Rose's parents, Marie and Joe, met at Liggett Farm near Tiptree, while their families were fruit picking, the nearest many of the London working class then came to a holiday. In the following two years, Joe regularly walked the five miles from Vauxhall to Camden Town to maintain contact until the couple married in 1937. Their first child died after measles led to encephalitis.

Joe volunteered for the Royal Navy in September 1939. When Marie knew that she was pregnant again, she wanted to leave London, more fearful of infections than bombs as the blitz had not yet begun. She returned to the farm where she had met her husband. After having Rose, Marie did heavy work while Mrs Liggett looked after the baby during the day. Joe died in the Battle of the Denmark Strait before he had seen his second child.

The new baby flourished in the country. Rose's earliest memories were from Essex and all happy. She said the love of the farmer's wife must have helped to counter Marie's grief, which later Rose learned had almost led to hospitalisation. Mrs Liggett had kept the books of her own children and delighted in introducing Rose to them. By the age of four, she read Beatrix Potter tales and a mastery of Winnie the Pooh and other children's classics followed.

What restored Marie was the satisfaction she got from her work, the relative peace of the countryside and the support of Mrs Liggett, emotional as well as childcare. Marie would have liked to remain on the farm or find other agricultural work, but made way for men returning to civilian life. The disadvantage of her war-effort was that Marie had acquired no skills to help her get better paid work in London. She supplemented a widow's pension through charring. Her parents shared their second-floor room in a large house in Kentish Town; their former home having suffered a direct hit. They child-minded and cooked most of the meals. It helped that the grandparents could start preparing the dinner early because the kitchen was shared by three families and a single woman who had a small room, also on the second floor. After this woman left, Marie and her daughter took over the vacated room. Both grandparents died before their only surviving grandchild was seven but, as Rose put it, not before they had given her a great deal of love.

Marie and Rose moved into the larger room and the landlord let their old one to Stan, who became Rose's stepfather. She loved her mild-mannered new Dad and thought herself lucky to have his room as few children at her school had their own space and many shared beds. Stan had fought in the infantry through North Africa and Italy and longed for an uncomplicated life as a civilian. He took the first job offered to him, labouring in a bakery, and joked that he had acquired a taste for heat in the desert. If Army comrades looked him up, he was pleased to see them, but avoided getting drunk, which was what many old pals wanted to do. He would say he was working an early shift, even if he was not, and leave after a few pints because the unpredictability that goes with heavy boozing did not fit his idea of a quiet life. When not working, Stan was happy to spend most of his time at home listening to the wireless and smoking one cigarette an hour. The family managed on their small income by living very simply; tobacco and sweets, when they could get them, were among their few luxuries.

Marie and Stan began to use Rose's superior literacy when official mail arrived at the flat or a form needed completing. As a result, their daughter as an adult never mistook poor English for a lack of intelligence.

She taught others, including me, not to assume too much from another's reading or spelling by asking, "If it hadn't been for Mrs Liggett, how would I have done better than the rest of my family when it came to literacy?"

Her form filling and letters helped the family to move into a fourth floor flat with two bedrooms on a council estate in Finchley, six miles to the north of Kentish Town. They revelled in the luxury of having their own kitchen and bathroom. And Rose no longer had to lock herself into her room overnight to prevent an intruder.

For reasons that she never understood and her parents did not challenge, Rose went to a secondary modern while her classmate, a chartered accountant's daughter who had failed the Eleven Plus, went to a grammar school. Rose knew that something was amiss because their teacher had said that passing the exam meant getting a better education. However, the grammar school's teaching of Latin, more expensive uniforms and the accents of those who wore them deterred Rose from querying the jiggery-pokery with the exam results. By the end of her first week in the secondary modern, she regretted not protesting. Some of her new teachers struggled to control classes and even those who coped went far too slowly for a pupil who relished unabridged Dickens and annotated Shakespeare. Her one attempt to ask a teacher if it was possible to change schools confirmed that it was too late; the only option was to wait for the Thirteen Plus Exam, which sometimes enabled students to transfer to a grammar school. Rose became dispirited and retreated into books, often spending much of her school day reading whatever stories she could get her hands on. As a result, her maths never advanced much beyond the arithmetic she had mastered at the age of ten.

The idea of changing schools receded because her family could not afford a change of uniform. Stan had fallen from the back of a moving bus as it sped around a corner. He was returning from the dentist after having had his last eleven teeth extracted. A woman holding packages began to wobble and he moved to grab her arm. She dropped her parcels and caught a rail. Stan, groggy from the dentist's gas, missed the pole and fell to the road breaking his right femur, hip, and arm.

The injuries did not mend well. His hip in particular was always painful and his arm ached at the first sign of damp or cold. The hospital discharged him to the fourth floor flat, where he became a prisoner despite the letters Rose wrote requesting a transfer to a property that could be accessed with no or fewer steps. With no lift, he was unable to get to physiotherapy. After the accident, the wireless that had once brought such pleasure came to signify all the things he could not do. He stopped listening to football, cricket, music and comedy. Stan had never attended a sporting event or a theatre, but now he resented these activities because he no longer had the choice of going. Rose said his bitterness did not spill over; Stan did not lash out at others. Yet months before he died, Marie and Rose were grieving for the man they had known. He had lost the will to live and hated to be a burden; the more they showed their love by caring for him, the greater his depression. He blamed sugar for his loss of teeth and therefore the accident. And when he had no teeth for sugar to be a threat to, he gave up sweet things and consumed far more tobacco. His smoker's cough became louder and more frequent until he died from acute purulent bronchitis.

Rose had never known Joe, and his parents had died in the blitz. She had also lost the grandparents who gave her a home, Stan's mother and then Stan. So much death combined with some of the books she had read made her question the religious sentiments that had helped when she was younger. Atheism took root.

Marie, devastated by the loss of Stan, again teetered on the brink of a breakdown. Rose learned about the near hospitalisation in Essex and struggled to prevent her mother's re-admission. Rightly or wrongly, Rose was convinced that Marie would never return to an ordinary life if she entered what many then still called an asylum. I wish I had taken the time to discover how the teenager supported her mother emotionally. Each time I try to picture this, I see Rose with her adult skills and confidence.

The oldest photograph I have of Rose comes from the Festival of Britain and includes Marie and Stan, not long before his accident. Both adults look very shy; their closed-mouth smiles convey more embarrassment than pleasure. Rose is an excited and pretty child. Two years later, not long after Stan had died, a cousin took a picture of Rose and Marie at a wedding. The mother is haggard and seems to have aged ten or more years. Her daughter, not tall but taller than Marie, has lost her childish features, looks tired and uncomfortable. Her arm is around her mother's shoulder suggesting the child has become the carer. How easy it would have been to have asked Rose for her interpretation of such pictures.

Rose started a Saturday job in a department store to contribute money to the household. A manager thought well enough of her to offer a fulltime position, which she started as soon as she could quit school. She continued to read most evenings after leaving school and no week went by without visiting the local library, which one of her primary teachers had taken her to because Rose had read most of the books in the school.

When I was first getting to know Rose, I asked, "What authors did you like around the time you started fulltime work?"

When she spoke of books, her hazel eyes shone more than usual. "Novelists I'd heard of at school, like George Eliot and Thomas Hardy, but hadn't read. Then I saw a man who looked like Gene Kelly returning Priestley's *English Journey*. I took it out knowing nothing about the author; just because someone with film star looks had handled it. I loved the way Priestley wrote about the present and things that were familiar to me. I read his other works, fiction and non-fiction. When I'd exhausted the library's Priestley collection, I started to browse more widely. One day on the bus, I picked up a discarded newspaper and saw a book review for the first time. After that, I started to look at papers in the library for reviews and kept a list of the books I fancied."

"Why list them?"

"Because it would be a while before the library acquired them and I didn't see the point in owning more than a dictionary. No one at home had ever thought of buying a book apart from the odd Christmas annual. And I wanted to spend the money not handed over to Mum on clothes, make-up and going out."

"Did you ever ask a librarian for suggestions?"

"At first, it took all my courage just to be in the library. No one was unkind. I just felt out of place with so few teenagers and most people having accents different from mine. Perhaps some good came from it. If I'd asked a librarian, she probably wouldn't have mentioned writers like Koestler, Russell and Shaw. And without discovering them, I wouldn't have made the leap to atheism. But I didn't have the confidence to join any organisations or move into new environments. No one I knew belonged to anything other than a trade union or the Co-operative Movement. And the people around me joined them for what they could get, not to change the world."

This is another point at which Perry resembles Rose more than I do. While my parents were never political activists and their sympathies lay with conservatism, they communicated to me a sense that gradual change was desirable and possible. The upbringing of Perry and Rose was far more constraining, yet both sought as adults to make a difference, one to relieve pain and the other wrote what were in effect prescriptions for discomfort.

P There you go again, comparing me to Rose.
N Do you want me to ignore you, when I see an opportunity to contrast?
P How am I meant to win if Rose is the comparator?
N I'm not your lawyer or PR agent. I never undertook to represent you in that way. All I can offer is a bigger picture to help make more sense of your actions and outlook.
P I would like to delete this conversation and the one at the start of the chapter.
N But how can you expect others to take anything that I say seriously if they were to discover that I hid dialogues at your bidding?
P Do you have to use any dialogues? And if you're worried about them undermining your credibility, why mention them?
N The way I see it, part of my unique insights into you come from our conversations. And the most liberating thing about my impending death is not worrying what others will make of what I wrote. I'll be gone before anyone living sees this.
P Have you considered that your suicide will amount to killing me?
N You're already dead by your own hand. Whatever dies with me is not another human life.
P I didn't know that you could be so harsh.
N I don't seek to be harsh, but I will not yield to you except where you convince me without browbeating.
P That's just another way of calling me a bully. Still, I'll leave you alone. Perhaps I'm to blame for making you so tired and crotchety.

A manager spotted that young Rose had perfect skin and a talent for selling. He transferred her from haberdashery to cosmetics, one of the store's most lucrative departments. Although she longed for more interesting work than selling perfume and make up, she regarded her dissatisfaction as a personal weakness because other women behind the counters made no mention of career aspirations other than saying they wouldn't mind getting a supervisor's pay packet. With hindsight, she realised that wanting to be one of the girls held her back; the norms of the group did not encourage self-improvement. There was little malice in this apart from a clique of younger women who called Rose a college pudding after she had enthused about a book of short stories by Dylan Thomas. After that, one of the girls occasionally would ask in mocking tones if Rose had read any good books recently.

Rose spoke about her first marriage without her usual vivacity. It suited me to interpret this as a sign that she did not want to dwell on Rodney Gates, but really it was my general reserve, a particular reluctance to ask personal questions, and the insecurity that came from knowing her ex-husband was very handsome. She had several friends who gave her the space and encouragement that I withheld. At least three living confidantes are bound to know far more about what led up to the divorce than I do. And yet I have not phoned any of them.

If Rose did pour out her heart about Rodney, the women may think that she had her reasons for not wanting me to know and believe that confidences must be respected even after death. Or is this an excuse to save me the embarrassment of admitting to the friends that I ignored this aspect of Rose's life and know only the bare bones of what happened?

Rodney was twenty-four when he first spoke to seventeen year-old Rose at the perfume counter. He came back the next day, but in the meanwhile, a shop assistant had warned that he had refused to marry a girl after getting her pregnant. Rose declined to go out with him, which only made Rodney keener. He kept coming back to the counter until she said the supervisor had forbidden her to speak to him in the shop. He started waiting for her at the staff door after work.

After she had refused to go to a Bill Haley and the Comets concert with him when most teenagers in the country were in hysterics about the band, he said, "For God's sake girl, what do I have to do to get a date with you?"

Rose was attracted by his looks, confidence and persistence. "Tell me you accept that I'm going to be a virgin until my wedding day."

"Is that all?"

"You haven't said it yet."

"OK. I accept."

Her first inkling that Rodney was despicable came three months later in his flat when he lost his temper just after she had agreed to marry him. He assumed the acceptance of the engagement ring entitled him to penetrative sex. Rose reminded him of their understanding. On that occasion, his outburst was limited to verbal abuse and throwing condoms at her.

"I forgave him. I was fighting my own urges so it wasn't hard understanding his frustration. But I never imagined that the next thing he flung at me would be far weightier. Our compromise was to bring forward the wedding date."

They were married in a registry office seven weeks later. Rodney insisted on paying for the reception because his parents wanted to invite a lot of people. Among the guests of the groom's family were the Naysmyth brothers. Rose noted how the Gates and their other guests treated the Naysmyths with great deference. She overheard two women in the toilets discussing how a shop owner who refused to pay protection money to the brothers was roughed up and had his window smashed.

During their honeymoon in Jersey, Rose asked about the Naysmyths after Rodney had ignored a publican's warning about the strength of the local cider and downed a second pint of it before lunch. The drink made him unusually talkative.

"My Dad does some business with them. He's known the oldest for a long time. They used to knock around Hoxton together. Then their family went into scrap metal in East Ham and they do all right from it."

But after this snippet, Rodney was evasive and got ratty if she sought more details. Rose desisted. After all, Rodney had left Hoxton for West London three years before he met Rose and he liked to emphasise how he was different from his male relatives. His dad, for example, could barely write his name and worked as a porter in a spice warehouse. Rodney had gone to grammar school and achieved reasonable results until asked by the head to give back his prefect's badge for smoking. Rodney bent the badge, dropped it on the floor and quit school. He got a job in a Hackney record shop that was part of a chain. The other employees, who tended to be much older, did not like popular music and some detested anything other than classical. Within a year, Rodney was selling more than anyone else in the shop because teenagers came to him.

He evaded National Service on spurious medical grounds. All Rose knew was that he had taken something before attending the medical. At the age of twenty, he took over the company's Earls Court branch as a temporary manager and changed the window display to attract teenagers. The weekly turnover shot up, he became permanent manager and took a flat in West London. He reduced the floor area for classical records to expand what appealed to the youth market, got rid of the older staff by giving them sales targets they could not meet and hired younger people. Such was the success in terms of revenue that the company put him charge of their twenty-two shops in London.

After the honeymoon, Rose and Rodney moved into a spacious and well-appointed flat at the top of a house in Westbourne Green. She reluctantly gave up work because that was what her husband wanted and no one gave her any encouragement to keep her job. Many colleagues at the department store said she was lucky not having to go to work.

Rodney proved to be far more moody than she had expected. He became irritable if asked what had delayed him or even where he was going when he went out for an evening.

In her second month as Mrs Gates, Rodney came home in a taxi with a steel trunk, large padlock and an electric drill.

"What's all that for?"

"Never you mind. But I want the walk-in cupboard cleared."

"Where will I put the cleaning stuff?"

"There's room in the kitchen for it. Buy another cabinet if you like."

That night he drilled the bottom of the trunk and screwed it to the floor of the walk-in cupboard. She never saw the trunk again because he kept the door to the cupboard locked.

Rodney left many things lying around, but never the keys for the cupboard and padlock. In fact, he bought a chain that linked from his belt to a leather pouch that held the keys.

She tried a moment when he was more relaxed. "So what is it about the trunk?"

The relaxation went in an instant and his voice was harsh. "Leave it alone. Remember what happened to Mrs Bluebeard."

She suspected that the trunk had something to do with the evenings when Rodney gave her a five pound note.

"Here girl, take yourself to the pictures and don't come back before nine. I need a bit of time to myself."

When she came back there would be more butts in the ashtrays than usual and two or three glasses that had contained whisky.

Rose learned she was pregnant a few weeks before she turned nineteen. Rodney was pleased and, when reminded that two flights of stairs would be difficult for a pram, said he would sort out family accommodation. They soon moved a few streets to a three bedroom house he had bought outright. The smallest bedroom became his study and he had a safe fitted, which replaced the tin trunk. He handed Rose a roll of notes for furnishings and increased the household allowance to pay for a gardener and a cleaner because he wanted her to take it easy.

"I don't see how we can afford all these things on your salary."

"I get bonuses for sales."

"It still doesn't explain how you can afford to buy the house."

"You don't have to worry about money, just spend it. As long as there is good food on the table, you wear nice clothes and the house is clean, I don't want to know what you do with your allowance. If I don't ask, why should you?"

"Because I'm worried for the baby. What if something goes wrong?"

"Like what?"

Rose stopped because there was a note of irritation and it was clear that he would not reveal the source of the money. She had never heard of a gambler who was shy when it came to boasting about winning, so the money had to be illegal. The fear of losing everything, a husband in jail and her struggling with a young child would not go away.

Rodney often left notes and coins in clothes discarded around the house. Instead of leaving the money next to where he put his wallet at night, she placed the coins in her purse and the notes in a chocolate box at the back of a kitchen drawer. Rose bought a sewing machine to make most of her own clothes and some for other women as well. She sought cheaper foods and prepared them to disguise the economising. The cleaner and a gardener came on a casual basis and, apart from the last two weeks of her pregnancy and the first two weeks after the delivery, Rose did the work herself. She deposited the coins in her savings account once a month and when Marie came to visit she left with a much larger sum in notes to bank under her own name at the North Finchley Post Office.

In Rose's sixth month of pregnancy, Rodney came home late several times with traces of the same perfume and got angry when asked where he had been. She noticed other perfumes after that, but said nothing until she saw a trace of lipstick on his collar. She pointed out the mark and recited the names of the different scents that he had come home with.

"I'm not prepared to risk getting VD from you and least of all while I'm carrying your baby."

Rodney responded with a curse and then a punch that missed her face only because she swerved. It hit her shoulder and she fell backwards. As she was getting up, he threw a heavy silver picture frame at her, slammed the room door and then the front door. He came home drunk hours later and never apologised or even mentioned what he had done.

When Rose was in her late thirties, she came home from a course on domestic violence that had stirred the anguish of her marriage to Rodney. It was not that I invited her to talk so much as her feelings, especially guilt, spilled over unbidden.

"He hurled the picture at me without any hesitation. His face was pure evil. I deflected it with my hands from the baby. The next day my arm was bruised from the impact and I couldn't stop thinking what might have happened otherwise. After that evening, he never even pretended to love me, just controlled me through fear. It was like ice giving way after you've ignored the reality of how thin it is. There was no going back to the illusion that he loved me or even knew what love was. I wanted to flee and never return, but I was afraid because he didn't let go of things easily.

"I didn't tell Mum in case she tried to intervene and Rodney went for her. When he lashed out at Colin for the first time, I wanted to flee, but where could I hide with a baby? He would pester Mum, hurt her even to try and find me, whether she knew or not. And Mum had just settled into her new one-bedroom flat. If she ran away with me, she stood to lose it and would have spent years waiting for the council to give her another one. I thought the best that I could do for Colin was to try to placate Rodney and take the brunt of his violence. It worked to a point, but then Colin started crying a lot because he was so anxious. Mum took him for days at a time to keep him out of Rodney's way. Colin had brought an end to her depression and they were more than happy together, but Rodney said proper parents don't farm their kids out. He was worried what others would say. I was near my wits' end when the police arrested him. His detention seemed too good to last and I pretended to be loyal in case he got off. But the day after he was sentenced, I saw a solicitor."

The trial revealed that Rodney had replaced the staff in the Earl's Court shop with less reputable people in order to sell records obtained from the gang run by the Naysmyths. He had worked hard to boost the legitimate sales to prevent any drop in takings that might raise suspicions at head office. After Rodney became Area Manager, the gang moved from stealing records to pirating copies of best sellers. In shop after shop, Rodney replaced the manager with a person who could be relied upon to support the scam; some were new to retail and few knew the music business. Rodney had to induct, support them, deal with their mistakes and help get rid of the existing staff. And all the time there needed to be an increase in turnover to deter suspicions at head office. In that sense, he worked hard for his money.

The company suspected nothing until a record label noted curious sales figures for top twenty records in the shops managed by Rodney. Private detectives identified the racket and the factory making the pirated copies. During a police raid, Rodney's safe yielded two handguns, a large amount of cash and lavish jewellery, some of which was traced to armed robberies.

Rose and I got married with the blessing of CARE while Rodney was in prison. I had notified my boss at an early stage because marriage to the former wife of a criminal was no small matter and withholding the information could have led to my dismissal. I worried for years about Rodney turning up, perhaps using the pretext of seeing his son, but there was not so much as a birthday card, let alone seeking to meet Colin. After another spell in prison for handling stolen property, Rodney went to live in Spain. He disappeared without trace from Puerto Banús in 1973. I used to hope his corpse would turn up so that I no longer had to fear seeing him.

Rose was uneasy about living on the stash of ill-gotten funds, but Colin's needs came first and the guilt she felt about the money was insignificant compared to what came from not having done enough to shield the child from Rodney's cruelty. She knew Colin's frequent nightmares, the way he startled so easily and his hitting other children who annoyed him were all linked to his father's irritability, harsh voice and severe slaps. Colin responded at first to Rodney's absence by repeatedly asking when he was expected home in the way a child might ask if the bogeyman is coming.

Rose would say, "It might be a long time."

After the trial, Rose took her son to the Port of London and explained how the ships were so big because they travelled to faraway places. She said that because Daddy had gone on a long voyage and would not come back for many years they would move to a smaller place near to Marie. Soon after renting a modest private flat in Finchley, Colin's nightmares fizzled out, his edginess decreased and he stopped hitting other children. Yet, just when it seemed he had got over his father he began to idealise him.

He would ask Rose to show how tall Rodney was and ask questions like, "Was he strong enough to push a car up a hill?"

"If it was a small car, he could have pushed it up."

"Will he have to fight pirates on his ship?"

"I don't think so. But if he had to, he would probably manage."

In trying to sound neutral in response to questions like these, Rose discovered too late that Colin had begun to revere Rodney.

For a time, she had wanted nothing more to do with men. Then she began to think that Colin needed a decent stepfather to help him forget about Rodney. I have long suspected that she, consciously or unconsciously, looked for opposite qualities in a new partner; someone short, swarthy, plain, who would not domineer, mock her love of reading and lacked the gift of the gab. Her aversion to what reminded her of the man who had made her life miserable worked to my advantage. In what other way could we have ended up together?

She did not go to work after we married in order to provide more support to Colin. There was still over £1000 in Marie's Post Office account. It continued to prick Rose's conscience and she asked for my advice.

"If you told the authorities, they might want more of the money back. A donation to a charity would be easier. But what about your mother? She's worked hard all her life and has so little to show for it. And it won't be much longer before cleaning work gets too hard for her. Doesn't charity begin at home?"

"She does deserve more, but giving it to her still feels like stealing."

"What if you let Marie have the money and you gave your time to a charity as a volunteer. Think how much you might earn an hour, divide that into the sum and commit to working that many hours until it's all paid off."

Through another mother with a son at Colin's school, Rose heard of a charity supporting victims of crime and became a volunteer. You might expect that having a rotten husband who went to jail and dealing with other casualties of crime would turn a woman against all criminals. Not Rose. A Quaker volunteer at the charity got paid work in an organisation that befriended prisoners and persuaded Rose to try a different form of volunteering. There was the option of not seeing certain offenders. Murderers, rapists, wife beaters and abusers of children – she saw them all, provided they wanted to see her.

Rose was in and out of prisons, as she liked to say, for over thirty years. That so few others put themselves out for inmates was part of what attracted her to the clientele. It took a lot of effort for her to get a paid job with a prison charity, yet she thought little of returning to unpaid visiting when she reached sixty. And she continued the prisoner befriending after her election to the council despite suspecting it lost her votes.

Colleagues admired her ability to charm old lags and hard cases that others found unapproachable. She took counselling courses without pursuing certification.

"Most of the people I see don't think much of mental health professionals," she would say to acquaintances on the outside who asked why she had not bothered with qualifications. "If they thought I was a counsellor, they would be less likely to speak with me. They're much more impressed that I left school at fifteen to be a shop girl and had a husband who worked for the Naysmyths and did time."

People often challenged Rose about her prison work.

She would say, "You have to think about after they come out. When I help someone not to reoffend, that doesn't just help him or her. It's fewer victims and their devastated families. And if the prisoner has a family, it helps them as well. And even if the people I see never leave prison, I can still try to reduce the chances that they hurt an officer or another inmate."

It was a game of probabilities for her. She did not expect to divert from crime everyone she met, but believed that a proportion would respond to being spoken to as a human being. Nor did she predict with whom she would succeed. She spoke of inmates and other people having days when, for often unfathomable reasons, they were open to influence. What was important to Rose was to develop a relationship that might just allow one of those windows for change to let in the light.

I can feel Perry brooding.

N What is it? I have not compared you this time. Why are you sulking?
P You set up the comparison earlier so that it's already in the mind of the reader. And I had already made known my loathing of the jail population. What chance do I stand against St. Rose?
N It's no good trying to rile me, Perry. You said yourself that we all have choices. Rose chose to help others rather than scheme against them.
P But she had one bully and I had dozens.
N I could say that the first man she loved betrayed her while between you and the people who made you suffer there was no love.
P I never lived off immoral earnings the way she did.
N So she wasn't a saint. But my point was about dealing with hurt. Why was she able to respond so differently? I don't know the answer. Perhaps part of it is being a woman? Perhaps she got a better start with her mother and Mrs Liggett than you did?
P You mustn't blame my Mum for what I did. She would have died of shame if the police had come to her door and reported any of the things I got up to.
N Parents affect us in two ways. There is what they knowingly teach and the vulnerabilities they impart, often unwittingly. Look at how I learned to fear lightning before I could understand speech.
P Yes, there's that. But my parents did a lot for me. Especially given the circumstance of their childhoods. Look, Norman, you're tired and you should have taken tablets an hour ago. Do it now and go to bed.
N Right you are. The rest of the chapter can wait till tomorrow.

One of my most vivid recollections of Rose comes from a week or so after I had provided Ann Groves with the decoding. I mentioned over breakfast that Perry had not gone away.

"If it's bothering you, we could talk about it in the dining room."

This meant sitting on the two easy chairs there without distractions. I agreed.

She must have looked much the same earlier and later that day, but our time in the dining room stands out. Her eyes were wide and welcoming. Some might find it strange, but I loved every line on her face; I still love them. If you see a plant every day, you do not see the changes in the same way as someone who looks at intervals of a week or more. Often I forgot that her skin had aged. Her body remained supple and strong, which she attributed to Pilates, but she had arrived at her first class five years earlier in good condition from decades of walking and swimming.

She slipped off her shoes, brought her lower legs onto the seat and tucked her feet under a voluminous skirt. The principle colours of the paisley fabric – teal and light grey – matched her cashmere sweater, on which sat a necklace of grey agate beads. Once she settled, I passed her mug and sat opposite with my coffee. From the first sip during these conversations, time became slower and richer. And this was all the more remarkable because when I had begun to talk in this way, not long before my retirement, I had been frantic to conclude our sessions.

"I thought Perry would go once the work was finished, but perhaps he intends to stay. It's like he wants to live on through me."

"So what's been happening with your muse?" She sounded curious rather than worried.

"I don't hear his voice unless I deliberately imitate him and I've stopped doing that. But I have this sense that some thoughts are his."

"Could you give me an example?"

"When I was cleaning my teeth last night, the radio mentioned David Kelly. He seemed like a good man and his death was so awful. I felt sad and Perry's thoughts came to me. He said bullying contributed to David's death and I acknowledged those were my suspicions. Then Perry wanted to know if I intended to do more than feel sad about it. He wanted action. I made it clear that I had limited information about what had happened and no wish to write anonymous letters. He insisted letters weren't the only option. The flow of thoughts between was confusing so I went to my PC. I typed this before I went to bed."

I handed her a folded page from my shirt pocket.

N You think I should do something about David Kelly, but it doesn't have to be writing anonymous letters. I hope you don't mean planting evidence or bugs.
P There are protests within the law.
N So how come you acted illegally?
P At least I did something. You vote in elections and the rest of the time you wring your hands. You don't even support Rose with her work on the District Council. I appreciate you dislike public speaking, but you have never even written a letter to an editor or signed a petition.
N Taking a public stance wouldn't have helped my career if it led others to wonder what made me bolshie.
P But you're not making up for lost time now, are you?
N Retirement was difficult at first and now that it's comfortable, you want me to do something that suits you and not me?
P Point taken, Norman. I do accept that it's your life.
N So why badger me about David Kelly? Why are you still here?
P But you conjured me up. It's not for me to return myself to the bottle.

Rose looked up from the paper, smiled and said, "He seems to accept that you have the final say."

"But this isn't normal. Am I going doolally?"

"You don't sound mad to me and being concerned about an unusual experience is a long way from being certifiable."

"But you were worried about me taking on the Vitriol assignment."

"When you discovered Perry was bullied in the Army, I was afraid that your nightmares would return."

"Perry seems a whisker away from being a voice that I hear."

"Even if you did hear a voice, lots of sane people do that. A Welsh GP found it was common, normal and helpful among the widowed."

"So when does hearing a voice become an issue?"

She had this way of fixing me with a smiling stare that made me listen yet more closely.

"I'll check if you like, but I think an enlightened psychiatrist would be concerned only if it made you very unhappy or caused problems for other people. I don't see how this impacts on anyone else. Are you unhappy other than being concerned about Perry?"

"No. In many ways I've never been happier. I like having time for myself. And I got a fillip from being involved as a backroom boffin in something so much in the public eye."

"I don't know of any way to expel Perry and I'm not sure there's a good enough reason to do such a thing when we're talking about part of your imagination. He's had his uses and even now he provides another perspective. He needs to be reminded of boundaries. It seems to me that when you have put your foot down, he's taken some notice. What about that as a way forward? If he stirs you up too much, remind him that you have your limits. Refuse to engage with him if the topic might upset you, especially in the evening. House train your muse."

"And if that doesn't work?"

"Then we'll discuss and look for other options. You look unsure."

"You make it sound matter-of-fact. But if anyone else knew about Perry's presence they would want me locked up."

"Lots of people assume hearing voices is a sign of madness because sometimes a hearer is very disturbed. But many hear voices without problems, provided they don't tell people who then rush to judgement. No one else needs to know about your relationship with Perry."

She waited a few moments before adding, "And Perry is wrong about you not supporting me. There are women councillors who complain about their husbands being obstructive or expecting to have the final say when an issue is voted on. You've never sought to influence me like that. And if you take a call from the council or one of my electorate, you always leave a message that I can make sense of. Of course, I'd love you to come canvassing with me, but it's my hobby just like I don't get involved in your Lions' fundraising. Don't let Perry worry you on that score."

"Thanks." I meant it, but perhaps my concerns about Perry made me sound half-hearted.

"Do you know about Tesla?" she asked.

"The inventor of the fluorescent tube?"

"And much else. He was prolific. One part of his creativity was not being afraid to harness his imagination. If he had an idea, say for an electric motor, he not only designed it in his head, he also created an imaginary test bed, left it running and came back weeks later to this figment to check on wear and tear. He said it helped him improve the real thing."

"How do you explain that?"

"There's more to us than the stuff we bring at will into our conscious mind. People stumble upon ways of accessing information stored in deep recesses. I don't think what Tesla imagined would have worked if he hadn't filed away mentally all sorts of observations and insights. What feels like Perry to you comes from many different sources; the press coverage and TV clips, his house, the decoding, and other experiences that you've accumulated over a lifetime. What you've described doesn't worry me other than you being uneasy with it, but I could talk to people who know more about these things, if you want me to."

Although I would have liked more reassurance, I was not prepared to see someone and nor did I want Rose describing my experiences to a third person. And there was still the hope that Perry would disappear over time.

About a week after that discussion, I had this sense of Perry hovering voyeuristically, as if he was a fly on the wall, while Rose and I were making love. The awareness was momentary, just as she guided me into her. Then the pleasure and my efforts to please soon distracted me. All ended well and I never mentioned to Rose what had happened. I felt I could deal with it myself and did not want to risk upsetting her. The next morning, I sat at the keyboard.

N Perry, there are limits to my hospitality.
P I know what you mean. I'm sorry. It won't happen again. But you must understand a virgin's curiosity.
N You never saw a blue movie?
P Of course. I know what sex looks like, but making love is different. You're a very lucky man.
N I'm an exceptionally lucky man. But Perry, you had looks that I didn't have. You could have been as lucky.
P I see that now, but when I was alive fear ruled me. And I never found a Rose to help me overcome my phobias.
N Nor did you seek help.
P I'm not exactly alone in that, am I?
N Touché. But there's a difference. You were deliberately hurting other people and putting yourself in danger of disgrace, if not grievous bodily harm. And you spoke of the grief for your parents that would have followed had you ended up in court.
P I agree. I see now that I should have waited till they were both dead, at least for the riskier actions.
N But what about protecting yourself?
P After Gatgash, it was too late for that. The damage was done. Once I stopped feeling completely numb, what mattered most was revenge. I never thought of seeking help. Had someone suggested counselling, I would have said, "No way". I couldn't have confided and, in any case, I wanted to avoid anyone who might try to dissuade me from vengeance.
N And if you had your life again?
P That's too painful to contemplate. To say that I wished I had sought help would be like admitting my life was a mistake.

Chapter 10: Perry ~ The Great Reversal

In April 1945, Mrs Kyte said Mum was coming to take me home.

"But I want to stay here."

"And we'd love to have you, but your mummy and daddy miss you and you belong with them now that it's safe."

"Can Tilda come?"

"No, she's going to wait here for her daddy. But you can come back and see us. You'll always be welcome here."

When no one was looking, I found the child harness, put chips of wood into the bells and wound the straps into a ball, which I carried to a rabbit hole. If Mum asked where it was, I heard nothing about it. She was in good spirits. There had been no bombs for some weeks, Germany was almost overrun, she had quit her job at Kodak and Dad's hours were down to fifty a week. Local women came to Raventulle to see her, or possibly for a slice of the cake Mrs Kyte had made with the bounty brought from London. There was even a bar of chocolate for me to share with the girls.

Grace said, "You're lucky to be going to where the shops still sell nice things."

Moving back to Rayners Lane was anything but lucky. I missed the girls, the easy-going ways of Mrs Kyte, goats, chickens, the orchard and roaming further afield. Our cottage seemed to have shrunk; rows of vegetables limited the space for play outside and Mum would not let me stray beyond the garden fence. I spent a lot of time sulking in the Anderson shelter until Dad, at the instigation of the council who wanted the corrugated sheets, took it apart and filled it in.

The only consolation was visiting Raventulle for a fortnight in August to give my lungs a rest from the London air, as Mum put it. In truth, the relatively low density of housing in Harrow, its distance from the Thames Valley and the prevailing winds meant we seldom suffered from fog the way central London did. Mum, weighed down with black market gifts, accompanied me on the holiday. Within minutes of arriving, the girls had whisked me away and freedom was restored for two weeks.

By the time we went again in 1946, Mr Kyte was back from India. He had resumed his former job as a maintenance engineer in a fertiliser factory. What I remember most about him was a thick fair moustache that stretched almost to his ears. He must have been home for some time because while we were there he had a week's annual leave, much of which he spent tinkering with his motorbike, catching butterflies and chatting with whomever was handy, including me.

One day when I was the only other person in the parlour, he looked up from his newspaper and jabbed his pipe in the air. "Britain is on its uppers. What the Germans didn't bomb hardly works anymore. The country's going to the dogs."

"What dogs?"

"It's just a saying, Perry, for when things are falling apart."

I thought it odd that he worried about the state of the country while he ignored the crumbling house despite Mrs Kyte reminding him of what needed fixing. Dad had done more in two days than Mr Kyte did in the two weeks I was there and little had changed at Raventulle by the next summer.

Mrs Kyte smiled as she mentioned any outstanding repairs, but it was a tighter smile than her best pleased one.

"Yes, yes. It's on my list." The husband smiled without reservation.

If she was busy at the stove or sink when she mentioned what required fixing, he sometimes stood behind her, pinned her arms with a hug and said, "I'll get around to it", or "Your wish is my command."

Then he would nuzzle her with his moustache to the giggling delight of the children. If we sniggered too loudly, he would grab one of us and rub his whiskers against a cheek. I was not used to this kind of behaviour, but I liked to watch the couple being affectionate and the way he extended the embrace to the child he caught.

With Mr Kyte returned, Mum could no longer share the double bed. As the third bedroom remained unsafe, she had to sleep on the sofa downstairs, which she found uncomfortable. From my third summer visit and onwards, Mum stayed only two nights, one on arrival and the other before taking me back.

I preferred her not to be there. With Mum present, the girls and I did not boast of our adventures, such as taking a shortcut through a field with a bull at the other end. Mr and Mrs Kyte, while disapproving of such larks, did not get all jittery. For one wonderful fortnight, I roamed and was relaxed with the other children. To the Kyte girls, my being the smallest in the house made me special in a good way. They made allowances for my shorter legs struggling to keep up with them. I was one of the gang and part of every adventure and chinwag.

We talked a great deal, especially away from the house or in the bedroom. Lucy and Grace, and sometimes Tilda, explained the world and cited the evacuees from Selly Oak as the source of some of their knowledge. This included why the bull jumped on the backs of cows, the way parents did something similar to make babies, and how the village regarded the Kyte family. Being outsiders was bad enough, but a family that never went to church or chapel was most peculiar.

On my second summer visit, the girls described a big row that happened between their parents not long after Mr Kyte returned.

I was incredulous. "What did they argue about?"

Lucy said, "We don't know. Dad got a letter and went red in the face. He sent us to the orchard and said not to come back until he called us. We could hear him shouting. When we went in, Mum had been crying. They wouldn't say anything. The next day they were canoodling again and said parents sometimes need to clear the air."

Raventulle was dusty. Motes often danced in the sunbeams coming through the windows and clouds emerged from rugs beaten outside. I assumed that clearing the air had something to do with getting rid of the dust.

"What's canoodling?" I asked.

Lucy made Grace demonstrate on me, which I did not mind, not even when the others giggled. However, I would have preferred Tilda's hugs and kisses.

Perhaps they mentioned this to their parents after I had left for London because Mrs Kyte said when I next arrived that I was too old to share a bed. Tilda had to squeeze into the bigger single bed with her sisters. I missed not having her next to me at night, but at least our bedtime conversations continued. And while the girls had become shyer about undressing in front of me, their affection was undiminished.

The August holidays were important for another reason in addition to freedom from Mum's fussing. Bullying at school had begun in my first class. Boys called me a sissy after I picked up a doll to play with and the girls, rather than befriending and caring for me like the Kytes, either giggled or walked away. Playground brouhaha, cliques and horseplay made it hard to talk the way I did at Raventulle and left me feeling alone in the crowd. The roar of sixty voices inside and the noise outside created enormous longing for the serenity of the countryside.

When I went to join the girls at a pretend tea party in class, Miss Thimby, my first teacher, directed me to where the boys wielded tiny mallets to knock small pieces of wood through various shaped holes cut into a block. In Rayners Lane, only Mum thought it better for me to play with the opposite sex. She regarded girls as kind, yet it was Shirley Morris, also a new entrant, who first mocked me with *Lickle Grin*, adapted from *Little Peregrine*. I stamped my foot and her two friends, Jenny and Meg, started chanting the name with her until I cried. The incident taught that showing I was upset encouraged more teasing, but by then too many other children had seen my tears and knew that Lickle Grin had started them. The name, or variations on it, such as *Lickle Cry Baby* and *Lick*, followed me through primary school.

Not crying when hit took longer to master. During my first term, Jimmy Reece, who was eighteen months older, terrorised the playground with his harsh language – "I've found bigger things than you, daft baby, in matchboxes" – and sly kicks.

Not content with calling me "daft baby", he insisted that I answer to this name. If I did not, his gang crowded around me and Jimmy slipped from sight to deliver a kick from behind. He then cited my crying as evidence that I deserved the name.

A teacher once asked, "Why are you crying?"

Her concern was enough to stop my blubbering. "Jimmy Reece kicked me."

"Jimmy!"

"It wasn't me, Miss. It must have been one of the other boys."

"Did you see Jimmy kick you?"

"No, but..."

"You mustn't say you know something when you didn't see it."

After the teacher had moved on, the gang gathered round to yell "daft baby" and assault me till I cried again.

Jimmy was not big compared to most others in his class yet he would have been far too strong for me to fight even if he did not lead a gang. His unpredictability and a need to act out his aggression several times a day made him a terror. When dared to eat a worm, he did so. And on the one occasion another boy hit him back, Jimmy went berserk until restrained by two teachers. The only sure thing about him was that he would wreak violence on anyone he suspected of getting him into trouble.

The last day I saw Jimmy was in my eighth week of infant's school. He made me stand feet apart with my back against the privet hedge in a corner of the playground while he threw a knife into the sparse grass. Each time I had to move a shoe up to where the blade had landed a few inches from my foot. He mocked when I shook with fear and, just as I was about to fall back into the privet because my feet were so far apart, he made me put them back together again in order to continue the torment.

A teacher saw him about to throw and shouted. Jimmy sheathed the knife and slid it into his trousers with the handle covered by his jumper. She demanded he hand it over. He refused and when the teacher stepped towards him he waved the blade and threatened to stab her if she tried to take the knife off him.

"Don't be ridiculous!"

He lunged at me to show that he was serious. I fell into the hedge to avoid the glistening steel and began to cry.

He laughed and shouted, "Daft baby."

The teacher grabbed my hand to pull me away. She told two older children to take me to the school hall and a third to get the head teacher. I was sobbing by the time we got inside, partly from being scared by Jimmy and partly from fear of punishment because teachers sent children who misbehaved to the hall. Within minutes, all the children with the exception of Jimmy came running inside, some screaming. There was no blood, just hysteria.

It was only when Miss Thimby spoke kindly, took me back to class and stamped the back of my hand with a purple leaping tiger – her reward for good behaviour – that the threat of punishment receded. Towards the end of the afternoon, the head called an assembly and told us we did not have to worry about Jimmy Reece because he would not be returning to our school. When Mum came to collect me, the head was waiting near the gate. She invited Mum to the office and I sat outside while they spoke in hushed tones before emerging with forced smiles. My parents were extra-kind for several days apart from Mum having an even greater reluctance to let me out of her sight.

While I was happy to imagine Jimmy Reece shivering in a prison cell, his gang missed him and blamed me for what had happened. The boys continued to humiliate and assault. Daft baby was another name that followed me for several years.

Miss Thimby saw part of her role with new entrants as getting them used to school discipline and one part of this was banning talk for long periods. As I found the clamour of so many children oppressive, I welcomed the silence, but not the sitting still with arms folded that often accompanied it. Nor did I like putting up a hand for permission to answer a question. Toys, books and other fascinating objects were so near and yet forbidden for most of the time. Not only could we not touch these things without permission, we had to keep our eyes to the front for long periods. Miss Thimby was attractive even to my young eyes, but I did not want watch her all day long. Boredom and strict control of access to the contents of the classroom sparked the same sly resistance as Mum's stultifying regime at home.

My desk was next to the nature table and its treasures. One morning, as the class sat upright with folded arms, Miss Thimby dropped a box of pencils. All eyes gaped at the spillage. In a flash, I scooped a scallop shell from the nature table and hid it under my jumper. For a time, I was content to finger the shell as it pressed against my stomach. Then I placed it behind my waist band and pretended to need the toilet. In the privacy of a cubicle, I sniffed and viewed the shell from every angle before returning to class. During another distraction, the scallop reappeared on the table.

I did the same on other days with a magpie feather, a pinecone and a piece of glittering rock. Returning the items undetected after examining them at leisure doubled the pleasure of my disobedience. I relished having my way and proving that Miss Thimby's beautiful green eyes were no more all-seeing than Mum's.

Not long after the incident with the knife, Shirley Morris spotted my fifth borrowing from the nature table and shouted out, "Miss, Miss. Perry took the sheep's horn off the table".

Miss Thimby made me open my hand and took the tip of a ram's horn from it.

"What were you going to do with it, Perry?"

Trembling lips muttered, "Look at it".

"But you can see it on the table. When it's the right time, you can even hold it. If you take things without asking and hide them, people will think you're a thief. I don't want to think that."

My ears burned. Along with the shame, I felt betrayed by Shirley. The Kyte girls never told tales to adults, not even when we bickered. I wanted revenge, but Shirley was bigger, popular with other girls and teacher's pet. Then during a chilly February lunch hour, I went from the playground to the cloakroom to get my mitts. Nervous giggles came from the classroom. Shirley, Jenny and Meg were at Miss Thimby's desk and taking it in turns to use the tiger stamp on a large sheet of paper. No one had accumulated more tigers than Shirley and most weeks she achieved the ultimate accolade of a tiger on the back of each hand. On the one occasion Miss Thimby awarded me this honour, I had spent ecstatic hours wriggling my fingers to make the tigers twitch as if they were about to attack each other.

Not only were classrooms out of bounds after the teacher had left but also Miss Thimby had instructed us that nobody should interfere with what was on her desk. My first idea was to run and tell the teacher on playground duty, but the girls would be angry with me if they learned I was the informer. Then an idea popped into my head.

I waited out of sight until the three girls left, by which time the sheet they had used was scrunched up and in the bin. Unfolding it revealed almost as much purple ink as white paper. The desk was in perfect order with the stamp resting on the closed lid of the inkpad tin. I opened the tin and used the stamped sheet to hold the tiger end while I brushed the handle across the pad. Then I left everything as it had been with the exception of the paper, which I folded and placed out of sight on the teacher's chair under the desk.

Miss Thimby pulled out her chair long after we had started class, opened the sheet and asked who had used her stamp. Shirley pretended to look surprised and disapproving, but Meg and Jenny blushed, trembled and soon named Shirley and said it had been her idea. Miss Thimby ordered the three to the front and while they were coming forward she picked up the stamp and tut-tutted at the purple stains it left on her fingers.

"I'm very disappointed because I trusted you girls and you let me down. And Shirley most of all because you pretended to know nothing about it when you were the ringleader."

All three were crying. Shirley's suffering and loss of standing pleased me no end. What made revenge sweeter still was no one suspected that a fourth child had played a part. The girls assumed Miss Thimby had found the paper in the bin and Miss Thimby did not ask why they had left it on her chair.

Throughout my school years, a lack of sufficient allies and the fear of responding to insults led me to take advantage of similar covert opportunities to retaliate. Had my torment ceased, I might have outgrown such behaviour. But in every class and each corner of the playground bullies lurked.

Another source of grief at school was Dad's lack of military service. Other children, especially the boys, boasted about members of their family who had fought in the war, or at the least had worn uniforms. When I was seven and asked my parents, they said nothing about relatives in the services and Dad looked sad. The one time I pressed for an answer, Mum got angry. I waited until I was watching Dad in his shed adjusting the gear cable on his bike. He was never more at ease than when he worked with his hands.

"What did you do in the war, Dad?"

He looked up and said in a matter-of-fact way, "Why do you want to know?"

"Boys at school are always going on about what their dads did in the war. Why didn't you fight?"

"Britain hadn't prepared for war like Germany. They'd been re-arming for years. So toolmakers making what the armed forces needed were not allowed to join up."

"So what did you make?"

"I had to promise never to talk about it. But you can be sure it helped to win the war. All the factory's output during the war was for the military. I worked long hours and never less than six days a week to make sure the men doing the fighting had all we could give them."

"A secret weapon?"

"You could put it like that."

But when I told boys how Dad had worked around the clock making a secret weapon, they were unimpressed because there was no name or details of what the weapon did.

Dad did one thing that helped my standing. He did some joinery as a private job in Mr Beaufort's home and returned with a large pre-war collection of Meccano; more pieces than anyone else at school had. This kit attracted boys to the cottage. After tiring of the Meccano, we often indulged in friendly rough and tumble, which led to Mum going on about my fragility and fretting what might get broken. The resulting embarrassment led me to prefer going to the homes of others to play.

She reacted by limiting the time I could spend away from the cottage. To sidestep her restrictions, I took advantage of her conviction that girls were gentle and therefore unlikely to hurt me.

"Where are you going Perry?"

"To Susan's."

Susan was the sister of Dan and I would say nothing to her while in their house. Some of my friends did not have sisters. The idea of saying I was going to a family with an invented daughter was tempting, especially when Mum did not know the people. However, an outright lie then was more difficult.

Mum urged, "Be good for Jesus", which included telling the truth. But as I got older, her exhortations became less convincing. Rev. Newelm had imparted his faith, but not his way with words. In time, I began to suspect God was no more all-seeing than Mum was because lots of kids did naughty things, wicked even – such as the boys who boasted about smashing windows at a factory under construction – and got away with it. The prospect of everlasting fires in hell, worried such boys less than an earthly thrashing.

For me though, playing sly boots had attractions beyond merely avoiding punishment. The success of getting my own way through deviousness, lent a sense of power with both adults and children, provided no one suspected the extent of my slipperiness. It suited me to let others regard me as ineffectual rather than hint at my capacity and eagerness to retaliate on the sly.

When Mum was in hospital and complaining that the ward was too hot, which it was, she reminded me of another thing that had prompted religious doubt.

"Mum, remember that winter in 1947?"

"Snow from January to March. Weeks without seeing the sun. And we couldn't get coal for love nor money. I didn't want you to go out into all that ice, but your school had some heating and it was better to save ours during the day. What made you think of that winter?"

"I used to think there was something odd about God being so wasteful. Why go to all the trouble and expense of heating hell when cold was just as good a torture?"

After looking at her fellow patients to see if they had overheard, she said softly, "Oh, Perry."

Her embarrassment puzzled me. How did she, and Dad for that matter, get so caught up in a faith that its influence continued long after religion disappointed them?

A nurse came with a hypodermic needle and after Mum's face softened in response to the injection, I asked, "How did Dad get involved with the Newelms?"

"A friend of his had died and he took it hard." She was smiling. "He heard that the Newelms were mediums. They said his friend was at peace and your Dad became a regular on Sundays. That's how we got to know each other. Until Mr Newelm's politics got in the way, your Dad looked up to him."

"What sort of politics?"

"Mussolini, then Mosley, Hitler and Franco. Your Dad went along with it to a point, but he'd lost a brother in Flanders and wasn't happy about Hitler sending troops into the Rhineland. Still, it was hard to break completely from the Newelms because of their messages from the other side. And after we moved to Harrow, your Dad and I used to think that the Anglicans were too soft."

Her talk became more rambling and repetitive, but the overall message was clear. After moving to Rayners Lane, my parents had reverted, at least in terms of Sunday attendance, to the Church of England that had christened them. Although their vicar thought the Sabbath should be free of earthly distractions such as sport, they found his acceptance of moderate drinking, occasional gambling, dancing and acting too liberal. Newelm had allowed radio for refined music, but urged his flock to avoid popular songs and drama, which he saw as passion-inflaming. One wonders what he made of fascist orators.

As a result of Newelm's puritanism, I was the only child in my street forbidden to listen to the BBC's *Dick Barton*, a detective so decent that today he could only feature in a spoof. We never went to the cinema and my mother checked every book that I brought home to ensure that it was wholesome.

The big attraction of the Church of England was its respectability. No one in Harrow knew that Mum and Dad had worshipped at the Church of the Upper and Lower Tables. Not only was spiritualism unorthodox, but Newelm's fascist sympathies, publicized in his letters to newspapers throughout the 1930s, had become less popular after Hitler bullied his way into the Sudetenland. By not mentioning their former minister, my parents had no need to disown him. The Newelms were educated people whom my parents wanted to keep as patrons they could tap for advice or a letter of support. And while other mediums practised in Harrow, Mum was keen to keep the door open to the couple in Watford who had such ready contact with her mother in heaven.

I was not aware that Mum had living relatives until, at the age of six, I overheard her chatting with Dad about a spiv she visited that day.

"It's a shame. He has some good stuff, but not if my brother works for him."

Dad's response was unambiguous. "I hope you didn't tell him where we lived."

"No, but the supplier knows."

"Let's hope he keeps quiet," said Dad.

"Quiet about what?" I asked as I pushed open the back door without letting on that I had heard about the brother.

"Don't be nosy, Mr Parker," said Mum.

Mum always ironed and often did other chores while listening to classical music on the radio. In the hospital, she recalled standing in the shadows near the door of the Newelm's living room to listen to their records and wireless.

"It was all proper music, none of your Gracie Fields or George Formby malarkey. So when your Dad got a wireless, I was made up not having to listen through a closed door. It felt so good having the same kind of music as the Newelms in my own kitchen.

The end of a concert while Mum was ironing was a good time to ask questions. Not long after the mention of her brother, I looked up from my homework as the applause began.

"There's only one other boy in my class who doesn't have a brother or a sister. I wish I had one."

"You've got two parents who love you. And you've got a room to yourself. Not every child has that."

"But I want to share a room. I liked sharing a bed with Tilda."

"You might like sharing when you're young, but not as you get older. I couldn't wait to leave home and have a room to myself.

"So who did you share with at home?"

"I had to share with my brother and he didn't like it any more than me." Mum suddenly frowned. "You're not to tell anyone else about this."

"So where's your brother now?"

"In Watford I expect."

"Does he have any children?"

Impatience crept into her voice. "Yes, three."

I was especially interested in cousins who might deter bullies.

"How old are they?"

"A bit older than you."

I wanted to know their names and ages, but the number of questions that I could ask was limited. I waited for ironing to soothe Mum a little.

"Why don't we go and visit your brother?"

She paused a second before answering, but without stopping her work or looking up. "When I accepted Jesus, he mocked me. And his family don't live like Christians. But you're not to tell anyone that."

Mum's accompanying sigh meant any further query would provoke her anger.

The part about not living like Christians made no sense when Mum was happy being friends with anyone who was at least her social equal, including two Jewish housewives and the Kytes who never said a prayer.

I reverted to taking Christianity more seriously, inspired by a new Sunday school teacher who preached against bullying and spoke of the need to be kind to all. Her censuring a boy for calling me *matchstick legs* proved to be a turning point. I saw a new benefit in religion, if only everyone could be persuaded to be kind. But after just a few weeks of my renewed interest, events that overtook my parents led to what I came to think of as *The Great Reversal*.

I was eight. Late in the afternoon on a Tuesday that had brought sleet, Mum and I were in the kitchen when we heard the rap of the brass knocker on the front door. She put down her darning, took off her apron and swapped her slippers for the shoes kept in the kitchen in case the caller was the sort to be received with all dignity.

The small parlour had only two doors, the front and the one to the kitchen. In her haste, she did not quite close the latter and as soon as the front door opened the chill wind widened the gap. The continuing draught meant she had not invited the caller to step inside. I grew curious about the wavering voices. By the time I got up to peek, the front door was closed and Mum and the strange man were hugging. Before my shock at this had settled, she broke away and dabbed her eyes with a handkerchief retrieved from the sleeve of her cardigan.

"Come into the kitchen, it's warmer."

I rushed to where she had left me and feigned surprise when the stranger entered.

"Maurice, this is my boy Perry. Shake hands with your uncle."

The weasel of a man – skinny body and pointy pasty face – forced a small smile, offered nicotine-darkened fingers and spoke in a flat voice. "Nice to meet you, Perry"

"We need to talk. Take yourself to your bedroom and read. Put the quilt over you to keep warm. I'll call you down to say goodbye".

Her uneven breathing along with a voice struggling to suppress emotion ensured that I pretended to shut the bedroom door and crept back as far as I could without being seen. Both were too agitated to speak softly, yet the meaning of their conversation was unclear. They spoke of Gertie, Luton, a Medical Superintendant, Fairfields, Asylum, Chief Female Officer and senile. I could tell these words had great significance for both of them, but their meaning escaped me. The way the same terms kept surfacing reminded me of ducks diving under dark water; you never know where the bird will next appear, only that it will.

After many minutes, I gathered that my grandfather had died recently. I had been reluctant to accept Maurice saying this earlier because for as long as I could remember Mum had claimed both of her parents were dead. As the siblings' discussion continued, it became clear that she had known before Maurice came to the door that her father had died from a liver failure eight days earlier. Why had she told me that my grandfather had died while she was living with the Newelms and then said nothing about his actual death? And had she lied to Dad as well? I was shivering and not just from the cold.

Mum also struggled to make sense of new information. "You're saying Gertie always knew?"

"Yes. You know the way she is after a few drinks. Well, you can't have a funeral without providing a few bottles for the mourners. Towards the end, she started crying and saying she wouldn't get anything because they weren't properly married."

"The shame of it! How could Dad and that hussy live in sin like that year after year? And not let on to us that Mum was still alive. What was Mum like when you went to see her?"

"Not a pretty sight, Maud. I could hardly bare to look at her. It was upsetting enough finding her after all these years, but the state she was in. And then the nurse saying she's worked there fourteen years and I was the first relative to visit."

"This is breaking my heart. Do you think I should go and see her?"

"It won't make any difference to Mum. If she doesn't know her own name, she's not going to know who you are. The nurse said that Mum is happier now not knowing who she is. That before the war she was still fretting about her children."

"And she ended up there because of a breakdown?"

"She tried to kill herself twice. Once before and once after she arrived at the asylum."

Mum gasped at the thought of suicide and my body trembled at her response.

"The poor thing." she said. "Dad and his drinking drove her to despair. Gertie only coped because she was a sot like him".

"You're right, but we have to remember Dad wasn't always like that. Anyone who knew him before he joined up said the trenches changed him. I hope he's at peace now."

"And Gertie always knew about Mum?"

"She must've. Otherwise she would've married Dad."

"God knows what she saw in him."

"Gertie was no great shakes as a mother, but when Dad lashed out, she took the brunt of it. I'm grateful for that."

"But she bought drink when we had no food in the house. What kind of woman does that to children? I'd starve myself to a skeleton before I'd let Perry go hungry. If it wasn't for him, I'd never have got involved in the black market."

"You don't have to justify it to me, Sis. Just take care you don't get caught. Take it from me, kids suffer more than the parent who goes to prison."

A cold feeling crept up my spine because only bad people went to prison. Then there was anger. I did not know the word *hypocrite* then, but I resented being beaten for petty things while she broke laws that could land her in jail. I lost some of the anger when a pale Mum tugging relentlessly at the cuffs of her cardigan called me to say a brief goodbye to Maurice.

She put stew and a loaf on the table, said she was not hungry and did not notice, a first I believe, how slowly I finished only half a bowl and ignored the bread.

Shortly before Dad was due from work I volunteered for bed. As soon as I heard him enter the house, I returned to the top of the stairs. Mum said nothing beyond "Food's ready". She sounded flat, but he did not respond to her tone.

Had she found a sack of sovereigns while Dad was out, she would only have told him after sitting opposite him over a served meal. By the time he started to eat, I had to clench my teeth to stop them chattering.

"Gordon, I've got something to tell you."

Hard of hearing from factory noise, Dad could not understand the quiet speech that I could follow at a distance.

"Speak up."

"You won't believe it. I can hardly credit it myself."

"Go on, surprise me."

"Maurice came here tonight."

"What did he want?" There was a note of anger.

"He came to tell me my mother's still alive." Mum started to snivel. "She's been in an asylum since Dad moved us to Watford."

For the only time in my hearing, Dad swore, "Bloody hell!"

On the rare occasions that he displayed emotion, Mum spoke with awkward pauses.

"I'm sorry. I didn't mean to spoil your dinner. It's just that I feel so angry. First Dad dying. And me not going to his funeral. I should have gone. That would have been the Christian thing. Wouldn't it?"

"He made your childhood a misery. You don't have to apologise for anything."

"Maybe you're right about that, but what about the Newelms? They said Mum's spirit was looking after me, but she wasn't dead. I believed them. If I hadn't, I'd never have evacuated Perry without me going too."

"That's the second time the Newelms have been wrong."

"You mean Calvin."

"I thought maybe they were too close to him and that's why the message about him surviving was wrong. But after today, I don't think I can believe in any of their messages."

"I'm a fool. I let myself be robbed of my mother and my son. And I thought the Newelms were good people."

"No more a fool than a lot of others. And he almost had me joining the Blackshirts."

She sobbed and Dad kept saying "There, there."

If he went to comfort her, I did not hear his chair scraping the way it usually did on the kitchen flagstones when he got up. I crept back to my room and started to cry with rage because Mum had kept me away from her relatives. I thought more about my living cousins than her dead father and mad mother because I was desperate for children who would protect me. Had Mum discovered the cause of the tears, she would have chastised my snooping, so I kept my head under the bedclothes to muffle the blubbing.

The next day, I felt selfish for not caring more about Mum. On top of the pain of her Dad's death and the news of her Mum, the Newelms had tricked her. Up until then, she had spoken of her former employers as if they were saints.

Mum said on the following Saturday, "We're not going to church tomorrow."

"But I need to go to get my attendance badge."

Only the children with current badges went on special outings.

She raised her voice. "You're not going to Sunday school anymore."

"Why?"

Dad rested the *Illustrated London News* on his knees. "Honour thy father and thy mother. Isn't that what they taught you? You don't need to know why. But you're not going again and we won't be going to church either."

"But you don't need to tell people that," Mum quickly added.

"What do I say if they ask why?"

Dad's face reddened and he sounded exasperated. "Tell them that if they must know they can come and ask me."

Mum said with conviction, "People can be good without going to church and some people who go to church aren't good."

"Even some ministers are not good people."

"Let's leave it there, Gordon."

On the next Saturday as I helped Dad to creosote the exterior of the shed, I asked, "Do you think God minds if we stop going to church."

"If He does, and it's a big if, you're only doing what I tell you to do. So you can't be at fault."

"But what if He sends you to hell for not going?"

"That's not going to happen. I can promise you that."

"How can you be sure?"

"The thing is, your Mum and I have decided some of the things we thought were true are false."

"What things?"

"I'm saying more because these aren't things for children."

His evasiveness reminded me of the secrecy around what he produced during the war. A little later, he stood back and surveyed what he had painted with a look of satisfaction. It was the sort of moment when he might be more forthcoming.

"How many hours a week did you work during the war?"

"Sometimes when you and your Mum were away, I didn't bother to come home. The manager gave me a roll-up mattress and I slept in a storeroom next door to a furnace, where it was always warm. If the canteen wasn't open, his wife would bring a meal so that I could keep working."

"But how many hours?"

"Often over a hundred a week but the highest was 125. There just weren't enough skilled people, let alone toolmakers. And then there was something I did that the government didn't want too many people to know about so only I was allowed to do it for the first two years."

I was staggered not so much by the hours, but that Dad had shared a national secret with me. I racked my brain for a way of encouraging him to say more.

"How many people were allowed to do it after two years?"

"I trained up two ladies who were especially vetted and between them they kept the Air Ministry supplied."

"Was one of them Miss Plasholl?"

"She was one and the better of the two by far. By the time the war finished, there wasn't much she couldn't turn her hand to."

Trying to sound casual and without ceasing to paint, I asked, "What did the Air Ministry do with the stuff you made?"

"We were never told and never asked. Besides, we made just one component."

"What from?"

Dad applied creosote – the pungent smell of it comes back to me now – for several seconds before resting his brush on the can and straightening his spine with hands pushed into his back.

"Can you keep a secret?"

I turned towards him and, too excited to speak, nodded.

He walked to the fence to check no one was on the other side, returned and bent towards my ear as if about to whisper, but what emerged from his lips was more like normal speech.

"Vitallium. It's a combination of metals, what we call an alloy. Sometimes when you mix metals what you get is harder, stronger and more resistant to heat. Vitallium is also light and doesn't corrode. Just like you, light as a feather, tough as old boots and can be out in all weathers without coming to any harm."

He would say no more about his wartime work yet my spirits soared because Dad had acknowledged in coded language that he thought Mum made too much fuss about my size and vulnerability.

Chapter 11: Norman ~ The Assam Tea Rooms

Daya drove from Raventulle at a speed that made it easy for Rose to follow her through the twists and turns of Vaulting Ryego. We angle-parked in the square with the Corn Exchange. There was plenty of room for cars. Three of the thirty or so surrounding shops were vacant and charities looked as if they had occupied two of the others for some years, judging by their faded fascia. Several stores had either a down-at-heel look or promotional signs suggesting proprietors desperate for customers. Daya said that local trade had struggled since a superstore had opened on the other side of Ryego Forest.

She led us to the Assam Tea Rooms, which looked pristine compared to its neighbours and more sympathetic to the square's Georgian architecture than most of the frontages. Fine strips of white-painted wood separated small glass panes on the windows. About one in four pieces of glass was a bull's-eye with matching flaws that made clear they were modern simulations from the same mould.

"Did a retired tea planter from Assam settle here?" I asked before realising the name could come from a fondness for Assam tea, or wanting to appear at the start of directories, or for a thousand other reasons.

Daya delayed opening the door to answer me. "The owners are Anglo-Indians from Madras, or Chennai as it is now. Madras might do as the name for a place that specialises in curries, but it isn't quite right for morning and afternoon teas. In India, they may well have called their tea rooms after somewhere in England."

Although nothing in the reply suggested she had found fault with my question, I told myself to stop leaping to conclusions. What was clouding my thinking? Not just the earlier assumptions about Daya; I was also apprehensive about wasting police time by persuading a Detective Inspector to come for coffee.

Despite the reference to *rooms,* the public space within consisted of one long area with a counter at the back. Spotless lavender gingham covered the tables while the chairs had an unconvincing adzed-finish that made it all too easy to imagine someone swinging a blade against sawn timber. Or did the manufacturer have a machine to create the hewn effect? I glanced to see if each leg or back was as identical as the bulls-eye panes or the faux-melted wax on the light sockets around the walls, but the timber needed more than a cursory inspection to decide and other things were on my mind.

"It's charming," said Rose to Daya, reminding me how easy it was to make conversation that was not fraught.

"Hi, Theresa," Daya said to the woman approaching our window table. "These people asked me where to get the best coffee." And turning to Rose and me, "Theresa's worked here since she was nine. Her parents started the business in 1955. India's loss was Vaulting Ryego's gain."

Rose gave me a quick look, which I imagined was a response to Daya not mentioning our names.

Theresa wore a gold cross on a chain that, along with her rosy cheeks and healthy-looking plumpness reminded me of matrons used to promote Italian food. While she greeted us all warmly, her smile for Daya was bigger.

How much did they have in common as the children of families with roots in India when they came from different religious backgrounds? Then it occurred to me that the cross could be piece of jewellery rather than a symbol of faith. Plenty of other people who were not religious wore crosses in much the same way that Colin sported on his upper arms tattoos of a pentagram, ankh, yin-yang and OM in Sanskrit. He had never said what he believed in, but it seemed unlikely that he could have subscribed to four different faiths in the three university years it had taken him to acquire the designs.

One thing was certain. Theresa would not mistake Daya's companions for police officers. I was too short and Rose's style, bless her, never approached the part. The heels she put on once the car had stopped and a skirt that limited strides were impractical for police work.

Theresa asked, to no one in particular, "So what brings you to town?"

We waited for Daya's response.

"I had to check on something at Raventulle and met these people there."

Theresa, turning to me, said, "We get a lot of customers who come because of Perry Gray and others because of the Ryego Forest murders. Well, it's only natural after all the reporting."

"I'm sure you do, but I'm here at the request of Chief Superintendent Grove."

This came out pompously. Daya's face stiffened. Then I overdid a grin in an attempt to compensate for sounding pretentious. Fortunately, Rose injected some levity.

"It's lovely to see an older property like this so well maintained; especially when I'm bursting for the loo."

"I think you're like me." Theresa said with laugh. "How can you have confidence in the toilets if the rest of a place doesn't look smart?"

Rose followed Theresa towards the back. Would Daya be more forthcoming with just the two of us? She sat facing her car and studied passing pedestrians as if looking for clues.

"Is Gray a suspect for the Ryego murders?"

"No. At the time of the first murder, he was at a computer centre in Aberdeen with scores of witnesses."

"I understand that no one really knew Gray, but which locals had the most contact with him?"

"The men he played poker with. They saw him regularly over several years, unlike his girlfriends who seldom lasted longer than a few months. Gray hosted more than his share of the poker games at Raventulle. The players also socialised at the Shoe and Anvil, where Gray drank with a lot of other people. And he used most of the other pubs from time to time. When you ask the locals what he was like, they often look confused. A poker player sheepishly admitted that he knew next to nothing about him. The one fact he was sure of was that Gray won far more hands than anyone else."

"Did the others resent that?"

"Not really. They played for small amounts and Gray was generous with food and drink; not just the quantity, but the quality. For most poker evenings at Raventulle, Perry spent more on food alone than he won and the wines were by all accounts excellent. One player said that after sampling the hospitality at Raventulle, he regretted that it had taken them so long to invite Perry to join. The rest of them are locals and they had hesitated about letting in an outsider."

Rose brought a tray with two cups and said, "I'm having mine with Theresa."

I was all in favour of this because Daya was saying more.

"What about before he joined the poker school? Who did he spend time with then?"

"He was a regular at the almshouses after he arrived in the village, especially with a woman who had dementia called Joan Plasholl. No one knew what he and Joan spoke about. Even had they asked her, she couldn't have said. Her Alzheimer's was at the stage where she remembered little from a few minutes earlier. Some thought Perry's frequent visits were pretty odd because she was away with the fairies. He did odd jobs for her and other pensioners that he never charged for."

"Did he chat with the more lucid pensioners."

Yes. He seems to have enjoyed chatting about local history. One person thought he was most interested in what happened here during the 1940s."

"Anything else he liked to talk about."

"There was another women at the almshouses called Mavis. She's been dead some time, but her relative, Lady Thellow, said Mavis spoke of Perry bringing Madeira and wanting to know about her life in India. Lady Thellow also mentioned another deceased relative, Eustace Troupe. Have you heard of him?"

"Yes. He was a solicitor from Vaulting Ryego found not guilty of possessing child pornography."

"He had the images in his house, but an anonymous letter sent to the police had some inconsistencies that led to him getting off. He did Perry's conveyancing and Lady Thellow claims that Troupe disliked Perry as person."

"Do you think Perry wrote the letter?"

"We suspect he did. What is established is that the same person wrote an earlier letter that led to a local teacher being convicted for offences against children. We know now that Perry had repaired that teacher's laptop. But back then we didn't regard allegations as malicious. Not only were they true, the teacher confessed to other crimes and revealed the names of other paedophiles."

"Do you suspect Perry of being involved in paedophilia?"

"There's nothing to indicate that. If he was attracted to any vulnerable group, it was OAPs, and nothing suggests he had any kinky interests in them."

"I'm puzzled that Perry was given access to the almshouses. Was no one concerned about a stranger spending so much time there?"

"The warden says he had no reason to suspect Gray took advantage of anyone; more the other way really. Gray did lots of repairs for the residents. A lot of people mention his ability to mend anything. One old dear showed me a stunning example. She had a statue of a pit pony sculpted from coal. When the ears got shattered, Gray made them as good as new and charged nothing for it. I imagine he was new to sculpture and working in coal, yet somehow he triumphed."

"The papers made a lot of his ability to fix things, but I can't remember any reports saying he did so much for free."

"He was open-handed with many, the people he liked I guess." She hesitated before adding, "Perhaps he was as generous as he was malicious, provided that people didn't cross the lines that he drew."

"What were the lines?"

"We're still working on that. Even now that we know who Mr Vitriol is, some of the recipients of his letters swear they never knew Perry Gray. We can't figure out what links them."

Her eyes followed something outside. I turned and saw a tall heavily-built man walking by. I wanted to ask if she was interested in him as a possible suspect for the murders, but she had agreed to the coffee because I claimed to have more questions about Perry.

"How did Gray know Knattmaw? I'm curious that there's been no mention of why Knattmaw was targeted."

Her face puckered for a moment at the mention of the name. "Knattmaw was in the Army before joining the police and the sergeant in charge of Gray when he did his basic training at Fort Gatgash. Are you OK?"

My mouth must have dropped. I spoke about being at Gatgash for my first six weeks of National Service and never being so unhappy.

"Would you like some water?"

"Thanks, I've still got my coffee."

I found myself adding two sugars to the half-empty cup. The sweet liquid made me nauseous or at least more aware of the agitation in my stomach. Daya looked concerned.

After waiting a while, she asked, "Did you know Knattmaw at Gatgash?"

"I don't remember hearing the name until Gladys Knattmaw went on television."

Attempting to conceal my continuing shock, I asked, "Do you know what contact Gray had with the sergeant after basic training?"

"They only met at Gatgash, as far as we know. Someone who was in Gray's hut remembers that he had two left feet, which didn't please the Knattmaw. Army records show that Gray was in hospital for his last two weeks at Gatgash for exhaustion. Then he went into the Pay Corps. Gray was bright and it seems odd that someone who was so dexterous had difficulty learning the drills during basic training."

"Many NCOs made bone-weary recruits more confused. When there's no let up and someone is shouting abuse into your ear or kicking you, you can't think straight and simple things become difficult to learn. The days are tiring enough, but sleep isn't always easy."

I forced myself to return to Perry rather than dwell on the memories that had flooded back. "Do you think bullying in the Army might have been Gray's motive for targeting Knattmaw?"

She bristled at the mention of bullying and did not reply for several seconds, during which I noticed that my breathing had accelerated.

"I didn't mention bullying."

"No. But take it from me, there was a lot of it at Gatgash. You'll find it in all the services from to time, but every so often there's a perfect storm; lack of senior leadership, junior officers who won't confront abuses, and a coterie of NCOs with sadistic tendencies. Unchecked, a brutal culture emerges."

Daya lowered her voice enough for me to realise that I had raised mine. "I don't rule out bullying as a motive for Gray's letter to Knattmaw, but there's no evidence."

Sensing that she knew more, I raised my eyebrows.

"Let's just say that when I played good cop to Knattmaw's bad cop during an interview, he was very convincing."

"Did Gray's letter hint that Knattmaw was a bully?"

"The letter lacked credibility." She sounded exasperated, quickly recovered and spoke even more softly. "Perry made himself out to be a sort of underworld criminal who had been assaulted despite not resisting arrest, but there were all sorts of allegations, including taking bribes to let a criminal go and fitting up others. Knattmaw was no saint, but none of his colleagues ever suspected him of going easy on a villain."

My brain still reeled from the mention of Gatgash. Vivid memories of a near drowning slopped around my head. They were not flashbacks, but in the past such images had preceded disorientation. I bit the inside of my cheek, using physical pain to distract myself from mounting fear. I searched for a question that took us away from bullying. The more I wanted to leave that topic, the more it filled my mind.

"Mentioning Knattmaw's bullying in the Army could have provided a clue. Perhaps that's why Gray used other accusations to hit back?"

Daya gave half a nod and looked peeved. Did she have her own unhappy experiences of Knattmaw?

Then she appeared to change the subject. "Remember the bugging devices? We wonder if Gray was spying on people and blackmailing them, as well as using some of the dirt he found for his anonymous letters."

"Any suspicion of him being an agent for another country?"

"MI5 considered it unlikely. On several occasions he turned down government work, including defence-related contracts. There's also something a competitor of Perry's pointed out to us; most of his work in the private sector was at computer centres with very large numbers of customers and all his government work was with departments that keep large databases."

"What about commercial espionage? Did he have any wealth that wasn't accounted for?"

"Not that we've found and there's nothing to suggest that he stashed money overseas. His income versus expenditure and assets pretty well tallies. If he had an illegal income, he might have banked it overseas, but my feeling is that when he was cornered he took his own life because he'd run out of options."

"What made him feel cornered?"

"My guess is the DNA tests we had started in this area. They were voluntary, but any adult male not giving a sample would have drawn attention."

"But he had an alibi for one of the murders. He could have argued there was no need to take the test."

"The first body was found badly decomposed. All the public had was a two week window when the murder was thought to occur. It took time to find other prostitutes and punters and establish when they had last seen her alive. Between them and forensics we pinned the death down to one of two days, by which time there was a second victim. Her body turned up within hours of her death and she was a nurse. It was easier to appeal to public about her and similarly with the third victim who was a student. We still haven't released the information about the time of the first murder."

Despite the further information being of interest, my thoughts kept returning to an abyss on Gatgash Fells that has featured in my nightmares. Leaning back, I tried to breathe deeper and slower. I studied the décor to distract myself. Why choose lavender gingham?

Before reaching any conclusion, laughter came from the counter. Rose was in full flow while Theresa inserted a roll of paper into the cash register.

The paper whirring through the machine meant I missed some sentences before hearing, "Norman's acting as a consultant to the police, but you'll have to ask him what he does. I'm just the driver."

"My money's on him being a psychic. I'm a bit of an intuitive myself," said Theresa.

When Daya glared at this exchange, I asked, "Would you rather Rose said nothing? Is it the prospect of Theresa telling the village that the police are using psychics? Or would you rather we posed as tourists?"

Before I had finished, I realised these were three more assumptions and felt like a schoolboy getting it wrong when he wants to show off to an attractive girl.

Her brow tightened, but the voice stayed calm. "Rose is free to say what she wants, but the Chief wouldn't be too pleased to learn that the public think she uses psychics. I witnessed her tearing a strip off a colleague who suggested a clairvoyant when a child was missing. Believe me, you don't want to hear my guvnor balling someone out. And I don't know about you pretending to be tourists. I wasn't briefed on that. The expectation was just to show you Raventulle."

"I'm sorry. I don't need to mention our coming here to Ann and I can honestly report that you were very helpful at the house."

Daya drove off expecting that Rose and I would be getting into the Volvo. Instead, I suggested we look inside the museum and Norman church because I wanted to make visiting Vaulting Ryego more of a day out. Rose was unaware that I had promised the police to work flat-out on the decoding.

As we walked to the church, I asked, "Did you learn anything from Theresa about Perry?"

"I thought it better not to ask in case she assumed that my interest was somehow linked to the police."

Why hadn't I thought to encourage Rose to use her ability with people to find out what Theresa knew about the man? I was all the more curious about Perry after realising we had Gatgash in common.

I hardly remember the museum and church because of the upwelling of memories from National Service basic training. As we were returning to the car, I suggested lunch in the Assam Tea Rooms.

As it was busy, we took a table for two between the entrance and the counter. Before the waitress, whom we had not seen before, got to us, Theresa came over.

"So what is it you do for the police, Mr ..?"

"Call me Norman." Then I spoke more softly. "To be honest, I'm not sure what I'm allowed to say and Daya was also unsure. But I'm not a psychic. I'm the sort of person who needs to be told about Perry Gray by people who knew him. If you could spare some time for a call this evening?"

Theresa brimmed with pleasure while she wrote her home number on a page of the pad she kept in her apron pocket.

Because she had not hesitated, I added, "And if you see a few other people today who knew Perry well, perhaps you could ask if they would mind taking a call from me tonight?"

"I'm sure others would love to help. I just wish I could stay and talk now, but there's someone waiting to pay. Ginny will take your order."

When I smiled with mock innocence as I studied the menu, Rose asked, "What's going on?"

"There's more to Mr Vitriol than the papers reported. The police are holding things back from me. Knattmaw was not quite the wonderful man that he was made out to be."

"But if you want other assignments from the police, you can't afford to offend by interviewing off your own bat. Why take that chance?"

I took a few moments to reflect on what was driving me.

"Daya said that Gray did his basic training at Gatgash and Knattmaw was his sergeant. It's possible that Gray was bullied by Knattmaw."

Rose reached for my hand and patted it because something like this had the potential to bring my cauldron of horrors to the boil.

"Bullying wouldn't excuse the hate mail, but I know how vicious the NCOs could be. And it's still going on. Look at what's emerged from Deepcut Barracks."

Rose reached for my hand. She had seen me splutter at every news item relating to the deaths of young soldiers at Deepcut.

"Do you think you should continue the assignment now that you know Perry was at Gatgash?"'

"I feel afraid and compelled at the same time."

"Ah!" This was one of Rose's invitations to say more.

"I'm agitated. It feels a bit like how I was before we began to talk."

"But you'll keep talking?"

"As long as you're prepared to listen. But let's wait until after breakfast tomorrow."

"Just one thing before we leave it. Is there anything I could say that would tempt you to walk away and let someone else do this work?"

"I may be wrong, but I feel the need to meet it head on. I'm stronger for talking to you, but the ogres haven't all gone. Each time I hear of bullying in the services, I ask why's it still happening? What's the point of defending our way of life if we can't eliminate such brutality among the defenders? If we can't stop bullying within the Army, no wonder we have groups of soldiers who act like animals with unarmed civilians and God knows what they do to anyone captured with a gun in his possession."

She squeezed my hand and tried to steer my thoughts by asking what I thought of the church.

My mind buzzed with questions during the drive home. Could the hate mail have been a response to lasting damage inflicted on Perry as a National Serviceman? How deranged was he? Was signing letters with Mr Vitallium a fantasy that owed something to comic heroes like Mr Fantastic and Iron Man? If bullying had been a key driver for his poison pen, why did others who had suffered from mistreatment, including myself, never even consider writing such a letter?

In other circumstances, my growing curiosity might have made me work late into the night at deciphering, but I sensed a need to pace myself after the mention of Gatgash had so fazed me. The thoughts and feelings aroused by my six weeks there had merely been submerged through studying and work. Expressing anger in front of others was rare before basic training and after it there was another reason to keep the lid on even when I was alone. Part of what had driven a sergeant to almost drown me was his uncontrolled rage.

Army Intelligence work had deepened my stoicism and reticence because anything that suggested mental instability or deviating from the narrow norms of those cleared to work with top secret information had implications for reliability. And the psychiatrist and psychologist interviews arranged at intervals for all CARE employees after 1972 were not opportunities to unburden so much as a test of one's ability to appear trustworthy. Even my social views, which were far from revolutionary, were better kept to myself when the prevailing attitudes were right wing. The sentiments shared with Rose at the tea rooms about defending our way of life would have been enough to make many former colleagues twitch. I had never considered betraying my country. The one time a Bulgarian agent approached me at a scientific conference, an event soon reported to my superiors, I asked her why she thought I would support a cause with a far worse record on human rights than the West's? Rather than argue, she offered me money and her body.

After I had left CARE, Rose heard me castigate successive leaders of the armed forces for not stamping out bullying. Her inscrutable mask for listening had slipped once with the shock of hearing a condemnation of the top brass for failing to eliminate this vice. For me, it felt like another person had borrowed my voice to get something off his chest. I see now how selfish I was to use only Rose as an outlet for such denunciations until Perry latched onto me.

Chapter 12: Perry ~ En Garde

In August 1949, Mr Kyte collected Mum and me from the station in a shooting brake bought with the proceeds of selling the orchard. It was my first ride in a car and so exciting that I insisted on accompanying Mum when he returned her to the station the next day. The girls, already used to the vehicle, chose to pick blackberries to make into jam with sugar lugged from London.

On the way back to Raventulle, I asked Mr Kyte if he would still be on holiday when Mum returned.

"The thing is, Perry, I'm not on holiday. The men are on strike and I don't know when they'll go back. Later rather than sooner, I hope."

"What are they striking for?"

"More pay, shorter hours and everyone has to join the union. I don't mind the first two, but I'll be beggared if I'll pay for someone to sit in an office and dream up more strikes. Still, it's worked out rather well for me. I turned up as usual and the manager said, 'Thank you very much, but stay at home for now on full pay.' And if the strikers win any concessions I'll still get them. No wonder this country's on the skids."

The strike continued and on a rain-sodden afternoon, Mr Kyte drove the children through Ryego Forest to a matinee at a cinema, the first I had entered. The show started with a newsreel about the London Olympics held a year earlier. I was surprised to see fencing was one of the games because I had thought swords in the twentieth century were merely symbolic. Two Tom and Jerry cartoons followed with a level of violence that was scary at first, but by the end of the second I was roaring with laughter. The feature was *The Wizard of Oz*. Tilda and I held hands during the tornado, witch and flying monkey scenes, but most of the time the fairy story unfolding before my eyes was astounding and joyful. I was much taken by the change from monochrome Kansas to Technicolor Oz within the film; it resembled the difference between the dourness and bullying of Rayners

Lane and the delight, adventures and laughter of holidays at Raventulle.

Mrs Kyte was in the middle of making a rabbit pie when we got back. Mr Kyte said how much he had enjoyed the outing. We giggled at his imitation of Tom sneaking on tiptoes and Mrs Kyte told him to stop, but only because her shaking from laughter had caused a sheet of pastry to tear.

The next day, I went with Mr Kyte to collect Mum from the station. By the time we returned, the sun was out and the girls were not in the orchard that we still played in despite the cowpats from the cattle of the new owner. I trudged back to the house and then trod softly after hearing adult conversation coming through the wide-open windows. Mr Kyte was describing how his troop ship had called at Cape Town on the way to India. Although flies landed on me as I listened, I kept quiet and moved as little as possible.

"There were lines of cars at the docks. The local English people all wanted to show any bloke from Blighty what a great place South Africa was. They couldn't have been more different from the sahibs in India who hardly wanted to know other ranks, just like some of the toffs around here now that the war's over. A couple from Leeds, the Peels, who said they'd sailed to Cape Town in 1936 with a trunk and £5, took me and two mates for a tour and lunch. He'd built up a business painting and decorating and they had a big house with servants and a daughter at university. I kept in touch with the Peels and they kept saying come and join us, we need more British here. We'll be staying with them till we find our own place."

"But aren't there a lot of darkies there?" asked Mum.

"No more than in India," said Mr Kyte. "And the whites in South Africa aren't going to hand over power to the wogs. If anything, the government is getting tougher with them."

"The sale of the house should be finalised soon," said Mrs Kyte. "That's when we'll tell the girls."

I cried silently that night. The one group of children I felt secure with was about to sail away, yet I dared not draw attention to what I knew. While the Kytes might well have laughed to learn that I had eavesdropped, Mum would have been angry and suspicious in future.

My family went to Waterloo Station in October to say farewell. The girls said they would miss me, but nothing inhibited their excitement at having travelled from another station in a London taxi and the sea voyage starting later that day.

Even Tilda was not thinking about what we had shared. "Imagine, Perry, we'll have another summer without a winter."

The girls were so giddy-headed that Mrs Kyte had to remind Lucy to present me with one of the cases of butterflies.

After Mum nudged me, I said, "Thank you."

Mr Kyte shook my hand and said, "Think nothing of it, Perry. There was a limit to what we could take on the boat and glass doesn't always survive a long journey. Besides, there are hundreds of butterfly species in South Africa."

The men shook hands and wished each other the best. Mrs Kyte hugged Mum and then I shook hands with the girls. I so wanted a kiss from Tilda, but youngsters at that age can find such intimacy awkward with adults and strangers about. The Kytes boarded. Ghostlike images of the two families waving appeared in a window of the poorly lit carriage. As the train lurched forward, the noise and gases that had thrilled me as a toddler seemed ominous. Mum lifted me onto a tall wicker crate and held onto my hips until the train was gone. It felt as if a part of my stomach had left for South Africa.

That evening, Dad screwed the case onto a wall in my bedroom. I shed bitter tears over several nights and even when I could not see the butterflies, my gaze was directed towards them. While I grieved for Raventulle and all of the Kytes, it was Tilda I missed most; her kiss in the cellar, the distant memories of falling asleep and waking up in a shared bed, and laughing at Tom and Jerry. The butterflies came to represent all that had been lost until I began to identify with them. Like their young, I wanted to grow, escape the cocoon that Mum sought to keep me in and stretch my wings. And like butterflies I lacked weight.

During her wartime stays at Raventulle, Mum saw how much I enjoyed being read to. She bought a book of biblical stories to mark my return to Rayners Lane. I much preferred fairy tales to the characters from the Old and New Testament and it did not help that Mum dragged a sluggish finger over the sentences to keep her eyes focused. Reading was never something she enjoyed, not even the Bible. The frown that appeared and her lips moving without sound revealed when her eyes had moved from pictures to print in *The Daily Sketch* or a women's magazine. Sometimes when she studied an unfamiliar word, I amused myself by guessing how long it would take for the tip of her tongue to emerge and curl against her upper lip.

Her slow reading and pointing at words, coming after much exposure to books at the Kytes, had helped me to learn to read, and not just books. I began to pay attention to print in other places. Not long before I started school, I pointed at an advertisement for Colman's Mustard said, "Man must," which was as much as I could work out.

Mum's jaw dropped before saying, "Well done, Perry. What a clever boy."

Everyone she spoke with over the next few weeks heard the story. Had I needed any further encouragement to read, the praise of neighbours and black market customers provided it. My school teachers found me grateful for any other ways of deciphering words that they introduced. And as I often finished my class work well ahead of others, I was allowed to keep a supply of books in my desk to read until the next lesson began. Soon my reading speed overtook Mum's crawl, a fact she acknowledged by letting me read in bed rather than reading to me.

She bought more books for me; all were religious before the great reversal. After my parents had lost their faith, an older neighbour hearing of my appetite for reading offered Mum a box of children's books. No doubt Mum culled titles that she thought unsuitable because abandoning religion did not end her concern that many a children's book was unwholesome. Among what remained was *The Wolf Cub's Handbook,* in which Baden-Powell ridicules Shere Khan for being a bully and emphasises the need for kindness. Reading it made me want to become a Cub. On hearing this, Mum drew in her breath, probably from fear of me camping in bad weather and being among boys determined to have adventures.

"Maybe when you're older."

"But other boys in my class are Cubs."

It had not occurred to me that joining did not make these lads any kinder.

"Tell you what, Perry, your Dad and I thought we might take you to the pictures."

I forgot about Cubs because, other than with the Kytes, the only films I had seen were documentaries at school and *Robin Hood* was returning to our local cinema. This film made me very curious because mention of it prompted local boys to wave imaginary swords at each other despite everyone knowing that the hero was a famous archer.

"Can we go and see *Robin Hood*. It's got Harold Flynn in it."

While Errol Flynn was just a misheard name to me, Mum must have known something about his off-screen reputation.

She frowned and said, "I'll have to ask your father."

That evening when Dad rattled the side gate, I rushed to offer to put his bicycle in the shed.

As soon as he smiled, I spouted, "Mum said we're going to the pictures and said to ask you about *Robin Hood*."

He looked surprised. "Let me talk to her."

By the time I had parked the bike, both were sitting in silence at the kitchen table with stiff tiny smiles that indicated a pause during a tense discussion.

"Your Mum's not keen on Robin Hood, so I'll take you." He made it sound like a chore.

"I don't mind going by myself."

"We don't want that," said Mum. "It's dark in the pictures and some people take advantage of it."

"How do you mean?"

"Never you mind that, just take my word for it." Something had made Mum flushed, goggle-eyed and created a tiny leak in the dam that held back secrets. "I'll never forget my first half-day off work. I didn't want to go home and I went to the pictures. It was horrible."

"That's enough," said Dad raising his voice.

"Was it a scary movie?" I asked.

"No more questions, Perry, or we won't be going."

Despite Dad ogling at Flynn kissing Olivia de Havilland no less that the other adult males and gripping his arm rest during the fencing scenes, when Mum asked, his vinegary tone suggested that the film had not been to his liking. The bitter taste of Newelm's theology remained long after my parents had spat out the gristle.

I was fourteen before they allowed me to go to the pictures alone. In the meanwhile, my choices were limited to what at least one of my parents was prepared to see. Dad sometimes agreed to a film about the recent war, such as *The Way to the Stars*, *The Red Beret* and *The Cruel Sea*. Mum favoured classics with a moral flavour, such as *Oliver Twist*, which was the first film I saw with both of my parents. As well as pitying Oliver, I envied the long trousers his benefactor, Mr Brownlow, had given him. Summer or winter, I wore shorts. Besides wanting to be warmer in bad weather and show that I was more grown up, I was desperate to hide the pipe-cleaner legs that prompted the taunt of *Bandy Ghandi*.

In the hand-coloured photograph of my parents' wedding, they are typical of working-class people of their generation in terms of height, but not girth. Especially for young adults, already they were chubby. Despite this and me being two weeks over-term, I popped out far lighter than most newborns of that generation. Although my childhood illnesses and recovery from them were unexceptional and no physical injuries required hospital treatment, Mum harboured an exaggerated fear of susceptibility to death. Failure to thrive, a term used when my parents thought I was out of earshot, triggered guilt in them.

In the year following the launch of the NHS, my trips to the local surgery became so frequent that the GP must have suspected Mum of hypochondria by proxy. Doctor Tuffelton had a Double Albert gold chain that drew attention to the roundness of his stomach. The pocket on the left of his waistcoat held the handsome hunter-case watch used for taking a pulse and on the other was a gold-plated lighter that patients were just as likely to see. The consulting room was often full of his cigarette smoke.

Unable to convince the doctor that he should do more for my weediness, Mum enlisted Dad for an evening appointment. He was as ill at ease talking to a professional as she was and Tuffelton grew impatient with their awkward pleading.

"Mr and Mrs Gray, your son has recovered promptly from every infection and there's no reason to think others will be more of a problem for him than for most children of his age. The lack of weight and height is not a medical condition. For whatever reason, your son is small, but he's not deficient, handicapped or ill and nothing suggests malnutrition. If you want him to make the most of what he's got, get him to exercise through a sport he enjoys."

Mum paled and froze while Dad flushed and wrung his cloth cap. I sat between them without letting on that I agreed with the doctor. After all, my grazes took no longer to heal than those of other boys.

After dragging on his fag and returning it to a cluttered ashtray, Tuffelton spoke as if I was the only other sensible person in the consulting room.

"So, young man, what sport do you fancy?"

Other children always chose me last when they formed teams for football, cricket and rounders because I had no talent for them. Athletics did not suit my little legs and scrawny arms, and Mum would never have allowed me to take part in boxing or wrestling no matter how much I craved skills for self-defence. Then I recalled the swordfighting in *Robin Hood* and the newsreel of the Olympic Games.

"Fencing, sir."

"What an excellent choice. You'll have the advantage of being a smaller target and it will build up your mental as well as physical fitness. So how about it, Mum and Dad, taking him to fence rather than to see me when he's quite healthy?"

Dad bit his lip.

Mum, fearing an outburst promised to look into the sport, propelled me towards the door and said, "We can put on our coats in the waiting room. No point in delaying the next patient."

They did not speak during the walk back to the cottage.

"I'm going to read," I said, knowing that a discussion about the visit would begin once they assumed they had privacy.

After banging my door, I opened it quietly and, avoiding the floorboard that creaked, crept back to the top of the stairs.

While Mum made a pot of tea, there was no conversation.

After she sat down, Dad shouted. "That jumped-up quack. How dare he speak to us like that, and especially in front of the lad. He treated us like idiots."

There was a pause filled by the sound of pouring. I imagined Mum seeking a way to contain Dad's anger.

"It wasn't right. I can only think the doctor was cross with me. I've taken Perry there such a lot and then we both turn up."

"But only because you'd said he wasn't listening."

"Maybe I didn't listen. I wish I had, but it's hard when your only child looks half-starved and just can't put on weight."

"You're not to blame, Maud. And anyone who knows us knows we've done everything we could to build him up."

"I'm worried about him exercising. Using up more energy won't help his weight. And the idea of kids his age using swords!"

There was the sound of slurping. Except in company, Dad poured scalding tea into his saucer to cool the first few mouthfuls.

"The swords don't have blades and they have a button on the end. And fencers wear masks and special clothes. I've never heard of any injuries when people have the right stuff."

"Is it always indoors?"

"As far as I know."

"Then he'd be away from the rain, cold and the fog. And he won't get his leg broken the way he might at football, or hit on the head with a cricket ball. But what about the cost of kitting him out and getting someone to teach him?"

"I can do more overtime or jobs for others if needed."

When Dad asked if I was still interested in fencing, I jumped up and down with excitement. They had found a class and the fencing master had even suggested where to find used kit to fit me. Mum rang from a phone box before taking me to a detached house in Pinner. A sad-eyed lady answered the door.

Though not unfriendly, there was a forced jollity to her polite and posh voice. "You must be Mrs Gray and Perry. Perry, there's a swing out the back, if you would like to try it while I make some tea."

The garden was large and the swing, hidden from the house by bushes, hung from a branch. The seat was mossy, as if unused for some time. I made my way stealthily until I was next to the open French windows. There was silence until the sound of crockery rattling on a tray.

"Perry's a lovely boy," the woman said. "Almost the same size as Rupert, but he was two years younger."

"I'm so sorry for your loss. I don't think I could cope if anything happened to Perry. Could I ask you, is fencing dangerous?"

"Not in a well-run class and Captain Latinak is first rate. The children learn safety before anything else. I just wish Rupert had stuck with fencing."

"How do you mean?"

"We think he caught polio at a swimming pool. He loved to swim. Now, let me fetch the kit. Would you like to call Perry so that he can try it on?"

"No, we don't need to try it on. I'm sure it'll be fine."

All the way home, Mum insisted on holding my hand. She squeezed hard at times, sighed and was deep in her thoughts. She would not let me touch the half-sized kitbag or anything in it until she had disinfected and aired every item in the sun.

When I protested, she said, "We don't want to take any chances, Perry. You're too precious. You can try them tomorrow."

The next Saturday morning, Mum took me via two buses to a memorial hall rented by the fencing school. Well-dressed women chatting outside with each other looked us up and down. In the hall, a tall man duelled with someone almost half his size. I was stunned when they removed their masks. The youngster who had fought with such energy was a girl and the forty-something man resembled Errol Flynn until he turned his head to reveal scars running from temple to socket to cheek. Captain Latinak, formerly of the Free Czech Army, had represented his country as a *sabreur* before the war that had disfigured and left him with a glass eye.

He politely explained to Mum that he preferred not to have parents in the hall during classes.

"A few of the mothers wait outside or go to the Lyons Tea Rooms in the High Street."

She took me aside and asked if I could find my way home. When I told her the numbers of the buses we had caught, she looked relieved, handed over the fare, warned me about talking to strangers and left.

Despite Latinak's curious accent and the shock each time he took off his mask, I liked him. He spoke as if we were old friends and was patient when he coached. Some of his sayings have been lifelong companions.

Feints have their uses, but require two actions rather than one.

Hiding intentions is better than disguising them.

The essence of fencing is to give, but by no means to receive.

Because the Captain did not allow harsh comments about another's efforts, unkind students only mocked me out of his hearing. They jibed at my lack of strength, the way I spoke, the generous fit of my jacket and breeches and the everyday clothes that I wore. There were children younger than me, but no one smaller or punier. Their speech suggested they would grow up to be newsreel commentators or BBC announcers. Many arrived at the hall and were collected from it in cars, two of which were driven by chauffeurs. All had clothes that looked newer, smarter and cleaner than mine. In those days, I changed my shirt, underpants and socks on Sundays and Wednesdays and had always thought this adequate because Mum looked down on the families that made these clothes last the week.

There was a girl fencer who looked upset each time she witnessed the other students baiting me. Another girl and her brother walked away when it happened, but no one challenged the perpetrators or alerted the Captain. School already had taught me that it was safer not to report such behaviour. And any mention of the bullying at home would have given Mum an excuse to stop me attending. In addition to fears for me, she was unhappy that the students and their parents were not "our kind of people". She was right in that respect, but I wanted to prove to the Captain that his tuition and encouragement were not wasted on me.

Much practice at home developed skill and sinew if not muscle until I tired no more quickly than most and began to hold my own with other novices, yet never enough to deter the snubs and teasing. One day when I was coming from the toilet to the male changing room, a boy was inviting the rest of the lads to his birthday party, which would have a marquee and a magician. I waited out of sight until the hubbub had died down; my drawing attention to being excluded would have served no useful purpose. Later there were looks, some smug and some pitying, but no one mentioned the party.

During my second year of fencing, I arrived one Saturday to find the hall locked and no one outside. A woman wheeling a pram noticed me first on her way to the shops and then on the way back. She took me to the flat of the caretaker, who said Captain Latinak had suffered a stroke and his wife had arranged for her brother to take over the class from the next Saturday. The caretaker understood that Mrs Latinak had phoned all of the students. When I told my parents this, Mum bristled so much that I withdrew to eavesdrop.

"I'll bet we're the only ones who weren't told," said Mum. "Poor little mite, he could have been sitting out there for hours."

In a half-hearted way, Dad replied, "Mrs Latinak might've overlooked us because her husband's so ill."

"It wouldn't have taken five minutes to write a letter, or at least tell the caretaker to put up a notice. Because we don't have a phone, she thinks we don't count. We should apply for a phone."

"It's a lot of money and we don't have much need."

"Even if we don't use it, people take you more seriously when you've got a phone number."

I had never heard Mum so insistent with Dad.

"What about the fencing?" Dad asked. "Perry's cut up about Captain Latinak, but still seems to want to go."

"I still worry about him going."

"What? Getting hurt?"

"I mean the other kids aren't like him. What if he gets ideas? They live in another world from us."

"You're not a servant any more, Maud. Our money's as good as theirs."

"But it's not just money, is it."

"Now you're sounding like a socialist."

Although Dad did not speak harshly, it was enough to end the conversation.

The new fencing master said that the return of the Captain was unlikely. I had assumed that Mrs Latinak was also Czech, but her brother, little more than a teenager, had an English public-school accent.

Once he heard me speak, he mocked my pronunciation. "So you live in 'arrow do you? In an 'ouse, I suppose."

When I fenced, he said, "Where's your attack, Titch? Given you're tiny, you have to make up for your lack of height with vigour."

Students noted his attitude and began to add their own abuse in his hearing. By the time the class ended, I was so close to tears that, rather than catching a bus straightaway, I stood behind a tree in a park to cry. That afternoon I told my parents that I had lost interest in fencing. They did not question this and Mum sold the fencing kit within a few weeks.

The experience of being ridiculed at fencing led me to fail my eleven plus by inserting wrong answers and misspellings. I imagined that a grammar school would be full of the sorts of pupils who had made fun of me at the Memorial Hall. A less academic school, I assumed, would provide an easier passage through adolescence and a better route to a trade, preferably my father's or as a locksmith. Classes in wood and metalwork, rather than dead and foreign languages, seemed likelier to secure an apprenticeship.

What Dad had saved from his colossal overtime during the war enabled him to buy our cottage after the landlord died in 1947. Dad had made some improvements as a tenant, but as the owner he put everything in order and added a single-storey back extension. His home improvements increased opportunities to observe more of his skills and try my hand at the less physically demanding ones. There were shortages of building materials and on occasions Mum called on her black market contacts to obtain them or Dad did a job in exchange for supplies. Before the great reversal, he had never worked on the Sabbath in peacetime. After breaking with the Newelms, he laboured on Sundays provided our neighbours were not aware of it. Noisier tasks and those outside took place on weekday evenings, Saturdays or during his annual vacation.

He turned his hand to carpentry, wiring, plumbing and bricklaying; whatever was required. Some customers valued his standard of woodwork to the extent that they would wait months for him to do a job rather than employing a joiner. A manager at the Hoover factory in Perivale bribed him to come sooner to tile a bathroom by providing a washing machine at a discount when most of the output was exported.

Although the cottage remained much smaller than the surrounding houses built after the Great War, its decor and contents began to match the standards of the majority of our neighbours in semi-detached houses. Linoleum-topped floorboards covered our kitchen's flagstones. Wall-to-wall carpets appeared in the other three main rooms. Mum delighted in showing her friends and customers the new wallpapering, washing machine, pressure cooker, electric stove, fridge, vacuum cleaner and food mixer. A Post Office engineer installed a telephone and Mum was always happy to receive a call despite seldom making them for many years other than for her black market dealings. Yet we were one of the last local families to acquire a television set.

Despite my parents attending films after the great reversal, something of Rev. Newelm's abhorrence of acting and popular programmes persisted. Dad had acquired a car, a twenty-year old Baby Austin, before we finally rented a television in 1955. Mum sought to limit our viewing to the news and documentaries until *Emergency Ward 10* started her addiction to television soaps.

Not long after Coronation Street became her favourite programme, it was just the two of us in front of the box one evening watching an episode.

I said to Mum during the break, "Remember when you thought TV and acting were wrong?"

"Did I?"

Her reply so confused me that I thought that she was distracted by the advertisement and its jingle until I guessed she was wondering what would happen in the second half. It was then that the appeal of the soap operas for her became clear. These programmes were full of tensions between adult characters that led to them speaking their minds and other disclosures, the sorts of scenes largely absent from the cottage. I thought of switching off the set and challenging Mum to be honest with me until I recalled how much in my life I concealed from my parents. How could I ask for revelations without being prepared to reciprocate?

Chapter 13: Norman ~ Constabulary HQ

The Lychinclay Valley Road during dry weather follows a gentle stream fed by several brooks. Newcomers who arrive after heavy rain often suggest calling the torrent a river and some, noticing that the ridges of pine-topped hills merge without a gap, ask how the water escapes. The catchment flowed into a lake that filled the lower end until, aeons ago, part of the underlying limestone collapsed. Since then, the Lychinclay Stream has disappeared into a swallet towards the end of the dale. This giant drain soon gives way to miles of caverns that dyes have shown link to at least two rivers above ground. Narrow sumps near the swallet frustrate would-be explorers and have killed two cave divers.

While the sumps are no barrier to the water escaping, they do not admit air and this contributes to the valley's microclimate. In a sun-filled hollow, temperatures soar when no breeze penetrates and relief is limited to thermal currents rising and cooler air trickling down the sides of the hills. The trickle is woefully inadequate on a warm still day. When the weather chills, the only thing that displaces Lower Lychinclay's cold air is even colder air; hence the frequent mists, hoar frosts and hard frosts. Sometimes as the mercury plummets, chimney smoke from the village rises in a thin column before mushrooming as if encountering a great horizontal sheet of glass. A pane that, were you not so cold, you might be tempted to watch descend until the smoke hardly rose at all.

No one built grand houses in this terrain so loved by Jack Frost. Upland neighbours use the same honey-brown stone, but the lower valley's modest dwellings weather far more quickly with the help of the yellow and orange lichens that prosper here. And while soil at the swallet end is silt-enriched, extremes of temperature and reduced sunlight take their toll on flora. Villagers, resenting the theft of light by the valley walls and lingering mist, plant nothing that might blight a window and sometimes bicker about shade from a neighbour's garden.

Since the shop-cum-post office closed, the last commercial building is the *Cul-de-Sac*. The pub's sign shows the upper part of a jolly chubby man with his arm pushed against the end of a sack to reveal the outline of a fist; a suggestion that pleasant enough inhabitants can be riled. The name harks back to when all wagons came and went via Upper Lychinclay. Only in 1873 did navvies cut through where the ancient lake's outflow had cascaded to make from a steep bridle path what locals still call the New Road. Sadly, the cutting was not deep enough to allow the coldest air to escape.

Before Rose and I arrived with the pantechnicon, our three visits to Lower Lychinclay had coincided with sunny May and June lunchtimes. We never thought to come earlier or stay later, which led us to assume that the climate differed little from London apart from having less pollution. Our August moving day was cloudless and so still that when no birds sang we heard the shuffling stream. Soon sweat oozed and not just from carrying loads. During a late lunch inside, the heat kept us perspiring.

The afternoon sun dipped behind a ridge making the top line of conifers resemble a black paper cut-out of Christmas trees. The air began to cool and by the time lights were needed it was chilly enough for sweaters indoors. Later, as I closed the upstairs windows against the cold, a tiny sliver of moon was surrounded by extraordinarily bright and numerous stars.

"Rose, you must see this. We have a bonus. I'll open some wine and show you."

We took glasses into the garden to toast the ravishing sky and our arrival. As we shivered, the relationship between geography and climate occurred to me. Not wanting to spoil her first night at Foxenearth, I said nothing about suspecting we were in a frost hollow. The next day after neighbours had confirmed my fears, I still hesitated to tell her. It was always hard for me to share news that disappointed unless asked outright. Like Perry as a child, my adult conscience struggled with direct lies, but in other ways I was very dishonest. One lie in particular will be the second hardest thing to write about here, but not just yet.

If you suspect Perry infected me with his slyness, consider this. The professional standards that had guided me through my career dipped before his haunting. I shared with Rose details of the police assignment, manipulated Ann Grove to gain access to Raventulle for two tourists, and instead of hurrying back to complete the decoding I delayed Daya and blatantly overstepped my brief by letting villagers assume the constabulary wanted me to interview them.

Nor did Perry prompt me to keep unauthorised files. The idea arose with the delivery of the police documents and seeing that what I signed made no mention of copies. But that was a line that was too well marked by my years in Intelligence to pretend that crossing it did not matter. After sending several instalments of the decoding to Daya, I emailed her Perry's complete text in a Word document.

The accompanying message included, "Please confirm that you can read the full document and have created back-up copies, so that I can delete my files."

The next day, she gave the go-ahead. But before eliminating the decoding from my PC, I copied it onto a CD using a different form of encryption. This security was not for the benefit of the constabulary. On the contrary, in the event of the police searching my house the encryption would make it difficult for them to discover the copy.

I emailed Daya that my PC held no files relating to Perry. Along with this half-truth, I mentioned that I awaited further instructions for the documents supplied by the police. She replied that she would consult Ann. I heard nothing for twenty-four hours, by which time I was again a man of leisure, a readjustment made more difficult by Rose playing Mahjong in Brighton. She came back late and left early the next morning for the first of two days of meetings at County Hall where she was representing the District Council.

Daya's emails had ended with her telephone number. Curious about how the police were using the transcription, I rang. Thorsen answered and said Daya was with Ann. Then he chatted about the decoding, referring to Perry as Dolly and avoiding anything that would have made sense to someone bugging the line.

"Do you need to be so coy? Dolly didn't mention any ministers or departments by name."

"No, but he's put a few noses out of joint in this building. Hold on, I've just seen Daya."

There was a largely inaudible exchange between them that included him asking, "Are you alright?"

"Hello, Daya. Are you OK to talk?"

"Hello, Norman. How are you and Rose? I won't be here after today. So if you want to talk, now may be the only time."

Her voice lacked the expected composure. Yet because I thought so highly of her, I assumed that she must have got a promotion or a secondment.

"Congratulations. What's your next step?

"I can't tell you everything, Norman. What I will say is that my parents are both unwell and need looking after. My sister has been the main carer. I'm going to take over."

"But your career?"

"I'm ready to leave the police," she said with a hint of anger. "And in Indian culture, letting non-relatives look after parents is frowned upon."

"I think the constabulary are mad to let you go."

"They are mad, but not in the way that you think. I wish I could say more, but I can't. Give my best to Rose."

My surprise at her news meant that I forgot to ask about the use made of the transcription.

Later that day, Ann Grove rang me. I wanted to ask about Daya, but Ann, while polite, had an edge to her voice harsher than the tone that previously had signalled *time is short*. She wanted me to bring to her office the next day the documents delivered to Foxenearth in return for another day's fee added to my invoice. I imagined that she could not spare someone to collect them, perhaps because of Daya's leaving.

"I'm happy to bring them. Could it wait a few days? I'm just catching up on a few things." The truth was I wanted to make a day out of the journey for Rose.

"It's important you bring them tomorrow. Could you get here for eleven hundred hours? I would like you to hand them to me in person."

I agreed, although puzzled by the urgency when the police had the originals, my full transcription and a list of the symbols with their meanings.

The constabulary's headquarters building was a product of the brutalist architecture that had emerged in the 1950s. Years had darkened the concrete to the colour of slush, the five tiers of aluminium window frames had acquired a dismal patina, and an array of antennae on the roof of the squat building brought to mind a cornered porcupine. The structure would not have looked out of place in a Soviet industrial centre built immediately after the war. Unfortunately, the headquarters blighted a wonderful Gothic church and other magnificent remnants of ages past, rather like a faecal mound placed on a royal banqueting table.

Once inside the Stalinesque bastion, there was colour, wood and works of art that spoke of humanity, but a sense of tyranny from the exterior aspect persisted. Ann's office was at the top. A central lift lobby divided the fifth floor. On one side was the canteen with sun-lit linoleum, melamine walls, lively chatter and the aroma of fried bacon. On the other side and beyond a door with wire-reinforced glass and a coded lock, were carpet tiles oak veneer and displays of trophies reminiscent of school. But neither wood nor metal glinted; there was no sunlight, only a few small ceiling-mounted spotlights sending faint cones of light to the floor.

An office junior led the way down the short corridor and through fire doors into a large central office with two rows of women, most of whom were touch-typing at speed, some from documents and others via headsets. The facilities for the typists smacked of battery farming. There was little space between their desks and even the space behind them was cluttered by tall lockable cupboards and filing cabinets. The secretaries relied on fluorescent lights for the most part because the offices for individuals on either side of the large room had veneer walls and the only sunlight came from the small panels of glass inserted into the doors.

I mentioned my surprise at the set up to Ann after she had closed her door.

She said with a shrug, "If I ever get to be Chief Constable, providing daylight for the secretaries is the first change I'll make. If I bring it up now, I won't get another promotion."

Ann was in uniform, but jacketless and wearing a short sleeved blouse. While very slim and not particularly tall, the wiry arms and square shoulders made clear her physical strength. Allowing for a crinkly face, the kind that has had too much sun, I guessed she was in her mid-forties. Short brown hair and minimal make-up added to her no-nonsense image. One wall was devoted to Aikido prizes and photos of Ann in her thirties in a martial arts jacket tied with a brown belt.

"Do you still compete?"

"It was my career or the practice needed to get to the next level of competition. Thanks for coming, Norman. I've read your transcript and there are a few things I want to discuss. How confident are you that you've captured Perry word for word?"

"Most of his writing was clear enough. The rest I am more than ninety-nine per cent sure of."

"If you were in court with a hostile barrister, would you still be so certain?"

I felt panicky, but on reflection it was a reasonable question and Ann did not sound hostile.

"Yes. I've had lots of experience translating Russian and decodings and being quizzed about accuracy. There may be an odd word to quibble over, but I have no doubt that I've captured Perry's meaning."

Ann's slight frown was puzzling. Why does my assurance not please her? I considered mentioning the help that Perry had provided before recalling my fears for the statistician who was chums with Pascal.

"It might be possible to pay you a higher rate, say an extra two hundred pounds per day. However, we would expect something in return."

The smile was frozen and she had also spoken more quickly than before.

"And what would that be?"

"Other police forces and some government departments want to see your transcript. Once copies go from here, they could end up anywhere. There are references to Knattmaw that we want deleted. Also, some comments about serving officers could be amended. Our reputation is at stake. We can do a better job when people have more faith in our policing."

I said nothing and sought to be pokerfaced. A large part of me strained towards compliance with only a fragment hanging onto ideals. My breathing was speeding up.

Ann braced her muscled shoulders. "You did a great job. Now we're asking you to help us do a good job."

The way she said *we*, revealed this was not her idea. I do not think she deliberately communicated this. Rather, her discomfort affected her usual poise. She tried hard to be persuasive, but acting under duress can make people less convincing. I was grateful that she did not use David Stancher's name to add to her persuasion. If she did not cite him, this probably meant our mutual friend would not approve of the favour she sought. It also crossed my mind that Daya's resignation could have something to do with what Ann sought from me.

"But you have an electronic copy that you could edit? Why do you need me?"

"It would look better if you signed it off. And if we distributed copies with your details that could help you to get further work."

It was unlikely that they would destroy the evidence of Perry's original pages. Should someone compare the coded pages to an edited version, they would soon find the deletions and any discrepancies would be attributed to me rather than the constabulary. Her proposal was outrageous. Nevertheless, I had been so devious with Ann that taking the high moral ground would be hypocritical.

"I feel uneasy. It's a bit like tampering with evidence."

Ann's face relaxed. "I assure you that nothing we seek to amend has any relevance to court proceedings."

"Maybe not court, but what if Perry was right about Knattmaw?"

"Gray caused the Knattmaws a great deal of grief." The irritation in her voice was unmistakable. "Establishing if there's any truth in allegations about what happened decades ago would be difficult, if not impossible."

"For what it's worth, what he wrote about the Gatgash and the boiler house struck me as credible."

"But without corroboration, it's not fair to smear the reputation of a man who gave thirty years of service to the police when Perry Gray was without question as devious as a sack of stoats."

"I appreciate that his account is unreliable, but I don't want to be part of any airbrushing of history."

"Are you sure you won't consider the offer?"

She looked me in the eye and sounded stern. I stopped to consider if there was a hint of menace in her question and concluded that she was acting from habit.

"I would have liked the extra money and the chance of more consulting, but not in return for what you ask. While I can be economical with the truth at times, I draw the line at altering a dead man's words, even someone like Perry."

"I need to leave you for a minute. Would you like some tea or coffee?"

I declined. Ann picked up her mobile on the way out. I guessed that she was about to report my decision to the Chief Constable. Would I be on Catchpole's carpet next?

To counter my agitation, I looked around. Apart from the Aikido memorabilia and a photo on the desk of Ann with two teenage boys who bore some resemblance to her, nothing was on view. I would have bet a fortune that every drawer was secure. Her approach to office confidentiality reminded me of my old workplace, except that at CARE we never have left a visitor alone.

She returned looking peeved. I suspected Catchpole had growled his displeasure at the failure to persuade me.

"If you haven't changed your mind, all that remains is to check that you have returned everything."

She unlocked a drawer and took out the chit that I had signed. I handed over my bundle and she ticked the items against the list.

"That's all in order. Do you have copies of anything?"

I fobbed her off with a look and then felt both awkward and smug. She trusted me; probably because I had come recommended by David. Yet despite her reputation for not suffering fools, I had avoided answering her question.

Looking cross, she said, "I know provincial policing hardly compares to what you dealt with in your former skunk works, but I had to ask."

Perry made his presence felt as soon as I left Ann's office. On reaching the car, I jotted down a conversation.

P Thanks for batting for me and not surrendering to their censorship.
N It's got nothing to do with what you want.
P I still appreciate it. Christ! If you can't trust the police not to fudge and whitewash, who can you trust?
N You weren't exactly a shining beacon of truth when it came to writing letters.
P Feeling the pressure, are we? It's not like you to be so snappy.
N You're probably right about the pressure. But Ann's standards are way above yours. I won't join you in mocking her.
N As you wish. Just one more thing. I reckon she didn't pursue the question of copies because she thought you were so moral for refusing the extra money.

I got back to Foxenearth just before Rose. I made tea and we dunked biscuits in our cups – a habit we both enjoyed when no one else was around – while sitting at the breakfast bar in the kitchen and discussing my meeting.
"What do you think the police will do?"
"I expect Catchpole will make the amendments he wants. I'll talk to David and see what he thinks."
I left a ginger snap for too long and more than half of it fell into the cup.
"Mucky pup," said Rose. Another of our private habits was to use such language, as if correcting a child with affection. "Are you worried?"
"I was at the time. Now I feel disappointed. It was seedy and I'm not used to being bribed, least of all by the police! And Ann wasn't happy doing what she did. I think Catchpole bullied her into it. But then maybe Ann bullied Daya in turn?"
Rose feigned exasperation by looking at the ceiling before staring at me.
"But you *would* suspect bullying. One minute you're saying Ann's as tough as old boots and Daya a smart cookie, and the next you think they're being leaned on. Come on, you haven't got any real evidence."
"How come only women are allowed to use intuition?"
Rose stood to get more tea and kissed the centre of my bald pate in passing. "You've got a point, but even

unusually incisive women get misled by prejudices. You've got to keep an open mind."

I called David that evening. A grand-daughter had just told him that she would be playing football for her country. I shared his delight at the news, but also recognised that he might well have objected to women playing soccer when I first met him. His form of Christianity had little time for women wanting to do things that men had reserved as their province. He was so full of a Stancher wearing an England shirt that, rather than share my work concerns when he was so happy, I simply arranged the lunch that I had promised. The earliest opportunity would be after he had returned from a holiday. Thus, I saw David for the last time three months ago.

Chapter 14: Perry ~ The Stoning

Tonight I am Mr Vinous, flush with words and drunk in charge of a pen. I tasted an Otago Pinot Noir so exquisite that I could not resist opening the companion bottle. While drinking my cellar dry is not part of the countdown to cashing in my chips, there is no longer any reason to save the finest wines for special occasions or to worry about liver damage. Only the need to write provides a reason for not opening a third bottle.

I imagine someone reading this might want to know whether I have any regrets about the letters sent and my other machinations. No, is the simple answer, but life is complicated. For a start, after I have done so much to expand my life choices, they are now reduced to suicide or arrest with inevitable hullaballoo and humiliation. But let us take that type of regret as read and concentrate on the subtler and less selfish varieties.

Imagine that Satan is less preposterous than other religious myths and not only exists but also has a job description. Among his key duties would be maximising the misery of mortals. How convenient for the Prince of Darkness that many vices provoke a shame so toxic that only more of the sin can counter the poison. We see this in junkies, alcoholics and other addicts, such as gamblers and wife beaters. For a while, the addict is lost in his habit or its afterglow. As they come down, self-hatred kicks in, guilt threatens to overwhelm and prompts further indulgence of what prompted the self-loathing. Lucky old Satan sows a single seed of temptation and harvests crop after crop of sin.

When I say that at times there were misgivings about the rough and ready justice I dispensed, guilt was not a factor; my loathing was for bullies, not me. I disliked being short and slight and the way these things invited mocking, but as the Kyte girls with their height, intelligence and good looks had befriended me, I knew that size was an excuse for bullies to act out the dictates of the mental poison that had accumulated within them.

Vengeance drove me, but I was not hooked. I could desist for a month from doing anything of potential interest to the police without experiencing any of the discomfort that can come from giving up a familiar pleasure. What usually led to a resumption of seeking revenge was either an opportunity to look for a name on a database or some fresh insult.

My regrets are limited to hurting the feelings of people who were not my quarry, such as the wife of a target when it is more than likely that her husband was also a bully at home. But then governments routinely apologise for collateral damage after high explosives rain on innocents, yet continue to order further sorties and barrages against areas that include civilians. Politicians, generals and their public relations flunkies put more effort into spinning the stories of carnage than preventing the slaughter. And all but a tiny minority of citizens of the country that did the damage lose no sleep about the non-combatant casualties; we know modern wars tend to lack clear-cut battle lines and accept it would hardly be worth sending troops abroad if their caution was so great that ordnance never goes astray. So why should I have stopped launching letters that were damp squibs in comparison to the mayhem of one shell, bomb or missile?

And speaking of governments, I have little time for the elected leaders of a political system that legitimises backhanders. What company would allow an employee to sell his favours by acting as an advisor or consultant for those seeking deals with the employer? I have even less respect for those in the House of Lords because of the degree of corruption involved in their appointment. Many of the hereditary peers have titles because some ancestor slept with a king and a high proportion of the life peers have made so-called donations to the party that ennobled them. All that sort of sleaze is bad enough, but Ministers and their departmental staff are addicted to throwing tax payers' money at whatever fad catches a minister's attention. I should know, having witnessed so many ill-conceived and ill-managed Whitehall computer projects. Warning signs appear, whistle-blowers jump up and down, but admitting a mistake could jeopardise promotion or lose an election. Better to bodge on and apply for a job in another ministry or position yourself for the next cabinet reshuffle.

Over the ages, those who govern have largely ignored human anguish in both conflict and peacetime. Lethal poverty still exists in much of the world, just as in England before the Second World War. A combination of cold dwellings and poor nutrition killed Dad's parents before either reached forty-six. Four of his five siblings did not make thirty-five. His eldest brother died two days after his nineteenth birthday on Messines Ridge in 1917. The youngest succumbed to starvation and exhaustion following the surrender of Singapore. Those deaths you might see as regrettable casualties of war, but in the 1920s Dad's two sisters died of TB and another brother of typhus.

While Mum hid her surviving kin from me, Dad had none of his original family. In the 1940s, when I asked him about his relatives, he changed the subject. If Mum was there, she threw me warning glances. Dad once spoke in his shed about a school friend, Sid; how they had played soccer with a tin can for a ball, learned to swim in the River Colne and explored the Chilterns.

Only after doctors had drugged Mum did I learn about Dad's family and why Sidney was my middle name. At the time, Mum was nil by mouth apart from rationed slivers of ice; a drip into her arm provided fluids without preventing her throat rasping from the ward's dry air. It surprised me that she made the effort to talk at length.

"Near the end of their last year at school, your Dad and Sid walked to a lake near Rickmansworth. Two kiddies toppled a canoe. Your Dad brought a girl to shore. When he looked for Sid and the other kid, they'd drowned. Your Dad got a medal and the parents of the girl he rescued arranged his apprenticeship. But he never stopped missing Sid."

"What happened to the medal?"

"He gave it to Sid's parents. He said Sid deserved a medal more than him because he tried to help when he wasn't a strong swimmer like your Dad."

"I wish he'd told me this himself."

"It wasn't something he felt good about. I met him because he wanted to know why Sid died and not him. The Newelms said that Sid was at peace and asked only one thing; for your Dad to be a good Christian. Later, Mrs Newelm said she had another message from Sid; that your Dad should propose to me. He wouldn't have married otherwise. He felt that if Sid wasn't able to have a wife, why should he. I was lucky he didn't see through the Newelms until long after our wedding."

She gasped and coughed. I placed ice on her lips and helped her to move up the bed. She was more comfortable semi-sitting, but forever slipping down and too weak to reposition herself.

"After we saw through the Newelms, your Dad felt haunted again. Why was he too young for the Great War and not called up in 1939? He linked his exemption back to Sid. Without the canoe accident, your Dad wouldn't have started the apprenticeship. And he felt funny about earning so much during the war when most of the blokes he grew up with were paid a pittance for facing the enemy. For the same reason, he didn't like my dealing, but it was the one thing I insisted on because I was so worried about your health and him working so hard."

Mum breathed more heavily from talking so much and about such matters. The effect of the drugs fluctuated. One minute they lifted her inhibitions, then she became more reticent or stupefied, and at other times the force of painful emotions penetrated the haze of her medication. On that occasion, I sensed that she felt not just her grief for losing Dad, but also regret at the way life had hurt him.

As the cancer grew, more potent doses allowed other wayward sheep to slip the pen of Mum's mind and bleat. Among the last of her revelations was the way Rev. Newelm had promoted Mosley as the only way of avoiding Soviet godlessness ruling the roost in Great

Britain. And she smiled to recall the minister interpreting King Edward's abdication as a sign that the world was about to end, much to the alarm of the congregation.

More than anywhere else, Dad spoke to me in the shed and garden. For a start, Mum was usually inside and could not look daggers at my questions. But Dad had his own ways of avoiding topics, not least of which was the way he focused on teaching me his skills and encouraging my efforts.

He asked only a few questions of me, such as, "How's school?"

The Kytes had shown that not all families are so stilted and guarded. The girls kept some secrets from their parents, but disclosed much more than I did at Rayners Lane. And Mr and Mrs Kyte shared issues and views with their children and me. Thus, I knew of his dislike of *toffee-nosed* people and the names of several of them from what he said at the meal table. Mrs Kyte was less free with names, but complained about the *squirearchy* and their *lick-spittles,* and made me laugh with her explanation of such terms when I asked. The couple answered with good grace questions from the mouths of babes. They must have steered the conversation at times, but I cannot remember them doing so with forbidding looks or sharp comments. Not even on the morning when I touched on a very sensitive topic.

I had got up early and gone for a walk alone. On my return, breakfast was underway and no one was worried that a child had wandered from the house.

Mr Kyte looked up from his *Punch* and said, "Blimey, Perry. You were up with the birds."

"I'm sorry if I woke you."

"You didn't wake anyone," laughed Mrs Kyte, who was stirring scrambled eggs. "You were so quiet we thought the fairies had taken you."

I said, "Tilda didn't use to like me getting up early, but now she doesn't notice."

"Well, there you are," she said without looking away from the pan. "That's another reason for a young man to have a bed to himself."

"And I'm not frightened to get up now, because I know all the voices,"

Lucy asked, "What voices?"

"The first time I stayed there used to be a man here at night. If I hear a man's voice now, I know it's your dad. And, if we didn't know who it was, we could go and look because there's no blackout."

A worried look flashed over Mrs Kyte's face before she turned to the stove. Mr Kyte looked solemn and studied his wife's back. The girls were busy dribbling and stirring golden syrup, which Mum had brought, into their bowls of porridge. Something novel and uncomfortable was happening between the parents and I expected one of them to say something harsh, the way my parents closed down many a conversation.

"There were all sorts of funny noises during the war, Perry," said Mr Kyte, ruffling my hair. "It's all different now, no more fighting, new rules and new beginnings."

Mrs Kyte smiled at her husband while speaking to me. "That's right, Perry. Let's look to the future. How about you and the girls pick gooseberries after breakfast so we can make a crumble with the sugar your Mum brought?"

The difference with tensions at Raventulle was that the adults quickly dealt with any argy-bargy before relaxing again. And when one of the girls got angry because I cheated at Snap or claimed privileges as the only boy, I knew that they would soon forgive me.

Mr Vinous has rambled from where he started. Let me try to make amends. Had the great reversal not happened, would Christianity have restrained my hand from sending the letters?

I suspect that my parents' abandonment of religion made no difference. Before Uncle Maurice appeared at the cottage, I already had been wilful and enjoyed covertly hitting back at Shirley Morris and other children. While Sunday school briefly tempted me to be a sunbeam for

Jesus, I have met many who outgrew such sermonising. Had I continued to attend, I expect that I would have escaped from that form of superstition come adolescence or at least become the sort of Anglican who treats his religion like the Grand National or the Chelsea Flower Show: an annual outing with opportunities to socialise.

Mum and Dad never said to disregard the commandments. They continued to condemn lawbreakers great and small, presumably with exceptions made for supplementing their rations and refurbishing the cottage via the black market. After the shock of unmasking spiritualist charlatanism, they questioned the sincerity of other preachers and the worth of other religions when they thought their conversations were private, but without any hint that their new outlook gave them greater moral licence.

My occasional trips to the cinema more than compensated for the loss of Sunday school. The only real disappointment linked to the great reversal was that Maurice's visit did not lead to contact with his family when un-Christian behaviour was not an issue. One day when I asked about relatives, Mum kept her eyes on the ironing board.

"Is Uncle Maurice coming again?"

"If he wants to or needs to."

"Do you want him to come?"

"Neither want or don't want. It's up to him."

"Could I go to Watford and see my cousins?"

"You can't go to someone's place uninvited."

The rhythm of her ironing was faster, a warning sign.

"I could write to them."

"There's no shortage of children around here. You don't need to write to Watford."

The sharpness of the last sentence and the vigour with which she pressed on a pleat meant that she would be cross for the rest of the day if pushed further. I retreated to the shed and turned the energy of my frustration to taking apart an old padlock, studying how it worked and adapting one of the hundreds of keys in my collection till it turned the mechanism without the need for force or jiggling.

Mum not only disapproved of her brother's criminal record and heavy drinking but also of his family relying on unskilled work and rented accommodation, a state of affairs she expected would continue from generation to generation. In her mind, the drinking was causal, not the result of unfavourable circumstances. The stigma of my grandmother's mental illness provided another motive for Mum drawing a veil over her relatives in Watford. I learned of granny's death only by nosing through letters in my parent's bedroom. She died of pneumonia eight months after Maurice had found her.

The Pritchard family helped me to understand Mum's attitude towards those who struggle on the basic wage of an unskilled occupation. Adda Pritchard first came to Harrow in 1937 as an eighteen-year-old. He swapped tending cows in Caernarvonshire for a dairy round in Wealdstone, a job secured for him by his uncle who had made the same transition sixteen years earlier. After serving as a sapper in North Africa, Adda wanted to be where flooding was more frequent than drought and only gave up Pwllheli's reliable rain because work was easier to come by in London. In 1947, he brought his wife, Gwaldys and one-year old Padarn to the cottage next door to ours.

He seemed untroubled by drizzle and downpours on his milk round; smiling just as much as when the sun shone. Apart from Adda's occupation, the family being Welsh and speaking English as a second language, the Pritchards' respectability was beyond question. Mum could find no fault with next door's housekeeping or modesty. Padarn grew to have exemplary manners and the three went every Sunday to a Welsh-speaking church that disapproved of drinking and smoking.

Mum was outwardly charitable to Gwaldys, passing on some of my old clothes, toys and books. The two mothers would speak in the street and over the back fence, but the Welsh woman seldom came into our house and the

Pritchards never entered through the front door despite this being handier for them than the side gate. Nor was Gwaldys among the ladies Mum invited for tea. And despite the abstinence of the Welsh couple, they did not attend the alcohol-free Saturday night gatherings hosted by my parents every year or so.

From my listening post on the stairs, I picked up threads of conversation that gradually embroidered a picture of social distinctions. Mum stitched while Dad was more the canvas for her needling. He seldom added his own thoughts or even agreed. Given how easily he could have got her to drop the subject by harrumphing, he seemed not to be bothered enough to dissent. She complained that while Adda worked and was sober he would always be unskilled and the tenant of a landlord who did little to maintain their cottage; no matter how presentable Dad made our property, the neglect next door spoiled his efforts. And to make things worse, in Mum's eyes at least, Adda made no attempt to disguise the fact that he worked at the dairy. He wore his uniform to and from work and only put on a tie for chapel.

I did not understand Mum's concerns. The outside of our cottage had been scruffy before Dad bought it, Adda had defended our country and delivering milk was a useful job. What was the problem? Not that I said this aloud, though I did remind her that Mr. and Mrs. Pritchard were always kind and Padran had never teased me, not even once his height shot past mine.

After Padran went to study veterinary science, Mum forgot she had predicted he was doomed to unskilled work and renting. Rather, she spoke of how she had always known he was brainy. Dad and I said nothing. We understood that her snootiness and inaccurate recollections, like her over-protectiveness, were foibles in an otherwise loving person. Besides, saying nothing and dancing around the issues was the way of our family. What was unsaid did not need to be undone, a notion reinforced by my first crime.

With two nine year-old classmates, neither with a reputation for loutishness, I cycled towards open land to the north of Harrow. I stopped on a bridge over a road and pretended to find the flow of vehicles below fascinating rather than admit I was struggling to keep up. The boys came back and one of them dropped a piece of gravel onto the back of a moving lorry. The other lad found a similar sized stone and aimed, he said, for the roof of a car. It bounced off the boot. To counter my reputation as a wimp, I picked up a stone the size of a matchbox, but I deliberately missed a car by some distance.

"That was truly feeble, Gray. Who'd want you as a bomb-aimer?"

"Bloody hell, Perry. All you had to do was let go. It's not like you need muscles to do that."

We re-armed. Stung, I made sure my stone was by far the biggest, the size of my fist. I knew that a shattered windscreen could lead to a serious accident, yet I took that risk. The stone bounced off the roof above the driver's head causing him to swerve, brake sharply and stop at the side of the road. We did not stop to see what he did next, but raced to the opposite footpath where we would not be seen and pedalled as fast as we could. The one in the lead turned onto a common and towards a weeping willow. We sat under the tree gasping and checking every so often through the curtain of leaves that policemen were not looking for us. Even after catching breath, my heart pounded with exhilaration and then with dread.

"That was brilliant, Perry."

"You sure gave him a fright," said the other boy. "We should call you Bomber Gray."

I tried to look nonchalant, but what if they used the name later, other boys asked why, heard the story and then gabbed to an adult? I imagined the shame of my parents and condemnation of teachers and neighbours when they learned of such recklessness. In that moment, acting alone made a lot of sense in matters best kept secret. I cannot think of a time sicne when I invited another to break the law or when others successfully tempted me to join them in questionable activities.

Chapter 15: Norman ~ Kent

Both sides of my family have their roots in East Kent, the area now promoted to tourists as White Cliffs Country, despite much of it being miles from the coast and laced with coal seams. Grandpa Midlin joined the local regiment, The Buffs, at the outbreak of the Second Boer War. He received a Distinguished Conduct Medal for valour and became a sergeant. As a local hero he caught the eye of a village belle in 1912 despite being almost twice her age. She agreed to marry on the condition that he gave up soldiering. He found the return to farm labouring tedious and re-enlisted soon after the start of the Great War. After rejecting an offer to remain in England and train recruits, he died at Loos in 1915 when his only child, Cedric, was not quite two. Cedric, my father, grew up idealizing a hero he could not remember meeting.

While the fighting continued, my grandmother turned down several offers of marriage from service men because she dreaded being widowed a second time. Come the armistice, she married a Royal Marine based in Kent with the expectation that the government would discharge him before long. Instead, the Admiralty sent him to Russia where he died near Archangel fighting Bolsheviks. Granny turned to religion and against anything that smacked of socialism, values she imbued in Cedric. However, she was less successful in her attempts to stem his fascination with the military. As a teenager, he wanted to join The Buffs and would have done so save for his mother's uncontrollable weeping at the idea.

My father grew up three miles from Eflinwood Colliery. The Bligh family, who owned the mine, countered union activism by recruiting conservative workers. They knew young Cedric fitted that bill and employed him to sort coal above ground. He did not like the job or the rough ways of the other workers, but year-round farm jobs were scarce. And while Cedric read well and had a good head for figures, he had the misfortune to be left-handed in a school that decried his preference. The punishments for using his left hand and the poor results with his right turned him against any occupation that required a pen.

Lily Nutwand, my mother, went from school to domestic service before she was fifteen. She seldom spoke against others, yet disparaged the family who had first employed her. The master and mistress, who were never short of money for a new motor car, fur coat or work of art, expected a staff of seven to do what then would have been the work of a dozen or more in similar-sized households. Food was adequate when the family were in residence as much was returned from the dining room to the kitchen and the cook had a talent for making soups from trimmings and bones. However, when the family went south for the winter months, meals for the servants who remained were sparse and dull.

As an *in-between maid,* Lily took orders from the cook and other servants, got up before them and had the least pleasant tasks, such as emptying chamber pots. From five in the morning until late in the evening, she ran between the demands of duties above and below stairs; hence the job title.

For her parents, their eldest daughter's live-in position meant more room and food for the other children. Her father, a sailor on a ferry, could not afford a larger house and struggled to provide for his eleven living children. He was not particularly religious; just enough to hesitate when it came to family planning. Contraception attracted a bad press and, many believed, thunderbolts for queering God's pitch. The number of births in the Nutwand house suggest that Lily's parents did not tempt divine retribution. Nevertheless, while I was still in nappies, death came from the heavens and obliterated the Dover home of my grandparents.

Teenage Lily, marooned in the country mansion near Deal, missed her family, if not their congested rooms and pigging, what sharing a bed with several others was called. Once a month on her day off she took buses, spent a few hours catching up with her parent's news, gave them half of her wages and pressed ha'pennies into small hands.

Lily's employers required their servants to go to church every Sunday. Domestics sat at the back regardless of the ample places in the family's private pew near the altar. A mesmeric vicar sparked a new level of faith in Lily when he spoke of the enslavement and deliverance of the Hebrews. Cedric Midlin, who was already a committed Christian, also sat at the back of the same church, the one he had attended all his life. When the sight of Lily did not distract him, the passionate vicar's sermons added to Cedric's fervour. After many Sundays of shy smiles, he and Lily began to have brief words. Two years passed before they spoke for more than a few minutes at a time. Their first extended conversation took place after Cedric arranged to accompany Lily to Dover. He waited in the town while she visited her parents. On the return journey, during the long walk from the bus stop to the mansion, he proposed.

Though Lily was desperate to escape skivvying, it was a love match between a handsome, if somewhat modest in height, couple. Apart from her work-chapped hands, my mother had fine skin; dark brown hair and blue eyes complemented her face's complexion. Cedric's oval face, once the coal dust came off it, was olive even in winter. People might have thought he was from a Mediterranean country, but for the fair hair, eyebrows and moustache. In addition to the looks that attracted them to each other, a commitment to piety, hard work and abstinence cemented their relationship.

Mr Bligh thought well enough of Cedric to rent the newlyweds a terraced two-bedroom terrace house in Eflinwood Village. Living among other colliery families was awkward because Cedric's politics made him unpopular and Lily, despite her experience as a domestic servant, did not vote Labour. She fared somewhat better than her husband because women appreciated her generosity. Many sought her help with letters that needed writing and, sometimes, reading. And if a miner had spent his wages on beer, his wife knew that my mother would not let children go hungry.

I do not know if my parents ever sympathised with Mosley, but they were not anti-Semitic; quite the opposite. Thanks to the beguiling vicar, they became British Israelites, a movement attracting supporters from many Protestant churches. British Israelites held that the *Anglo-Saxon races* were Jewish tribes and the House of Windsor descendants of King David. At least before

Pearl Harbour, some followers also considered the Japanese to be Jews and therefore entitled to rule over other races. Whatever views my parents had before I was born in March 1940, by the time I understood such matters, they felt no need to stray beyond mainstream Anglicanism. As far as politics was concerned, Churchill came to represent for them the qualities that made England superior. After Labour came to power, they feared for the country and gave prayers of thanks on hearing that the 1951 election had returned a Conservative government.

My mother's one and only pregnancy made her so ill that my father delayed joining the Buffs at the outbreak of war. Bligh heard of this and, worried about falling coal output because of the number of miners enlisting, spoke to my father.

"Stay where you are and you could be called up at any moment. Start working below and, if it's like the last war, they'll want coal so badly that miners will be exempt. It's a fair trade. It's always wartime for miners."

My father accepted the offer on the understanding that once my mother was well he would join The Buffs. But by the time she had regained her health, the government insisted that miners were vital to the war effort. He hated working in the dark and cramped conditions where near naked men mocked his refusal to curse and drink alcohol almost as much as his politics. He lacked friends underground until given his own gang of Bevin Boys, many of whom sent him Christmas cards long after they returned to civilian life.

Lily's uncle Norman was a merchant seaman who died in a torpedo attack. News of his death arrived shortly before my birth and prompted my parents to give me his name.

"Norman was a strange choice for a child born into a country fearing a brutal invasion," Rose joked the first time we travelled on a bus together.

"I don't think my parents ever thought of that. Their main reservation was that there is no St. Norman, so they added George, Andrew, Patrick and David. Thank goodness they didn't know the patron saints of the Isle of

Man, Jersey, Sark and Herm or they would have added Maughold, Helier, Magloire and Tugual."

Rose laughed till she shook and then asked, "Are you really named after four saints?"

"No. My only Christian names are Norman and George."

"I'm going to have to be careful with you. I can't tell when you're lying."

When bombs fell on another Kent colliery, Lily began to worry about living so close to Eflinwood's winding tower, which she saw as a giant sign beckoning Nazi planes to dump their loads. As my parents could find no alternative accommodation, she reluctantly went back into service. Such was the shortage of domestics, the Lodeleys, who had a large farm five miles from our village, took her on with a baby in tow. Dad shared the house with two Bevin Boys and cycled twice a week to visit us. My earliest recollection, or possibly a collage of memories, is of my mother holding me tight underneath the big table in the Lodeley's kitchen while she chanted psalms. Usually unflappable, she had a terrible fear of thunderstorms, which she said ran in her family. At about the same time, I remember her reading to me from a variety of children's books that she had access to at the farm. The Beatrix Potter stories became my favourites.

While Perry played at Raventulle with children he loved to be with, I had only Cuthbert Lodeley, twelve years older than me and the chubby spoiled heir to the estate. Every so often as an adult, a child reminded me of Cuthbert. Usually it was the girl or boy's harsh tone that triggered the association, but occasionally the rough handling of a toddler by a child brought him to mind. When such behaviour came to my attention on holiday, I spied from a distance, worrying about how far the miscreant would go when no one appeared to be observing. I found it hard to sit easy when a little one's tears loomed, despite a part of me saying, *Don't get involved.*

Often I would emerge and speak solicitously to the younger child, but my words were also for the bully.

"Hello there. You look a bit unhappy. Who's been making you cross? What have they been doing to you?

Don't they know how to talk to a youngster? Now you're beginning to smile. See how easy it is. Anyone could make a child smile, if he just tried."

After my mother understood that Cuthbert frightened me, we moved back to Eflinwood. By then the German threat came from flying bombs that, if they fell short of London, could fall just as easily on the farmhouse as the colliery. She was all too aware of this because a doodlebug had obliterated her childhood home. An RAF pilot had used the wing of his plane to destabilise the V1 over the Channel. The Nutwand house had been unusually full that morning because it was the day after my grandfather's funeral; he had been hit by the swinging hook of a crane. My mother lost the rest of her family that day with the exception of two brothers who were at sea and one of these died in the Atlantic two months later. Yet I cannot picture her wartime face without a smile except for her terror during thunderstorms. Perhaps she found solace in the fact that my father and I survived, for we had all been in the Nutwand house the day before the explosion. If anything, the tragedy of the bomb and the later loss of her brother deepened my mother's faith.

News of Cuthbert Lodeley's conviction in 1974 for cruelty to animals prompted my mother to say why she had left the farm.

"I liked Mrs Lodeley. Her husband was moody, but I didn't have much to do with him. She was always pleasant and not just because the war made her desperate for staff. But she couldn't see Cuthbert's faults for what they were. His boarding school had expelled him for goodness knows what and he was cruel to animals even then. And too often, when the two of you were alone, you had an accident. One week your fingers got jammed in the door, the next you fell down a bank, and then Mr Lodeley found you in a field with the bull just about to come through the gate.

"I knew it was Cuthbert. You couldn't have opened the gate, but you can't accuse people without proof. The only option was to work my notice and not let you out of my sight when Cuthbert was at home. Mrs Lodeley thought I left because of my family. I never had the heart to tell her the real reason."

By the time of Cuthbert's court case, only a few acres remained from all that he had inherited; the rest he had sold to fund drinking and gambling. The RSPCA had intervened after ramblers witnessed a drunken Cuthbert beating a dog with a stick. Inspectors told the court of two other dogs and three horses severely underweight and surrounded by excrement. Some of the animals were also without water. My mother's reasons for leaving the Lodeleys, the news coverage and my unease with aggressive children who reminded me of young Cuthbert, unsettled me for several days. Then as I was shaving I asked myself if he had done other things to me.

From another part of my brain came a very insistent thought that left me chilled, *Don't go there!*

And I did not until looming death allowed me to ask, *What fear prompted my censoring response?*

The emotion in my voice confounds speech recognition software and makes it easier to type that I dread that Cuthbert sexually assaulted me. The news surrounding his court appearance contained no suggestion of such abuse, but the idea flashes like a lighthouse through a moonless night, both alerting me to the suspicion and warning me away from it.

Where has such a notion come from?

Either the reporting of myriad cases of paedophilia in the last twenty years has prompted my speculation or Cuthbert did something so unpleasant that I chose to forget it. I do not expect to find any answers in the time available. The important thing now is accepting abuse as a possibility rather than avoiding the question. There is no point in writing this account if I avoid awkward facts and questions.

Perry was very fortunate to have ended up with the Kytes. Nothing suggests that anything untoward happened to him at Raventulle other than the accidental discovery of bodies in a barn, a ghastly incident but not one that involved wilful cruelty to him. Yet surely it is detrimental for toddlers to be separated from parents on whom they have depended for emotional security?

He recalls preferring to be with the girls when Maud visited. I think this might be what happened towards the end of his wartime stay. What was the impact on him of the first separation from his mother? I doubt that he gave her up so easily. Young children can enjoy playing with new friends, but initially they want familiar faces nearby. Did he really settle in so quickly with the girls and Mrs Kyte?

In the months before he first stayed at Raventulle, Perry portrays his mother as highly anxious. Imagine the impact on the child of Maud's prolonged agitation followed by her abandoning of him. An older child might be relieved to escape someone who constrains, but witnessing distress in their mothers makes pre-schoolers fretful and therefore more dependent on them.

Did Maud's fear of bombing, exaggerated but hardly irrational, and their separation contribute to Perry's anti-social behaviour? Others might say that the government evacuated over a million children, some to houses a lot less welcoming than Raventulle, and yet there was only one Mr Vitriol. However, I am not suggesting a simple causal relationship, just pointing out a possible factor that none of the others writing about Perry have discussed.

My father returned to surface work as soon as he could. Despite having intelligence and reading widely, his quiet manner and aversion to writing prevented him becoming more than the supervisor of the sorting shed. His ambitions and my mother's came to revolve around their only child. Thanks to my parents' love of books and the library of children's classics that Cuthbert had outgrown, I could read before I started school, just like Rose and Perry. Like Perry, formal education came as a shock to me. I now suspect that my first teacher was severely depressed following the loss of her husband and only brother in the war. Her constant scowl and harsh voice seemed threatening. If she spoke directly to me, my breathing stopped. She seldom used corporal punishment and never on a child like me who was obedient to a fault, yet I sensed the anger and dreaded that it would lead to her flying off the handle at whoever was nearest or caught her eye. My parents had never hit me. They had no need to. Their rebukes triggered shame and a determination not to repeat a misdeed. They created a craving for acceptance as a *good boy* that meant teachers' reprimands invoked enormous guilt.

My second year at infants' school was relative sweetness and light with a young teacher who smiled a great deal and even laughed at times. The following years were dull, but without any particular sense of menace from the staff. However, my classmates were growing fangs, claws and sharp tongues. Their most common nicknames for me were *Dumbo, Pig* and *Radar.* The second was short for *Pig Ears,* and the third prompted by pictures of the new invention with dishes on either side of an antenna. Children also accused my father, via me, of sucking up to the bosses and of being a *Tory toady.* They said he was a *coward* and a *scrimshanker* who only went into the pit to escape enlistment and that his return to surface work proved these claims. I was never beaten up, but many of the boys and some of the girls delivered individual punches below the neck, kicked my heels when we walked in line and used rough play as an excuse to hurt me. At grammar school, the other boys from Eflinwood who attended smeared my father's reputation there and prompted others to use the same unpleasant names for me.

One reason my family had stopped going to the cinema was that in the darkness, louts from the village threw pellets of paper at my father. All the same, my parents, who disapproved of what they considered lax censorship, had no interest in the films I most wanted to see, such as *Robin Hood.* And as in Perry's home, many popular wireless programmes did not meet my parents' high standards; much BBC comedy they found coarse. My father listened mostly to the news, weather forecasts and cricket. For the latter and when he had time to listen to ball by ball commentary, he preferred to close his eyes. The emotions displayed on his face as a match progressed fascinated me as a boy.

Mum encouraged me to read books such as *Kidnapped,* yet she feared that these stories as radio dramas or films might over-stimulate me. Not even the coronation on television, watched with great reverence as guests of a churchwarden, prompted my parents to consider getting a set. The small number of films that I watched, restricted access to wireless, and later the lack of a television set at home separated me further from other children.

Perry and I were also victims because we were small, unathletic, good at schoolwork and habitually polite. When another child felt the need to discharge pent up feelings, tiny lads like us were easy targets. Yet I had one cross to carry that Perry does not refer to; I was and remained ugly.

I imagine that Perry also told his parents at first about being picked on at school and his Mum, like mine, spoke to teachers. While staff expressed concern about the tales of bullying, they had no effective ways of responding to the issue as a whole. Classes were large and it is often difficult to distinguish between boisterous and vicious. And as children age, they become wilier in their tormenting and more skilled at intimidation that deters confiding to the teacher. My bullies became adept at avoiding adult witnesses or they communicated taunts in ways that did not draw fire from a teacher, such as smirking while scratching the side of the head. This might have mystified an adult or not even registered while still drawing my attention to prominent ears.

What enabled me to cope was the stability of home and the unfaltering conviction that Jesus and my parents loved me. Dad was not physically demonstrative, but that was the norm then. I always knew that he cared, not least because at weekends the two of us would walk, bike or fish, or some combination of these, for the best part of an afternoon. Even before I could cycle, he fashioned a seat for his crossbar where I rode feeling quite safe. Not long before I started school, my mother went to an evening church meeting. He fed me and asked if I wanted to go for a ride. I was almost asleep by the time we arrived at an area of swampy ground. The dim light from the bike's dynamo disappeared as we stopped. He nudged me and pointed. Faint lights floated among the dark clumps of vegetation.

"What are they?"

"It's the fairy light of Will-o'-the-Wisp. You can't see it every night, but I had a feeling we would tonight."

"Is it magic?"

"It makes me feel lucky."

Because he had grown up locally, he knew where and when to look for such things. Several times he took me to watch badgers emerging from sets and we would squat downwind so quiet that every noise in the woods seemed unnaturally loud. *Mr Brock*, as he called them, appeared so often that a photograph of a badger, or even a cartoon, has brought tears to my adult eyes. He loved the countryside as only a man who has worked underground can. To see a skylark or find a wild orchid filled him with joy.

If the weekend weather was too foul to go out, we shared my toys for an hour or two. He also read to me at bedtime as often as Mum did. If I had a question and waited until he finished listening to the news or turned the page of his paper, he was usually informative, if a little biased.

"Why do we have rationing?"

"It started in the war. The Germans sank boats bringing food to England. It wasn't fair that sailors like your uncle Norman lost their lives so that landlubbers could get fat. Then the fighting cost so much, the government kept rationing to save money. At the end of the war they began to ration bread so people in Europe didn't starve. Now rationing's become a habit for the Labour Party, but the people are sick of it. They'll get rid of Attlee, just you wait and see."

Another time I asked why people had to die.

"All our lives we climb towards God and when the time comes we fall off the mountain into His hands."

"What mountain?"

"It's just a way of describing life. From birth to death is a like journey, but not one on a flat sealed road. It's more like spiralling around a mountain where the tracks can be steep and narrow. God wants us to keep climbing rather than use the easy paths that would take us down and away from the light."

"If you live a long time do you get to the top?"

"God's mountain has no summit. The journey continues until you fall. And then the angels catch the good people and take them to Heaven."

"And bad people?"

"God wants to catch everyone and always helps those who regret their sins. But if someone keeps choosing the easy path they're not climbing towards heaven and when they trip or walk blindly over an edge no good angels guide their souls upwards."

Miners who would credit Cedric Midlin with little else acknowledged his skills in the allotment he started during the war. When I asked to go with him, he kept me busy and was pleasant enough, but he seldom invited me. After the garden at Foxenearth became a refuge for me, I recognised that he valued the solitude and silence of the soil; at work, clatter, shouts and oaths surrounded him. Before I discovered the tranquillity of gardening, I had suspected that he did not encourage me because manual work was not in his plans for my future.

My mother was generous with her hugs and talkative without prompting, but never said anything in front of a child that she would not have announced to the village as a whole. As a tot, I loved her flow of observations. When I was older, her prattling in front of other children embarrassed me.

"Look at that ginger tom walking in our yard as if he owned it. He's not even afraid of the dogs around here. Mrs Sladden told me she saw him stare down a vixen. Now he's sniffing the rubbish bin. You'd think he was never fed. Oh! He just went for a sparrow and missed. Now he's cleaning himself to pretend he's not bothered."

The running commentaries on her modest slice of the world happened mostly while she worked at the scrubbed table lit by the south-facing kitchen window and without her hands taking a break from peeling, sewing or ironing.

Her best local friends lived in a much older village two miles away and were regular attenders at its Anglican church. I was happy worshipping there with my parents and the Sunday school was a sanctuary where other children did not abuse me, not even when the teacher was out of earshot. Religion seemed to offer an excellent deal; not only would God reward you in heaven for being good, but also associating with other believers meant one encountered more kindness.

Chapter 15: Perry ~ Gobstoppers

For many a saying another exists with an opposite meaning. *It's better to light a penny candle than to curse the dark* is countered by *Waste not, want not* or *A penny saved is a penny earned*.

My parents invoked all three maxims, but as survivors of childhood poverty, the Slump, wartime *make do and mend*, and the austerity that followed victory, economising was more instinctive than spending. Food and acquisitions to help their social standing were the major exceptions. The amount of protein we ate in a week during rationing was far greater than coupons alone would have secured, but Mum's idea of nutrition was limited in other ways. Her vegetables were overcooked – though to be fair no more than in most houses then – and potatoes dominated unless other weighty produce, such as turnips and carrots, cost less. Fruit and fibre in general were less important to her than portion sizes. We had salads for a few weeks each year because she could not imagine one without tomatoes, lettuce and cucumber and all three had to be cheap at the same time. And what had been luxuries or treats for modest families before the war, such as the tins of salmon or pineapple that often lay under her bed, only appeared on our table if we had guests.

For over a year we ate tinned snoek at least once a week simply because it was marked down; the government had assumed people would be hungry enough to eat this fish despite its muddy taste and a smell reminiscent of stale urine. If butchers provided a choice, Mum took the cheapest cuts. And long after the end of rationing, nothing that was edible or could contribute to stock was thrown away.

When Dad rewired the cottage he provided two power points for each of the four main rooms. No longer did we need to trail flex from the light socket in the ceiling for the iron or the radio. One of my Christmas presents in 1948 was a pre-war reading lamp. Why buy new when used items are so much better value? Dad fitted it onto on the wall of my bedroom so that by swinging the arm the light was available for both bed and the desk he had made from a plywood case. A peeling sticker on the lamp warned not to use more than a fifteen watt bulb, but it still made a difference because no room in the house had more than a forty watt bulb dangling from the ceiling.

Mum boasted about her young eyes having sewn by the light of a single candle, yet had I mentioned that I preferred more light for homework and reading, my parents would have provided a brighter lamp. What stopped me asking was both the fear that Mum would have regarded such a request as further evidence of sickliness and my parents' constant fretting about the cost of electricity. Every time I left a light on and sometimes even when I switched one on, they would say something like, "This isn't Rockefeller's mansion," or "No wonder the bill's so high," and leave the impression that my profligacy could bankrupt them.

One dreary winter morning in 1952, Mum wanted the vacuum cleaner bag emptied. Although drizzle dampened the dust that came from the bag as I shook it over the dustbin, some particles irritated my nose. She heard the resultant sniffing as I was putting on my mackintosh to go to school.

"Peregrine, gentlemen don't make a noise like that. It sounds like a cold coming on."

"It's only the dust from the Goblin."

"Have you got a clean hanky?"

"I've still got one hardly used from yesterday."

"Your Dad didn't get me a washing machine for you to carry a dirty hanky. Go and get a new one. There's some I ironed yesterday on the middle shelf of the airing cupboard."

Dad had added the cupboard to my bedroom after replacing our outside toilet with an internal one and a plumbed bath. Hot water came from a new fuel-efficient coal stove that also supplied radiators and aired clothes. Because the door to the cupboard swung towards the window and stopped at ninety-degrees, even on a bright day the shelves were gloomy. On that morning with the sky full of solid cloud, I could see almost nothing and should have switched on the main light. But the history of exhortations not to waste electricity persuaded me to feel with my fingertips and stuff what I took to be a handkerchief into my trouser pocket.

The school day began with woodwork. Dad's coaching meant that I handled tools with confidence and finished ahead of many boys with far more muscle who had to wait for Mr Gower to help them put right bodged work. Towards the lesson's end, Mr Gower complimented the T-Square I had finish sanding and set me to cleaning the benches. John Thrusham stepped away from his vice while I brushed beneath it. Sawdust and chippings rained on my head and shoulders. John was looking elsewhere with a smug sneer that meant he had sprinkled the debris on purpose. As I was slapping off the mess, a sneeze threatened. From my pocket came a duster cut from an old petticoat ironed so that the irregular remnant formed a neat square with a fragment of lace trim concealed in the pressed folds. Perhaps it was from Mum's wedding trousseau as none of her other undergarments had such frills. Thrusham caught sight of the rag before I hastily palmed it.

"I saw that. Look what pygmy's got."

Mr Gower heard this and snapped. "Thrusham! You're further behind than anyone else. Cut out the cackle and keep your mind on the job."

He walked to the bench, picked up the pieces of John's T-square and held them together. "How do you expect to mark up anything accurately with something so crude?"

The teacher's intervention allowed enough time for me to act behind Thrusham's back. I brushed wood shavings into the pan, moved to the bin, dropped the cloth and tipped the rubbish over it.

At morning break, Thrusham, all beefy ten stone of him, found me in the crowded hall used during bad weather.

"You're a loony, Gray, keeping a pair of girl's knickers in your pocket. Where'd you steal them? Did you take a ladder to reach the clothes line?"

Showing hurt invited further abuse while lashing out or giving lip meant a battering. The best course was to respond in a low key manner, but I always feared not being able to carry this off. And at that time, my voice wavered between soprano and tenor and had invited yet more teasing from classmates, all of whom had made the full transition.

I strained to prevent squeaking. "What knickers?"

"Empty your pockets then."

"What will that prove?"

Thrusham shouted, "That you're a lying nancy boy."

I had have never been called anything like that before and it shocked me. The accusation turned heads and within seconds a crowd surrounded us. Stung and panicked by the prospect of a mob scenting blood, I shouted back.

"And if it's all in your imagination, then it proves you're lying and twisted."

He prodded my shoulder with two fingers that felt like a chisel being hammered. "You're afraid to show."

When my turned-out pockets revealed only lint and three-penny bit, the tormentor looked confused.

A tall boy jeered, "John's lying and twisted."

Thrusham grabbed my arm, lifted up my jumper, and said, "I know the tiny twerp has it!"

As he began to pull my shirt from my trousers, someone yelled, "Pansy!"

The throng took up the cry, forcing Thrusham to retreat in humiliation, something he never forgave me for. I undid the bottom buttons of my shirt, bared my belly and shook my head as if in disbelief.

The boys regarded me as a weedy swot, but I was dull and inoffensive whereas most of them disliked Thrusham's snide remarks and the way he used his size to push people around. To some extent, peer pressure prevented Thrusham from hitting someone less than half his weight too hard or too often, but with even a single blow being painful, I spent much time trying to avoid him or at least the reach of his limbs. However, little deterred Thrusham's verbal digs at me and his taunts were harder to escape because he had a loud voice that carried across the schoolyard. He was not the only one at the school to bully me, but after the petticoat incident he took every opportunity to rain down misery. I sought a covert way of hitting back.

Inspiration came from a reading of Bleak House on the radio after Mum had said it was too cold to be in the shed. She allowed me to take apart a clapped-out gramophone at the kitchen table while she darned socks and listened. I was so engrossed in the clockwork mechanism that spun the records that I hardly followed the story until my ears pricked at the word Dedlock. Thinking this related to keys, I paid attention and discovered that Lady Dedlock feared that letters might lead to her disgrace. I did not appreciate straight away that she had written the letters. Rather, I assumed they were forgeries created to embarrass her, a misunderstanding that led to the idea of an accusation delivered anonymously. The prospect of wounding Thrusham in this way was so exciting that I lay awake well past midnight wondering what mischief might seem credible, who to send it to and how to disguise my involvement.

Our headmaster had decried shoplifting in assemblies after complaints from store owners about boys wearing the uniform of my school. One incident had involved two lads creating a distraction while a third stuffed his pockets. The head's furious response to this blotting of his school's name led me to settle on an accusation of stealing from a shop. After many mental drafts, I took an envelope and sheet of paper from the small supply kept at home. To disguise my writing, I used the stick and ball letters taught at infant school.

Dear Headmaster, Last week I saw John Thrusham stealing gobstoppers when the shop owner was not looking. Perhaps I should have reported him, but I don't want to get involved with the police and if it got into the newspapers, my old school would get a bad name. I hope a few wise words from you now will mean that John does not end up in a borstal.

I collected sweet packets. If they came from the gutter, all the better, as long as the dirt was not too obvious. The morning after posting the letter, I slipped a used toffee packet containing three gobstoppers into John's satchel before our first class and discreetly watched him. He discovered the items during maths while reaching for his ruler, was about to say something, but thought better of it. As he walked out at morning break, a gobstopper was in his mouth and the bulge in his trouser pocket meant the others were there. He could not finish the sweet before the next lesson. Rather than trying to conceal it in his mouth during the next lesson, what I had hoped for, he slipped the gobstopper into his pocket, wriggling his fingers to open the cellophane without extracting the packet. I had begun to doubt my plan and was cursing myself for providing treats for a bully when the head sent for Thrusham.

His classmates next saw him entering the dining hall scowling. Later, word spread that he was fuming about the head calling him a liar for insisting that someone else had placed gobstoppers and a toffee packet in his satchel. I hid my delight until I was outside the school gate. I had been prepared to slip more packets into John's satchel in the hope of a teacher catching him with a gobstopper in his mouth and word of this getting to the head. Instead, the letter had prompted the head to call for John.

I got much pleasure that day speculating the exchange of words during their meeting. Indeed, I played in my mind over and over again for months scenes like the following.

"Do you have any sweets on you, Thrusham?"
"No, sir."
"What's that bulge in your right pocket?"
"Conkers, sir."
"Show me the conkers. As I thought, you're a liar. Where did you get the gobstoppers and toffees?"
"There were no toffees, sir, just the packet with three gobstoppers. I found them in my bag during maths, sir."

"Don't provoke me, boy. You don't really expect me to believe some fairy brought you sweets?"

"But it's true, sir. Honestly."

"And were you honest about the conkers? If what you say was true, which I don't believe for a minute, you would have tried to find the rightful owner."

"It was sort of *finders, keepers*."

"Had you found them, it would have been dishonest to keep them. Given your dishonesty is beyond doubt, I believe you stole the gobstoppers, a packet of toffees and goodness knows what else."

The day after the head interviewed John, we had a whole-school assembly. The head shared how disappointed he was in John Thrusham and not just for stealing but also for being so stupid as to think he could deny his theft. It became clear that John's parents also did not believe him and had promised to keep him on a tight lead both to prevent further crimes and as a punishment. In the days that followed, the more Thrusham protested to boys that he had told the truth the more they teased him for being an incorrigible fibber. *Gobstoppering* became school slang for telling stupid lies. The bigger lads taunted John with the word and smaller boys joked about him behind his back. I relished both forms of mocking without revealing any feelings. A classmate noticed that I did not make fun of Thrusham and asked why.

"It's not sporting to kick someone who's down."

"You're daft. Thrusham's picked on you more than anyone."

I shrugged, but felt an extra thrill at adding another layer of deception that would protect me. In all of my later letter writing, appearing aloof from the devilment that I had started was a bonus. You might compare my enjoyment of revenge to eating. Although one can enjoy good food without feeling that hungry, it tastes better after a hard day's slog. Covertly hitting back at someone as loathsome as Thrusham was comparable to working up an appetite. Knowing that others thought me charitable or at least disinterested, rather than Machiavellian, was like adding a good wine to the feast.

I considered sending a second letter about another school bully. There were plenty of targets to choose from, but I was fixated on the need for physical evidence, like the gobstoppers and packet. After spending much time thinking about what else I could plant and who else might fall for an anonymous letter, I parked the idea. It took some years to realise that a cleverly worded accusation by itself sometimes could be effective.

I increasingly opted for solitary pursuits during my teens rather than risk being bossed around, insulted and assaulted. The few boys I trusted gravitated to larger groups and in every gang at least one lad threw his weight around. If I could not be with people who did not bully me, self-entertainment was preferable. Dad allowed me free range in his shed, provided I did not use certain power tools unsupervised and limited myself to scrap materials, of which he had a good supply. Often I was happy enough taking household objects apart and reassembling them. In those days, you could see how most things worked, even electrical goods. A library book taught me the basics of building and repairing radios and Dad was thrilled when I identified and replaced a faulty valve in our wireless. He felt that his genes were shining through because I had not just imitated his clever hands, but broken new technical ground.

"When I was young," he said, "There wasn't a better trade than tool making, but now my money's on electronics."

How right he was, but the career Dad suggested came to nothing. My exam results, while good by the standards of a secondary modern, were not enough for the Post Office to accept me as a trainee telephone engineer. TV rental companies also turned me down. Locksmiths thought me too short to stand at a key cutting machine and most other trades wanted brawn as well as brains. Along with my parents, I wondered what employment I would find until a neighbour, Mrs Ovesian, shut her front door with the keys still inside the house.

Chapter 17: Norman ~ Croydon

The oddly named Congregation of the Upper and Lower Tables prompted an Internet trawl that revealed Peregrine Newelm's father was a minister in a millenarian sect with another curious name, The Church of the Last Epoch. Newelm senior led his household in prayer three times a day, six if you include grace before meals. Rules for the Sabbath meant cold food on Sundays, a day devoted largely to church services and Bible reading at home. Newelm junior graduated in theology, became a minister in Watford and supported every tenet of the sect until the Great War took two brothers and Spanish flu killed his wife, their three children, a sister, and both of his parents. Presumably grief and doubt prompted him to investigate spiritualism. The second Mrs Newelm, the one who hired Maud Owens, was one of the mediums consulted.

The Epochite leadership regarded *séances* as on a par with devil worship and suspended Newelm from the list of approved ministers. Excommunication for heresy followed his refusal to renounce spiritualism. Part of the Watford congregation, many of whom had found solace for their losses through messages from the other side, followed Newelm's call to join a new church. A supporter who had amassed a fortune from the manufacture of casings for artillery shells provided the minister and his new wife with a substantial house, part of which was used as a chapel. As the congregation grew, a hall was rented for Sunday services until a chapel was built.

Part of Newelm's success is linked to the number of families with a loved one who had disappeared in the carnage created by high explosives. He convinced people that smithereened human residue and the consequent lack of a body in a grave trapped spirits on earth, claims confirmed by messages from the deceased passed on by the Newelms. To provide release and direct lost souls to eternal rest, Newelm provided *Ethereal Funeral Services*.

Unlike most spiritualist leaders, Newelm continued to preach hellfire sermons alongside the messages of hope from the other side. And he continued to condemn pleasures that most of the country took for granted even then. His church used music for services, but warned that popular songs might arouse unwholesome passions. He forbade the children of his followers to perform so much as a nativity play and condemned as ungodly any woman whose hair when let down was less than twelve inches long.

If Perry's portrayal of his mother before the great reversal as neurotic and suffocating is accurate, her faith crumbling could only have aggravated her symptoms. I imagine her clinging more desperately to son and husband because the Newelms, who had become parental figures, had failed her just as her father and stepmother had. Gordon's loss of faith at the same time would have made him less of a resource for Maud. Moreover, respectability for both had in part depended on passing themselves off as good Anglicans. After the great reversal their status depended on occupation, owning and improving their cottage, accumulating possessions and Perry's success. However, I suspect that Maud's unease with the middle class and concern for her son's health limited the extent to which she pushed her son to achieve. And after he failed his eleven plus, Gordon lowered his ambitions for the boy to entering a skilled trade.

The parents never suggested to Perry that anything goes because their religion had gone out the window. Yet just how shattering it could be in that era for a lad to have to find his own way without former absolute beliefs is illustrated by my own loss of faith.

Grammar school revealed different interpretations of the Bible and taught me that proving one over another, or faith over atheism, was not easy. Yet for three years after passing my Eleven Plus, I continued to pray with fervour at the foot of my bed each night. Some sermons added to my zeal and one made me consider becoming a minister. The motivation for such a vocation included, along with pious notions, the prospect of pleasing my parents, having the title of reverend and other boosts to status. However, the thought of having to preach sermons and other public speaking acted as a powerful deterrent. To put an end to months of mental toing and froing, I decided that God would call me to the priesthood if that was His wish. How odd that Perry arrived unbidden, yet when I listening intently for an inner voice, nothing happened.

The National Coal Board took over Eflinwood and my father had to admit that working conditions improved a good deal under Labour. Safety became no less important than productivity. The provision of hot showers meant that he and his clothes no longer came home filthy. Public ownership also brought to the mine a flow of technical experts, regional and national union officials, trainee colliery managers, politicians and those they invited.

The NCB-appointed manager, like Mr Bligh, saw Cedric Midlin as a safe pair of hands and my father continued to supervise the sorting shed. But the new manager also saw him as a safe pair of lips, someone who could act as a reliable guide to the lesser visitors who warranted a tour. Dad's courtesy, discretion and ability to answer questions about work above and below ground made him an ideal choice. On April 26th 1954, Head Office summoned the manager at short notice to London. He barely had time to brief Cedric about three visitors from Yugoslavia wanting to see a modernised pit.

While the party were on their way to a coal face, a fault in a compressed air machine sparked methane. Word spread rapidly through the village and Mum and I prayed for those underground and the safety of the rescuers. We assumed Dad was one of the latter when he did not come home at his usual time. A deputy manager knocked at the door. We thought he would ask my mother to go with him to break bad news to another family.

After the manager had gone, we prayed again. My knees ached from the cold stone that seeped through a thin rug, yet I would have put up with far worse to help my father. As the chance of his survival withered, I resisted as unseemly the urge to offer God future personal sacrifices, such as becoming a monk at Alton Abbey, in exchange for Dad's safe return. Who was I to offer heaven a deal?

Instead, I tried to imitate my mother's forbearance by telling God that I bowed to divine will. This submission did not withstand the discovery of Dad's crushed body and the distress of waiting for his burial, which enquiries into the disaster delayed. The more I heard religious expositions on death or phrases like, *We cannot understand the will of God*, the more doubt crept in. By the time of the funeral, I was doubly bereft because I no longer believed that my death would reunite us. And for many years I had the sense that a large part of my head was hollow because nothing replaced the religious certainties of childhood.

Because my mother would have regarded my loss of faith as another catastrophe, I kept quiet. There were no teenage friends in the village to turn to and boys at the grammar school might gossip about my atheism, which was unique among the students as far as I knew. As well as not wanting to provide a further excuse for bullies to pick on me, had the pious choir master heard of my apostasy he might have sought to reconvert me through unwanted fireside chats. Worse still, he might have said the chapel choir was no place for a non-believer. Singing with others, if anything, became more important after losing so much. Although church rituals made no more sense to me than a desert dweller dancing for rain and the language of worship had become mumbo-jumbo, the music could still be sublime and the harmonies were the only time I felt integrated with my peers. The way I saw it, a non-believer being part of a church choir was not much different from singing a song in an unfamiliar language. Looking attentive during sermons and services while my mind roamed was easy enough. And, if the words of a hymn seemed banal, I treated it as a form of folk song worth preserving and let the music and other voices lift me.

After the pit disaster, bullying at school eased for a time. The reaction in the village was longer lasting and more marked. Death erased distinctions and the community supported all of the bereaved households. Lads who had never missed an opportunity to torment, greeted me like a friend and girls who had ignored me after primary school stopped to chat. If anyone shunned, I did because the only people in the village I felt a connection with were those who had had lost a loved one underground. And yet I seldom said more than hello to fellow mourners because it seemed that our shared experience of bereavement created understanding without words.

Walking or cycling near Eflinwood reminded me of Dad and his love of nature in a way that swelled sadness. To escape the house, which at times felt like a mausoleum, I caught a bus to town on Saturdays, watched two films and then trudged the streets with shops until closing time made me feel too conspicuous in the near deserted centre. Still not wanting to return, I walked the residential areas for an hour or more, usually seeing no one that I knew. If I spotted a boy from school, I tried to avoid him before he saw me. How could I say that I was wandering his street because I hated Eflinwood and the countryside around it?

The shortening days increased a sense of being excluded. Houses either had drawn curtains or windows that showed a smiling family bathed in light. I felt especially forlorn at the sight of someone of Dad's age and not once did I consider what became obvious later; many men had gone to war and not all had returned. There must have been dozens of boys at my school who had lost a male relative, including fathers.

In the New Year after the explosion, my mother said, "Uncle Ed has invited us to stay with him for a fortnight during your next school holiday. If we did, we could easily visit London most days. What do you think?"

Edmund Nutwand was four years younger than his sister. They had been close as children and being the only survivors in their family had brought them yet closer. After serving as a wireless operator in the Royal Navy, Ed drifted to London where he had great success as a salesman whatever the product. The last time he had visited Eflinwood, his Jaguar had attracted children who had never seen such a splendid car in the village after the Bligh Lagonda disappeared following nationalisation.

My mother's voice was tense when she asked about staying with Ed and there was a strained smile. I knew she worried about my Saturday excursions, which I avoided discussing, and the school results that had dropped from promising to mediocre as I sank into self-pity. I hated to think that she suffered even more because of my lack of application, yet this failed to provide sufficient motivation to study as before.

In response to her question, I feigned enthusiasm to please her. "That would be great."

I had nothing against Ed, whom I liked. What I feared was a repeat of Christmas when all that should have been pleasurable was tainted by Dad's absence.

Ed made himself available to whatever selling offered the best potential for income. He had worked for many companies and claimed all had regretted his going. I think his flair came from hiding his determination to sell under a genial mask and an ability to imitate accents without appearing to mock. This skill first became apparent when I heard him speak with neighbours in his leafy Croydon street. He talked just like them; not the way he chatted with his sister, for which he used an East Kent accent and localisms such as *another when* for *another time*, *buck-fisted* for *clumsy*, *hicket* for *hiccup*, *out of doors* for *unfashionable*, and *swimmy-headed* for *giddy*.

For a fortnight, my mother and I explored London, which neither of us had seen before. My father was with us because, as well our grieving, we knew that this holiday would not have happened without his death. Yet for many of the hours I was happy. I liked my uncle not just for his generosity, which he said he had learned from Lily and her ha'pennies, but also for his ability to make us smile. Ed had a fund of jokes and shaggy dog stories and knew where to draw the line with a pious sister. He was only slightly more *risqué* with me when she was not there.

He drove us to Windsor Castle on our first Saturday. Often when the car stopped for more than a few seconds, he did impressions of different accents and encouraged me to try my larynx , as he put it, at Scouse, Geordie, Cockney and what he called Wardroom and I called posh. In the evenings, he had me imitate comedians on the radio. He was particularly fond of the Goon Show and we held conversations in the voices of its characters. My mother disliked such programmes, but welcomed the smiles they brought to my face.

Ed's bespoke shoes were designed to add to his height. Smart attire was as much a feature of him as his pencil moustache and thin body. Ties and matching pocket handkerchiefs were all silk and colourful, though never striped, as he always wore a striped shirt or pin-stripe suit – never the two together – to make him look taller. The cotton hankies he actually blew his nose on carried his interlinked initials embroidered in red. If he did not wear a tie, there was always a cravat as if a naked neck was offensive. Until the 1960s, he never left the house without a hat, usually a trilby.

I assumed Ed was waiting for the right woman because he owned a four-bedroom house. Thus his invitation to Lily to stay on as his housekeeper confused me. He had said he enjoyed her cooking and the way she made everything far cleaner than the woman who came in five mornings a week.

"But what will happen when he gets married?" I asked after Ed had left for work.

"Not all men get married. Even if he did, he wouldn't do anything that would hurt you or me. But I want you to decide. We won't move leave the village if you want to stay."

I thought of the reminders of Dad around the village and the bullying at school that had returned to its former level and said, "I want to leave Eflinwood."

She looked at me in a different way, a stare, but not one intended to force me to do something. For the first time, I felt that she invited me to be an adult.

"So the question is, where do we move to? I'm sure I'll get a job anywhere they need unskilled hands but, you see, all I really know is being in service and housework and that won't earn much."

All through life whenever I had to make important decisions, my mind turned to that moment of choosing for both of us. If my transition from childhood requires a marker, the sense of responsibility for our future at that point is as good as any. I did not want the village, but the scale of London, its grubbiness and the grimy buildings as black as the coal from Eflinwood also repelled. Ed's part of Croydon, where all the homes had gardens front and rear, was attractive as suburbs go, but it was still densely populated. And not yet having Ed's ability to hide my accent, I would be a conspicuous yokel among city folk. Moving to a town in East Kent would have suited me better, but my mother would then struggle to find housing and a job.

I cleared my throat to speak with a deeper voice. "It makes sense to move to Croydon."

My new grammar school had twice as many pupils, harsher discipline and, by and large, less effective teachers. The most memorable lesson was unscheduled. I took a wrong turning on my first afternoon and entered the school hall. The elderly man with puffy bags under his eyes who had taken my German class in the morning stood watching a sign writer add a name in gold paint to a long list of the war dead. He beckoned me over.

"Norman Midlin, isn't it?"

"Yes, Sir. I'm sorry, I got lost."

The teacher sounded tired and sad, unlike during his class. "Well, Midlin, I hope we never lose you. You can see this school has lost far too many boys. The latest was in Korea. If you look back to the First and Second World War lists, you'll see the same surname, his grandfather, father and uncle. I knew them all."

The golden names attracted my eyes during assemblies in the months that followed. Some of the old boys would have died virgins, but many would have left behind children or at least a pregnant wife or girlfriend. My grieving did not stop, but the illusion that I was the only fatherless pupil was shattered. I thought also of my father growing up without knowing his Dad and I appreciated the years my family had been together; not even the war had separated us for more than a week at a time. As a result, I began to work hard at school and especially at German from respect for the teacher.

While I stopped feeling so sorry for myself because of the pit accident, bullying classmates continued to depress me. I was never their chief target the way I had been in the village because the main gang of bullies in my year picked on two boys with Italian parents. Fear of attracting more attention from the thugs, if I objected to their racism, made me walk away from the persecution.

Unlike my former school, bullying continued in the classrooms when the teacher wrote on the blackboard.

The boy behind once jabbed a compass into my backside and on another occasion a shoe ground my hand when I was retrieving a protractor from the floor. The shorter the temper of a teacher, the more the gang sought to provoke him through causing a boy to make a noise. Nothing made the bullies – who were confident that their victims knew better than to incriminate those responsible – happier than to see an innocent punished by an irascible teacher.

Outside the classroom, verbal abuse was frequent and most weeks saw me bruised, by a single blow if I was lucky. As much as I blamed the bullies, there was a suspicion that I too was at fault for being ugly, attracting abuse and not standing up to it. Such was my disappointment with the viciousness that I told my mother I wanted to leave at the end of the school year that I turned sixteen.

"But your father wanted you to go to university. The school says your German could get you a scholarship. I want you to get a degree. Ed does too. Why waste your chances like this?"

I said things like, "It's time I was earning".

Had I mentioned my real reasons for leaving, Mum would have gone to the school, which would have made things worse. The bullies were more than capable of continuing to harass me whether I was at school or not.

Chapter 18: Perry ~ Global Typewriters

After I had picked the lock on Mrs Ovesian's front door, she insisted that I tread on the immaculate and thick hall carpet and enter her gleaming kitchen for milk in a cut crystal glass and homemade biscuits served on a gilt-edged plate. She took off a navy blue coat while leaving on a small matching hat that covered her brow with a veil. The hem of the black gauze created the illusion of her pencilled eyebrows meeting over her nose, a comic effect that did nothing to erase the sadness in her dark eyes. No matter how much warmth in her voice, the sadness remained on her face.

"When my little ones are at university, I have no one to feed until my husband comes home."

She made my consuming sound like a favour. The accent was not strong enough to stop her sounding posh and she had the confidence I then thought all well-spoken people shared. The family were Armenian. I wanted to ask where Armenia was, but she was too busy ordering me to eat another *mamoul*, putting her shopping away and asking her own questions.

Finally she sat opposite still wearing the hat, which seemed rather exotic. "So Perry, how did you learn to open doors like that?"

"Dad got me interested in how locks work and brought home old ones for me to take apart. He used to help me make skeleton keys and lockpicks, but now I make them for myself because he's taught to me use the tools in his shed."

"And what else do you make in this shed apart from things that a burglar would find useful?"

She was smiling and not for a moment did I think that she doubted my honesty, but it was a lesson never forgotten. People want to believe that their security measures are effective and it disturbs them to discover how easily another can circumvent locks. After that day, when neighbours who already knew about my skills called on me, I took fewer implements and pretended that certain types of locks defeated me. And once I had left Rayners Lane, I said nothing about my locksmithing skills.

"If we need something for the house, like a new coal scuttle or a replacement window sill, I help Dad to make it. Simpler things, like a new handle for a saucepan lid, I make by myself."

"And what do you want to do when you leave school?"

"I tried for an engineering apprenticeship with the Post Office and then for one mending TVs, but no luck. Fixing wireless sets is the one thing I can do that Dad doesn't do."

"So how did you learn?"

"From books and then taking sets apart and putting them back together."

Her olive face crinkled with a big smile. "And you can always reassemble a wireless that you have disassembled?"

"Yes. I was already used to taking things apart, like the engine of an old lawn mower, and then putting back together.

"But how do you know where everything goes?"

"I leave all the parts along the bench in order and make notes and sketches. And the more things you take apart, the more you sense how they work and are held together."

"Have you ever taken a typewriter apart?"

"No, Mrs Ovesian."

She spread the previous day's Daily Telegraph on the table, refilled my glass and said to eat up while she fetched a typewriter. It was a portable in a battered grey leather case with a metal badge that read *HEMHOrO*.

"This is damaged. Perhaps you would like to look at it. It's alright if you can't put everything back together. As long as you keep the parts, my husband can fix it."

"I'd love to try."

"Take it for a week and when you bring it back, I would like to see any notes or drawings you make. By the way, the keys are in Cyrillic."

I thought *Cyrillia* was another name for Armenia.

By rewinding the ribbon, I found a small section that still had enough ink to produce grey letters from the typebars that were not jammed, letters that resembled the Greek symbols seen in maths books. I made more notes and diagrams than usual because the typewriter was novel, straightened misaligned typebars, brushed out decades of paper dust and used a fine oil to ease movement.

Mrs Ovesian tested the machine and then asked to borrow the sketches and notes. That evening, her husband returned them and invited my family to tea on Sunday afternoon. Mum glowed at her first invitation to what was easily the best-kept house and garden in our street, but as the hour for the visit approached she became so tense that she feared her stomach would misbehave.

After I had enjoyed three different kinds of Armenian cake, Mrs Ovesian suggested I look at the back garden. The adults talked earnestly while frequently glancing outside. Their smiles allayed any fear that I had done something wrong, yet I would have listened had there been a way of doing so without making it obvious.

Dad joined me in the garden and said, "The Ovesians have taken quite a shine to you. He wants to know if you would like to fix typewriters for him when you finish school. He's not offering a proper apprenticeship, but I think it would still be a good trade to learn. The money's not bad for a youngster and he's told me how much it will go up every six months until you get what he pays his adult repairers after four years. Your Mum said she wasn't keen on you doing heavy lifting and he's promised you don't have to lug anything that might be unsafe."

I fought back tears of joy. Only one boy in my class had lined up a job with prospects and most had no idea what unskilled future awaited them. Working with typewriters suited my practical bent, fixing them required little strength and my small hands would be a boon. The last month of school passed far too slowly.

Global Typewriters occupied four rooms on the second floor of a dilapidated building five minutes from Great Portland Street Station. Mr Ovesian sold new and second hand foreign typewriters. If you lived in London and wanted to type in Farsi, Tamil or Kana, or your exotic machine needed attention, Global Typewriters would help. The mechanics also serviced typewriters from Britain, the United States and Europe. In the front office were the only two women employees. Both were old enough to be my grandmother and their appearance dampened the sexual arousal that followed travelling on the tube from Harrow to Central London with young women I could barely bring myself to look at. Sometimes a passenger's perfume excited me and other times the rush hour crush brought either fleeting contact with a beauty or the heat of her flesh sitting alongside mine between several stations.

Global Typewriter's largest room was the workshop, which included a wall of shelves for machines awaiting repair and those ready for collection, plus spare parts and, accessible only by ladder, part-cannibalised typewriters. Three other men, all ex-soldiers, taught me their skills. Cliff and Dan had completed a year-long training after the war to become typewriter mechanics and they grumbled about me coming straight from school. Fred had learned on the job before the war and pointed out how quickly I picked up skills.

As the youngest, I also made the tea, swept up and did errands. All three men expected deference, even after I matched their level of ability and then overtook them. My success was due to Dad's coaching in many skills, a decade's experience of taking things apart and a relish for new challenges. Because the old hands preferred not to work on an unfamiliar model and were wary of electrical components, within little more than a year I was regarded as the expert on electric typewriters, a growing part of the business.

I accepted my junior status. What I resented were the jokes that Cliff and Dan played on me, such as sending me to a hardware store for a "long weight" and to a cake shop for "buttered ovaries". One great relief was that the mechanics did not tease me about my size; they were all men of modest height.

Mr Ovesian had warned staff that they must not let me strain myself. At first, people yelled if I went to lift the heavier machines. However, the need to lug typewriters and supplies up and down the stairs when the lift was yet again not working built up my appetite and my strength. Sadly, my weight increased by only a few pounds each year.

Mr Ovesian insisted that his mechanics tested all repaired machines by typing on a sheet of scrap paper. When work was slow and the typewriters featured the Roman alphabet, the men typed silly letters. The first I read declared that Cliff had Lurgy of the groin and needed six weeks off work with both hands in plaster. I knew the disease was an invention of *The Goon Show* yet somehow the typed page lent credibility to patent nonsense. Another test-letter warned that the police were looking for a left-hand drive typewriter that had run over the slow brown fox. In the ensuing discussion between the three men, I learned that the police could match a typewriter to a letter.

After seven months in the workshop, Fred took me to service machines at an insurance company.

As we walked along Marylebone, he said, "These service jaunts are funny. Most of the time, we're not doing anything the typists couldn't do themselves. But Mr Ovesian is a wizard at selling maintenance contracts and most managers being men know bugger all about typewriters."

"I hope I don't make any mistakes."

"Chances are, all you're going to do is clean the machines. If you do find a problem, there's not much you can't fix. You've got more to worry about with all the women in the typing pool. They can get a bit silly and come out with things you wouldn't expect a lady to say."

I nodded without understanding what he meant.

"Tell you what, I'll work from the back and you work from the front. That way I can keep an eye out for you. It's only the herd you have to watch out for. Once we get to the upper floors the girls are all much better behaved."

We heard the curious rhythm of many manual typewriters as we climbed the stairs towards the typing pool on the first floor. Forty-eight women, most of whom were under twenty-five and several of whom were very pretty, sat in eight rows of six. At the end of the first row, a stunning redhead not much older than me yet much more womanly than I was manly, stood to let me access her typewriter.

She smiled and said, "Hello," in an enticing voice.

Then she stood in front of her machine close enough for her perfume to register over the methylated spirits used for cleaning. I avoided looking up because her cone-shaped breasts stared back at me.

I prayed to the God I no longer believed in. "Oh, Jesus. Don't let me go hard."

To distract myself, I read the letter to one side of her machine; a reference for a Personnel Assistant to be signed by Reginald Brown, Personnel Manager. Among the qualities commended were reliability, discretion and honesty.

The redhead attempted to make small talk about what I was doing and why until the typing pool supervisor appeared.

"Rather than wasting this young man's time, go and check the stock in the store cupboard. It seems we're again out of pencils and rubber bands. Where are they all going to?"

As the supervisor turned on her heels, the youngster mouthed what I took to be "cow" and then said aloud, "Yes, Miss Splicer."

As she spoke, a fleck of her spit landed on my lips. Had this happened with anyone less beautiful, it would have been nauseating. To my astonishment, sexual excitement drove me to the Gents by the stairs where I climaxed within seconds of pulling down my trousers. I leant back on the cold tiles to enjoy the waves of pleasure and appreciate the pristine surroundings and their privacy. I had masturbated only in my bedroom before this and even there in moderation because of the rumours about self-pleasure enfeebling the body and mind. After removing the semen from my body with shiny sheets of tissue and replacing the top of my coveralls, I checked in the mirror for any signs that might let on to others what I had been doing. Cold water helped to reduce the redness in my cheeks, but not the ears.

Back in the typing pool, I was surprised to find that proximity to the women, continued to arouse me. Some said nothing or little, others greeted while the keys did their bidding unwatched. Mercifully, none sought to say more than a few brief pleasantries to me. As I started on the third row, Fred walked past winking. Did he have a need similar to the one that had taken me to the toilet?

Two voices in the row behind me cut across the keystrokes, perhaps taking their cue from Fred's departure.

"Oh, he's so cute. Look at those pink ears. I want him at the altar with me for my wedding."

"Like a small one, then, do you, Maisie?"

"Of course not! Give me Victor Mature any night of the week. No, I want him to be my page boy."

There was giggling. I dared not turn round and tried to put all my attention on the typewriter.

"Silly me, I thought you'd taken up baby-snatching."

"Ah, look at him, his ears are boiling now and his little cheeks as red as beetroot. We've embarrassed him now, Lottie."

"Best leave him alone then."

"Oh, I don't know," said Maisie raising her voice. "Maybe the little fellow is enjoying it. You know what boys of that age are like. They can't say what they want, but that doesn't stop them having sheep's eyes and panting like an old goat."

Their jibes reminded me of my disappointment with the girls at infant school who were not like the Kyte sisters. I thought of how I had hit back at Shirley Morris and John Thrusham and wanted a similar sort of revenge.

I slowly took the carriage return off the next machine. There was no need other than wanting Fred to service the row behind. During the reassembly, my burning ears overheard a reference to Maisie living in Finsbury Park and the supervisor called her, "Miss Manners".

At home that night, I drafted a letter to the Personnel Manager.

Dear Mr Reginald Brown, I regret contacting without saying who I am, but there are reasons for this that I cannot go into. What I will say is that I am grateful for a reference you wrote that encouraged me to employ someone who has been as reliable and hardworking as you stated.

One of your firm's typists, Miss Maisie Manners, is well known in Finsbury Park for her dishonesty. Recently I saw her in a pub selling pencils and a box of rubber bands and heard her boast how she and another light-fingered colleague in the typing pool called Lottie take advantage of your company's stationery cupboards.

My advice is that you do not let these girls have access to any supplies that might be pilfered and sold on. I hope that none of Miss Manner's colleagues have been puzzled as to why money has gone missing from their purses. She is clever enough not to take large amounts. A well wisher

I typed this on a portable about to be collected from the workshop and posted the letter from Finsbury Park. From the moment the envelope dropped into the Royal Mail box, a sense of satisfaction ensued that intensified with imagining Mr Brown studying the details. At the least, I expected him to discuss the letter with Miss Splicer. The thought of them beginning to doubt the two women created a pleasant warm tingle.

Two weeks after posting the letter, I called the insurance company from a phone box and asked for Miss Splicer in as deep a voice as I could muster.

"Typing pool supervisor."

"Is Maisie Manners there?"

"She no longer works here. But why are you calling? We don't allow personal calls."

"Sorry. It's just that someone said she might have some pencils for me. Is there someone there called Lottie."

"Miss Courtenay has also left us. There is nothing for you here. Good day."

Although I was delighted and had no doubt that the letter had been effective, I called the firm again and asked for Mr Reginald Brown. A woman answered.

"I'm Errol from Finsbury Motors. My boss has asked me to check on a woman seeking a job with us as a typist who said she worked for your company until recently. He thinks it strange that Maisie Manners doesn't have a reference."

"Miss Manners did work here and she did leave without a reference. But you would need to speak to Mr Brown for more details and he's with someone at the moment."

"Perhaps you could answer a more general question? Do many typists leave your firm without a reference?"

"We always provide a reference when asked unless there is a particular reason not to."

"I think the boss will understand without me needing to call back. Thank you."

The second call added to my sense of accomplishment, but not enough to compensate for the anxiety of being on the phone. It was hard to believe that someone would not recognise my voice or that I inadvertently would give myself away. After that, I only made extra calls if the earlier ones were inconclusive.

Fortunately for me, the other men enjoyed working in typing pools and the next time Fred suggested I go, I made excuses and he took Dan. My biggest fear was that Mr Ovesian would negotiate a contract for a pool with electric typewriters, but this only happened shortly before I was called up and by the time the visit came round I was in the Army.

Chapter 19: Norman ~ Probett's Print

When my mother was out, Ed allowed me to pour and sniff brandy and whisky. Tasting was out of the question because his teetotal sister would have regarded giving any alcohol to a minor as sinful. I often served drinks at the start of one of his evenings when a friend of Ed's would call before they set out. Occasionally a show or film in London was mentioned and other times the plans appeared vague. Although most of the men who called were married, their wives never came to the house or took part in these outings. Ed went out most often with another bachelor, Gerald Probett.

The first time we met, my mother was at Evensong and Ed was upstairs when the bell rang.

"That'll be Gerry." He shouted. "Show him in and say I'll be down in five minutes."

I tried to make small talk in the front room while the guest's much nicotine-stained fingers lit an unfiltered Capstan with a gold coloured lighter.

"Do you live in Croydon?"

"Yes."

His curtness encouraged deference. "Do you mind if I ask how long you've lived here?"

"All my life apart from the Navy. It was Ed who followed me here, not the other way round."

Ed could have said something similar and made people laugh. His friend's tone and frown left me feeling stupid.

"He usually offers me a drink." And when I moved to the table with the decanters and syphon, "A large whisky and soda."

By the time I had presented the glass, the cigarette was half smoked thanks to frequent and powerful drags. The last of the drink was knocked back as Ed entered and another declined. Probett often left the impression that he was keen to get away from the house and especially when my mother was there. I suspected he was uncomfortable with her piety.

As far as I know, only Ed called him Gerry. My mother used Gerald. I always referred to him as Mr Probett and heard no invitation to do otherwise. However, many of the other men who called insisted on first names and some on nicknames such as Kiddo and Mac.

Ed's friendship with Gerry stemmed from the comradeship of war; they had served on the same frigate for four years. Apart from that and both having prospered on Civvy Street, there was little similarity. Not even physically were they alike. While Ed was slim, short and fresh faced, his friend had height, a drooping belly, pudgy jowls and a florid complexion. What beauty he may have been born with had been lost to excessive eating, heavy drinking, and chain smoking. More than that, there was only a veneer of civilisation, whereas the other men who came were not just polite but also showed an interest in whomever they met. The tailored suits and overcoats draping Probett's lumpy proportions, rather than making him a gentleman, seemed to say *clothes do not maketh a gentleman*.

The day after first meeting Probett, I asked Ed what he did.

"Gerry's trained non-union members to run printing machinery. He pays above the going rate for unskilled work, but far less than print union members would expect."

"Is that fair?"

"It depends how you look at it. He's got twenty or so people earning more than they would anywhere else and his customers can't see any difference in the finished product other than Gerry does it cheaper."

"What do the unions say?"

"They hate Gerry because he trains someone in a few months rather than a four year apprenticeship. And Gerry tries to run his equipment non-stop, which is a lot more difficult when you have to deal with shop stewards."

As my parents and Ed had made me wary of unions abusing their power, I admired Gerald's enterprise and let this overcome my reservations about his uncouthness. When my mother failed to persuade me to stay at school and I had no idea about what work to seek, Ed arranged a job at Probett's Print in Mitcham, an easy enough cycle journey from the house. I would have preferred a job with another of Ed's friends, but I accepted with gratitude having no other options or plans. The idea of much overtime paid at time-and-a-quarter also appealed. Ed had said that Gerry expected long hours when the order book was full because there were only two shifts and a dozen or so casuals who were mostly available at weekends.

Overlooking the clattering machinery was a mezzanine floor with two offices. Mr Probett, as his employees called him, occupied one when not out seeking more orders or down on the shop floor. He entered and left his sanctum through the other office where Melchiorre Zammit kept the records and files. Behind his back he was known as Milky to the hands; only the boss used this to his face and not when they were downstairs. After all, during Probett's absences Zammit was elevated from bookkeeper to acting manager. He said he had left school at the age of ten in 1897 and boasted a lack of formal qualifications. Yet he had a phenomenal memory and could simultaneously total columns of pounds, shillings, pence and farthings by running his eye down the page, a skill that he insisted was common in his native Malta.

Each morning during my first week, he showed me an office system, let me get on with it for an hour and then inspected. He acknowledged my accuracy, but warned that he would keep checking. If I had a job title, no one told me what it was. Only when the Army asked me to give my occupation on a form did I decide on Accounts Clerk, not realising how a little dollop of information this can have lasting consequences. I was lucky not to end up in the Pay Corps like Perry.

It would seem that Probett made an exception for Zammit's brown skin and curly hair because all other applicants who did not look like northern Europeans were told there were no vacancies even when the shop was short-handed. And curiously, Probett employed no women, who then counted themselves lucky to earn half of what a man received for doing the same task.

Employees did whatever was needed; demarcation disputes were unheard of. Few got the sack, but not from Probett having any reservations about exercising such powers. Rather, existing employees recommended new people – jobs were never advertised or listed at the Labour Exchange – and workers knew that their reputation would suffer if the boss found lacking a recruit they had recommended.

After two weeks in the job, Probett said, "Zammit's happy with your work, which is just as well. It would've been embarrassing to dismiss a mate's nephew. But mark my words, there will be no passengers on this ship. Now how are the lads treating you?"

"They're OK, Mr Probett."

Just as in school, it was better to say nothing about the ragging in case it made things worse. Besides, was it reasonable to complain that others called me *Big Ears*, when most hands had nicknames? Nick was called *Tin Bum*, derived from pronouncing his full first name as *Nickel Arse*. Alf from Burnley was *Cloggie*, Ken from Swindon was *Turnip,* Bald Len answered to *Coot*, and the older workers referred to the obese, 56-year old day shift foreman, Oliver Saxon, as Sexy. But as well as name calling, I attracted an excessive proportion of the insults and horseplay.

On my first afternoon, as I walked past Nick on my way to the toilet, he was bent over a dismantled press. He asked me to hold a large spanner for him. As I went to take it, he pointed to the ceiling. In the second that my eyes glanced upwards, he turned the tool to offer the end covered in grease and ink and I grasped before registering the switch.

"Spread that about a bit in the khazi and you'll have a nigger's prick to show for it," leered Nick, loud enough to be heard over the working presses."

"Yeah, but wash yer palms after the wank," roared Alf.

I only used the work's sit-down down toilet once. It was towards the end of my second Monday and Gerald had gone out. Someone stopped near the cubicle door. There was the smell of paraffin and the scratch of a match. Then a ball of flaming newspaper rolled under the generous gap at the bottom of the door singeing the hairs on my legs before I could kick it back out. Someone booted the burning ball back and the sound of at least two men giggling trailed away.

When I emerged, all eyes watched and Alf triggered much laughter with, "Drop of paraffin does wonders for constipation."

Had anyone challenged this sort of behaviour, the old hands would have said something along the lines of, "It's just a bit of fun. I was the greenhorn once and it didn't do me any harm. If someone doesn't like such larks, he should sling his hook. You've got to have a bit of a laugh to break the monotony."

Had I said to the men that I felt humiliated, it would only have encouraged them to push for the breaking point. Unfortunately, the men saw me as a way of hitting back at Probett, Zammit and the ruling classes. Like the two bosses, I wore a white shirt. When asked how Gerald had recruited me, I had made the mistake of saying he was a friend of my uncle. And the fact that I had attended a grammar school and lived in an affluent area somehow linked me to the country's elite.

Urgent orders required me to don overalls and work downstairs, sometimes for twelve-hour days, packing, counting, trimming and any other routine tasks. Probett being on the premises made life more tolerable because then the men would not waste time playing tricks. Zammit knew what went on in the boss's absence, but chose not to confront the foreman. Saxon not only did nothing to stop the others, he used his position to send me on the delivery bicycle with spurious purchase orders to a jeweller for angle iron, to a hardware store for glass nails and Woolworths for *effing* tape. Overtime at short notice meant that I took food orders. Until I knew what was available, the men delighted in seeing me write down bizarre requests such as a kosher ham sandwich, a cheese roll with no crust, or a Cornish pasty with extra corns.

As in school, the print workers threatened to hit me for no good reason, but unlike classmates the men never thumped me. They jostled and someone put grease on the firm's bicycle wheel rims so that the brakes failed. I fell on the crossbar avoiding a car because my legs were so short. Bruised testicles meant I could hardly walk, yet I rode back into the loading bay rather than give anyone the satisfaction of knowing the prank had hurt me.

Working downstairs meant sitting with the others in the grubby cramped tea room rather than fetching tea to drink with Zammit before the men took their break. The older hands had chairs at the one large table. The rest sat on benches with backs against walls covered in girly pictures. I favoured sitting behind the foreman's huge frame where he could not see me and his bulk blocked the views of some of the others. This position was also next to the draining board where I could place my mug, allowing me to hold up an old newspaper to further limit who could see me. I especially wanted to avoid them noticing my shocked reactions to some of the conversations.

Len was the first to stun me in the tea room. "These two trollops came into our local last night. My mate and I went up to them and they let us buy them a drink. After a bit they go for a piddle and we saw they has ankle chains. So Lefty says they must be on the game and I says let's not waste time buying them drinks to get our leg over if what they really want is cash. He can't wait until they've sat down before he asks how much? Quick as a flash, one of them says ten bob for fifteen minutes round the back of the pub and out they go. The slow one says, how about you and I says, yeah, give me ten bob and I'll give you a good seeing to. Nah, seriously, she was worth half a quid. What are you gawping at, Titch? Would rather pull your little pudding than spend a bit of money on nice bit of crumpet?"

It was not so much his use of prostitutes or the idea of sex in a dark alley – after all, teenage hormones and ignorance prompted all sorts of fantasies – but more the sense that he disliked women other than using them for gratification. Some weeks later, I heard worse from one of the casuals.

"I might have to scarper soon. The wife's gone back to her parents. She got the hump when she found out I'd knocked up next door's teenager. I smacked the missus to calm her down and now she's threatening me with the police."

"Is she bruised?" asked Nick.

"Black eyes and broken arm. So you can see why I might need to slope off."

"Can't she see reason?"

"Nah, the mother-in-law has never liked me. She's the one pushing to involve the blue bottles."

"Maybe you should give the mother-in-law a smack or two?" said Alf.

"I might just do that as a parting gift."

"What about the girl?" asked Nick.

"I didn't tell her to get pregnant and with a bit of luck she won't know who the father is."

I hid my face with a newspaper during the laughter that ricocheted around the tea room. How could they be so indifferent to a badly beaten wife and mock the plight of a pregnant teenager?

In one way, I am grateful to the printers. Unlike Perry, the nastiness of the adult brutes I encountered in the Army did not come as a complete shock. Perry's workmates were less malicious and at Global Typewriters his main fear was of women mocking. Perhaps the viciousness of National Service came as an even bigger blow to him?

P I wasn't prepared, but would it have made any difference? The NCOs were out of control and the Owls thought they were untouchable. And did you suffer less on your worst day at Gatgash because the printers had prepared you?
N No, not that day.
P You haven't followed my lead and written about your worst memory first.
N I'll get to it. Are you afraid I'll stop work when I reach that point?
P It would be a shame, given all your efforts so far.
N Is there anything else you want to say?
P Such as?
N At the end of the first chapter you felt I'd stitched you up.
P I'm sorry if I over-reacted.
N But is there anything that strikes you as needing correcting?
P Not that I can think of just now.

The only time that I spoke out with any force at the print works happened in the month before my National Service started. During a busy period, Nick had left me to clean the rollers of a press, returned a few minutes later and ruffled the hair on my bent head with inky fingers.

"The Army will clip away these curls and sort out the rest of you."

"Get off."

When I resumed cleaning, he prodded my backside with the sharp end of a broom, making an indent in my pants. I thought for a second something was about to enter me.

"Why don't you grow up?"

"That's rich coming from a short-arse like you. What's the matter? Is Big Ears saving himself for Mr Probett? Or has he buggered you already? Oh! You do look surprised. Didn't you know what kind of friends your uncle has?"

I stammered because by this time I had guessed that what Ed and Gerald had in common their homosexuality. "What are you saying about my uncle?"

"If the sailor's cap fits, wear it. How old's your uncle? Is he married? Has he even brought home a girlfriend? Come to think of it, how come he wants a little lad like you to live with him?"

The eyes of the workshop were upon us and some men moved closer to hear better over the din of the presses. The idea that Ed wanted to molest me brought back memories of the calumnies against my father. I was incandescent; my ears felt as if they would burst into flame. What I most wanted was to batter Nick to a pulp, but not only was he much bigger, stronger and armed with a broom, the others would intervene if I somehow got the better of him. And if a fight resulted in some major injury the police might want to know what had prompted the altercation and that would carry risks for Ed. It was tempting just to walk away, go outside and cool off, but Ed had been kind and deserved better than that.

"If you really believe these things, say them in front of Mr Probett or my uncle. If you can't say them to their faces, why should anyone believe you?"

Nick looked daggers. "The Army'll soon take the wind out your sails, Big Ears. You're way overdue for a few lessons in respect and discipline. And if you haven't been poked up the bum already don't say I didn't warn you about the buggers."

The incident made me think about how society treated men who were homosexual. For some time, I had assumed that Ed and the men who called to see him were queer, which is the term I used then. As most of them had served during the war, I thought that they deserved to be left in peace so long as they did not disturb others. None of them had bothered me. Apart from Probett, all had tried to put me at ease. And it wasn't as if I had any religious objections to same sex partnerships.

Tolerance was as much as I could manage at that age. Acceptance of homosexuality took much unlearning of the negative messages that anyone of my generation had taken on board in great number. For example, at secondary school it was not enough to know that I was heterosexual; fear of name calling made me avoid what other boys might link to being gay. Perry was no different except that his fear of others assuming he was homosexual persisted. He also made use of society's intolerance of gay people in some of his malicious communications. Daya pointed out that he did not use racist or sexist language, but he did appeal to homophobia.

P I might have made the same progress towards acceptance of homosexuals as you if it weren't for the Owls. And it was easier for you being married. One of my fears was that some thugs thinking I was gay would lead them to attack me. Being beaten up would have been bad enough, but what if they had sexually assaulted me? Can you imagine how I dreaded further rape or another object being inserted in me? It doesn't matter how heterosexual a group of hate-filled men are, they might still force something into a victim as a punishment for being different.
N I hadn't considered the way your terrible experience left you more fearful in that way. Perhaps that's because I'm not sure that the Owls were homosexual.
P How could they not be?
N There's no question that they were sadistic. But were they like prisoners who use men for sex, but maintain heterosexual relationships the rest of the time?
P I don't know. Gatgash was isolated, but the NCOs got leave most months. Now you have me wondering if the Owls also preyed on women.

N I would be surprised the possibility of them assaulting women crossed anyone's mind back then. Things were much more cut and dried. If a man raped another, the rapist had to be a homosexual.

Chapter 20: Perry ~ Back Squadded

At the station nearest to Fort Gatgash, two-hundred motley youths in civilian clothes climbed into lorries. NCOs fired words like shotguns, spraying threats and sneers, but without swearing as there were women nearby waiting for a bus. I did not like their contempt yet still felt relief to be away from Mum's fussing and her outrage that I had passed my medical.

The Gatgash Fells appeared through the canvas flaps at the back of a lorry, glimpses of greenness that evoked memories of Raventulle. Yet even the lads from inner city slums must have understood that the upland soil lacked fertility. Trees became an oddity and then nothing living stood taller than a stunted wind-sculpted bush. Road signs with words like *Barugh*, *Cleugh*, *Lonnen* and *Upgang* suggested the local language was not English. Climbing another few hundred feet brought a chilling mist that soon turned into drizzle. The raw coldness and landscape merging into cloud added to the sense of being in a forlorn wilderness. Remoteness would make us prisoners regardless of any other security measures at the fort.

Our driver's speed on the dips and twists made no allowances for passengers on wooden seats encumbered by luggage. It was safer to brace with arms on the metal frame that held the olive canvas keeping the rain at bay, and press feet against the floor ready for the next lurch. By the time we arrived many were sore and some nauseous. A sergeant noticed my wobbly descent from the lorry and launched the first salvo of the personalised abuse.

"Gawd all fucking mighty! It's bad enough they send us tiddlers, but now we've got a cunt who can hardly stand. What's your name, midget?"

I gathered myself as best I could. "Gray, sir. Perry Gray."

"Are you the fucking queen, Gray?"

"No, sir"

"Then you fucking can't make me a fucking officer, can you?"

I didn't know what to say. The sergeant walked to me and oozed bad breath as he bent to shout into my ear.

"If I ask you a fucking question, I expect a fucking answer."

"Yes, sir."

"Don't fucking call me sir, you pathetic excuse for a man. I wasn't born with a silver fucking spoon in my mouth. I worked for my rank. These three stripes mean I'm a sergeant. Got that, short-arse!"

"Yes, Sergeant."

He was about to speak again when a lad threw up close to a lorry. The vomit flecking a tyre prompted a corporal to scream obscenities at the youth despite the rain that would soon wash it away. From the corporal's menaces, you might have thought the puke had hit his uniform rather than a wheel. While the other NCOs grinned at the lad reeling from the invective, I stepped away from the sergeant. A recruit whispered his sympathy at my bollocking and another glanced upwards to suggest the sergeant and corporal had been unreasonable. I thought, I'll cope here with a few mates.

After all the urgency to get out of the trucks and into ranks, the freezing rain soaked us while the NCOs in their ponchos took their time. The nearest buildings, which turned out to be typical, had something in common with the cottage before its refurbishment. Everything gleamed that could be cleaned, but you cannot make rotting wood or rusting window frames and corrugated sheets look good with either paint or elbow grease.

My optimism was as thin as a shadow before the end of the day. Some of the kit issued to us was more than used, it had been to war. Our parkas, among the more recent items as they had probably been made for Korea, carried the marks of being brushed and scraped to remove the mud, blood and grease of war. However, the decrepit and often ill-fitting clothing was the least of my concerns because the other occupants of hut D3 soon made it clear they had no time for me. Our squad consisted of fifteen teenagers and one twenty-one year old. Three factions, none of which included me, quickly emerged and gave each other names.

The Snots, two former grammar school students and a university graduate, admitted to hopes of getting commissions. This attracted abuse not only from other conscripts but also later gave NCOs an outlet for their loathing of officers.

The Delinquents were seven lads who boasted about shoplifting and other offending. Halton trumped Warren's boast of being fined by announcing he had been in a borstal. That first night, four of this group said that they had never before been in a bed without sharing it and two admitted that their army pyjamas were the first they had worn. I kept quiet about always having had a room of my own at home and owning sets of pyjamas for winter and summer.

Five men required to repeat their six weeks basic induction became known as the *Rejects*, which was hardly fair. Two had been hospitalised following injuries during training and one of this pair had a medical chit to say he was excused boots because of an inflamed Achilles tendon. The other three had failed their training. Yet in the days that followed they demonstrated competence in every skill and task asked of us. NCOs had back squadded them, made them repeat basic training, as punishment. One of the three had sworn at a corporal who had ignored protests that standing still with sodden and numb feet on icy ground risked frostbite. Another had argued with a sergeant about whether the mug deliberately smashed during an inspection, which the private had to replace from his meagre pay, was dirty. And the third had been overheard reciting a bawdy limerick in a mock-Scouse accent about a man called Divis. The Sergeant Major was a Liverpudlian with the same surname.

Although little social difference existed between the Rejects and the Delinquents, military tradition insisted nothing should be done or shared that makes a greenhorn's life easier. The old hands quickly bonded and resented the mouthiness of the Delinquents, especially the jibes about failing basic training. Rejects and Delinquents united to mock the Snots for their ambition, while the aspiring officers detested the unruly Delinquents and showed no sympathy for those having to repeat their six weeks. Only the threat of Halton and his cronies ruling the roost made occasional uneasy allies of the two smaller groups.

  The Snots never saw me as officer-grade material, the Delinquents rejected anyone who did not brag about crimes, and to the Rejects I was despicable simply for not joining the Army six weeks earlier. In a better-run camp, a good NCO would have seen how fractured we were and how isolated I was and done something to develop camaraderie. But the point of Gatgash's basic training, at least then, was to knock the spit out of individuals so that they accepted any order or abuse without dissent. And not only did our squad lack a single good NCO but also Knattmaw was our sergeant.

  He seemed to blot out what little daylight existed from the first time he stood just inside the door of Hut D3. He was tall, broad shouldered and without an ounce of fat. The blue-eyed face might have appeared handsome to a girl with a penchant for men who sneer. Before he spoke, his age – he was young for a sergeant – stirred hope that he would be fair as well as firm. The Rejects stood at attention by their beds at the far end; the rest followed their lead. Knattmaw abraded us with his Birmingham vowels, alternating between loud and deafening as he strode backwards and forwards while we all shivered despite wearing mothball-scented long johns and cold weather vests under our woollen khaki sandpaper suits.

  "I'm new to this camp, but not new to SKIVERS AND BACK-SLIDERS. The Sergeant Major asked for a volunteer to sort out THREE PEOPLE IN PARTICULAR and make sure they don't CONTAMINATE the rest of the squad. Believe me, you lot will have twice as much of my attention as my other three platoons. Now, when so many sergeants' hands went up, why choose me to look after the awkward squad? It's because I see it as a personal failure when one of my men fails to learn and has to repeat basic training. AND I DON'T TOLERATE SLACKERS! And guess what? The Sergeant Major handpicked my corporals BECAUSE THEY SHARE MY HATRED OF TOSSPOTS!"

Knattmaw stared one at a time at the five who had led us to stand before moving back to the door and taking in the rest of us.

"Now you're all slime, but if the new slime has any sense they'll make certain the old slime does not BRING DOWN A TON OF BRICKS ON ALL YOUR PRICKS. Already, you may be aware that you have the worst accommodation. You have the back squadders to thank for that. BUT THAT IS JUST THE BEGINNING of your troubles if you let the shirkers drag down your standards the way they FUCKED UP THEIR FORMER SQUADS. And I don't like cunts who get injured during training unless it's me doing the injury. Who was in the hospital?"

He glared at the two Rejects who had taken a step forward. I already knew anything that resembled an independent thought would invite a tirade, so kept quiet about how unreasonable it was to blame trainees for accidental injuries.

The sergeant introduced Lance-Corporal Redfarn. "He's like me, keen to have a go at sorting you lot out."

Redfarn, a chubby man of about thirty, puffed out his chest. His ample jowls were darkened by black stubble. We learned that his facial hair grew apace because each morning he arrived with a jaw scraped pink that turned black during the afternoon. We saw more than enough of him in the days that followed, but other NCOs replaced him for activities that involved the squad in sustained exertion and he was strangely absent in the evening, his role being replaced by one or both of the Owls. He showed no deference to the corporals at handovers and they treated him as an equal despite his single stripe. Trainees speculated about how Redfarn got away with this, what he did in the evenings and how he wangled exemptions from more onerous duties. Was he somebody's pet? Did he buy favours or obtain them through blackmail? However, we welcomed the daytime swaps because the bites of a dog are preferable to those of a bear like Redfarn and, apart from the Owls, none of the replacement NCOs were so unpleasant.

By the time the occupants of D3 were shivering under their bedclothes on their first night, there was no mistaking the rough ride ahead. Halton teased the Rejects about how Knattmaw would sort them out; we all expected the three who had crossed NCOs would take the brunt of the abuse. But that was before I understood how the hatred and irrationality of our overseers was boundless, or the way group punishments for individual failures, or alleged failures, were just as much standard issue as our dark blue berets.

NCOs encouraged platoons to punish individuals, especially those held up as the cause of a group punishment. And while this happened to most trainees, it was more common in Knattmaw's four platoons. On day three, Redfarn inspected us before breakfast and growled that my bed was not made up to standard.

"Permission to speak, Corporal." He nodded as if amused by the request. "Please, Corporal, which part of the bed needs redoing?"

He tipped over the bed and all the kit arranged on it, ordered the others to do the same to their own beds and said he would be back in forty minutes to re-inspect.

At the open door he turned and said, "If I was one of you, I would want to teach someone a lesson for creating all this mess on the floor."

The lads came and punched me one after another on the arm. Most vented their frustration with force. After that, such assaults became common and my arms permanently bruised. Some of the lads hardly needed the NCOs to hint that comeuppance was due. And while the form of punishment was never specified, the NCOs knew that the Delinquents were vicious and needed clear boundaries rather than incitement to violence.

As the pressure on the squad mounted in the second week, the spontaneous assaults began to happen more frequently. In addition, the members of the Delinquents and Rejects who found themselves at the bottom of their cliques' pecking orders began to bait me with names that alluded to my height. All too often, others then joined in. It was as if the one thing that could unite the three factions and dissipate the simmering tensions between them was to have someone to scapegoat, ridicule and harass. No aspect of my performance as a trainee, other behaviour or anatomy was exempt.

The standard day was long enough, but no other squad came close to ours in terms of re-inspections, extra drills, running, jankers and mind-numbing tasks such as scrubbing a latrine floor with toothbrushes. The first week left me so tired that confusion set in. NCOs responded to the errors that followed as wilful failings; outpourings of vile abuse and physically demanding punishments added to my exhaustion, clumsiness and ability to learn simple tasks. Knattmaw especially lashed out at me with his hands, baton or boots.

Assaults never took place if an officer was nearby, which led me to think about making a complaint. But it would have been my word against the sergeant as none of the privates would have admitted to witnessing anything. And whether my complaint succeeded or not, every NCO at Gatgash – and, for all I knew, wherever I ended up for the rest of my time in the Army – would delight in beasting a private who dared to complain about a superior.

The coldness of D3 aggravated the tiredness of its occupants yet we never lit the stove because Redfarn had said, "The supply of coal is erratic. Besides, it's hardly worth bothering when you think of all the extra cleaning you will have to do because of the smoke and dust. Of course, the choice is yours. Just don't expect any lowering of standards during inspections."

After Knattmaw found fault with the layout of my webbing in the third week and penalised the squad, the others made me set out my kit on my bed and spend nights for a week on the freezing floor. No one else who triggered collective punishment slept on the floor for more than one night at a time because others in their subgroup would not allow it. Sheer exhaustion meant that the cold boards did not keep me awake for long, but I woke with yet more aching and stiffness; it was as if I could only accumulate unease.

The ex-servicemen at Global Typewriters had warned that Gray would invite the nickname *Dolly* and Redfarn used it as soon as he knew my surname. The Reject with a penchant for limericks came up with the following.

There was young wanker called Dolly
Who stroked his dick with an ice lolly
When it began to feel numb
He shoved the ice up his bum
And farted a volley of hail by golly.

Halton and others chanted this over several days. Soon most of the new intake had heard it and many faces I could not put a name to called me Dolly. But at least Dolly without the limerick was not personal abuse like Pygmy and the other names that referred to my height. And while the lads sometimes said Dolly with a smirk, no one really thought that I was queer.

Almost everyone in the hut had a nickname, most assigned before the end of the first week. Some were predictable, such as Don Warren being called *Bunny*. Bernie Halton, the daddy of the Delinquents, became known as *Dodger* due to boasting about his family avoiding rent payments and other debts on a Leeds housing estate he claimed was known to locals as Dodge City.

Bunny came from Sheffield and a similar background to Dodger. They certainly shared the same level of viciousness. It was Bunny who, while we were polishing brass and boots, came up with a new nickname at the end of our third week, perhaps because I did not respond enough to the limerick and Dolly. He explained to the squad that I should be *Duckling*, because I was even shorter than the comedian Charlie Drake.

Dodger responded, "Peregrine Duckling doesn't sound right. Too many fucking feathers. Best make it Fuckling."

At first, when a private used it, I tried not to answer to Fuckling, but I gave in after NCOs started to use this name.

As well as the Rejects and me, Knattmaw had it in for Dodger who smiled too often at the wrong time and had made the mistake of being cheeky in the second week after Bunny had asked Redfarn what the sergeant had done to get his stripes so young.

"He was in the right place at the right time and did the right thing. He was the only private who didn't mutiny."

"What do you mean?" asked Dodger.

"When the men in his unit complained about getting ready for Suez and got all bolshie, he didn't and got promoted for it."

"You mean he was a scab?" Dodger made it sound more like a fact than a question.

Redfarn screwed up his eyes and yelled abuse. Although Knattmaw never mentioned the incident, it was obvious that he resented the slur from the way he picked on Dodger after that.

With my background, I should have found it easy to strip and reassemble weapons. I mastered my rifle and the Sten gun, but by the time we trained on Brens in week six, my brain was too scrambled and being paired with Dodger only made things worse.

After Knattmaw's curses and a kick to my thigh had not worked to improve my time, he said, "I'm giving you one last cunting chance. If you fuck this up again, you'll be back squadded."

It was five days from the end of basic training and I was desperate to leave for Aldershot where I would be a clerk. The idea of another six weeks of hell made me tremble. With so much to lose, I fumbled again and again until Knattmaw kicked my shoulder so hard the Bren gun rolled over.

"You useless little fucker. Have it your way then!"

He was not just angry with me. His threat had not worked and he would lose face. Either he would have to admit that he had failed to train me adequately in a weapon or others would see him as making an idle threat about back squadding. He called Redfarn over and spoke to him too softly for others to hear. The corporal ordered everyone except Dodger and me to jog to the armoury and back and strolled after the running pack.

"Halton, what do you think of Fuckling's efforts and what he has done to the reputation of the squad."

"He's a disgrace, Sergeant."

"Come with me."

He led us to where a building meant no one could see us.

"Why don't you have a word with Fuckling to sort him out?" He had put an odd stress on *sort him out*.

Halton grinned at the novelty of a polite request and the chance to win favour by beating me up. "My pleasure, Sergeant."

"Good. Set him straight."

Knattmaw strode round the corner. Halton started punching as I cowered with hands over my face. But less than twenty seconds after Knattmaw had disappeared, he came around the corner with Redfarn.

"Corp', put these men on charges for fighting."

"But Sergeant," whined Dodger, "You said…"

Redfarn was waiting for this. "Who gave you permission to speak. Don't be so stupid as to try and suggest you were ordered. That would only make things worse you stupid cunt."

Dodger had only one card left to play. "Ask Fuckling, then."

Knattmaw and Redfarn stared at me. I shrugged my shoulders because I had no energy and least of all for futile protest. The only comfort came from the gutted look on Dodger's face.

Knattmaw saw to it that our punishment for fighting was another six weeks of basic training. That way he got his own back on Hatton for being cheeky and did not lose face for having one of his trainees back squadded because he had failed with a Bren gun. The new squad, again in D3, was much the same in terms of background as the previous occupants. I got an easier ride at first because, unlike Dodger, I helped the new recruits learn the ropes. Gradually though, he established himself as the daddy of the less reputable half of the squad and from the end of the first week directed their hatred and violence towards me until everyone called me Fuckling.

In the second week as the new platoon was cleaning the hut, Dodger looked at me and said, "How's it going, Tad?"

His snigger meant it was better not to ask why he suddenly called me this name with enough volume and tone to make sure the rest of the hut looked up from their bull. After he grew frustrated with my lack of response, he explained anyway.

"So little Taddy, do you know why you deserve the name Tad. Suit yourself, but the other lads want to know, don't you? Do you know what a tadger is, Tad? Well, I've seen yours and it's tiny. Just the *Tad* and no *ger*. I can't work out if it's so small because you've never pulled it or you tugged it so much it's worn away."

Raucous laughter followed and Dodger imitated a squatting chimpanzee masturbating. All I could do was continue to polish the futile stove, but pretending to be indifferent was not helped by my blushing. Others at the Fort began to call me Tad and many made jokes as if it was surprising or relevant that the shortest recruit also was short between his legs.

NCOs picked up the name and what it referred to and during one square bashing, when I turned the wrong way, Knattmaw said, "It seems your brain is as about as miniscule as your prick, Private Tad."

Much of my recollection of Gatgash seems like a foggy ocean of misery and exhaustion in which only the episodes of greatest pain, the most intense cold or the worst of the humiliation stand out like island peaks visible above the sea mist. One of the memorable moments concerns the firing range, where I wished for a pistol rather than a rifle too long to turn on myself.

Someone would have spotted me taking off a boot to use my toe on the trigger and there was nothing else to hand that would have fired the gun with the muzzle against me. Other means of suicide came to me as I lay in bed, but overtiredness soon brought sleep that, despite its depth, never lasted long enough to refresh body or restore spirits. I was in a parlous state long before the outrage committed by the Owls.

In the boiler-house, a lance-corporal, corporal and then the Corporal of the Guard ordered me without success to stop crying.

Knattmaw arrived and after his yelling at me made no difference, said, "Fucking hell. I don't need this. Why couldn't you keep your legs closed, you useless cunt? Open the fucking furnace."

Fearing that he was about to hurt me, I turned my head. The lance-corporal covered his right hand with his parka sleeve to lift a brass handle and pulled back the door to reveal a bed of glowing coals. Knattmaw threw the larger part of the broken broom inside; sparks from the bristles danced before bursting into flame. He disappeared from view and then reappeared with the cudgel, which he carried to the flames at arm's length using a sack to hold onto the less stained end. The jute caught alight as soon as it entered the furnace and for a moment the room was well lit. Then after a clang the gloom returned and seemed more profound. Even the polished brass handle looked dismal.

Knattmaw got the men to put on my long johns and sit me up. Being moved added to my pain and I cried all the louder. The sergeant slapped my face hard on both sides and looked exasperated when his blows had no effect on the wailing. The stinging cheeks and ears were nothing compared to the agony radiating from the centre of my body. As soon as hands let me go, I collapsed onto my side and passed out from the pain of the jolt.

The next I knew, Sergeant Major Divis had arrived and I cried as soon as I saw him. Not even his Scouse bark – something along the lines of *Be a man and pull yourself together* – could silence me. He took Knattmaw to a corner where they conferred before sending two men away.

The Corporal of the Guard returned to report only one empty bed in my hut and that a private had seen Stace and Payner getting me up.

"I'll settle their hash," said the Sergeant Major. "Take two buckets of cold water to their quarters and wait outside with them till I get there. Then you're going to run them fucking queers ragged with forty pound packs until the Sergeant relieves you."

The lance-corporal returned with a stretcher. Four sets of hands lifted me. It felt like horses were dragging me apart until I again passed out. When I came round, there was much painful jerking and the blanket that covered me from head to toe did little to keep out the bitter damp wind.

Light penetrating the blanket and a change in temperature meant that we were in another building. A Geordie accent told the bearers where to place the stretcher. Hands rolled me onto my front and the pain made me start crying again. More lights were turned on.

"You can go," said the Geordie voice, and boots tramped away. "Because movement is painful for you, I'm going to use scissors to remove your long johns. I need to see what it looks like."

The examination and swabbing were agony. At last, he pulled the blanket back over my body.

He went outside and said softly, "There might be an internal injury. I'll have to wake the MO."

Oaths followed; one set distinctly Brummie and the other Scouse.

I felt relief that a doctor was coming. My crying became softer, more like whimpering. I was alone for some time before footsteps came into the room.

A brisk Scottish voice, face unseen, said. "I'm going to examine you. It will hurt, but I have to find out what it's like in there."

Two pairs of hands were involved. The Geordie spoke and the other addressed him as Corporal. Then the pain became so great that I stopped breathing and grew faint before passing out. When I came round, the Scot, whom I later knew as Captain Maddan, was talking with someone he addressed as Major. They stopped their discussion as soon as they realised I had stirred and went into the corridor. Then their voices came from an adjoining room. The major was asking for something, which puzzled me when the Scot had sounded deferential. Why did the major not just pull rank and say it's an order?

Maddan returned and placed a chair so that his eyes were no more than twenty-inches from mine as I lay on my front with head turned. He showed no signs of tiredness and was clean-shaven, despite it being early morning. The face was stern and nor did his voice convey the least trace of sympathy.

"You were lucky you used Vaseline. Without it the damage might have been far worse."

I stopped breathing for some seconds before saying, "But I didn't do it."

He did not blink before responding. "Think very carefully, Private Gray. You have no witnesses. If you accuse others, whatever you allege would feed the rumour mills at the Fort and further afield. You must know by now that the Army for all its rules and regulations has never succeeded in stopping tittle-tattle. Do you want people to think that you're homosexual?

"There are other ways of punishing people. Stace and Payner are now privates. The Sergeant Major inspected their rooms and found them in possession of unauthorised supplies. They are out in the cold carrying packs around the perimeter of the camp and their punishments will continue until they depart for separate unpleasant overseas postings.

"You, on the other hand, could be diagnosed as suffering from exhaustion and stay in the warm here for a couple of weeks. If you're a co-operative patient, you will be signed off as having completed basic training, have some home leave and get a congenial onward posting. Have a think about it for a few minutes."

He left the room. His icy tone had made clear that retaliation would follow if I complained about the outrage. I was gutted and furious with the ploy that I was somehow responsible for my injuries, but it was hard to resist the prospect of being able to avoid my tormentors, stay warm and rest for several days.

Whatever I did the story would be all over the Fort anyway. Maddan was right about rumour, but disingenuous to suggest that the absence of a complaint would prevent soldiers gossiping. Keeping the story from my parents, the last people I wanted to know the truth, was the clincher. In any case, even before the boiler house I had lacked the energy for fighting a conspiracy, let alone one that involved a major.

Maddan rewarded my compliance. "I'll give you a knock-out injection that will get you through the worst of the pain." As he swabbed me for the needle, he said, "I'm so glad you're being sensible about this."

When I woke after midday, more than anything there was a general numbness that I assumed was the tail end of the medication. I later ascribed my blunted emotions to the pills the orderlies doled out, but the sense being divorced from my feelings continued long after the medication and some of the numbing fog never lifted. After waking from the injection, I seldom cried again in front of another person; tears only followed nightmares or the re-experiencing invoked by splinters in my hand, sacks spread on floors or coke dust. As far as possible when overcome by the reliving and panic, I sought to be alone, if only in a toilet cubicle.

While recuperating I was the only occupant of an eight-bed ward, as if infectious. The orderlies, who mostly said little more than was necessary for basic care, were wary more than hostile. I suspected they were under orders not to discuss what had brought me to the hospital. They insisted on keeping drawn the window curtains on the side facing the more public areas of the Fort and allowed me to go no further than the bathroom. After I did not eat two meals, they brought better quality food. I still ignored it. Just drinking required an act of will. After a painful motion on the third day, they brought soup and threatened to force feed me if I did not finish the bowl. I had little appetite, a state of affairs that persisted over several years, during which one modest meal a day sufficed. And for some months after the incident, I suffered from intermittent constipation, a new complaint.

I had a bath three times a day during the first four days. Hot water eased the pain and suds countered the sense of contamination. While the physical pain became more bearable, the sense grew that no amount of soaking or soap could erase the stain left by the Owls. My kit, minus my razor, arrived in perfect order; someone had taken pains to ensure the clothes were clean, pressed and packed with care. When I realised being presentable entitled me to walk no further, I stayed in pyjamas and hospital dressing gown all day and ignored the electric shaver provided. Twelve days after the assault, an orderly gave me my razor and told me to be ready for a visit.

Two officers came to the ward. I stood to attention and saluted the CO and Lieutenant Rogers, who had briefly appeared on my second day to welcome his platoons to what he had called "Gatgash Holiday Camp" and had rarely been seen since.

Colonel Montana asked, "How are you, Gray?"

"Very well, sir." I was too frightened to say anything else.

"I understand the Army did not make enough allowances for your physique and you needed bed rest."

"Yes, sir."

"Apart from that, have you any complaints about your time here?" His voice had acquired an edge.

"No complaints, sir."

"Make a note, Lieutenant. Private Gray has no complaints about his time at Fort Gatgash. Now, having reviewed your record, you are designated as having satisfactorily completed basic training. The charge of fighting is dismissed following Private Halton's admission that you offered no resistance after he had assaulted you. The reason now given for repeating the course is to build up your physical fitness."

"Thank you, sir."

His tone had indicated that he was generous, yet I felt relief rather than gratitude.

"I understand that you serviced typewriters."

"Yes, sir."

"After home leave, you'll join the Royal Army Pay Corps at Hounslow Barracks, which I understand is not far from your home, and continue there with your former occupation. I trust that being stationed in Middlesex and resuming your former work is satisfactory."

"Yes, sir."

I answered mechanically and from fear but, on reflection, being allowed to do what I knew best and avoiding further training with the licence it gave to bullies was as much as I could hope for during the rest of my National Service. Besides, the amended record and the onward posting were as close as the Army would get to an apology.

That evening, Douthwaite, the Geordie corporal who had first examined me was less taciturn than usual. "Who says there's no justice. I just heard that two very tired former corporals are on their way overseas. One's going to Aden and the other to Malaya. They won't like it, but they'll be glad to see the back of Gatgash after all the miles in the snow they've done at the double in the last fortnight."

I must have looked unappreciative because he added, "They're punishment postings. I know what I'm talking about 'cos I've been to those countries. Stace is going upcountry in Aden where he'll have sand in every orifice and tribesmen who use Tommies for target practice. And Payner is going to Kroh on the Thai border, which is more dangerous if anything. And they'll never get another promotion. One of the clerks told me what's in their records."

I did not ask for more information because, whatever the files of the Owls said, they would not list their crimes against me. Instead I asked for the name of the major who had spoken with Maddan not long after my admission. Douthwaite hesitated before saying it was Major Peebes.

Douthwaite woke me at three the next morning. Heavy snow was falling until just before I left the hospital for the station in the back of a Landrover with shovels, blankets and emergency supplies in case we got stranded. We followed an Army snow-plough until we reached a road already cleared. A corporal drove the Landrover and a lance-corporal sat next to him. The pair had different shoulder flashes and hard faces. They offered no greeting, avoided looking at me and only spoke to each other as needed. I suspected that an officer had ordered them not to communicate with their passenger and had sent men from different units to reduce the chances of this happening.

The headlamps picked out sheep with just their black faces clear of drifts piled up by dry stone walls. We were making good time, but there was no point suggesting we dig them out. Apart from any ban on talking, I reckoned the NCOs were not only indifferent to the plight of the sheep but also they would be chary of a man expressing compassion for farm animals. And the last thing I wanted was to add to any suspicions that the Owls had targeted me because I was queer.

Chapter 21: Norman ~ Helgrund Foss

If nicknames are common enough in civilian life, they are rife in the forces. Some do not particularly lend themselves to abuse, such as Smiler, Lofty and Geordie, although a lot depends on how they are said. One recruit who reeked of Bay Rum in the lorry on the way to Gatgash was christened Stinker and another with hay fever was called Sniffy. Both happily answered to these names when said in a friendly way. I became *Meddle* during basic training, derived from mispronouncing Midlin as *meddling*. The name was also a reference to a putdown – "What do you want, a medal or a chest to pin it on?"

I much preferred Meddle to names such as *Shorty* and *Dumbo* that drew attention to my features and hurt, especially when said with animosity over and over again by the Gatgash NCOs and some of the privates. While school and Probett's Print had made me used to mockery, during basic training, you were likely to hear insults for as long as you remained awake. And not only was there no respite other than sleep, but also verbal bullying might escalate to include assault. It still rankles to think about what people called me then and the blind hatred behind their lashing out.

Perry recorded abusive names that others called him at Gatgash, which were no less hurtful for him. Yet words like *rape* or *buggered* do not appear in his account. Of all that I decoded, the boiler-house incident appears the most factual. Not because I heard of anything similar during my National Service, but because the language Perry used was different from the rest of his writing. However, I cannot discount the possibility that Perry made up or distorted the attack by the Owls to blacken the names of Knattmaw and others. And he might have checked to ensure that all the people he named at Gatgash were dead and therefore unable to contradict him.

Perhaps he had good reason to hate the sergeant, but there was also Gladys Knattmaw's accusation that Mr Vitriol contributed to the death of her husband. What if Perry invented the sergeant's reaction to the rape and disposal of evidence in an attempt to justify his allegedly fatal letter to Knattmaw?

Perry protests angrily now, but he can communicate later.

If the rape did take place, the way officers and NCOs are reported to have conspired to deal with it does not surprise me. The Army makes much of honour which, like patriotism, can also provide a refuge for scoundrels. When soldiers and officers fear censure for what happened on their watch, cover-ups to protect the honour of a unit often coincides with self-interest. The Fort's commandant and others under him would have feared for their next promotion had news emerged of two NCOs at the Fort carrying out a brutal rape on a conscript. Tabloids would have played such a story for all it was worth and there had been questions in the House of Commons throughout the 1950s about the mistreatment of recruits.

I started at Fort Gatgash in late May, four months before Perry. On the trip from the station, lambs gambolling in the sunshine cheered me for a time. Then civilisation ended other than the road. The unkempt moorland appeared alien after the chocolate-boxy countryside of the Home Counties and each winding mile further unpicked boyish notions of occasionally slipping out of barracks for a drink at the local.

Vicious shouting and swearing began as soon as the trucks stopped in the middle of the Fort. Even though the lads expected tough discipline, we were shocked to find that stripes entitled a fellow human being to cast vile aspersions on our parents and inflict physical pain. We were lined up and told not to talk. Sniffy, who was only a few inches taller than me and in the front rank, muttered an oath after a sixpence dropped as he pulled a handkerchief from his pocket. A very tall and burly sergeant came close and ordered him to pick it up. The giant of a man turned around as if something in the distance had caught his attention and pretended to be unaware of Sniffy's fingers trapped between boot and ground. Had the sergeant not been aware he could easily have broken a finger. And instead of an apology, there was a knowing sneer.

While my squad was as mixed socially as Perry's, we were never as riven as he described, not that I think his account of the relationships in D3 is far-fetched. Some lads were always friendly to me. Stinker, Mike Lapgood, often intervened to stop other privates bullying. His father was a Durham miner and as soon as he knew that Dad had died underground, Stinker was my mate.

Our squad occupied one of the newer accommodation blocks, which made cleaning rooms easier. We would have had central heating, except that it was turned off between March and October. Much time and elbow grease were still needed to ensure everything passed inspection. Perfect or not, the mood of an NCO determined whether he found fault, the scale of his reaction and whether punishment was individual or group.

Perry's tiredness is understandable. Lads who arrived at the Fort fit from training for sports were exhausted and sometimes ravenously hungry because the food served often turned the stomach. Summer sun sweated us to the point of fainting, yet idiots forbade us to drink for hours as a punishment, not to teach us anything about the importance of conserving what might be a scarce resource on a battlefield. One lad had convulsions following avoidable heat exhaustion and dehydration. The marching, hiking and running stretched the likes of me even more. We carried the same loads as the others, but short legs worked harder to cover the distances, especially over rough ground. Perry not only had this to cope with, he also faced bitter cold without any fat to insulate him.

The two NCOs who most often hounded me in my basic training were both below average height. I was the one person in my squad for them to look down on. Unlike most of the other name callers, this pair did not refer to my size. Rather, they drew attention to my ears and lack of stamina. And every mistake I made they cited as proof of stupidity.

"Are you sure you went to grammar school? If you ask me, your Mum was fucked by the village idiot. Does your local half-wit look like Big Ears?"

Taking the hint from NCOs, our squad responded to a careless failure during kit inspection that led to collective punishment. After that, we required an offender to sleep one night on the floor. I slept by my bed on two occasions, but only when I had been careless with my kit and not when it was freezing. Most of our time was spent square bashing and cleaning. The prospect of learning other military skills for a few hours a week was something we all looked forward to until the sergeant who had stood on Sniffy's fingers took our squad for fieldcraft.

If Sergeant Roibeard knew about camouflage, the first topic he lectured us on, his expertise was well hidden. No matter how we paid attention, his brief and often poorly linked sentences short-changed us. Why couldn't he just show us a *ghillie suit* or even a picture of one rather than trying to describe it? Except when bawling someone out, his tone was flat. Roibeard's abuse stood out simply because he was the only NCO heard at Gatgash with an Irish accent. No one would have suspected him of having kissed the Blarney Stone; every expletive and expression that came from his lips during a dressing down was army standard issue - such as *Have you got shit for brains?* and *You 'orrible little man*. In the latter he dropped the h yet was never heard to drop it with other words. His language was so timeworn we called him *Cliché*.

One day my squad stood outside while Roibeard explained that the Army only recognised three types of trees when identifying a target. As there were no trees for miles, he had drawn crude outlines on a blackboard of bushy, fir and poplar. Yet still he felt the need to use mangled words to explain the differences. Lapgood heard a commotion in the distance and momentarily turned his head. The sergeant ordered him to stand and face the distracting squad who were yelling as they bayoneted dangling sacks of straw. While Stinker enjoyed a better view of the distraction, our instructor walked quietly over the turf, viciously clapped hands over Lapgood's ears and kicked his right heel enough to make my friend's boot slide forward several inches.

Roibeard smirked. "Thems that don't pay attention don't see what's coming."

Others laughed. The sergeant noticed my scowl and came at me with blazing eyes.

"What's your problem?"

I stood at attention to convey deference. My brain desperately sought a way of placating the anger coming towards me without condoning the violence. Given a few more seconds, I would have said, "No problem, sergeant."

Before I settled for pure appeasement, his fist took my chin by surprise. It may be that I avoided a broken jaw because, with feet planted together, my body readily toppled backwards onto the ground. I landed with splayed legs and saw his right boot swinging towards me. The lads around me had instinctively grabbed my arms as I fell and I was unable to break free of their hold in time to protect my crown jewels. The agony was eye-watering.

As I writhed, the sergeant yelled, "I was warned this was a bolshie squad. Well. I won't have it. You hear me, I won't have it."

He marched with swinging arms back to his blackboard, which must have helped to calm him down because he resumed his dreary teaching voice while I was still gasping from the pain in my scrotum. I have no way of telling if he derived sexual pleasure from either inflicting hurt or connecting with my groin area. What I do know is that other NCOs made jokes of this cruelty, which suggests that Roibeard had boasted about it.

The next morning, a corporal encouraged my third attempt to strip and reassemble a Sten gun at speed by saying, "Get it wrong this time and I'll give you two black eyes to go with your two black bollocks."

Darker forces drove the less competent NCOs. It is likely that many came from disturbed families, some were mentally battle-scarred and others brutalised simply by years in the Army. The officers might have limited the effects of these things but, of course, rank does not preclude them having had the same experiences. In any case, our lieutenant, like Perry's, had little input. I only saw him for more than a few minutes at a time during Sunday Service.

After inspection on the first Sunday morning, a Staff Sergeant yelled, "Jews, Hindus and left-footers, fall out."

Going to church was optional in theory. A few men in other platoons did fall out, but not from mine and the parade ground was the last place I wanted to be conspicuous. Several Catholics and three Jews – no one was of obvious Indian descent – attended the Anglican service rather than risk annoying an NCO. The hymn singing was execrable, a combination of massed, untrained and embarrassed voices along with men who expressed their displeasure at being corralled in a church by exaggerating disharmony and, judging by the sniggering that broke out at intervals, substituting bawdy words.

Based on my experience of Gatgash, Perry's claim that he was afraid to pursue a complaint about the everyday mistreatment makes perfect sense. The Fort's culture tolerated and even celebrated abuse. None of the NCOs would have shopped one of their own for striking an inductee and nothing suggested the officers or Sergeant Major were unhappy with the state of affairs. Recruits believed that reporting an assault, like anything else construed as not respecting those giving orders, would invite gross retaliation from every other person left in charge of the complainant.

Let us assume for the time being that the corporals did rape Perry. As NCO cruelty at Gatgash was widespread and unchallenged, the first mark the Owls overstepped was engaging in gay sex. Had it been a woman, they may well have claimed that she was willing and others could have believed them at least as far as the use of their penises were concerned. It is also possible that the Owls would have got away with gross torture of Perry provided there was no suggestion of sexual gratification, no need for the MO to get involved, and no obvious marks. Indeed, if Perry's account is true, his treatment over several weeks amounted to torture.

Once the Sergeant Major linked the corporals' assault of Perry with them being queer, the Owls' cards were marked. Divis may well have dealt with them differently had officers not got involved. My guess is he would have preferred to keep the secret limited to a few NCOs and hounded Stace and Payner as privates until they cracked or provided other reasons for dishonourable discharges. It would have looked better for Divis, and Knattmaw for that matter, to prevent officers knowing about the rape.

Once the doctor was involved, the cat was out the bag and the best the Sergeant Major could hope for was nothing going further than Fort Gatgash. Perhaps the officers becoming aware of the outrage committed by the Owls had one advantage for Divis; making onward postings easier. *Out of sight, out of mind* might have applied. By scattering the rapists and Perry, there was less chance of anyone else gathering the testimonies. I wouldn't be surprised if some of the others who saw Perry in the boiler house were also transferred away from Gatgash in the following months to reduce the chances of an outsider unearthing what had happened. The incident by itself was bad enough, but the CO and other officers also would have feared an exposure of their cover-up and outsiders learning the extent to which the Fort's NCOs were involved in assaults on recruits and inciting violence among them.

Many British men still respond with revulsion to the idea of any sexual contact between males. Back then, homophobia was far more rampant and the few voices speaking up for tolerance reached small audiences. Those conspiring to hide the fact that a particularly vicious male rape had occurred might in part have been motivated by a deep sense of unease. Most soldiers and officers would have felt at a loss after stumbling upon someone like Perry in the boiler-house. I met many in during my National Service, some of them decent enough in most ways, who would have had no idea how to deal with a sobbing male rape victim. Holding his hand or hugging him to offer support would have been a step too far and even words of comfort might have aroused the same fears that Perry experienced in the Landrover when he wanted to help the snow-bound sheep.

One last thought on this matter; did the broom handle save Perry's life? Without this final act of savagery, he might have left the boiler-house on his feet. Long before this attack, bullying and over-exertion had depleted his spirits and energy. Being so drained, ashamed, shocked, confused and lacking a single friend to turn to he might have sought to take his own life or simply wandered in the dark until he succumbed to hypothermia.

Sergeant Major Divis was at Gatgash while I was there. He wore a cap with a drop-down visor, which should have blocked half of his vision, yet he missed very little. His iron-grey moustache, though small enough to fit under a gas mask, had a life of its own when he quivered with indignation. Our corporal came to the hut one night drunk and voluble and let slip that towards the end of the war Divis, then a young sergeant, had fired over the heads of his platoon in Italy when the soldiers protested against the Army using them to unload ships, while local labourers were desperate for work. The gun had come from the holster of a recently commissioned lieutenant who had lost his bottle after privates, battle-hardened by Monte Cassino and North Africa, had jeered him. The corporal speculated that Divis favoured harsh discipline more than most of his rank because of this experience of stemming a mutiny.

Perhaps this was the case, but plenty of younger men with stripes on their sleeves and who had never confronted stroppy veterans were also martinets, even when it was counterproductive and possibly dangerous. The worst I witnessed was in my third week at Gatgash in the underground rifle range, a dank concrete box that thrilled most recruits because none of us had fired a real gun before. Private Gerrison was one of few not happy to be there. He suffered from claustrophobia, a condition he had kept secret.

Corporal Dowglas stopped soon after beginning to instruct us on the procedure for shooting and walked up to Gerrison.

"When I'm fucking talking I want you watching with both eyes and listening with both ears, not grimacing and looking at the exit."

"Yes, Corporal." Gerrison sounded unwell.

The corporal continued as if he was trying to pad out his act. His instructions were lost in a welter of anecdotes, such as how the Boer War had taught the importance of the prone position for shooting, and witticisms punctuated with obscenities. Finally, the first eight collected their five rounds of .22 ammunition and prepared to shoot. I waited my turn animated by the echoing gunfire. Gerrison responded by placing his hands over his ears.

"Get those fucking hands off your sodding head. You've got to get used to the sound of gunfire, not avoid it. How are you going to shoot the cunts firing at you with your hands over your fucking ears?"

The white faced recruit gripped the sides of his trousers and gritted his teeth.

"What are yer? Some sort of nancy-boy who doesn't like loud noises?"

Gerrison being popular with the other privates did not stop most of them laughing at the abuse.

After the next group had collected their rounds, we lay on the floor to load. There was a kerfuffle after the corporal booted Gerrison's left ankle for having a toe cap on the ground rather than both feet splayed. The private groaned loudly; it had been a hefty kick. To hide his embarrassment at crying out he made himself busy with his rifle.

Then the Corporal shouted, "Who told you to remove the fucking safety?"

There was too much quiet and when I looked over my shoulder Gerrison had rolled onto his back and was waving the barrel of the rifle toward Dowglas and the lads behind him.

Lapgood was next to Gerrison. He kneeled and lifted the gun until it was pointing at the ceiling, reached over with his other hand and put the safety on."

He was just beginning to remove Gerrison's fingers from the gun when Dowglas lurched forward cursing. Gerrison snatched the gun away from Lapgood, thought better of it, dropped the weapon and raced outside.

"Christ. A fucking nutter. That's all I need," said Dowglas.

That was the way an MO saw it after Gerrison attempted to hang himself in the gymnasium a few minutes after leaving the rifle range. None of the privates from his squad saw him again. He was in the Fort's hospital for a time and word emerged from there that he had suffered a breakdown. Privates worked out that that he was claustrophobic from the way NCOs began asking if anyone had a fear of confined spaces before taking a group into the range for the first time. My squad concluded that Gerrison opted for suicide because he dreaded the prospect of spending time in a military prison.

Lapgood was never thanked for what he did by Dowglas. Instead, the corporal boasted about staring down an armed man until he threw down his gun and ran away, or so we heard from Redfarn while he was under the influence.

It was not unusual for NCOs to have boozy breath. Sometimes it made them more sociable or indiscreet, but more often than not they were nastier when tanked up. I discovered that the extent of NCOs with drinking problems also concerned Divis. At the time, five of us were on hands and knees cutting grass with nail scissors as a punishment for having taken off our blousons without permission while waiting outside a lecture theatre. The voices of two men came through the part-open window of a latrine.

The booming Scouse of the Sergeant Major was unmistakable. "There'll be two boffins on the tent trials and I don't want any fuck-ups like last time. Select NCOs who can get by for three days without a drink and check their kit before they leave to make sure they're dry."

He strode past a few minutes later accompanied by a Staff Sergeant. After our intake had paraded the next morning, the Staff Sergeant ordered all the privates who had ever slept in a tent to step forward. Well over half of the two hundred moved. The sergeant dismissed those who had stepped forward and ordered the rest of us to form three lines. Then he dismissed the front two rows and turned to Redfarn, who had been standing behind him.

"I'll leave it to you to whittle them down. Pay attention to the Lance-Corporal."

Redfarn asked, "Are you all absolutely sure that you have never slept in a tent?"

"No, Corporal."

"So none of you were in the Boy Scouts?"

"No, Corporal."

"Did you ever help to put up a tent or take one down?"

Three hands went up and he told these men to go. The rest of us waited while he noted names and squads, but he stopped after writing the twelfth name and dismissed the rest.

"You've just volunteered for a scientific experiment that involves spending three nights on the fells. Report here with full webbing at fourteen hundred hours."

Lapgood and I were among those selected. He was thrilled to be chosen because he had hiked on the public part of Gatgash Fells over several summers, staying in an old school owned by the Boys' Brigade. The reference to a scientific experiment had made the others apprehensive because of stories about soldiers exposed to noxious chemicals. Wanting to put them at ease, I repeated what Divis had said in the latrine.

By the time I reported back with the required kit, Redfarn was livid because one of the lads has asked him about the tent trials and identified me as the source of this information.

"You snotty little runt. Who asked you to eavesdrop on Sergeant Major Divis."

"No one, Corporal."

"Who asked you to fucking repeat what he said."

"No one, Corporal."

"Five fucking times round the parade ground at the double then report to Stores C."

I ran until I got a stitch on the second lap and then walked as fast as I could until the end of lap four. No one else had been counting so as I passed the brick building that was Stores C I joined the privates outside. They were packing their rations and a sergeant almost as plump as Redfarn and wearing full webbing was going inside. I followed him, but by the time I got through the door no one was in sight. The bare wooden counter that ran for almost the width of the building suggested going no further. Cricket commentary floated through the open door of a room behind and to one side of the counter. All the rest of the space consisted of tall loaded shelves. The commentator's voice was so comforting after all the shouting at Gatgash that I stopped to listen and remember Dad's enjoyment of cricket on the radio. Then the radio went silent and live conversation replaced it.

"So you don't fancy a few nights on the fells, Redfarn?" The accent was Welsh.

"There's nothing I would like more, but you know how it is, Taffy. The ladies would miss me."

"Jammy bugger," said the Welsh man.

"That's rich coming from someone who works in stores. Think about all the prattle I have to listen to. And what if something went wrong. I mean, Mrs Montana's hair is hard work. Makes me wonder how curly she is where the sun don't reach. What if my straightening treatment turned out wrong or she didn't like the colour or the cut?"

"What do they give you by way of refreshments?" asked a deeper voice with a London accent.

"A bit of cake now and again, but not even a sherry at Christmas. I might as well be a wowser like you, Cecil. Still, it helps me keep my hand in for when I give up the Army."

"I thought you had given it up," said Taffy. "You already spend more time being Mr Teasy-Weasy than soldiering."

"C'mon, where's your heart. Think what it's like for the wives being posted to Gatgash. If it wasn't for me it doing their hair, it would be like Siberia for them."

By this time I was retreating as quietly as I could towards the door to avoid another punishment for eavesdropping. I knocked on the architrave and slammed my boots down on the way back to the counter. A stores lance-corporal, who turned out to be the Welshman, came out of the office followed by the sergeant and Redfarn.

Had any other private heard the conversation, he would have blabbed and every recruit in the camp would have known within a day that Redfarn was a ladies hairdresser. But it was not in my nature to gossip about people because of the way facts had been distorted to blacken Dad's name. Moreover, there was the risk of being identified as the source. Of course, those with rank must have known that Redfarn spent a fair part of his time doing the hair of the wives who lived at the Fort, but they kept this from the recruits. Perhaps, in their eyes, the standing of NCOs was demeaned by a profession in which male practitioners were often assumed to be gay.

The plump teetotal sergeant, Cecil Mayhew, was so unfit that the pace we went frustrated Lapgood's wish to see as much of the army part of the fells as possible.

He said to me, "If we go at this pace, what's the point of having a tent as light as a feather?"

The low weight came from a thin tough fabric, wispy cord and alloy pegs and pole segments. Everything fitted into a small draw-string sack made from the same synthetic as the tent. But it was not just Mayhew's pace that frustrated Lapgood. Stinker had not counted on us stopping every two hours to put up tents and unpacking our equipment in them. As soon as we had pretended to sleep, repacking began. One site was chosen because it was rocky and they wanted to see how we coped with tent pegs there. At the next site, we had to erect the tents as quietly as possible and without talking.

The two observers watched and made notes. They hardly spoke with us and did not say much to the two NCOs. Swearing was at a minimum because Mayhew, who was a Bible-thumping Christian, did not indulge and looked daggers if any of us did. Even the corporal gave up swearing when the sergeant was nearby. Besides, the NCOs were not meant to comment on how we coped with the tents. While we did not see as much of the fells as Lapgood would have liked, there were compensations. Peewit calls filled the air. The tarns were still and reflected the blue sky in their brownish mirrors. We dipped hands and the edges of our sleeves in them to cool off.

On the first day we pitched camp for real on springy soft ground in half-light. It was pitch black before we stopped for the second evening and many of us slept badly on the uneven and pebbly ground. Then we had to get up and pack while it was still dark, march two hundred yards, set up again and wait for enough light to check if we had left any kit behind. Mayhew complained about poor sleep and backache from jutting stones and the drizzle that arrived mid-morning made him yet more irritable. For me, the smell of rain falling on dry earth and the scent of damp heather was comforting. My only worry was that the clouds would darken and bring lightning.

When the NCOs complained about finding the map difficult to read with so few landmarks, Lapgood was too eager with his assistance. At first, Mayhew welcomed this, but soon resented the private's lack of humility. Stinker should have kept his voice down and sounded more tentative about what around us might be found on the map. A private shows up an NCO in front of others, especially outsiders, at his peril. Often an NCO would retaliate directly, but not Mayhew. However, on our return, he must have mentioned to others that Lapgood was getting too big for his boots.

The corporal who took my squad for map reading two days later asked Lapgood to identify himself and then attempted to prove the private was ignorant. Perhaps because bullying had not featured to any great extent in Lapgood's childhood, he lacked sensitivity to the moods and foibles of others and instead of placating he continued to parade his knowledge. At one point, he was all but arguing with what the corporal had said about contour lines. Then Chaille, a former boy scout, threw fat on the fire by backing up a point made by Lapgood. The corporal replaced his abuse with tight lips and refused to be humoured by my feigning ignorance and fawning.

Payback began three days later. After breakfast the squad was ordered to don full webbing and marched to a truck where we waited several minutes. The lance-corporal escorting us would not say what was in store other than a cryptic comment about hoping our boots were broken in. Sergeant Roibeard, the map reading corporal and another lance-corporal appeared in webbing and with grim smiles. The first lance-corporal got into the cab and started the engine while the second ordered us in the back, jumped in with us and took the kit offered by the corporal and sergeant. They went to the front and the remaining NCO fastened the flaps from the inside so that we could not see out. All he would say was that we would be on the fells and that the NCOs had food, unlike the privates.

The lorry drove for forty minutes, the latter part being unsealed. The lance-corporal got out the back and ordered a third of the squad to join him. He closed the flaps and after a further ten minutes of driving, another third got out for the corporal. He fastened the flaps and warned us to be ready to jump out as soon as the lorry stopped again.

The driver left us and the sergeant in the middle of nowhere and, confusingly, did not turn around but continued to follow the ruts that ran through the heather. There was rolling moorland for miles in every direction and not so much as a tree as a point of reference. It was beautiful and yet so bleak. The high cloud was continuous and thick enough to hide the direction of the sun. Beyond a thin line of blue sky were approaching banks of tall dark clouds that made me even more anxious than being with Roibeard.

Cliché gave Lapgood a compass and Chaille a map of the Fells. "OK, smart alecs, if you're so clever with maps, find your fucking way back."

He stood to one side smirking while we conferred. Chaille whispered that the drop off points all shared a lack of landmarks.

"I think we're in a public part of the Fells," Lapgood said. "Even if we get our bearings, it'll be a slog to the Fort."

I wanted to ask if others thought there would be an electrical storm, but instead contributed what only I seemed to appreciate. "Roibeard won't help us until we've made fools of ourselves."

"Let's make a start and get it over with then," said Lapgood.

Chaille took the map to the Sergeant and pointed to a spot. The smug look that crept over the giant's ruddy face meant that the guess was wrong.

"So what direction is the Fort?" he asked.

"South west, I think," said Chaille.

"Get moving then!"

After twenty minutes, drizzle started. We stopped to put on our ponchos before bigger drops fell. Wind made the folds of fabric blow one way and then the other. By the time we reached a hillock, the weather had reduced visibility and no one could identify any distinguishing features. Roibeard happily watched us stew.

Chaille was reluctant to choose blindly with the weather deteriorating. "Sergeant, we can't make out where we are so we don't know which direction to go. What should we do? I mean, can you see any landmarks that we could use?"

My heart stopped when I heard the last sentence. No one could see through the greyness, but Roibeard would never admit that he was similarly disadvantaged.

He roared, "So what happens if you six twats are stuck in fucking enemy country and you don't have an NCO to help you read your cunting map? Get marching."

Chaille turned to his right and led the way into the thickening rain that gusts blew almost horizontally. The air chilled my face, hands and where the wet had penetrated my neck and lower trousers. Then the clouds opened every valve. With thunderbolts seeming inevitable, I strained to abate panic. After fifteen minutes, Roibeard called a halt in the lee of an outcrop, the only possible shelter for miles. He looked annoyed.

Lapgood turned away from him and said just loud enough the privates to hear, "Silly sod, he didn't check the weather forecast and couldn't read the sky when we got out the truck."

"Do you think there'll be lightning?"

"Yes, but look at the positive side. Cliche's by far the tallest. If we keep away from him we'll be able to enjoy the fireworks when he goes up in smoke."

Others laughed as loud as they dared with the sergeant nearby. My stomach heaved at the images others found so funny.

We missed the worst of the deluge by hugging the rock. Others appreciated the shelter, but I expected the crag jutting only a few feet above us to attract lightning.

"You're lucky the rain fucking stopped play because you're heading away from the Fort," said Roibeard. "You sods wouldn't know a contour if it bit your 'orrible arses. We'll wait here till the rain eases off."

He tried to light a cigarette, but the air was too wet from spray.

As he spat the sodden fag away, I muttered, "That won't help his temper."

However, he did have food. A package of sandwiches appeared from a kidney pouch and after working his way through them, he ate cake and a bar of chocolate from the other pouch.

After the rain became less like a waterfall, a private held up his poncho to allow Lapgood and Chaille to study the map without it getting soaked.

Lapgood whispered to me as he approached Roibeard, "We know where we are. It's in the public part of the fells."

Roibeard looked surprised, but not altogether annoyed by whatever Lapgood said. By this time, Cliché wanted to get back to the Fort as quickly as possible.

"Right, you lot. After the fucking scenic tour Chaille and Lapgood have taken us on, we're heading home. You're wet and cold so keep yourself warm by going at my pace. If I have to come back and chase you it will be with my fucking boot."

And away he went at a clip that meant I had to run at intervals to keep up with him and the others. The going got harder after we descended into a vale because the ground was sodden with not just the rain that had fallen there but also with run off. The runnels soon became more pronounced, fuller and faster than the ones passed before the outcrop. Then the heavens opened again and the flows down the hill became torrents. Before long we were alongside a significant stream that would have been a dry bed two hours earlier.

Lapgood stopped for me to catch up and shouted. "We're near Helgrund Foss."

"What the fuck is that?" I did not often swear, but cold and fear of storms had got to me.

"A great chasm that leads to a system of caverns. It's popular with experienced potholers, but only if there's been no rain for several days."

Roibeard saw us, looked daggers, waved the others on and waited for us to catch up to him.

"Who said you cunts could stop and chat?"

Lapgood said. "Sergeant, I think we should cross here. The other side of Helgrund Foss drains a much bigger watershed. It'll be a raging river with this rain."

"So you still think you know it all?"

"No, sergeant. I just thought…"

I knew what was coming. How could Lapgood forget the mantra that his reply invoked?

"You're not here to fucking think, just to follow orders. Now if you dawdle again I won't waste words. Move."

He swung his boot to make his point. We raced as fast as the sodden peat would allow until we were in the middle of the others. I looked back at intervals to make sure Roibeard stayed out of kicking and lightning-strike distance. At one point, pea-sized hail pelted down for some minutes, stinging exposed flesh. On a rock pavement, our boots rolled on the pellets. After no longer crunching ice underfoot, we heard and then saw a raging torrent.

"The last time I saw that stream it was a trickle," Lapgood said.

The leading man turned his head, stopped dead in his tracks and the rest of us looked for what had grabbed his attention. The current conveyed a struggling black-faced lamb, its eyes a mixture of panic and despair. We looked on in horror, disturbed that we could do nothing as it sailed past.

Lapgood put a hand on my shoulder. "Poor thing. In a minute she'll fall hundreds of feet. If she manages to survive that, she'll drown in an underground river."

I thought of my father buried in the mine. When all hope of him surviving had gone, we feared that his body was lost forever. After several days, corpses started to arrive at the surface. With news of each discovery waiting to be dug out came an agonising tension; I felt pulled apart by wanting to know that the latest find was my father and not wanting his death confirmed in this way.

A deafening roar came from Helgrund Foss, the noise of water hitting a pond deep below the ground and the eerie echoes that bounced to the top.

"Jesus fucking Christ," said Roibeard when he saw the streams cascading from all sides into the abyss.

He led us uphill for twenty yards to ford where the geography caused one of the smaller streams to spread itself over a wider area. All the same, we formed a human chain to cross. The fording further chilled me and the water in my lower legs added to the weight already absorbed from sweat and trickles down my neck. Once we were across, Roibeard stayed at the rear and no matter how hard I pushed myself he was always near my heels. I expected his boot at any moment. But neither this nor the thought of his height attracting lightning that would kill both of us could speed up my exhausted legs. He probably would have kicked me before long if Chaille had not slipped. It was soon apparent that no amount of clichéd cursing could prevent him hobbling in agony.

Roibeard checked the map and said. "Not far from here is a track that leads to a farmhouse. If they don't have a phone, we'll ask the farmer to drive to one. All we have to do is cross that fucker."

He pointed downhill to raging water that was at least fifteen feet across and laughed at the fear on our faces. "What's the matter? Afraid of getting wet?"

Lapgood asked, "Have we got a rope, sergeant?"

"Did you bring one? Is there a fucking shop handy that sells ropes or are you going to knit one? You berk!"

"But the water's too fast." There was panic in Lapgood's normally staid voice.

We all feared that Roibeard was mad enough to make us cross there and then.

He shouted at the three biggest privates, "You take Hop-a-long's gear and you two help the fucking cripple. This way."

He led us to a dry-stone wall that ran from the top of the hill towards where the flooding filled what had been pasture a few hours earlier. A five-strand fence ran from the end of the wall through the stream to another wall on the other side. It was clear that the locals knew better than to damn the dip with stone. The top strand was barbed wire and where the water was deepest only this was above the flood.

Roibeard had me to walk with him to the water's edge. His leer could only mean he wanted me to cross the torrent. I racked my brains for a way out, but every idea would have resulted in the sergeant battering me. When we were two feet from what was a river in every way but name, he ordered me to take off my poncho and webbing. He rolled up my poncho and threw it and then the rest of my kit across the water.

"Now you go after it, using the fence."

He must have seen my fear, because he said in a more measured tone, "Lapgood will be next and then the two of you will go to the farmhouse to get help for Chaille."

I was terrified. How could I keep my balance? If I tipped over the barbed wire, would I be able to swim in sodden clothes and get ashore before Helgrund Hole? It seemed safer to place my feet on the bottom wire with the water holding me against the upper strands. With a little luck, I would at least keep my upper chest above the water.

I was relieved that the cold current pressed hard. It seemed unlikely that I could drown while pushed against the fence. Then I wondered what would happen if lightning struck the water or the wire. Hand over shaking hand I avoided the barbs.

Near the middle, someone shouted, "Look out."

My comrades gesticulated at something behind me.

My lower body added resistance to the strain on the posts, yet they probably would have held had it not been for the live sheep that struck me from behind before I knew what the others were pointing at. Moving at the same speed as the water, the animal's side hit my back. Its impact felt more like being stuck with a plank than a mass of wet wool. The fence moved forward as if elastic rather than metal before a slurping sound came from my right; a post being pulled from the ground. Currents of water and fear swept me clear of the wires. If I did not drown before Helgrund Foss, the fate of the lamb through impact or submersion awaited me. As I struggled to breathe, I feared that no one would ever see my flesh again, that my body would lodge rotting in some sunless sinkhole.

At times, my feet touched something solid, but without purchase all I could do was bob to the surface for a gulp of air. Brief contact with rocky banks slowed me enough for the sheep to overtake. When all hope had gone, a protruding rock saved me. The water painfully pressed my back against jagged stone. Eddies drove me into a recess where my soles found a surface. While I paused to spit water and catch breath, a lamb raced towards me, neck stretched high, black head jerking from frantic paddling. I could have reached out and rescued it, but I was petrified. I cried not knowing whether the sobs were for the animal or me.

After a time, I stood and found to great surprise that I was almost half-out the water. As I clambered, the mud gave way under my boot and, with water-heavy clothes I fell awkwardly hurting my right eye on the rocky ground. Both eyes still worked, but keeping the right closed was more comfortable. Slithering like a snake bloated by oversize prey, I finally reached ground on which to stand upright. The others were out of sight and, if they were shouting, too far upstream for the sound to reach me. I went to yell, but little more than a whimper emerged.

Although shock and exhaustion demanded rest, hypothermia ruled this out. But I could not move fast enough to warm myself. Even if the others walked downstream, they would not be able to help me. My best chance was to find the farmhouse. When I got to the track, I saw no buildings and, guessing wrong, walked away from the house. Only the farmer returning home in a shooting brake after moving stock to higher ground saved me.

I said others were across the water, including someone unable to walk.

"I'll go and get help for them once my wife is taking care of you. You'd have been a goner if I hadn't found you."

Never again did I experience such cold, but each time I feel thoroughly chilled it is more than a physical thing. Others have been astonished how quickly and violently I start to shiver while beads of sweat appear.

As we drove, the farmer established where I had left the others. After handing me over to his wife, he raced to the nearest phone to alert the Fort.

That evening Redfarn arrived at the farmhouse with dry clothes for me. He said the others were all safe at the Fort and his orders were to drive me back.

Once the farm lights were out of sight, he stopped with the engine running and looked me up and down.

"Very good of you to volunteer to get help for Chaille."

"I'm no hero. I was ordered."

There was grit in his voice. "No, Sergeant Roibeard was very clear. You're a brave man. You suggested going alone to the farmhouse to get help for Chaille. You might even get a medal. It's a shame they can't give you a chest to put it on. Still, your size makes you look even more of a fucking hero."

I understood then that someone had told Redfarn not only to collect me but also to prevent Roibeard facing the full consequences of his recklessness. All the warmth of the farmhouse and the good company of the couple there drained away. I hated lying, but my remaining time at Gatgash would be even more miserable if I failed to go along with what Redfarn had said.

"OK, I'm not going to show up Roibeard. I'll just say that I can't remember much about what happened."

"He's Sergeant Roibeard to you, Private, but it looks like you've learned something in the last few weeks."

An MO, not Maddan, examined me and ordered me to stay in the Fort's hospital for forty-eight hours. On the second night, after screaming in my sleep and waking with the blankets askew from kicking – I thought I was thrashing water and about to follow the sheep into the abyss – an orderly came. He calmed me down, tidied my bed and stayed when I asked him to.

"Don't feel bad about the nightmare," he said. "It goes with the job."

"Do you mean yours or mine?"

"Both I guess."

"So you've seen action?"

"I've seen what it does to the ones who survive it, mentally as well as physically. We're better at treating the bullet and shrapnel wounds. Part of the problem is the soldiers who suffer in silence. They won't admit to their friends, let alone see an MO about the strain they're under. And they'd rather give up drink for a year than see the loony doctor."

"Do you have to record that I had a nightmare?"

"What would be so terrible if I did?"

"It might stop me getting into the infantry."

"Then it might also stop you getting killed."

"It's family thing. I want to join my grandfather's regiment."

"I'll put it down as fitful sleep then."

"Thanks. Where did you treat casualties?"

"Aden, including a stint near the Yemen border, and the north of Malaya. Both were pretty much bandit country."

The orderly had a Geordie accent and was a corporal called Brian Douthwaite.

The nightmares continued. Lapgood and Chaille comforted me. Others, who normally would have abused anyone waking them, said nothing because they knew I had come close to dying. Chaille suggested seeing a doctor about the nightmares, but a combination of not wanting to talk and not wanting anything recorded that might suggest mental instability prompted me to steer the conversation to another topic. My hopes for getting into the Buffs were high because, while there would be no medal and the rank and file knew that Roibeard had ordered me to cross the torrent, officers believed that I had volunteered. Or so I thought until the day of my interview for an onward posting. I waited outside while the lieutenant quickly dealt with several others.

When it was my turn, he said to his lance-corporal clerk, "Take a cigarette break and close the door on your way out. Have a seat, Private."

After we were alone, he smiled and said, "I'm going out with a local girl. Her version of why you crossed on the fence was quite different from the one told by the NCOs. She got it from the wife of the farmer who found you and I spoke to the farmer. He reckoned you said you were ordered to cross the stream. Is that what you told him?"

"I might have. I was in a pretty bad way from the cold when he found me and probably rambling."

"But what do you remember now?"

"It's all a bit of a blur."

He looked disappointed and opened my file. " It says here you did well in German at school. Können Sie mir das auf der Karte zeigen?"

He had probably picked up a few phrases while serving with the Rhine Army. Otherwise, I cannot explain why he claimed to be impressed with the rusty vocabulary and grammar with which I replied.

"These days we have more need of chaps who can follow Russian. I'm putting you down for the JSSL, Joint Services School for Linguists."

"Sir, I was hoping to join the Buffs. My grandfather served with them during two wars and my father wanted to join them in 1940, but he had to keep working as a miner."

"Let's face it, you're not exactly cut out for the infantry are you? You didn't even have the guts to tell me the truth about what happened on the fells."

I said nothing and tried to conceal my emotions. I was angry with myself immediately after the interview. What if the lieutenant had wanted to stop bullies like Roibeard? But the opportunity had passed. By the next day, I was warming to the prospect of the JSSL. Language teaching would take place indoors and after the fells I was wary of the kind of terrain infantry training might involve. I had also heard that many of the instructors were civilians and it was hard to imagine NCOs as unthinking as Roibeard being assigned to the School. And my mother would be delighted to know that I was returning to a form of education rather than acquiring fighting skills.

The JSSL was on a former airbase near the Fife coast. Discipline at the school was more relaxed than basic training, yet the language classes were demanding; students who persistently failed the regular tests returned to their units or other duties. I hoped to do well enough to earn one of the university places that awaited the best performing students until I understood that just completing the course when I was so tired from disturbed sleep would be a challenge.

My fellow trainees were very different from the majority of inductees at Gatgash. One way or the other, the three services had found bright and less brutal lads to learn Russian. Some already had degrees and many of them you might describe as cultured. By and large, my fellow students were kind men who tolerated my nightmares. In particular, David Stancher, who had come from basic training in Colchester, was concerned by them. One night we sat outside looking at the sky to the east where, without a single light upon the North Sea, the stars were exceptionally bright and glittering.

"When did your nightmares begin?"

"Quite recently."

"I won't ask more if you'd rather not say."

It surprised me that someone tall and athletic could be so caring.

I feared holding back would lose his friendship. "A lunatic sergeant ordered me to cross raging water because he'd been too stupid to listen to someone who knew the terrain. I got swept away for half a mile or so and thought I was going to drown."

"Who wouldn't have nightmares after that?"

"It's not just nightmares. I lie awake for hours before sleep comes. I'd much rather be reading, but it would disturb the others."

"I'll pray for you. Do you pray?"

I spoke of the pit disaster and the loss of faith that followed.

"I can't judge you," he said, "I've never been tested in that way. Do you mind if I pray for you?"

"I'm touched that you think about me at all. It reminds me of the kind of Christian my mother is. She's a very active Anglican. Always doing things for others."

"My family are Baptist and my Dad says that if Jesus was here today He would have his sleeves rolled up and would seek out those who need help."

Even though the inference that I needed help was true, it miffed me.

"I appreciate you talking with me. The thing is, I'm not going to change my beliefs and I don't particularly want to discuss religion."

"It wouldn't be much of a friendship if I insisted that we did. Let's make a deal. I won't talk about Jesus and you won't tempt me to do things a Christian shouldn't do."

We shook hands on it and then he said, "Would you take it amiss if I tried to get you a room to yourself?"

"How?"

"Find someone with a bit of clout who's a Christian and tell him it would help you and others."

His intervention got me a room of my own. By studying into the small hours, sleep came more easily and passing the tests was less fraught. Over time, the nightmares became less potent and frequent until it took a particular event, such as seeing a dead sheep at the side of the road, to trigger one.

An elderly Russian tutor who heard the reason for getting a single room offered advice. "I had nightmares for some years after seeing massacres. It seems there are two ways of dealing with them, work or alcohol. I don't recommend drinking. I tried that for some years and vodka brought its own problems."

I made a point of drinking modestly, something helped by David's continuing friendship. On the evenings we drank back then, both of us settled for one or two half-pints.

N I have this sense there is something you want to say.
P Well done! You finally got it off your chest.
N I wondered if you were still angry with my comments about your possible motives for blackening the name of Knattmaw.

P I was upset. You seemed unable to take my word.
N You asked me to lend you credibility. If I accept you at your word, I will have no standing with others. People will have their doubts about me simply because of these communications with you. In any case, I have to say what feels right for me.
P I see.
N Is there anything you want to add.
P Not now.
N I sense resentment.
P Let's leave it for the time being. You should have been in bed hours ago.

Chapter 22: Perry ~ Unhobbled

Four hours after leaving the hospital at Fort Gatgash, the sun appeared in a blue band separating two dull elongated clouds. The unexpected rays reaching the compartment of the rattling train ended a stupor and made me look through the opposite window. I was aware of the world outside for the first time since boarding. Cattle on flat fields trod unimpeded by snow with wisps of vapour escaping from their mouths, hides and effluent.

My breath came more easily thanks to a modicum of ease; I had felt nothing comparable for many weeks. The word that came to mind was unhobbled. Like a horse long restrained and then freed, I could test my legs. The Army still corralled, but there was no need to return to Fort Gatgash and the most brutal of my persecutors would soon be in other countries where I hoped they would die slow and painful deaths after months of privation. I also looked forward to getting home and removing all traces of khaki for a week. As my relaxation increased another notch, it triggered an urgent end to constipation.

After the toilet and some minutes back in my seat, I took in that I shared the compartment with a grey-haired man. A broadsheet partly obscured his head and I had no idea what the bottom part of his face looked like, though I must have seen it at some stage. Nor I did know if we had greeted or chatted. I forgot he was there and returned to some kind of reverie in which the anger that had been suppressed by shock and fear kept bubbling up as the desire for revenge. I was furious not just with Stace and Payner, but the regime that had promoted them and tolerated wholesale bullying. Knattmaw had tyrannised at the instigation of Divis and with the connivance of officers. Maddan, Peebes and Montana had conspired to suppress the truth. I imagined Montana rewarding the officers for suppressing the story. My dishonour counted for nothing compared to their reputations; a private's feelings were no more relevant to them than displays of chinaware to frisky bulls.

"Did you say chinaware?" The man opposite set aside his paper. "Are you alright? You seem to be perspiring rather a lot."

I had spoken aloud yet did not know how much had passed my lips.

"I'm sorry. I've been in hospital for the last two weeks and came over a bit funny."

It was me talking, but it sounded like another person.

The man chortled. "The Sergeant Major tucked you up in bed, did he? Well I hope whatever you had is not catching."

Douthwaite had collected samples of urine and blood, "Just to be on the safe side. You know, VD."

No one had shared the results with me and while this suggested there were no infections, the passenger's joke panicked me. What if there were bacteria gnawing away and multiplying like crazy inside me? The spectre of such contamination sent me to the toilet again, this time running and to puke. When I returned to the compartment, no one else was there. I did not see the grey-haired man again until the platform in London where he kept his distance and avoided eye contact.

Mum had shifted from dreading my call-up to wanting to show off her son the soldier. She insisted that the uniform stayed on until Dad got back and that in the meanwhile we went to the local shops. I agreed rather than risk revealing why I abhorred the Army and sought to avoid thinking about Gatgash and the boiler-house by quizzing Mum, her friends and then Dad to prevent questions about the training and the Fort. By asking them so many questions, how much was unsaid at home became very obvious. Not just things avoided, but also ambiguous mutterings that resisted requests for elaboration, answers that did not address the questions, and looks, sighs and withdrawals that deterred honest exchanges. I felt angry and disappointed with their reticence and misdirection at times, but, following their lead, I bottled up these feelings.

Maddan's sleeping pills ran out on my third day of leave. I wanted more, but I did not wish to see the doctor who had taken over Tuffelton's surgery in case he decided to examine my rectum, found some vestigial injuries and thought I was queer. Before the call-up medical, no doctor had ever inspected the outside of my backside, let alone the interior. But knowing that my fears were quite irrational did not reduce them.

A chapter or two in a bed warmed by a hot water bottle had nearly always brought sleep. For a year or so after basic training, books that once would have been riveting did not distract enough, yet I read until my eyes could take no more. Then, even with the light left on, ghastly recollections danced in and out of consciousness as I listened to the wireless. Music did not help as much as spoken word programmes that could always be found on shortwave. Years of listening to what in effect were the debates between the stations of the west, such as Voice of America, and the programmes originating in Eastern Europe shaped my libertarian views. The Communists taught the extent to which democracies are undermined by entrenched interests that hi-jack government, while the capitalists made clear that socialism brought its own problems. Both systems abuse power and the contrasting programmes along with the help of authors such as Ayn Rand steered me towards wanting a state that limits itself to the essentials, leaves people to stand on their own feet and allows market forces to work without impediment.

The sleep that came at three or four or o'clock was often punctuated by a full-fledged nightmare or, later, by fragments of bad dreams. The threat nearly always involved me being naked and approached by men who looked threatening. I awoke screaming as they were about to touch me. The first time this happened at home, Dad rushed in.

Disorientation suppressed my usual reserve. "Sorry, it was a nightmare."

"I know what you mean, son. I used to have them as a lad."

"Did I wake Mum?"

"No, not much wakes your Mum before the alarm clock. I'm by far the lighter sleeper."

"Do you not sleep well?"

"Well enough. Good night son."

He left quickly as if he regretted being indiscreet. Had he mentioned the nightmare to Mum, she would have fussed over it like every other possible sign that all was not well with me. To my relief, she only railed at breakfast about my lack of appetite and lost weight. Dad never responded again to a scream in the night and we said nothing more about his sleep or mine. The nightmares continued, becoming less frequent and less severe over the years unless something particularly upsetting triggered them, such as reading that the Moors Murderers had sexually assaulted their victims.

One other thing disturbed my sleep during the week at home that followed basic training. Leaving the light on meant that the butterflies presented by Mr Kyte, which I had always felt ambivalent about, were visible from my pillow. I covered them with a shirt for three nights before taking the case down. While Mum was hanging out washing, I took it out the front door and to a second hand shop in Uxbridge where I accepted the five bob offered without haggling. To cover up the holes in the wall, I bought a framed print of an orchard in blossom.

Mum asked the next day, "What have you done with the butterflies?"

"I sold them."

"But why? It was a gift. It's all we have to remind us of the Kytes."

"They stopped sending us Christmas cards years ago. Anyway, I'd always thought it was cruel to pin butterflies. I didn't like looking at them."

"And I thought the Army made men less fussy. How much did you get for them?"

Until sleep came more readily, hard exercise and keeping busy until I went to bed were important. On that first home leave, I strode a dozen or more miles a day and in the shed I sharpened all the tools and sorted containers full of screws, bolts and bits and bobs accumulated over the years. Mum had nothing that needed fixing, so I asked the neighbours. Mrs Ovesian had taps and a toilet cistern that needed minor work and she wanted additional electrical sockets. After I refused to take money for the day the jobs took, the next afternoon she left a package with Mum; a compact transistor radio, then still a somewhat novel and expensive item.

I reported to Lieutenant Rilling at Hounslow Barracks. He made it clear without being unpleasant that I was an imposition as his team of nine were flat-out on a project that contributed to the automation of the Army's payroll. I had arrived, he said, following a personal request from a major at Gatgash to the major that Rilling was under. The lieutenant's orders were to get me servicing typewriters and trained to drive.

He left the practical arrangements to Sergeant Cobden, a man whose patience, quiet voice free of bad language, and soft rosy face made him appear more like a vicar than an NCO. He explained that I was to tour Army offices to service typewriters.

"What about repairs?"

"We were only told about servicing and we don't have a budget for tools and there's no space for a workshop. We don't even have a spare desk for you here. So just keep yourself busy servicing and any minor adjustments you can do with your penknife, assuming you have one."

I guessed what had happened and could have kicked myself. During my call up interview, I had said that I mended and serviced typewriters, but only the servicing had appeared on the record consulted at Gatgash.

"The thing is, Sergeant, a good typist maintains the typewriter. Most of the time there's no real need for a service."

"That may be the case, but the lieutenant and the team are under the cosh and we don't have time to question what the majors have agreed. Keep your nose clean and you can go home every weekend on Friday at 17.00 and not have to come back until 22.00 on Sunday. The team are excused other duties because we're so busy and I'll include you in that if you also keep yourself busy."

Cobden gave me a list of army offices in and around London and said, "Start with the ones near stations. Phone up and find out how many typewriters each establishment has and arrange to visit. After you get your driving licence, you can go further afield. Each week you'll submit a report on where you've been and a schedule for the next week. If you feel under any strain, let me know and we'll review."

While not treating me as a friend, none of Rilling's men called me names, teased or bullied me. I imagine the lieutenant had warned his team that I was mentally fragile. The worst they did was curse when my nightmares woke them. I mostly saw in the bunkroom we shared. And to be fair, I avoided a lot of their chat there by listening to my transistor radio through an ear-piece, while covering the other ear with a hand or pillow.

In the second office visited for work on typewriters, I walked into a room where three bored National Service clerks were meant to be preparing files for their unit's Officer in Charge of Records, whose duties included ensuring annual reports on individuals were completed on schedule. The men were slacking more than usual because their corporal was on leave. They chattered about the ignorance and stupidity that abounded in the military. One had heard of an Egyptologist who turned up at a recruiting centre shortly after Britain declared war in 1939. He had ended up in the Faroe Islands because the sergeant had asked him what an Egyptologist did.

"I study hieroglyphics."

"And what are they"

"The language of the Pharaohs."

Another clerk said, "You could understand it then when everyone was panicking about not being prepared for war like Germany was. What gets me are the mistakes made when there's no war on."

And they reeled off stories of careers turned tragic by cock-ups such as information being added to the wrong file. One spoke of a clerk who had come across the file of a sergeant who had made his basic training a nightmare and had replaced favourable reports with damning ones.

"Could you really scupper someone's career like that?" I asked.

"You bet," said the most vociferous clerk. "A few little amendments to handwritten reports or replace a typed one, or add new pages. The thing is, most blokes never get to see what's in their folder. Anyone who's got any sense shouldn't upset a clerk doing our kind of work."

The potential of records for surreptitious retaliation was exciting and frightening. The problem was that units held the files of their men for most of the time. The records of Stace and Payner would have followed them overseas and, even had Rilling been prepared to authorise a typewriter-servicing visit as far north as Gatgash, no way would I have returned to the Fort. I had to accept that any doctoring of files would depend on chance and that the most I could do was try to befriend clerks handling personal records, and orderlies who might have access to medical files.

On my first weekend leave, I bought an army surplus toolbox and the few tools not already owned that were useful for repairing typewriters. I added to the box a pouch with a collection of lock picks. A typewriter mechanic might have wondered what they were for, but most people would have assumed everything was part of a typewriter repair kit.

When Cobden asked what was in the toolbox, I opened the lid saying, "A collection of penknives."

He laughed. "It looks very professional. Just make sure that if any typewriter needs new parts, the unit knows they have to pay for them."

I made it my business to observe what locks were in use where records were kept and began to collect at home keys and skeleton keys. Many surplus keys I found towards the back of desk drawers in the offices I visited. Carrying a large bunch or a selection of the jigglers was too risky. It was better to leave a typewriter in pieces and return after I had collected what was needed.

Feigning a naïve interest in how the clerks and orderlies kept records was usually enough to curry favour with them. If not, when they asked how I had learned my trade, rather than mentioning Global Typewriters I spoke of Dad and the way he had taught me his skills and the range of items I had repaired. Quite often someone would ask me to look at another piece of office equipment, such as a jammed adding machine, or fetch a broken camera or a wireless. When it suited me, I used such repairs as an excuse for a second visit and returned with a replacement part or a tool for the job.

I didn't eat during the day and far more often than not the clerks would leave me long enough to search for Gatgash names over lunchtime. The mental list I used was based on how much I hated people. It began with the Owls and then Knattmaw. For several months there were no opportunities to sabotage a career. Then during a visit to Chelsea Army Barracks I heard through an open window a tirade of abuse. When I went to look, it was a towering red-faced bull of a corporal tearing a strip off a private who weighed half as much.

A clerk stood next to me and said, "He's a right little Hitler. Always finds fault and makes it personal."

"What's his name?"

I asked having already decided to sabotage his folder. The frustration of not having yet found the people I most wanted to hurt drove me to target a stranger. After doctoring the corporal's file, I responded to other NCOs who bullied, officers ignoring such behaviour, and people who made fun of my height. I put up with banter about being a soldier who serviced typewriters and being part of the Pay Corps, but the name of anyone reminding me of the bullies in Hut D3 or the NCOs who hounded us went on my blacklist.

The files of the mockers, martinets and those who tolerated abuse that I discovered in and around London were usually easy to locate. Working on them developed a *modus operandi*. I learned to carry six pens, three fountain and three ballpoint to match the black or blue ink used on a hand written document, for example changing *suitable* to *unsuitable*; red ink drew attention to negative items, be they existing or my additions.

I kept a supply of forms and letterhead that might be useful. The only soldier who asked what these sheets were doing in the toolbox accepted the excuse offered; scrap paper for typewriter testing.

Reading annual reports on officers revealed that many of the unfavourable comments were understatements, such as "shows passable leadership for a young lieutenant". By and large, the further down the ranks the less subtlety an assessor used to express a negative view. One folder had a psychiatrist's comments on a former sergeant who had lost his stripes for repeated drunkenness. I made a copy of the contents and signature and looked up the meaning of unfamiliar words to ensure that I could use them appropriately in a forgery.

Maddan was my biggest coup while I was in uniform. Not only was he high on my list for revenge, but also officers' folders were harder to access. I spotted his at the Royal Army Medical Corps HQ, his posting after Gatgash, and gleaned from what appeared to be idle chatter with clerks that the pile had come from the Officer in Charge of Records and were awaiting filing. Three clerks left me in their office over lunchtime with a key to lock it should I need the toilet. I did need it, both to clean my hands of typewriter ink before touching any files and to clear my quivering bowels. Then I locked myself in the office. After studying the contents of the doctor's file, I noted the make and numbers on the filing cabinet locks. By the time the clerks reappeared, I had removed a carriage return from a typewriter. The men accepted that I needed a special tool and would return the next week to complete the repair.

That weekend at Rayners Lane, I collected keys for the filing cabinets and typed bogus documents. One was derived from a report that a leering clerk had shown me a few months earlier. It concerned an infantry lieutenant who had been in a road accident. His captain had gone to the lieutenant's room to collect personal effects for a stay in hospital and had found two letters. They had no address, were signed with a single initial and expressed much affection. In one letter, the author commented on the attractiveness of young builders working on a site opposite where he wrote, including references to bulging groins. The lieutenant had denied being homosexual. When asked to identify the author, he said he would prefer to resign his commission and was allowed to do so. I created a similar report from Bulford Camp, where Maddan had been stationed before Gatgash. However, my report concluded that the evidence was not strong enough for action to be taken. Then, drawing on what I had seen in the folder of a sergeant P.E. instructor, I fabricated a report into an investigation following a private's allegation of the doctor indecently fondling him during an examination at Gatgash. The document ended with the complaint dismissed because there were no witnesses and the private concerned, one Bernard Halton, was a known troublemaker.

Imagine the state of a windy person carrying and planting material that sullied the reputation of an officer. I was could hardly breathe as I took Maddan's file from a locked cabinet, removed his two most favourable annual reports and added calumnies, both typed and handwritten. The tremor in my hand made it difficult to amend *caring* to *uncaring*, *competent* to *incompetent*, and *agreeable manner* to *disagreeable*. The Military Police and their glasshouses had terrifying reputations. I also dreaded seeing Maddan again because of the memories he was linked to. And what if he saw me in the building and then, on being made aware of what was in his file, suspected me of the inventions? Only hatred and a quest to remedy injustice helped overcome the urge to abandon the reprisal.

Due to my trembling, reassembling the typewriter took ages. The good humour of the clerks on their return from lunch was difficult to respond to. After I was well away from the building, I parked and let myself shake and pant until the worst of the nervousness passed. Gradually, I convinced myself that by the time someone studied the file, either a new superior would be looking at it or the old one would assume he had missed the information last time around. |In either case, Maddan would suffer without him knowing what was in the file. By the evening, the fear yielded to the satisfaction of a job well done and I savoured the various ways in which the forgeries might disadvantage the doctor in the years to come.

The mental list of my abusers included where I had encountered them, what they had done, the actions taken against them and any news that filtered through suggesting a ruse had worked. As the number of targets increased, I started to keep index cards at home. That was the start of the code used here with its symbols remembered from foreign typewriters. For each of the ten most common letters and for very common words, I have two or three symbols to make decoding more difficult. But if you have decrypted this far, you will know this. The Gatgash names on the cards were in black, the more recent ones in blue and I recorded in red ink what I had done to retaliate and indications or confirmation of success.

Apart from the lasting effects of Gatgash and the states of high anxiety that went with being furtive, Hounslow Barracks was a soft billet. Rilling and Cobden resented the minimal time that I took away from their automation project, but neither made me feel uncomfortable and the sergeant was always polite. When I located their files, I did nothing other than remove some documents from them with less favourable remarks.

Chapter 23: Norman ~ Calling Theresa

Having met humane and effective officers and NCOs after my time at Gatgash, Perry's account of Rilling and Cobden's handling of a supernumerary foisted upon them for the convenience of others is plausible. They would have welcomed a bright youngster to help with the pay automation project, but orders stated the new man was to service typewriters. Some receiving units might have shown hostility to the person imposed upon them. Fortunately for Perry, the lieutenant and his sergeant were not abusive. Perhaps someone had warned that the new man was fragile, but many leaders reserve their support and goodwill for men who have been under them and proved their worth over time. My guess is the major in the Pay Corps selected Rilling's unit because the lieutenant and his sergeant were decent coves.

Much depends on how much truth is in Perry's story. Let us again assume for the time being that the boiler house rape took place and was hushed up. The conspirators would have been worried about Perry blabbing at a later stage, especially if he was showing signs of strain in the hospital – nightmares, withdrawn, lack of appetite, bathing excessively and then not bathing and shaving. Sometimes the families of recruits learned about abuses and kicked up a fuss. Even the cover-up story carried the risk of the Grays asking how a slight and physically run down recruit was made to repeat such a gruelling training to the point where hospitalisation was needed.

Keeping Perry in the Army and in a unit where a major was a friend of another major at Gatgash meant that the private would continue to fear repercussions if he spoke up. At the very least, he would have dreaded his relatively easy life in the Pay Corps being replaced with something more akin to his experience of Gatgash. It must have been tempting for the conspirators to post him well away from his home, but even if they did how could they prevent Perry communicating with his parents? I suspect a Gatgash officer or group of them weighed up the pros and cons of where to send him and decided that a cushy posting near to his home reduced the chances of

Perry suffering a breakdown that might prompt others to ask what had pushed him over the edge.

Perry's description of lax security in army buildings did not surprise me. Soldiers understood back then the importance of confidentiality in matters that might help an enemy, but the idea of personal information being sacrosanct had not yet taken root. And if officer's files warranted more measures to protect them from prying eyes, this came from wishing to avoid gossip about superiors that could undermine discipline. Most of the humbler clerks were counting the days to when they would return to civilian life. Often they were bored and the sharing titbits from soldiers' files was one way of countering the monotony. The larger picture was one of more conscripts than needed and over-manning was not unusual. In the more bloated units and the ones that were less well organised, skiving was rife, often with the connivance of NCOs, if not officers. In some settings, as long as a private appeared to be purposeful or had a half-way plausible excuse for an hour's absence, nothing was said. You might think that if an office had more clerks than it needed, they would complete work promptly and return files to locked cabinets or rooms. But often more than one person handled a folder – different clerks dealt with different parts – and it took days to circulate. Some items needed an NCO to check or an officer to sign off. I waited over two hours in one office for a corporal to return as only he had a key to the drawer with the rubber stamp that my request needed. The four privates there talked with me and between themselves non-stop. Much of what they said was gossip, including speculation about which officer had impregnated a lieutenant-colonel's daughter.

Did Perry tamper with files? The Army has chosen not to comment other than saying men like Maddan had an unblemished record. This was ambiguous and I suspect deliberately so. Were the records always unblemished or had someone weeded out the misinformation inserted by Perry? Understandably, the late doctor's family were outraged at the suggestion that he had neglected his duty and cited the many tributes offered by civilian patients, the people he had served for over twenty years as a GP. I never knew the captain. All I can say is that many institutions put pressure on individuals to ignore operating procedures and ethical standards. Protecting a unit's reputation, or its commander's, is often paramount even when this requires further ignominious actions. There is a sickening tendency to pervert the course of justice as if adding to the original shameful failing could serve honour.

During our drive back from Vaulting Ryego, Rose and I played Gilbert and Sullivan, a shared passion, loud enough to hide the traffic noise. In normal circumstances, she would have paused the CD after a track or two and commented on the environment we were travelling through. Instead, she said nothing and barely glanced at me because she appreciated that keeping my brain busy with code-breaking was calming. Besides, all the distractions of a moving car made it a hopeless place for the kind of discussion she was most interested in having.

Memories of Gatgash kept erupting and they continued to surface after we got back to Foxenearth. I went straight to my study to pursue the code as best I could, given the state I was in. Rose resurrected old habits, silently bringing me green tea and, with the third mug, roast beef sandwiches that made me realise it was past dinnertime. While I was eating, I remembered that Theresa was expecting my call, put down the food and put on a headset linked to the phone. I felt guilty for being so eager to talk to her after ignoring Rose.

Theresa answered within seconds of the phone ringing and quickly boasted that two other people were ready to take a call from me that evening.

"Tell me about the last time you spoke with Perry and said more than just hello?"

"That would have been about three months ago. It was a slow morning and he came in to order cakes for late the next afternoon. He did that about once a month, usually a mixed box of twelve for his poker group. He liked me to bake them after lunch so they were fresher. Sometimes he rang to order…"

As I was out of my depth, I let Theresa continue. She knew so much about Perry, but I was unsure of how best to help her cut to the chase. Investigative interviewing was new to me and all the more difficult when I was fishing without knowing quite what was there. I made a note in the margin of the writing pad to ask David how he had coped when questioning a well-meaning yet voluble member of the public. Then an idea came to me from an interview in which a security officer had questioned me about a colleague who had run up gambling debts.

At length, Theresa drew breath and I said, "So on that day when you last saw him, if you had been a very attentive stranger watching Perry for the first time, what might you have made of him?"

"Gosh, that's interesting. Firstly, for someone who buys cakes in bulk, he's very trim. His eyes are clear, but he has slight bags under them and fine broken veins on his cheeks. I mean, everyone locally knew he liked his wine, but I think most people would have guessed he drank a bit. Clean-shaven – can't remember ever seeing him with stubble. Clean nails – caterers notice hands like that. His fingers were a bit rough, from gardening I would think. Well dressed without being show-offy, a bit like his cars."

"And what would a stranger have surmised about his mood or personality on that day?"

"Not happy or depressed, a bit anxious. To be honest he always looked the same to me. But not enough to draw attention. A bit of sorrow, but who wouldn't have lost someone by that age?"

There was more than a trace of sadness in Theresa's voice that evoked grief for my parents and led me to conclude the conversation by asking for the other names and numbers. My next call was to Terry Williams, described by Theresa as a widower who did painting and decorating and someone who had often been in the pub with Perry.

Terry said, "I'm glad you've called now, I wanted to go out before much longer."

The slightly slurred voice suggested that he was a native of the county and fond of drink. Perhaps the latter would work to my advantage.

"Did Perry ever do anything that suggested he was not what he usually appeared to be?"

"There's people who never knew him half as well as me who now claim they thought he was odd. When I press them, they can't spell it out. I think hunches after the event are like fastening seat belts after the accident, pretty pointless. Perry has disappointed a lot of people, but we never saw the crash coming. I thought he was more than OK. I trusted him and thought he trusted me."

"Did he tell you things?" I tried to sound casual.

"No, it wasn't that kind of trust. I never asked him for money, but let's say that I'd needed cash in a hurry and my bank card wouldn't work; Perry would have loaned me whatever I needed and I'd have done the same for him."

"If everyone's got an Achilles' heel, what was Perry's?"

The noise suggested Terry shrugging as he sighed. "I guess his size. He never said anything when people teased, but you could tell he didn't like it. He'd go a bit quiet or sometimes try a bit too hard to jolly things along. Why should he have liked it? What's height got to do with anything?"

"What did he like to talk about?"

"Just about anything, but he seldom introduced a topic. You could tell he was a great reader. Yet he held back. One night in the pub, some out-of-town Jack-the-Lad was going on about Moore's Law as if he'd discovered it. I only knew about Moore's Law because Perry had explained it ages ago. Perry just sat there sipping his beer, not letting on that he knew more about computers than this bloke would ever know. Apart from poker, Perry didn't like to compete. He could if he needed and I guess he had to at work, but it wasn't what he wanted."

"Tell me about the poker."

"A group of us have played in each others' homes for yonks. Perry joined us some years after he moved into Raventulle. At first, he missed quite a few of the evenings because his work took him away. More recently, he wasn't away so much and almost as regular at turning up as the rest of us. He won more than he lost. I used to watch him when I had thrown in a hand. He didn't make it too obvious, but he was studying the people still in the game. I don't know what he saw, but he could usually spot a bluff."

"What sort of stakes?"

"We keep them low. No one has ever lost more than twenty pounds in a night. I wondered why Perry didn't graduate to a game with bigger stakes."

"Any ideas why he didn't?"

"I think we were the best mates he had. He certainly treated us well. He always brought two good bottles with him to someone else's house. I didn't know Shiraz from sherbet before Perry opened his cellar to us. And he also used to spoil us with fancy food and lots of it when we played at Raventulle."

"Did any poker players receive letters?"

"Not that I know of. Perry seemed to like us. We drank a fair bit, but it wasn't like the pub where people can get obnoxious. Even when we were squiffy, the poker players didn't joke about his height. There was a bit of banter, but it was good natured and everyone contributed and got about as much stick as anyone else. Except Perry, of course. He seemed to be above putting people down even in jest."

"Do you think his height was why he wrote the letters?"

"God knows, but he must have had some reason. I hate what he did, but I don't regard Perry as all bad."

My third call was to a woman who had gone out with Perry for a while.

Theresa had said, "Shelley will tell you how she is if she wants to, but avoid asking about her health. She's tired of explaining to everyone."

"Are you sure it's OK for me to call?"

"Absolutely. She said she was looking forward to speaking with you."

Theresa left me thinking that the health condition was an embarrassment. As I waited for Shelley to answer, possibilities ranging from a botched nose job to bunions went through my mind. I imagined she would be bashful because of the issue, but this assumption dissolved when I heard her voice. Added to the slow rural accent was a come-hither huskiness that led me to picture her as the life and soul of many a good party.

"Ah, the mystery man who works for the police, but isn't a psychic and isn't a copper. Theresa got me quite intrigued."

"The thing is, if I say what my role is it would tell you something that is not yet in the public domain and it's for the police to decide when and if it's publicised. Let me just say I have never worked for them before and my skills are technical. Even interviewing the public is new to me."

"You could pretend you've met me in a pub and you're chatting me up."

Her flirting reminded me of Rose when we first met.

"Is that how you met Perry?"

"Yes, but I had a husband back then."

She spoke of knowing Perry for years and barely saying more than hello. Then her husband had turned violent after becoming dependent on cocaine and alcohol. She eventually kicked him out and, as there were no children, moved to a smaller property to pay off the debts he had incurred. Shelley started to chat with Perry at the Shoe and Anvil, felt safe with him partly because of his size and gentleness, and liked the way he listened and questioned her about what she was doing.

"What were you doing?"

"Working in the museum gift shop and doing art history through the Open University. I had plenty of time once I stopped looking after a large house and a pig of a husband. Most men I met socially, if they asked me anything about myself, asked about the gift shop. Perry said he knew little about art, but that didn't stop him being curious."

Her voice conveyed a love of life even when she spoke of a difficult marriage and boring men. I pictured her as a handsome, forty-something plumpish woman with blonde hair and vibrant yet tasteful clothes. As she had gone out with Perry, I assumed she was probably on the short side. For good measure, I also had her down as a bit of a gourmet.

"I met my wife, Rose, in a shop. Her work was the last thing I wanted to talk about."

"You sound like a good 'un, Norman. How old are you?"

"I'm retired and Rose says we should live years rather than count them."

For the first time, the voice did not bounce back immediately. I heard an intake of breath and wondered if she found Rose's remark silly.

When she did speak, Shelley's giggle suggested that all was well. "Rose is onto something there, Norman. She sounds like a good 'un too."

Judging by the candour that followed, Shelley really did approve of me. She described how after her husband had left the area she enjoyed several unplanned encounters in pubs with Perry until he invited her to a Sunday ramble in an adjoining county. Towards the end of the walk, they held hands. After the ramble they mostly met where there was less chance of a local seeing them. Often it was a meal in an out-of-the-way pub.

"I started to peck him on the cheek to say hello and then I started kissing him on the lips to say goodbye because I thought he might need some encouragement given the age difference between us. Perry inviting me to lunch at his house on a Saturday seemed significant. News was bound to fly around the town that my car was parked at Raventulle. I expected him to make a play and I was up for it. I had on a new pair of frilly knickers, showed a bit of cleavage, dabbed perfume between my boobs and put a joint in my handbag.

"Perry knew that I smoked and I knew that he'd never tried drugs. But when I produced the joint, he said he didn't want it in his house and asked, nicely but firmly, for me to put it in my car.

"It wasn't the best of starts. Still, we recovered and had a great lunch. But by four o'clock, nothing had happened other than both of us being sloshed. We sat on the sofa looking at art books. I'd deliberately chosen Gauguin, Klimt and Modigliani. Can you guess why?"

"Er, no." I did not admit to being unfamiliar with even the name of Klimt and vague about Modigliani.

"They've all painted erotic masterpieces. Perry hung on every word and kept asking questions, but I was no longer interested in the pictures and put the books on the floor."

Shelley's voice had lost some of its sparkle. "At first I just stroked his cheek. He closed his eyes and seemed very happy. I moved closer and gave him a big moist kiss on the lips. His expression didn't change. I was surprised that his arms hung still, but I thought, there's no hurry. I rested my brow on his. I was looking at his lap, saw things stirring, dropped my right hand and gently touched his erection."

I squirmed in my chair. I was a cheat who had no right to such intimate details. If she discovered my lack of authorisation, she would have every right to lodge a complaint,

"He shot away as if zapped by a cattle prod, stood up and walked to the window. My first response was laughter, because his flight was like something from a cartoon, but that upset him all the more. I apologised and suggested he come back to the sofa and we go more slowly. He shook his head, as if too choked to speak. To buy time, I suggested we have coffee. He had made one for me when I arrived and had taken ages grinding beans and operating the espresso machine.

"When he came back with the cups, he sat away from me and still looked like he'd sucked a lemon, but didn't say anything. I said, 'Let's talk about it rather than pretend nothing happened.' He looked uneasy and I said, 'We don't have to talk here and now, let's just agree we will talk about it because otherwise I'll keep blaming myself.'

"That seemed to shock him. He was adamant I wasn't to blame and said that we would talk. I said that I couldn't drive for at least six hours, so what did he want me to do? He was happy for me to stay in the spare room. We agreed to talk the next morning. And, as if to seal it, he said let's have one more bottle of wine. He took me down to the cellar to pick one. I had this sense that he wanted me to kiss him again in the cellar. He stood there with the bottle in his hand, looking at me with a tear in his eye. But after what had happened on the sofa, I wasn't game to take another chance.

"I asked if he was alright and he said sometimes the cellar reminded him of his childhood. We got very drunk on opposite sides of the fireplace and laughed a lot, but nothing physical happened between us."

Thank God for that, I thought. Shelley seemed quite capable of providing a blow-by-blow account of lovemaking and already I felt like a peeping Tom.

"There was one other thing that day. After we'd returned from the cellar and got halfway through the bottle, his mobile went. It was from a panicking man at a computer centre. Perry immediately sounded sober and talked him through what to do. I realised later that he had never said anything to me that he might not have said before drinking, which wasn't what I was used to with other friends. You know, when people have a few drinks they tell you something about themselves or their family and others share gossip about mutual acquaintances that they would never mention when sober."

"So he kept his guard up?"

"To the point where he had few real friends; his phone rang mostly for his consulting work or someone local asking if he could fix something. He talked to people in the pub and I imagine there was some conversation at the poker nights, but I was one of the few he just chatted to on the phone. Is this helping?"

I still felt uncomfortable that Shelley had poured out her heart to a devious stranger. "It's very helpful. The police approached me only a few days ago. I'm not sure how much of this you've already told them."

She giggled. "Less than I've told you. For a start, nothing about the joint, frilly knickers and fondling Mr Vitriol's willy."

"So how come you're telling me?"

"You don't sound like a copper and I was still hoping to get the NHS to fund a new drug when the police were here."

I understood then that she had a life threatening condition and felt stupid that Theresa's hint had led me to consider only cosmetic issues. I pushed the phone's mute button to hide the gulp that I could not stop, then pushed the button again.

"Theresa suggested some health issue, but she didn't spell it out."

"She's good like that. It's breast cancer. I prefer to tell people myself. Not everyone. Just people I feel some connection to."

Somehow she had worked her illness into her flirting,

"It's spread and now I'm not fighting it anymore." She sounded matter-of-fact.

"Shelley, I'm sorry. You sound so full of life that I feel all the more stunned."

"I put up a good front. And I've always been more of an evening person. You wouldn't find me so lively at nine in the morning. Detective-Sergeant Thorsen didn't."

Her spark was back. How unfair that she jollied me along.

"I wish there was something I could do or suggest."

"I'm glad you can't think of anything. So many people have had ideas for cures or boosting immunity and others just wanted to soothe. I've enjoyed some of the experiences, but I don't want more novelties. Let me savour being in my cottage and enjoying the countryside around here."

"I'm so sorry to have intruded."

"It doesn't feel like that, Norman. We're all curious about Perry here, especially me. It would be nice if you could feed back."

"It's difficult for a number of reasons. As well as the usual confidentiality, the police are extra-sensitive because Perry worked for government departments and as yet no one knows the implications of that."

"What is it that you do, Norman?"

The seduction in her husky voice combined with my guilt to persuade me to say more. "I'll tell you on three conditions. You don't tell anyone else. You don't ask me any more questions about my work. And you tell me your age?"

Giggles then, "Why do you want to know my age?"

"Just humour me."

"Forty-two. Now what do you do?"

Her age made me feel sadder, but I tried not to show it. "I break codes."

"What's that got to do with Perry? No, I can't ask that, can I?"

"Shelley, your voice is so gorgeous that I can't understand a man not being attracted to you, let alone jumping away. Did Perry explain?"

"We spoke about it the next morning. I suggested we talked while we rambled and suggested a quiet path wide enough for two. Sometimes men find it easier to be honest when they don't look at you all the time. He said he really liked me, but he'd made a vow of celibacy. I said, 'But you don't go to church,' and he said it had nothing to do with religion. And that was about as much as he would say other than apologising for not stopping me sooner. So we walked on for a while before I tried another tack.

"I said he struck me as an unusually private person, even by male standards. He said some of it came from his parents, who were very tight lipped, and some of it came from being bullied at school and learning to stay below the radar as he put it.

"I said, 'It sounds like you can't trust me.' And he said, 'I'd trust you with my life or my money, but I prefer to keep my secrets.' And then he laughed and just said old habits are the hardest to change. You know, I believed him, I think he did trust me as much as anyone."

"What happened after that?"

"We still met up and cooked meals for each other half a dozen times as well as going to pubs and restaurants. Some assumed we were lovers and one woman who'd had been out with Perry congratulated me for succeeding where she'd failed. I joked about her being too young for him.

After a while, I accepted nothing physical would ever happen between us. I'd never fallen in love with Perry, but I was fond of him. I said others were asking me out and that it was only a matter of time before one took my fancy. Perry said he understood and hoped we could still be friends. Then someone a bit earthier came along and I moved on."

"Was Perry jealous?"

"Do you mean did I get a funny letter? I didn't and, as far as I know, none of the blokes I went out with did either. Perry seemed pleased for me whenever I was happy. He still bought me drinks in the pub. He gave me a great bottle of wine every birthday and Christmas. He was the first man I told about the cancer."

"How did he take it?"

"He was gutted, but he never avoided me like some of the men. He'd lost his mother to cancer. I think he found it hard to share the optimism that I had then."

"What do you think made Perry tick?"

"He never really relaxed. He could have done with a joint or two. And there are other ways of unwinding when you're by yourself, but somehow they didn't work for him. I can just switch off my mobile, sit alone and chill out. Or do Tai Chi or spend an evening mindlessly doing a tapestry while listening to records. Perry always seemed to be busy; if he wasn't doing work, he still thought about it. Then again, maybe that was what prevented him becoming dependent on alcohol. I used to worry about what might happen if he retired. You know the way some pensioners start hitting the bottle because they don't know what else to do."

"And what might have made him so tense?"

"Insecurity, not financial obviously. He was never at ease in his body."

"How do you mean?"

Shelley spoke in a voice rather earnest compared to what had gone before. "He never told me this, but he hated being small. You know, little men can have complexes. Some are Napoleons. Perry was a scaredy-cat. He never appreciated that he was attractive and that women can appreciate little men for all sorts of reasons. I felt safe with him and that was very important to me after leaving a violent marriage. I have friends who said that they liked him, but didn't want to be seen going out with someone so much shorter. One even said that she would like to keep Perry in a cupboard at home and discreetly take him out at night. But height wasn't an issue for me. If others saw us as an ill-matched item that was their problem."

The embarrassment of revealing that I was one of the cupboard-sized creatures prevented acknowledging how well I understood. "Thank you so much for your time and insights, which were very useful."

"You're welcome to call again if you think it might help."

That's really kind of you. My best wishes."

The last three words sounded hollow. Long after I had hung up the headset, I wondered what else might be said in such a situation. Now that I know that awkward response to terminal cancer from the other side, I would not take offence if someone said the same to me.

When the decoding leaked, I rang Theresa to check how Shelley was before ringing her to say its publication had surprised me. My plan was to say that I regretted not having sent her a copy of the transcript, or at least the section that appeared to refer to her. But she was dead.

I did not tell Theresa that the same metastatic express was conveying me towards the edge. Rather, we spoke about Rose's sudden admission to hospital – it was before any mention of an exploratory operation – and the great impression that Shelley had made in a brief call. I asked if Theresa could spare a picture of her friend and received an email that night with the PowerPoint presentation assembled for the funeral service. In photographs that spanned three decades, Shelley was well above average height and always thin. Her hair ranged from purple-red to Morticia-black, but never strayed into blonde. I was, however, right about her wearing colourful clothes and being a gourmet; several tributes referred to her wonderful and elaborate meals.

When I emailed my thanks a week or so later, I could not bring myself to mention that Rose was dead. I also asked if Theresa had seen Daya. An email came back that evening.

"Daya left the police to look after her parents. Then her father died. Three weeks ago, she brought her mother and an aunt to the village. I made a cake without eggs for them because the family are very strict vegetarians. I'll pass on your regards when I next see her. Give my love to Rose."

I wanted to ask Theresa if she had a telephone number, but Daya had met hundreds of people once through her work. Why did I have any more right than them to make contact? What did I want?

Reflection eventually brought the answer. Like Shelley, Daya reminded me Rose. They three women had in common intelligence, vivacity and the ability to captivate. And Daya was Rose's equal in terms of astuteness. At least my prejudice had not blinded me to this. And all three women had a beauty that was more than skin deep. The resemblances to Rose attracted and pained me in equal measure.

Chapter 24: Perry ~ Union Comptometers

Mr Ovesian wanted me to rejoin Global Typewriters after National Service, an invitation my parents welcomed not only from deference to our prosperous neighbours but also from faded parental ambition.

As Mum put it, "You could do a lot worse. Not just the money, it's nice to see you leave the house looking respectable."

By which she meant fresh shaved, suit, tie and white shirt. And provided I scrubbed my hands, there was no evidence of my manual occupation when I returned other than the coveralls brought home for washing on Friday night. Mum would have preferred not to display them on the clothes-line, but not enough to let me pay a laundry.

The prospect of working surrounded by women in typing pools was deterrent enough. However, I also wanted new challenges. Some army clerks had asked me to service tabulators. I admired the greater complexity of these machines and, having enjoyed some success with simple faults, I applied to Union Comptometers in Neasden towards the end of my stint in uniform. Rilling wrote a fulsome testimonial and extended my weekend leave for a Monday interview. I went in civilian clothes and relished not seeing a single person wearing khaki within the factory complex.

The personnel lady who conducted the interview reported that Mr Ovesian's reference had expressed regret that with my ability to learn and solve problems I would not be returning to Global Typewriters. She checked a few details on my application form with me before making a call and directing me to where a foreman would assess my mechanical aptitude. The Repair Unit, a self-contained workshop adjoining the end of an assembly line producing tabulators, dealt both with older machines sent for repair and ones just produced that failed quality control. I could easily see inside Repair Unit as it had large windows, skylights and ample fluorescent tubes. Twelve work benches lined the two side walls. Three feet away from each bench was a small solid table that allowed repairmen to do some of their work while sitting. Eleven men in grey overalls fiddled with tabulators and chatted to their neighbours. Many talked more than working.

I stood ignored just inside the door. As civilian workshops go, it was unusually tidy. A middle-aged man approached me from an office built into the back wall. The first things I noticed after his modest height and unhurried walk, were wiry eyebrows that merged over a boxer's nose. When he turned his head, there was a cauliflower ear. He wore a dust-coat that was a distinctive dark brown, a colour the firm reserved for foremen. He introduced himself as Joseph without removing or steadying his lit pipe. While his Irish speech was slow, he soon got to the point.

"You see that empty bench? The tabulator on it has a fault. I'm going to time you to see how long it takes you to fix it."

My heart sank. I had not seen this model before and it was larger than anything I had tackled before.

"If you need tools that aren't there, shout. I'll be in my office."

As the bench height was awkward, I placed the machine on the table, disassembled and placed the parts in order until I found a cog with a bent tooth. I took it to Joseph. He disappeared through a door next to his office that provided a glimpse of the end of the assembly line. Fifteen minutes later he came back cursing the storeman who had kept him waiting. I fitted the replacement that he provided, reassembled, tested and then reported that the tabulator was working. Joseph checked yet still looked unsure.

He led the way to the Unit's tea room adjoining his office, said to make a pot for two and left me worrying about what had displeased him. Five minutes later he returned and sat at a table. I poured, sugared and stirred both teas while he refilled his pipe.

"Perry, I'll be frank with you. You've done very well, but if you're going to fit in here you can't show people up."

Without the pipe clamped in his mouth, I saw that the edges of his teeth were black from tobacco.

"I don't understand"

"If we take out the time waiting for the part, you fixed the bugger in under half an hour. If management finds out a complete beginner can do that, what are they going to expect from people familiar with the model? Believe me, you'll have a much easier ride with the other fellows if we say you took 65 minutes. That will still get you the job."

I stopped myself from saying that I could have worked even faster had I been wearing overalls. This was a job I wanted. The modern look of the workshop and its tidiness appealed to me. After my initial nerves, I had enjoyed the challenge of the machine's complexity. The last thing I wanted was to invite resentment from workmates or appear cocky to the foreman.

" I don't have a problem with 65 minutes if it gets me started here."

He had lit his pipe and it wagged in the corner of his mouth as he spoke between sucks to keep it burning. "I can see we'll get along famously. Besides, I imagine you'll want overtime as much as the others. They don't give us the overtime unless the jobs are piled up."

We did get on well. It was a great relief to have the equivalent of the sergeant in my new workplace on my side or at least not against me when other repairmen threw their weight around. Half of the team could not resist at least an occasional jibe at my height and most scoffed at joining the Army to service typewriters. All bar one had either fought or been trained to serve in more warlike roles.

Simon, a few years older than me, was the only repairman who had not been in one of the services. He had a sense of humour that did not involve mocking someone who was present. What he most enjoyed was repeating salacious stories from the Sunday papers or gossip about famous people that had not appeared in the press. He often came to watch me work and, to begin with, made suggestions.

On my second Thursday he said, "You've got a knack for this kind of work. I used to fix typewriters and they're not that similar."

"My Dad's a toolmaker. He got me started early on fixing stuff."

"My old man's a merchant banker, but I don't have any money. No disrespect to your old man, but you're not taking enough credit for your skill."

Anyone would have known from our accents that we were both working class Londoners. Nor did his appearance suggest a wealthy background. He looked ill-fed, something his above average height suggested was recent. A neater version of the standard Teddy boy quiff and duck's arse topped his long head and pale face. Most of his tiny waist lurked behind an oversize belt buckle and what would have been drainpipes on most other men, flapped around his legs. He was the only member of the repair crew who never wore a tie.

"Which bank is your Dad with?"

"Are you having me on? It's rhyming slang. If you must know, he works on the docks, or did when I last saw him. Fancy a drink after work tomorrow?"

I was chuffed to be invited out at the end of my second week when I could count on one hand the number of times soldiers had asked me to join them in anything social.

Concerned about drinking on an empty stomach, I snacked on biscuits and crisps through the last part of the Friday afternoon. As we left, Simon surprised me by suggesting a pub he knew near Baker Street. I would have preferred one close to the factory or nearer to home, but acquiesced.

On the tube, I mentioned how I had sensed the men did not like Joseph.

"He came to England during the war. It was nearly all women in the factory then so after he'd got a bit of experience they made him the gaffer of the unit. The others reckon he should have given the job up when the servicemen came back. I've heard he made himself unpopular with the blokes because he wanted them to work flat-out like during the war, but they wore him down. He's just waiting for his gold watch and pension now."

"Simon says have a glass of Hock. Trust me, they do good wine here."

I had never drunk wine and to my surprise enjoyed the sweet slippery taste. The dry food eaten earlier made it easy to drink at the same rate as Simon. I soon bought another two glasses and within ninety minutes we were on our fifth round. Before then, I had never drunk more than a half pint of beer in an evening. Simon suggested going for a meal. Standing up brought home that I was tipsy.

The fresh air did not clear my head. He steadied me and kept an arm around my waist to lend support, or at least that is what I assumed until, as we were in the shadow between two street lights near an entrance to Regent's Park, his hand started to caress my side. I pulled away in panic. Then seeing how worried he looked, I guessed he was not going to try anything else. We continued to walk and only the gap between our shoulders might have suggested something had happened. To calm myself, I reviewed how his advances were different from the Owls. He was alone. He had never bullied me. We were in a street with other people, passing cars and houses. He was not strong enough to force me. And he was frightened of what I might say to others even though he had not got as far as getting his hand to touch my skin. Although these thoughts helped, I still felt panicky. Yet he was the nearest I had come to having a friend for a long time. Joseph was useful, but the interest he took in me was dictated by his job; he protected me at times to prevent me leaving. I did not want Simon to be as distant as the others in the workshop.

When I turned a corner, he followed me and said in a soft and anxious voice, "I'm sorry."

I kept looking ahead without acknowledgement.

"Is it just me or you don't generally?"

"I don't ever."

"Will you tell anyone?"

"Provided you don't try anything else."

This was an idle threat. I would never have gone to the police in case they suspected I was queer or they spoke with my parents who then began to have their doubts. And had I mentioned at work that Simon had groped me after we had gone for a drink, the other men in the unit would first have had hounded him from the company and then have teased me for attracting the attention of a homosexual.

"Thanks. Do you still want a meal? I'll pay."

The nervousness in his voice – I was still avoiding looking at him – led me to interpret the offer as an attempt to buy my silence. The sense of having power over another adult was novel and went to my head. I decided to make him wait for my answer by suddenly crossing a road. His footsteps told me that he was following. I began to see him paying for my meal as a kind of fine for his wrongdoing.

I slowed and he drew level. "If there's no more funny business, we can have a meal."

"Simon says let's have Chinese."

While I wanted no more alcohol, he consumed several lagers and became garrulous in a camp voice never heard at work. I was grateful that we occupied an isolated table tucked under the stairs and that the waiter's limited English meant he had struggled to understand our orders until we pointed to numbers on the menu. I thought Simon was mad to risk telling a relative stranger what he did, much of which disgusted me. Yet I did not ask him to cease because he described a world I knew almost nothing about.

His family had disowned him after his arrest at the age of eighteen in the gents at Paddington Station. He then had moved to digs near Finchley Road in a large house where all the men and the landlord were homosexual. One of the occupants had advised him avoid the call-up by acknowledging that he was homosexual and acting as camp as he could without laughing.

Simon said that in every large workplace men met for sex in a storeroom or toilet. Although they didn't want to be caught, the risk could add to their excitement. Outside of work, he had some lovers he returned to, but what he most enjoyed was the thrill of the chase. At times, he went either alone or with others to Hampstead Heath to look for new partners. Often he went on the Heath after drinking at a pub he called the *King Willy,* which was the source of much of his gossip as some famous men frequented it. He named several actors and a member of the House of Lords whom he often chatted with.

"What do you call him?"

"Everyone at the King Willy calls him Gloria."

"Why?"

"It's a queer thing. Some of us like using a woman's name when were among friends. Some men like to call me Simone. It doesn't bother me. You can pull a face, Perry, but it's been going on since the Ark and disapproval hasn't made any difference. Imagine if someone said to you, forget about girls, just have a cold shower instead. Could you turn off your sex drive like a switch? Well, why should we?"

"There must be a good reason why the majority object?"

"The majority used to think slavery was OK."

"What about protecting boys from men?"

"All kids need protecting. I'm talking about what happens between adults. Being queer has got nothing to do with it. I was raped by two men when I was fourteen and I hate them for it. The only difference is, telling my parents or going to the police was out of the question, because they would have asked why I had gone to their flat in the first place."

I was on the verge of crying. "Can't we talk about something else."

Simon looked surprised and upset, but said, "Sure," and described his dad being approached by a toff at the docks who asked where the urinal was.

"He said, I dunno, what colour funnel has it got?"

A stream of silly jokes and stories followed that made the rest of my evening enjoyable.

After leaving the restaurant, the cold drizzle seemed to sober Simon. "Are you going to say anything to anyone about all this?"

"I want something in exchange for keeping quiet. Don't tell anyone at work that we had a meal together."

"Why not?"

"If others find out what you get up to, I don't want them thinking I'm the same."

He looked hurt, but said, "I understand."

"Some of the blokes already niggle me and I don't want to be the butt of jokes about being queer on top of everything else."

"I know what it's like to be made to feel unwelcome."

Simon continued to natter with me at work more than the other repairers did. I welcomed his chats, but not enough to initiate a conversation when he might be caught *in flagrante* with another employee. I went to tea breaks after the others and sat away from Simon whenever there was a choice.

Three weeks after our meal, he did not come to work on the Monday. Personnel told Joseph on the Wednesday that Simon was in hospital after a serious assault had left him in a coma. I waited for one of the other workers to suggest a visit, a card or clubbing together for flowers. By the end of the week, it was as if Simon was already forgotten.

I went to the hospital the next Saturday afternoon without telling anyone where I was going.

A middle-aged nurse looked at me disapprovingly. "You're his first visitor."

"What about his family?"

"I've heard they don't want to come."

She led me to where Simon lay with closed eyes and his head swathed in bandages.

"What happened?" I whispered to the nurse.

"He can't hear you. He was near dead by the time the ambulance arrived and he hasn't regained consciousness and might never do so. The police suspect that he and another man were attacked by a gang while up to something in the dark on Hampstead Heath. A dog walker found them unconscious early in the morning. The other man has gone to a private hospital. He was less injured and his family arranged it."

Her tone and taut face made me wonder if she had a grain of sympathy for Simon. I suspected that she had little time for homosexuals and assumed I too was a queer. Her prejudice made me uncomfortable, not least because Simon had suffered an extreme form of bullying that stemmed from intolerance and loathing. Although I had not persecuted him, his fear of being exposed had allowed me to dictate the nature of our relationship. After enjoying the meal that he had paid for, I had kept him at a distance, which had echoes of his family's rejection. Among the people who had known Simon, the only ones I felt superior to were the thugs who had left him unconscious. Had the criminals been identified, I would have pursued some form of vengeance against them regardless of any court-imposed sanctions.

Some Sunday papers carried news of the assault and hinted that such an attack was the result of the victims behaving as they did in a public place. An inspector appealed for witnesses in what he said the police had no choice but to treat as attempted murder. However, his hopes for a lead were very low because men on the Heath at that time of night were not likely to come forward. I could not bring myself to contact the police and tell them what Simon had said about others from his digs being homosexual or the names of the actor and peer Simon said he had spoken with at the King Willy. I pretended this was to protect the men from the law, but I was more worried about what the police might make of me having a meal with Simon and knowing about his private life.

On my third hospital visit, a kinder nurse said that the consultant did not expect Simon to emerge from his coma. I saw no point in continuing the distress of seeing him when he would never be aware of my presence. By this time, the other repairmen had concluded that Simon was a *nancy-boy*. One said that it was no skin off his nose if the fucker died and others agreed his sort had it coming to them. I kept quiet. With Simon gone, getting by in the workshop would be hard enough without inviting further abuse for expressing sympathy for a queer. And had I told my parents about Simon, they would have wondered what led me to take an interest in him. Already I felt awkward with them and others in our street because I had never had a girlfriend.

Union Comptometer managers seldom stayed long where they might get dirt on their suits or shoes. They had their own canteen, as if eating with the rank and file might contaminate them. Rather than visit the assemblers and repairers, bosses preferred to call overseers to the office block, a practice the foremen were reputed to exploit by passing off ideas from team members for increasing productivity as their own. True or not, the rumour led workers to withhold suggestions. The other repairmen insisted that Joseph had pilfered the recognition that was due to them for suggestions over the years, but no one cited a specific example and I never heard the allegations when the foreman or a manager was present. I did not defend Joseph, grateful though I was that he never humiliated me. To speak up for him would have encouraged others to mock me even more.

Joseph acknowledged on the quiet that my output was way above average and helped to fend off the questions management had about the unit's productivity. If I wanted to work faster, that was fine so long as I slowed down when bosses entered the workshop, so as not to show up the rest of the men.

Someone senior must have rumbled that our efficiency was deeply suspect because at the start of my fourth month a white-faced Joseph returned from a meeting with news that for the first time the firm was bringing in time and motion men and they would be starting in the Repair Unit. Two days later, he handed out brochures from the Tempus Consultancy written by Julian Tempus. If you believed the puff, Hitler would have triumphed and Britain's post-war export drive would have failed without the contribution of Julian to efficiency. A week after the brochures, Joseph warned his assembled team that Mr Myrer from Tempus would spend the next day observing us.

The foreman took me aside and wagged the stem of his pipe. "Perry, me old China, if this boffin sees you working at your usual rate, there'll be redundancies, never mind no overtime, and those remaining won't have time to wipe their sorry arses. Be a good lad. Just work at a third of your normal speed, but make it look cautious, not lazy."

He brought Myrer to me the next morning and settled him into the workshop's only unstained chair. Anthony Myrer was not much older than me, very tall, had large gleaming teeth and was brimful of confidence in a well-tailored suit.

"Perry's still learning the ropes. I thought he'd be a good place for you to start as he goes a bit slower than the old hands."

I had fashioned a wooden platform to make working at the bench more comfortable, but to accommodate the visitor I lifted the machine that I was working on over to the table.

He sat alongside me with a clipboard on his knees. "Just carry on as normal, Gray."

From this I guessed Anthony had spent most of his National Service as an officer.

I wielded tools like unstable explosives and gawped at the mechanisms as if they were as alien to me as hieroglyphics. After a few minutes, a suppressed yawn and glazed eyes established that he had no inherent interest in machinery, which in turn suggested he had few clues for determining how long a technical task should take.

Without stopping work, I said, "Excuse me for asking, sir, are you an engineer?"

"Good God, no. I studied classics at Durham. Why do you ask?"

"Well, with respect, how do you assess work like this?"

Myrer bristled despite my deference. Part of what he prattled came from the Tempus brochure, as if he assumed I could not read. It was my turn to suppress yawns. His concluding remarks, however, grabbed my attention.

"What you don't understand is that a new pair of eyes sees things differently. Habitual responses prevent people from finding ways of working that are more efficient. I'm afraid you're limited by your outlook and habits. It takes a tall man to see over the elephant grass."

His volume had climbed and he glanced around to see how many men had heard the witticism. He was like the jumped-up soldiers who had used their rank to make jokes at my expense. I seethed to see others smiling just like the privates from Hut D3 who had laughed at every belittlement.

And yet the way he had spoken as if I was a cretin made me eager to demonstrate intelligence. I spoke quietly so as not to upset the others.

"I came here four months ago with a new pair of eyes. I've seen that the unit spends over half its time on machines that have just come off the production line, but no one keeps records of the faults we find, so we just keep fixing the same problems. I've seen delays, because stores are ordered after they run out. Sometimes the storeman has to collect rather than wait for a delivery. When he isn't in the stockroom, people take what they like without recording. Next thing you know, another item is short and the stockman has to go out again. It's a vicious circle."

Myrer said, "Anything else?"

I thought, Fuck you. I'm not letting you have more ideas to present as your own. In fact, watch out because you've joined my list.

Besides, some of the men were craning. I might get away with criticising the production line and stores, but my colleagues would have made life intolerable for any hint at their indolence.

"I don't get paid to think, do I? I'm just meant to struggle through the elephant grass. Anyway, I can't talk all day, I'll get behind with my work."

While Myrer remained in the workshop, I had to keep dawdling in case he noticed any change in pace. The slow pace of the rest of the morning gave me time to think about how I might get even. At lunchtime, I put the leaflet about Tempus in my jacket pocket and walked to a phone box near the factory gates.

A cut-glass female voice said, "Tempus Consultancy. How may I help you?"

I put on an accent that owed something to a camp character from a radio comedy and something to Simon when drunk.

"Is Tony there?"

"We don't have anyone with that name."

"Oh, I think you do. I met him a few nights ago. Lovely man. Very tall. Big white teeth. Quite a looker with his blonde hair."

"Do you mean Mr Anthony Myrer?"

"He didn't tell me his last name. He just said to ask for Tony when we met on Hampstead Heath. Anyway, can I speak to him?"

"I'm afraid Mr Myrer is out of the office."

"That's a shame. What time will he be back?"

"I'm sorry, but he's out all day."

"You're sorry! I think he's standing there now and telling you to get rid of me. Typical. Thinks he's so good looking he can do what he likes with my feelings."

After a long silence the woman said, "I'm afraid Mr Myrer really is out. He's on an assignment for two days. May I take a message? He may call later this afternoon."

"I suppose so. Tell him Persephone called and I'll be at the King Willy on Friday night, if he can be bothered."

"Excuse me, did you say Persephone?"

"That's right, as in Queen of the Underworld." I stressed queen.

"Is that your surname?"

"No, it's the name he wanted to call me. Tony said he's studied classics and wanted me to use a Greek name."

At home that evening, I typed out a letter on bond paper.

Dear Mr Tempus,

For reasons that I cannot go into I am using a pen name. What I will tell you is that I run a sizable business and we have met. In fact, your insights and methods were very helpful to us during the war. I wish to return the favour.

I learned by chance that Anthony Myrer has joined your firm.

A young man known to my family was at Durham University at the same time as your employee. He insists that there was a scandal with Myrer at its centre towards the end of his last year. To protect its name, the University did not involve the police and allowed the men involved to graduate.

Let's just say, if I had a young son, I would not want him left alone with Mr Myrer. Studying classics is all very well, but there are certain Greek practices that no decent person wants to see revived.

Please forgive the nature of my contact, but I hope a friend would alert me if I inadvertently employed someone who might damage the reputation of my business.

Mr Vitallium

A week after posting this from Knightsbridge, I rang the Tempus office and asked in a different voice for Mr Myrer.

"Mr Myrer is not with us anymore."

"But he asked me to ring only last week."

"I do apologise, but he had to leave rather suddenly. Can I be of assistance?"

"Had to leave?"

"I mean that he left at short notice." And even more flustered, the receptionist added, "Personal reasons. I'm not sure of the details. Is there anyone else you wish to speak to?"

I was delighted with the receptionist's indiscretion about the manner of Myrer's leaving and the success gave renewed impetus to the urge to settle older scores. But how could I locate the unpunished without access to their army files?

Joseph announced that he would be retiring to Cork shortly after my sixth month would end. If management had any sense, they would replace him with a foreman willing to sort out productivity and half the team would disappear. Any sane business would want to keep the most productive workers, but shop stewards would insist on *last in, first out*. In any case, the repair work had become familiar, I disliked almost all the other repair workers and it would be better to create some distance before targeting the most insulting of them.

A vacancy for a technician in the Comptometer Research and Development Unit, which spoke of varied duties, appeared in the canteen the week after personnel confirmed the end of the probationary period. CRADU, as the unit was known, occupied three linked prefabs on what had been the firm's sports field until the war. Rows of cars separated the prefabs from the more solid buildings, adding to CRADU's sense of isolation and specialness.

The CRADU manager, whose gentle manners greatly appealed to me, offered the post after a brief interview and a test that involved soldering resistors onto a circuit board to test manual dexterity. As the Unit's technician, I set up test systems that often needed items adapting or I fashioned parts from materials such as plywood and aluminium. I especially enjoyed helping to take apart and identify the innovations in the latest machines of rival companies. On occasions, I asked Dad for his advice or took home work, such as designing a gear train that benefitted from his level of skill and experience. Working together on small components made clear that his eyes were fading. I also noticed that a task such as sawing through metal had begun to tire him. I told Mum about Dad's sight and she made sure he got spectacles, but there was no easy remedy for the rest of his ageing. In the shed, I suggested he lose weight.

"I don't drink or smoke and you want me to starve myself?

"I want you to live to enjoy your retirement."

"I wouldn't know what to do if I didn't go to work."

"You sound like you want to die in harness."

"It doesn't sound bad to me when I never had the chance to die with my boots on."

"You mean not wearing uniform?"

"C'mon. Let's finish drilling. Your Mum's got roast hearts and roly-poly in the oven."

The CRADU boss made a point of mentioning the contributions of team members to the senior managers who took an interest in our work and often told them in my hearing that I had been a lucky find. He cited the way I contributed ideas as well realising the plans of others. As much I enjoyed the praise, I was even more grateful to the boss for the pleasant working environment that he had fostered. No one used unwelcome nicknames or harsh put-downs despite the rivalry. Half of the team were young graduates keen to make their mark and who might have failed to collaborate and descended into backbiting without a talented leader.

Our boss disliked the idea of separate canteens for different grades and encouraged his team to eat together in the CRADU meeting room, which had a small kitchen area. People brought food from home, some of which was shared. The conversations during breaks added to the team spirit and my education. I began to read novels, see foreign films and attended as part of team outings a classical concert and a jazz club.

Once a fortnight, we met to review a project. The manager insisted that good ideas can come from anyone and his secretary and I – the only non-graduates – also attended. It was largely due to his influence that the few women in the team felt so at ease. Between the project reviews was another meeting for the whole team at which one of the Unit or someone from another part of the company gave a presentation. I learned about such things as the science behind transistors, new alloys, the design of the Babbage Engine and the properties of Mylar.

Union Comptometers was building computers at a new complex in Uxbridge and during a presentation on storing data by an electronic engineer, I realised the opportunities for revenge that I had missed by ignoring the automation of the Army's payroll. I could have kicked myself. Lieutenant Rilling would have welcomed me assisting his team rather than servicing typewriters. And I was sure that his major would not have objected had the request come from me.

The way forward for vengeance was clear, but how best to gain access to the mounds of electronic data that existed and would grow exponentially, according to the speaker? At the same time, I was reluctant to leave a happy team and satisfying work.

January 1963 was unusually cold. One morning, the frost was so severe that Dad could not start his car after several minutes of turning the crank handle. I had already left for work and was not there to help him. While waiting in an arctic wind for a bus, no doubt fuming about being late for the first time in his life, his heart gave out. A doctor insisted it would have been over in seconds, but the idea of him falling haunted me. For many weeks, I could not stop the movie of him sprawled alone in agony on filthy slush with the bitter damp penetrating his clothes and an icy kerbstone for a pillow.

Mum was quiet and passive at first, apart from insisting on an Anglican funeral.

"If it's what you want. But why when Dad and you rejected religion?"

"What would people think if there was no minister? It wouldn't be proper."

I did not question further as a church service offered her a speck of comfort and made no difference to me.

After the funeral, Mum spent three weeks mostly sitting and staring at the blank television screen or shut in the bedroom she now had to herself. Then she began cleaning the house from top to bottom. She moved so quickly that she knocked things over and sometimes broke things in a way never witnessed before. I suggested at various times that she go out, invite some of her friends around or see the doctor. She nodded without committing herself.

I came back from work one night and she was sitting in her hat and coat.

"Have you been out?"

"I'm going out. I wanted to know if you'd come with me?"

"Where to?"

"To see a medium."

"If that's what you want, let's go."

"I don't know what I want. I don't really believe in it any more. But I so miss him."

"If you're not sure, you could wait a bit longer."

"Yes, I'll wait."

"Let me know when you're ready. I'm not having you go alone."

I feared Mum was ripe for exploitation and dreaded her falling prey as she had to the Newelms. To my great relief, she never mentioned going to see a medium again and slowed to her former pace after a few more months. Then she acquired a new pastime. One of the women in the street most admired by Mum, because the husband had risen from conductor to manager of a bus garage, persuaded her to go to bingo for an afternoon. This became a major social outlet and I was delighted. For relatively little money, she made many new friends, got away from what could only remind her of Dad, and eased her grief for a few hours. On the few occasions that I said I would be home late, Mum got a lift to the bingo hall and enjoyed an evening out just as much as the afternoons.

When I invited her to go regularly at night, she said, "Oh no. I couldn't. I've always put dinner on the table for men coming home from work."

"You could leave it in the oven or I could heat it up."

"It wouldn't be right."

"What if you invited some of your friends here. You could play cards."

"No. I can't invite people around when you need to put your feet up after a hard day's work."

Her other main form of relaxation was television. I tended not to watch the dramas that she most liked. In any case, I had things to do in the shed and books to read upstairs. When it came to providing company for Mum, our interests were different and I kept as much of my thinking and feelings from her as she did from me. I shared only the good news, such as the former repair colleague whose wife had a baby. I never let on that the same man had continued his name calling whenever he saw me at work or that the couple had split up a few months after his wife received an anonymous letter about an affair with a woman employed at his workplace.

On the few occasions that I went out on a Friday or Saturday night, Mum would fish for information. I told her about the CRADU annual dinners and outings, but I kept her guessing about much else.

"You look very smart, Perry. Where was it you said you were going?"

"I don't think I did. I'll just catch a bus into Harrow and see what I see."

Sometimes I said that, walked to a local pub and had a few drinks with people twice my age. In a way, I preferred the company of older people there. When I chatted with lads I had gone to school with, they were married and had children, or at the least had a regular girlfriend. The older people were married and parents, but being an unattached bachelor felt less of an issue for me with them.

Given how little I did for Mum, it seemed only right that she went out more. To get her to play bingo at night on a regular basis, I signed up for two evening classes in central London. When these courses in programming concluded, I found other ones that extended my knowledge of computing. Posts in Uxbridge, an easy journey from Rayners Lane, that might use my new skills, appeared on the CRADU notice boards, but I had taken a shine to one of my colleagues.

Róisín, a petite graduate in metallurgy, joined CRADU six months after me. Her parents were from County Clare, but she had only visited Ireland for holidays. Some say Irish hair as jet black as hers comes from Spanish sailors washed ashore from the wrecked Armada. If that is so, how does one account for her fine white skin and cobalt eyes?

While Róisín was shy with strangers, she liked to chat provided someone else initiated and nothing vulgar or irreligious was said. If asked, she shared that much of her life outside work revolved around the Catholic Church. Her religiosity was not a positive as far as I was concerned, but what she had in spades that was far more important was trustworthiness. For even though I never considered telling her any secrets, there had been no one since Tilda that I felt more at ease with. I never sensed that she had more regard for me than most other colleagues, but seeing and hearing her every working day prompted fantasies of going out with her and getting engaged.

One Saturday while I was mending the washing machine at home, my thoughts about Róisín became erotic. I found relief in the toilet, but disliked the way I had used images of her. The conclusion seemed obvious; if we were married there would be no need for grubby daydreams. The question that then dominated my waking hours was whether I could find the courage to woo her?

To begin with, I doubted that I was a fit person for her to know more intimately. Even before the Army, I had worried that I might not be adequate as a lover; that even someone as sweet and diminutive as Róisín might find my manhood disappointing. After Gatgash, I also felt polluted and unworthy of one so pure.

The next weekend, having got tired of the arguments going around my head, I resolved to tell Róisín that I wanted to marry her. It did not occur to me to suggest inviting her on a date in order to find out more about her feelings towards me. I assumed the main barrier would be that I was not a Catholic and was all set to promise to convert.

I arrived at work thirty minutes early in the hope of a chance to speak to Róisín alone. However, as soon as she arrived she asked the manager if she could speak with him and closed his door behind her. By the time she emerged, every other room was occupied. My proposal would have to wait. Róisín put her coat on at 11.40, slipped away and brought back boxes of cakes just as rest of us assembled for lunch. The manager announced that she had something to tell us.

In her quiet voice she said, "Some of you know that I went on a retreat last month. It helped me decide a big question. I want to share the answer with you. This morning I gave in my notice. I'll leaving here in a month's time to join a convent as a postulant."

The secretary asked, "What's a postulant?"

The manager's answer confirmed my fears. "It's an apprentice nun."

The secretary and another woman graduate hugged Róisín and even the team's outspoken atheist lined up to shake her hand. I went through the motions of congratulating, but shock prevented me from thinking about her feelings and future. Had I proposed that morning, how ridiculous I would have looked! Apart from my mother, I knew Róisín as well as any adult woman, yet I did not know her at all.

By the end of that evening the whole painful business led me to decide I would never risk making such a fool of myself again. A life of celibacy was the only way to avoid the same sort of mental havoc over another woman. My vow brought no sleep, as I was too full of regret. And there were other nights when I considered I was asking too much of myself. But in the end, I got used to the idea of never making love to a woman. I might dance or hold hands in the pictures, but I would never seek more than a chaste kiss.

Chapter 25: Norman ~ Meeting Rose

Some speak of the sixties as if the decade swept along the majority of those under twenty-five. In fact, a few who dared to be different got a lot of publicity and the bulk of young people took from the zeitgeist little more than changes to clothes, hairstyles and musical tastes. Once I felt secure in my post-army job, I let my locks grow a little longer to make less obvious my ears and nascent baldness, but continued to dress much as I had before conscription. Swinging London might have been a world away rather than a mere dozen miles from Croydon other than the feeling, which many shared, that most other young people were having a lot more fun.

Pictures of Perry taken in that decade show him shorthaired, without any of the fashions spawned at the time and always wearing a tie. Nothing I have seen or heard suggests he altered his lifestyle after returning to civilian life. When religious beliefs did not impede Perry and me, what prevented us from enjoying the liberation and excess that existed for some of our generation? National Service consumed energy that otherwise might have fuelled protest and, overall, the services promote traditional values. Yet some conscripted lads lapped up the freedom, if not indulgence, in the years that followed their stint in uniform. Bill Wyman of the Rolling Stones had completed three years in the RAF before I went to Gatgash.

Like Perry, I returned from the Army to a staid home. If my uncle had a gay sex life, he was discreet. The only suggestion I heard relating to it came from Probett's Print and that was probably spiteful speculation. As Ed's wealth increased he joined the Masons, Rotary, a prestigious golf club and the Tory Party. Once ensconced at the Conservative Club, he favoured its right-winger demagogues. None of this bothered my mother and I kept my reservations to myself apart from once, after Ed had plied me with Scotch. I pointed out that his antipathy to drugs did not prevent him investing in alcohol and tobacco companies.

"There's nothing illegal in that."
"What about the principle?"

"Booze and fags don't promote rebellion. In fact, there'd be a bloody revolution if we tried to ban them."

While I became curious about drugs, or at least marijuana, no one offered anything to me. If they had, I would have been too afraid of the law, losing my job and hurting the feelings of my mother. By the time courage outweighed inhibition, who would have thought to share a joint with an old fogey?

Height also constrained my social outlook, though I accept some men of a similar size are radical and extrovert. The degree of self-consciousness that Perry and I shared meant that we preferred dependable people and milieus. A key difference between us was the friendship David Stancher provided because the nearest Perry came to such a pal was Simon, whose life was all too soon extinguished.

David, unlike Simon, reinforced the social values of my upbringing. His faith was so traditional that one of his girlfriends, after a Babycham too many, cried on my shoulder about his insistence on chastity even after she had managed to obtain the pill by pretending to be married. The most exotic thing about David was the way he bothered about an unyielding atheist. Had he been asked why and answered honestly, he would have said that it was his Christian duty to care and that decent people don't drop friends simply because they have met others who are more interesting, better connected or less neurotic.

David and I studied Russian Radio Voice Intercept after Crail. Then the Signals left us kicking our heels for six weeks at the Intelligence Corps depot at Maresfield, a slum of a camp, in Sussex waiting for postings. David volunteered to help a padre and disappeared for much of the time. The idleness at Maresfield and the aggressiveness of some NCOs heard in the distance, which evoked memories of the brutes at Gatgash, made me anxious and prompted two consecutive nights of bad dreams. To distract and tire myself, I read and re-read Russian books and conversed with anyone fluent for as long as they would tolerate.

We had expected assignments to a routine listening mill in Germany. Instead, David and I ended up in an ultra-secret unit in East Anglia where I was fortunate to find a corporal from an émigré family. He delighted in coaching me to distinguish regional accents and first languages; many of the Soviet forces had not started to learn Russian until school. Before the corporal left the Army, he made the officers aware of how much my language skills had developed. As a result, I took over his role transcribing tapes that other monitors had difficulty understanding. Radio interference degraded the clarity of some, while in others people with an unusual dialect or speaking Russian as a second language made comprehension more difficult.

David quickly became involved in local sports and the only nearby church, which was Anglican. He reported that the choirmaster was talented and the standard of the music very high. When I said how much I missed singing, he facilitated my joining the choir. I am sure if anyone had asked David if I was a devout Christian, he would not have lied. Fortunately, no one asked him or me. With our CO a regular at the church, NCOs gritted their teeth and juggled rotas to ensure my attendance at every sung service, practice and even for the weddings that the choir supported for a fee.

David also invited me to social activities that often were linked to his sporting pursuits. I readily accepted the offers of home cooked meals and usually declined anything that involved dancing. When I did go to dances, I was a wallflower and felt shy with the women David introduced. It was easier watching from a distance as they hovered around him rather than engaging in small talk.

Gatgash had taught me to hate exercise and David undid that by getting me to run with him. "Think of it as a country walk speeded up."

We went no further than I wanted and at a pace that allowed us to chat. Then he escorted me back before he completed many more miles at a greater speed. And after an exercise room was set up in a Nissan hut, David introduced me to weight training. I continued to rely largely on study and reading novels in Russian for the exhaustion that helped sleep, but sometimes shift working or the strain of transcribing made physical exertion preferable.

While most conscripts were keen to say goodbye to uniforms and discipline, David applied to join the Metropolitan Police. At about the same time, a lieutenant and then the CO tried to tempt me to stay on by offering to make me a corporal. Nothing would have induced me to remain, even though I had no firm ideas for civilian life. Then in my second to last week, I received an order to report to the CO's office. The sergeant who announced this was the most officious NCO at the post. His sudden arrival and escorting me at the double had me fearing a charge.

My mental racking about what I might have done wrong preoccupied me and I was slow to realise that the thin face and Roman nose of the man behind the desk was familiar. He was a tall captain in his mid-twenties with dark hair that was long enough for the brilliantine to struggle to control his curls. The pale blue eyes conveyed an air of indifference; not boredom and not coldness, but a kind of lethargy that is reluctant to acknowledge surprise. He gave the impression that he would not have blinked had I begun a Cossack dance while claiming to be the son of Khrushchev. But he was not anyone I had seen before in uniform.

"Thank you sergeant. You can go now."

"I'm Captain Bligh."

After the door had clicked shut, he said, "Take a seat. I'm having a whisky. Do join me."

I found myself shouting, "Thank you, Sir".

"Let's dispense with the formalities and go back to being Norman and Grenville."

Then I realised it was Grenville Bligh, son of the former owner of the Eflinwood Colliery. He had come across me with my father when I was twelve and we were on our way to watch badgers one summer evening. Once he knew where we were going, he asked if he could come and spent an hour or so at the set. On the way back, he talked about how he missed the countryside while he was at Harrow School. The way he described it, I pictured an old building with a cricket pitch surrounded by endless small houses on a treeless plain.

To compensate for yelling, which seemed inappropriate given his low-key drawl and request for informality, I tried to make my perching on the seat less militaristic. Two possibilities crossed my mind: either the captain brought bad news from home or he wanted a favour. If the latter, the drink suggested any volunteering would be for something highly unpleasant, if not dangerous.

He took a bottle of Vat 69 and two glasses from the filing cabinet, poured and walked around the desk to hand me one.

"Cheers. I've been making some enquiries. Your work here is highly regarded. If your officers had a way of making you stay on, they would. Just as important, we know your family are politically reliable. My father was jolly impressed by your father. Can't have been easy for him when most miners are pretty bolshie."

The maritime significance of Captain Bligh then dawned on me. I felt decidedly dull-witted.

"We also know that the firm you worked for is decidedly non-union and the CO said you're a regular church goer. I chatted with the vicar who said you've been a brick and he'll be sorry to lose a good tenor. Were you planning to go back to accounts work?"

I had spoken with the vicar without discussing religion and David had not mentioned my atheism to anyone else because he knew that I preferred to keep quiet about such matters. I imagine the vicar assumed that, like my friend, I did not take communion because I was from another denomination.

The law said that I could have my old job, but if Gerald Probett did not want me, he would have found a way of circumventing it. In any case, I wanted to earn more, have better career opportunities and a much pleasanter working environment. Yet knowing what I did not want to repeat did not suggest what I could do.

"To be honest, I'm not sure about work. It's only recently I've realised that my training doesn't really lead anywhere in Civvy Street."

Bligh replaced his indifference with a widening of the eyes. "On the contrary, I'm here to make you an offer because of that training and what you've done to add to your Russian. Similar class of work, but far more congenial arrangements. No saluting or mindless drill. Based in London, convivial if somewhat Dickensian offices. More money than I expect you would make elsewhere, a civil service pension and further down the line there could be opportunities to travel. I can't say too much till you've signed up, but I'll try to answer questions."

Despite looking rather soft for a young man in uniform, he showed no signs of struggling with neat spirits the way I did. I took tiny sips while I wondered what might be involved.

"Is it risky, sir? I mean, are we talking about working behind the Iron Curtain?"

"Good gracious, no. You know too much already to have you plopped where Mr Bear could get his paws on you. The only Soviet risk would be if the KGB knew of your role. Then they might be tempted to blackmail you. You know the kind of thing, beautiful woman beds you and snaps taken. But if you're discreet and steer clear of Mata Haris, then you face more danger crossing the road."

"Could you say a bit more about the kind of outfit it is?"

"Let me explain with what sometimes happens in industry. If you have all your best engineers working flat out on the production line, they will come up with the odd improvement, but don't have time to redesign the whole shebang or invent new widgets. So companies put together a squad to keep abreast of science and new technology. The boffins conduct research and build prototypes for possible new products, or look for radically better ways of manufacturing the product. Now imagine that applied to cloaks and daggers."

"So they don't deal directly with intelligence, but find solutions that others can use?"

"That's the idea. In practice, if the building is on fire then it's all hands to the pump."

"I'm not a scientist."

"No, but you could scan and translate science journals and technical bumf. That's where you'd start. The rest of your career would be up to you."

After I had signed the documents he had brought, Bligh said to tell others that I would be a computer programmer at the Centre for Advanced Research and Evaluation, thanks to an old family friend.

"But what do I tell my family?"

"That's exactly the kind of awareness we want from you. Tell them you bumped into my father and he put you up for it."

Having time on my hands during the ten days I spent at home before starting at CARE made me so uneasy that I went to London to look for second-hand Russian novels in Charing Cross Road. I discussed buying and returning books with a proprietor who offered to refund seventy per cent of the purchase provided their condition had not deteriorated.

On the Saturday that I returned the first three books, a stunning young woman was behind the counter with a smile for every customer. I envied the man who had placed the wedding band on her hand and assumed he too was attractive in every way. Regular customers called her Rose and from overhearing their dealings with her it was soon apparent that she read as well sold books.

I spent time in the bookshop almost every second Saturday and the more I saw and heard Rose the more smitten I became. The shop could be busy, yet she was always courteous. If there was time, she went out of her way to be helpful. I especially liked it when she emerged from the counter, stood on the mobile steps and stretched to reach the top shelf. I could not stop admiring what could be seen of her legs or fantasising about the rest of their shape and where her inner thighs ended. She almost slipped once and, until she caught a shelf, she looked about to fly like Eros in Piccadilly. I bought books in English just to stand closer while asking for her help.

Unlike the smattering of women at my new place of work, Rose's accent was familiar. There any similarity between us ended. Compared to me at that age she sounded confident, mature and, if the situation called for it, could be playful. When customers bantered or flirted, Rose gave as good as she got.

In one exchange, I witnessed a *roué* old enough to be her grandfather commenting on a pair of Morocco bound volumes she was inserting into a lockable glass cabinet behind the counter.

"What a splendid pair you have there, Rose."

His fruity tone made it clear that he was alluding to her breasts, which were obvious even when Rose wore loose clothes. On that day she had on a twin set that did nothing to ease my blushing at the double-entendre. Nor did her reply.

"Aren't they, Frank. It must be very frustrating for you that they're in mint condition and priced well out of your league. Still, there's always the bargain bins across the road that anyone can rummage in." She looked towards Soho with its prostitutes.

My mother would have thought the retort was vulgar. I envied the panache with which Rose was saucy. It signalled, quite accurately as it turned out, that she was comfortable with sexuality. Yet for all that she attracted me, Rose might as well have been standing on Nelson's column in terms of attainability.

Compared to making sense of Russian mixed with static or thickened by an Uzbek accent, my new job translating printed text was undemanding. Yet I was far from bored. Part of each week was spent consulting textbooks in English that deepened my knowledge of science, mathematics and technology and sometimes I met with vetted academics and engineers to check on details and nuances. The least welcome aspect of the job was crossing the metropolis to Enfield, which like Croydon was on London's outer rim. CARE's base was to the north of the capital, while my home was to the south. While travelling along the spokes that convey trains to and from the hub of the city, I read. On one journey, a fellow commuter, a man born in Krakow, struck up a conversation about my copy of *The Heart of Darkness*. He spoke of how many writers from his country were virtually unknown in England. I also learned that he was using his commuting to learn Spanish, having already mastered other languages during his journeys. He inspired me to teach myself to read Polish because the work of CARE included Polish texts and I already knew one Slavic language. My spoken Polish was never elegant, but that was no barrier to enjoying the extensive literature.

Rose noticed that I had stopped buying books in Russian and when I brought back the first Polish novels she asked where I was studying.

"Actually, I've taught myself Polish."

"You're not just trying to impress me?"

When I was with an attractive woman, often my tongue got tangled. That day was different, although my voice was quieter and higher pitched than I would have liked.

"I can see why men want to impress you, but I have a long journey to work and learning Polish helps to pass the time. I can't speak it so well, but reading isn't a problem now apart from the odd word."

She looked sceptical and, as no other customers were waiting, she pointed to one of the books. "What's *Bunt* about then?"

"It's rather like Animal Farm in that an animal revolt to obtain equality ends in a bloodbath. But Reymont died in 1924, not long after winning the Nobel Prize for Literature, so he was two decades ahead of Orwell."

"I'm beginning to believe you. Hats off for teaching yourself a language."

The cockles of my heart could have boiled a large kettle.

The next week I attended a seminar in Whitehall. During the lunch break, I almost ran to the bookshop only to find Rose was not there. I browsed for ten minutes and when she did not appear, I feared that she had left the job.

I took a book to the counter. "Where's Rose?"

The proprietor looked as if he had heard this question twenty times already that day. "Rose only works on Saturdays."

"Oh!" I said, rather than ask the question that filled my head - What does she do the rest of the time?

Every spare minute before the next Saturday, I studied the Polish novel bought from the proprietor and the one Rose had sold me. If she asked me about either book, I wanted to be able to answer any question. Instead of staying in bed till ten as I usually did at the weekend, I was out of the house by eight-thirty. I raced up the escalator at Leicester Square Station and all but jogged to the bookshop. I walked past the window several times until Rose, too busy to look outside, came into view. I gazed until she moved out of sight and then walked for over an hour around the West End deciding what to do.

I said to myself, She's a married woman. What do I think I'm doing? And why would she be interested in me anyway?

I went inside still undecided. We exchanged smiles. I found a book and waited until no other customer was near the counter.

"Hello, Norman. We don't usually see you two Saturdays in a row."

That she recalled our last meeting took me to cloud level.

"Actually, Rose, I was also here on Tuesday. What do you do during the week?"

Her smile flickered and she spoke less confidently. "I've got a four year old. His Nan looks after Colin on Saturday so I can work here."

Rose looked undecided, touched her wedding ring and then twisted it. "What about you, any children?"

"I'm not married."

"That doesn't stop some."

"I guess it doesn't, but it's better for kids when they have proper parents." Her smile faded. "I'm sorry if I've said something to upset you. Dad died when I was fifteen. My mother is great, but it's not the same as having two parents."

"It wasn't you who upset me. I wish Colin still had a dad."

I could not imagine anything other than death separating a man from Rose. "Is he dead?"

"He's gone away and we're getting divorced."

I was too stunned to say more than, "Oh!"

"You look rather pleased." She had a broad smile. "I thought you wanted kids to have proper parents?"

"Do you get a lunch break?"

"A sandwich in the backroom when it's not too busy. I finish at six. You could travel back to Finchley with me. If my Mum's in a good mood, she'll look after Colin and we could go for a drink."

As I mooched around central London for the rest of the day, it was incredible that Rose had made going out with her so easy. Was she interested in me or just desperate? Yet how could anyone so attractive be desperate, even if she did have a child? But why else would she want to spend time with someone who had my looks?

Marie and I got on well from the start. She said to come back as late as we liked and had Colin whenever Rose and I wanted to go out. After two months, he started to stay overnight with his Nan twice a week while I shared Rose's bed. As soon as her divorce allowed, we were married in a Registry Office. Apart from my mother's disappointment that it was not a church wedding, I was full of happiness.

Chapter 26: Perry ~ Data Mining

The CRADU boss returned to the prefabs solemn-faced from a meeting for managers, gathered the team and announced that Union Comptometers was changing its name to U-Comp because the manufacture of tabulators would cease. The firm's decision to focus on expanding its range of computers meant that our unit was redundant and our prefabs would be allocated to a team of programmers.

A personnel officer reviewed work skills with me a few days later. "With your evening classes, you could stay in the prefabs at the same rate of pay. Depending on aptitude, your take home pay might double in a few years."

How quickly the atmosphere in the prefabs changed! My work earned respect, but not the person who did it. Provided we met deadlines and our code was free of errors, the boss sat aloof. Three young men, motivated in part envious by the bonuses my accurate output attracted, made frequent references to my height. I smiled weakly, desperately hoping that other colleagues would object. They either ignored the teasing or, more commonly, grinned at the jibes.

In particular, I hated Roger Noel, a lanky twenty-three year old with less sensitivity than a drunken elephant. Most knew him as Grassy, a ghoulish name that he was keen to encourage and explain.

"You know, President Kennedy. He got shot as he passed a grassy knoll in Dallas."

Besides leading the bullying, Roger disparaged my former manager and team as dodos. I soon learned to say nothing about the former occupants to him, but I was inclined to reminisce with less obnoxious programmers. Every so often Roger would overhear and express contempt at such nostalgia. His talk was often about girlfriends and sexual conquests and he encouraged the other young men to be just as bawdy. The few women who joined the team at intervals soon left and one who came for an interview turned around as soon as she saw the pin-ups covering a wall in the tea room.

Roger was curious about my life outside work, about which I said little. He began to quiz relentlessly, often appealing to others present to add to the pressure to disclose. The first January we worked together, he badgered me to admit that I had not gone out during the Christmas break.

"Haven't you got a girlfriend, Perry?"

"What's it to you?"

"We felt sorry for you staying at home on New Year's Eve, didn't we?"

With others looking interested, I wanted to curtail the topic. "There's no one special at the moment."

"Yeah, but is there anyone you've gone on a date with during the last twelve months?"

I panicked and invented. "There's a woman I go to bingo with sometimes."

"Bingo? You sure know how to show a girl a good time. What's her name?"

Yet more men looking at us ramped up my anxiety and queasiness

"Does it really matter?"

"Come on! What's the big secret? You're not making this up are you?"

"Tilda."

"As in waltzing Ma? Go on! What's this mother like?"

I imagined Tilda Kyte looking like her mother. "Blonde wavy hair and blue eyes."

"Yeah, but how tall is she?"

I could not bring myself to look around and see who was sniggering and how many simply sneered.

"She's a head taller than me, if you must know."

"Do you use the biscuit method then?"

I had no idea what he meant and no intention of taking it further, but one of his cronies said. "Go on, Grassy, tell us about the biscuit method."

Roger stood and simulated actions as he spoke. "It's a kind of contraception used when the woman's taller. The couple stand facing each other. Once the key's in the ignition, the guy lets his arms hang and the woman locks hers around him so he's pinned. When his knees begin to tremble she lets go and kicks away his biscuit tin."

His foot swung past my eyes. I loathed Roger for this and mocking Tilda. How stupid I had been to mention her name to someone bound to respond with the language of the gutter. I did not know how he would regret his insults, but my retaliation would be without mercy.

Roger was so mouthy that everyone in the team knew that he lived with two men of his own age in a ground floor flat within walking distance of Kilburn Station. I found the address and a phone number in his wallet, which he had left in his jacket on a chair. On most days, his bunch of keys sat on his desk after unlocking his drawer. I made impressions of all the keys that might be for entry to his flat, fashioned duplicates at home and compared them with the originals. The matches appeared satisfactory and I told the boss I would be taking leave the next day, a Friday, to see a dentist about a tooth that had kept me awake.

I rang Roger's flat just before leaving Rayners Lane Station at nine in the morning and again from Kilburn High Road. No one answered. His street consisted of Edwardian terraces on either side apart from a large post-war Council estate at one end. After pressing the three bells by his front door with a gloved finger and no one answering, I let myself into the foyer. The next lock, to his flat, turned after some jiggling.

Pictures from Kennedy's assassination identified Roger's bedroom. On a poster featuring Dealey Plaza, a crayoned green arrow pointed to the knoll and childish letters proclaimed in red crayon, *Grassy woz 'ere*.

By his bed were copies of Playboy. Two raunchier magazines depicting fellatio were in a zipped overnight bag under the bed. While such images were illegal at that time, they were not enough for my purposes. I would have to plant something. The wardrobe had a bottom drawer. I completely removed it and measured with my hand the height of the space underneath. My first idea was to plant a gun there, but where to acquire one?

The pictures of oral sex made me think of gobstoppers and Thrusham's accusation that I had knickers in my pocket. Simon had relayed a story from a Sunday paper about a man offering money to a thirteen year-old for the panties she wore. From these elements came a plan.

I went to Marble Arch walked along Oxford Street buying knickers one pair at a time in a range of styles and sizes, including children's. I also bought a purple biro because the colour was unusual. After Mum had left for afternoon bingo, I washed the knickers and while they were in the dryer searched the bathroom cabinet where she hoarded medicines. There was a largely unused bottle of tranquilizers from the time of Dad's death and another of barbiturates dated the week after I had gone to Gatgash. I removed the labels. From one of her magazines, I tore a picture of the queen and drew a bull's-eye with the purple biro on the royal forehead.

Taking care to avoid leaving fingerprints, I placed the knickers, drugs and picture in a slim biscuit tin, which I carried in a plastic bag along with the biro to Kilburn. It took less than five minutes to re-enter the flat, leave the tin beneath the drawer of Noel's wardrobe and place the biro in a pocket of the bag under his bed.

I typed a letter as soon as I got home.

Dear Police, You probably know that for some time women around Kilburn have noticed underwear missing from clotheslines.

Last Saturday, my daughter, who is under 16, was approached by a man she knows as Grassy Noel. She says he lives in Hanson Street. He bought a bottle of Tizer and, as they sat on a wall drinking, he offered her money for the knickers she had on.

When she said she wasn't interested, he showed her a filthy magazine with women using their mouths, but not for eating food. My daughter got up to go, but he grabbed her arm and asked if she wanted drugs rather than money. She broke away and ran to me in tears. I dare not tell her Dad because he would end up in prison for attacking Grassy.

For the same reason, I cannot risk identifying myself and will not give the age of my daughter. Please, please do something about this pervert. If you don't stop him for the sake of the kids, do so before a parent murders him.

One other thing. Kids say that Grassy talks all the time about shooting the Queen.

Concerned Mother

I sold my portable typewriter on the Saturday morning to a second-hand shop in Harrow before going to Kilburn and posting the letter to the local police station. A bus then took me to Cricklewood where I bought another portable that needed minor repairs. Just in case something led the police to suspect I had sent a letter, I often exchanged typewriters in this way over the years.

Roger did not come to work and for three days no one in the office knew why. When his friends rang the flat, the other two tenants said that Roger was away for a few days and claimed not to know why. His father rang on Thursday to say he had been in an accident. On the Friday two detectives examined the contents of Roger's desk. They spoke of routine enquiries, asked who knew Roger best and then interviewed the two young men who were closest to him.

After the cops had gone, one of Roger's friends let on they had asked if Roger ever talked about guns, the Queen or young girls.

On the next Monday, Roger appeared rather subdued and with a split lip that he attributed to horseplay getting out of hand, which had also left him concussed. He said his lawyer had insisted he say nothing to anyone until the confusion was all cleared up. The next day he said that he had moved back to his parent's place in Romford. When others commented on how much travelling this would involve, he said the move was just temporary because his landlord needed the ground floor empty for underpinning.

One of the programmers shared a rumour that the case was serious enough to go to a Crown Court. While others speculated about the charges, I pretended to be incredulous. Roger increasingly looked like a man reaching the end of his tether and another bully, sensing his vulnerability, pounced during a tea break.

"A little bird told me you could be going to prison. What's it all about?"

"I'd rather not say."

"Your colleagues have got a right to know. I mean, if you're light fingered, we need to make sure we don't do anything to put temptation in your way."

"It's got nothing to do with theft."

He looked to the two men who had been closest to him, but one of them said, "Spit it out, Grassy. You're only making it worse."

"The police planted drugs in my flat. Tranquilizers, which I've never used!"

"And why would they do that to you?" said the bully.

"Because they're bastards," he screeched. "I invited them to search my room and left them alone there. Then they planted stuff, called me in and one of them punched me and said I'd resisted arrest."

When others looked doubtful, I said, "In English justice a man is innocent until proved guilty in court."

Roger was not the only one to be amazed and almost choking he said, "Thanks, Perry. I can't ask for more than that."

A rosy glow engulfed me. Already he had suffered, prison beckoned, the tabloids would have a field day with the knickers and banned porn that Roger had not mentioned, royalists would thunder about him defacing a picture of the monarch, and psychiatrists would speculate on the source of his obsession with assassinations and whether he had been a threat to the queen or merely a fantasist. Sweeter still, no one suspected me of anything more than having a bleeding heart for a dubious character.

The shortage of experienced programmers meant that anyone who could write reasonable code was well rewarded. Within two years of the demise of CRADU, I had tripled what I had earned as a technician. Then my boss got a promotion and asked me to move with him to head up a team. But, having seen colleagues competent at producing code fail as managers and attract hostility, I decided to review the options open to someone with my experience of programming and systems analysis.

Some of the team worked on contract. I had thought those who matched my level of expertise took home more or less the same money until one explained how he had an accountant who ensured minimal tax. What also made going freelance attractive to me were the databases that could help trace people I hated even more than Roger. I gravitated towards assignments in companies and government departments that had or were moving towards electronic records that listed millions of people. One of my first illicit tasks at a data centre was to find out if the information system recorded searches. If that was the case, I aimed to take home enough information about the computer to devise a way of either suspending that function or removing evidence of trawling. Through extra-mural searching for such solutions, I gained the skills to become a computer security consultant just as hackers were proving that most systems were easier to crack than a DDT-laced eggshell. My day rate soared. An entrepreneur would have exploited the demand by employing staff, but schmoozing and tendering for work to be performed by others would not create the same opportunities to mine databases for the names on my list.

I never needed to use a phone line for my illicit searching because enough organisations gave me what you might describe as an all-areas pass. During computer emergencies, I worked through the night or at weekends and often I was alone or the staff nearby did not understand enough to suspect wrongdoing. My first find as a consultant was a car insurance policy for a Bernard Halton, who had been born in the same year as me and lived on Farm Hills Estate in Leeds. The records showed that the company had paid out in 1964 after this Halton had killed himself, his two passengers and caused serious injuries to another driver. A visit to Leeds to look at newspapers from that time confirmed that I could cross Dodger off my list.

In 1969, a Harry Payner who was the right sort of age to be one of the Owls appeared in a list of mortgagors as the owner of 18 Nasturtium Hill, Finchley. He was not in the phone book. After inserting the address in a government database, I obtained a telephone number that had belonged to a previous occupant.

I rang it that evening from a phone box near the hotel I was staying at. The West Country accent matched Payner's so well that I trembled. He grew tired of listening to silence and slammed the phone down. In my room, I practised imitating James Bond to disguise my voice. It sounded nothing like Sean Connery, but nor did it resemble Perry Gray. After more wine for Dutch courage, I returned to the phone box.

"You don't know me, but I know Wally Stace. I haven't heard from him for years. Do you know where he is?"

Harry slurped breaths and then puffed out in a short blast. "Jesus. Wally's been dead for three years. How well did you know him?"

I felt elated, but also cheated. "Well we drank with the other lads. It was about a reunion, but it seems I'm too late."

"What reunion?"

"Secondary school. Shame about Wally, but maybe you can help with something else?"

"Like what? You don't sound like a Mancunian."

"Wally mentioned a guy called Knattmaw. Do you know where he is?"

"Are you fucking me about? Who are you?"

"I'm sorry. Did I say something to upset you?" And I put the phone down.

I drove to Finchley the following Saturday morning. Nasturtium Hill was off a B road, but quiet at Wally's end. The terrace houses on both sides had been built to the same plan in the early 1900s. As often happens with such terraces, the residents were desperate to express individuality at the expense of architectural coherence. The miniature front gardens ranged from not a leaf or blade of grass to seven foot high privet thickets. There were also marked differences in the types of windows, roofing materials and levels of maintenance. A few houses had skylights and some of the red brick frontages were hidden by pebble dashing, stone cladding or paint. One entrance sported a pair of Ionic columns that were no more appropriate than bay windows on a Greek temple. I parked in a nearby street and walked around the block with a woolly hat pulled low and a turned up collar. Payner's place had recent paint on the masonry sills and entrance, one bell, one gas meter, aluminium double-glazing and a solid front door with two good locks. At the back was another street with a similar terrace. There was no easy way of getting in and, even if I could, I had no idea of the number of occupants or when they were likely to be absent.

The house opposite Payner's front door was in a poor state of repair. I knocked and an ancient and fragile woman came to the door.

"Hello. I do odd jobs at weekends. I wondered if there was anything you wanted fixing."

The skin around her watery eyes became even more crinkled as she smiled. "I'm not sure that I can afford you. Just paying the bills cleans me out."

"I'm sorry to hear that. Is there no one who helps you?"

"Not anymore. I live alone now."

I hoped that Mum would never be so careless with a stranger.

"It's not a good idea to tell someone you don't know from Adam that you live alone. I hope your neighbours look out for you."

She described the support provided by a woman who lived next-door. I said that I would provide two hours of my time for free, but only if her friend approved. A few minutes later we sat with tea and biscuits in the kitchen of the neighbour. She was no less trusting than the old dear. I steered the conversation for information about Payner by commenting on how well-kept the house across the road was. They said in passing that Harry lived alone, could be surly and kept a Jaguar in a nearby lock-up garage. He worked as a bouncer, the neighbour's son had seen him on duty outside a club, and came home after four in the morning at the weekend.

While I was fixing a jammed bedroom window, I saw a row of twelve garages beyond the back fence. The old lady confirmed that this was where Payner kept his car, but she was not sure which door was his. After finishing the repairs, I went to Nasturtium Close, which led to a potholed lane, the only access to the garages. An estate agent's sign advertised one for rent. The units had no electricity and there was no outside lighting. The nearest streetlamp was to one side of the entrance to the private lane and its light would be partly obscured by a poplar in a back garden.

I found a phone box, called the estate agent and said that Harry Payner had mentioned a vacant garage near Nasturtium Close.

"Yes, we do have one. Would you like to see it?"

"What number garage is it?"

"Number two, second closest to the street."

"It would be handy if it was next to Harry's?"

"No, he's in number five."

I pretended to be surprised at the rent mentioned and said I would think about it. Back at the garages, I noted the type of padlock securing number five and bought three of the same model on my way home. Taking one apart showed that while the body and shackle were relatively solid, the mechanism was cheap. I turned one of each pair of keys into skeletons that worked all three locks.

I told Mum I would not be back before three, dressed in dark clothes and went to a cinema in the hope that this would provide distraction. But my nerves kept jangling at the thought of an alert neighbour calling the police or an encounter with Payner. On the drive to Finchley, my stomach tightened by the minute as the possibility of seeing my tormentor dominated my imagination. He would never show remorse for his actions at Gatgash. If anything, he would blame me for his demotion, punishment marches in the snow and onward posting. My hatred and determination to avenge only just overcame the terror that urged flight.

After parking a quarter mile from the garages, I put on gloves and wiped with an ethanol-soaked cloth the fingerprints from my bag and its contents – a penlight, a large torch, the keys, a roll of wide tape and a long thin-tipped screwdriver. As well as taking precautions for dropping something in panic, I had to be prepared for the possibility of Payner discovering me and I would never allow him to overpower me a second time. Before that happened, I would stab him with the screwdriver and leave the blade lodged to reduce the chances of blood stains.

Every footstep seemed to echo no matter how softly I trod through Nasturtium Close and the dark lane to the garages. A grunting noise made me crouch under a bush where I waited until a teenage couple had finished copulating and walked past me. It was reassuring that no one had twitched a curtain or shouted abuse from a window at the lovers, but what if another horny pair came while I was in the garage?

The first key worked. No car was inside. Two shelves on the back wall held ten large brown cartons; the stouter ones had held wine and the others groceries. There was ample time to examine them before Payner was expected at four, provided my nerves held. I had to fight the tempting idea that the cheap padlock meant finding something incriminating was very unlikely. Holding the penlight in my mouth, I used tape to blackout the edges of the garage doors, forced the screwdriver blade into the wood of the lower shelf and suspended the torch from it to check each box. Most had *bric-à-brac*, much of it old crockery and cheap tumblers wrapped in newspaper, cutlery, rusting kitchen utensils and mouldy books. But under a layer of stained plastic saucers in a carton from the middle of the upper shelf were military issue syrettes of morphine tartrate packed in white cardboard boxes. I filled my bag with them and later counted twenty-seven packs of five. The remaining syrettes I placed on the floor and created a layer of cups from another carton before replacing the drugs so that Payner would not immediately realise that someone had looted part of his stash.

By the time I had removed the tape and relocked the garage, I was a mess of over-stimulated nerves, but my ordeal did not end there. What if the police found the morphine before I got to my car or stopped it on the drive home? Not just imprisonment for possession scared me. Under harsh interrogation my most shameful secret might emerge. And if the police heard what had happened at Gatgash then Mum was bound to find out.

The urge for revenge was so great that as soon as I got home I typed a letter.

Harry Payner of 18 Nasturtium Hill, Finchley N3 gave this box of syringes to my fifteen year-old son in exchange for sex. My boy is not homosexual, but had spent all of his savings on drugs, not to mention the cash and jewellery he stole from his family and friends. Payner keeps a Jaguar in a lock-up off Nasturtium Close. My son thinks this is where Payner goes to collect drugs to sell. Please stop this pusher and paedophile from corrupting other children. You will understand that I want to remain anonymous to protect my son. Be assured, my boy will receive medical attention and the strictest supervision now that we know what his problem is.

Along with a box of syrettes, the letter went into a heavy duty envelope addressed to the police station in Finchley and marked Urgent and First Class. To ensure there could be no delay, I was ridiculously generous with the stamps and drove at four in the morning to the sorting office in Finchley to post it.

When I emerged from my room on Sunday afternoon, Mum said, "What got into you last night? I heard you coming and going at goodness knows what hour."

"That's not like you, Mum, to wake in the night."

"I don't sleep as well by myself. But what was up with you?"

"I had terrible insomnia. I must be working too hard. I might take tomorrow off."

"You're just like your Dad, pushing yourself too hard. But you don't have his constitution."

After telling the computer centre expecting me that I was sick, I shopped for stout plastic containers, heavy duty plastic bags and ten lavender bushes. Mum smiled at the plants and the idea of planting them along the garden path. I spaced the pots of lavender and dug the holes deep enough for a bush to sit on top of a plastic container. Then after driving Mum to bingo, I took the syrettes from under my bed, distributed them among the ten containers, taped the lids and placed each box in a plastic sack. After a thin layer of soil on top of each cache, the lavenders went on top. By the time Mum got back, all she saw was the beginnings of a hedge.

Nothing about Payner or syrettes had appeared in the national or London-wide media by late Tuesday afternoon. As I was too impatient to wait for the local weeklies that would appear on Thursday, I took a box of chocolates to the old lady in Nasturtium Hill.

"What are these for?"

"I had a stroke of luck on the pools. I don't have to work weekends anymore and I thought I should share some of my windfall. Of course, the chocolates will cost you a cuppa."

I tut-tutted to hear her talk about a police raid on Payner's house and the rumours of drugs found in his garage. After his conviction for dealing made the news, I was disappointed that no report mentioned him preying on young men and his jail term did not satisfy me. Once I knew which prison he had gone to I bought a large-print Bible, used a scalpel to create a cavity within its pages and inserted syrettes along with a note.

Dear Harry, What a come down for you since our NCO days at Gatgash. All that fun we had with the best looking new recruits. Now we both take orders more than give them. You from screws and me from whichever gang pays the piper.

The money you arranged arrived with me no problem. I am happy to supply more of the same in return for similar payments. You're much missed on Queer Street. Still, I expect prison provides other opportunities. Best wishes, your old Gatgash sergeant, Bert

I was sure that prison officers would find the contraband. Payner could swear on a stack of solid bibles that someone had framed him, but he had no credibility. Then the police would work out who Bert was and bring some bother into his life.

After the county press reported on Mr Vitallium, I wondered if Knattmaw had made the connection between my letter to him and the note in the hollowed-out book. If he had, this might help to explain his obsession with me.

Though I was sure that the package increased Payner's woes, I had not finished with him. I intended to set him up repeatedly. For while I would only have physically hurt him in self-defence, there was no limit to other retribution. But then his death from renal failure made the national newspapers after his sister protested that the prison medical service had taken too long before allowing him to be seen at a hospital.

Although in one way it was a relief that both Owls had died, part of me would have preferred them to be alive and suffering. With them crossed off, Knattmaw became the top target on my list. Years rolled by without a trace of him and I began to suspect he was dead, but I never missed an opportunity to search a database for incorrect versions of his surname.

Chapter 27: Norman ~ Colin

N You put yourself in a position where you might have killed Payner with a screwdriver.
P I would have stabbed only in self-defence. Drawing blood would have made me sick. But what was the alternative? No way would I risk being at his mercy again.
N The thing is, you put yourself in harm's way in the garage.
P I didn't have any other ideas and felt compelled to act rather than wait longer. Believe me, if I'd thought of a way of getting at him without such risks, I would have used it.
N But not if it involved violence?
P I hate bloodshed. To see or imagine others physically injured brought back memories of the bodies in the barn and Simon reduced to a vegetable in hospital.
N But the police assaulted Roger and what do you think awaited him as a nonce in prison or after he finished his sentence and some self-righteous thug recognised him?
P If others flew off the handle and beat him that's their responsibility, not what I planned.
N Putting aside the beatings, you perverted the course of justice. How do you think jurors feel on discovering a person they helped send to prison was framed?
P Roger was a relentless bully. The public should feel uneasy about how much bullying goes on rather than occasional villain getting locked up on the wrong charges.

Sometimes I think that, other than his parents, the nearest Perry came to a lasting caring relationship was with Raventulle. He had little contact with children after he grew up and never had a pet to indulge as a child-substitute. As soon as I knew that Rose had a son, it was obvious that anyone fortunate enough to become her second husband also had to act as a father. Colin liked me after some initial shyness and I warmed to him enough to welcome the prospect of becoming a stepfather. I thought it would be easy enough to copy Rose's approach to nurturing, which better suited my liberal outlook than the love of my parents with its religiosity and guilt.

Nan looked after Colin for a week while Rose and I honeymooned in Bournemouth. He was pleased to hug his mother again and then came to me with a big smile when I offered a stick of rock. I read him a bedtime story that night and he was sleeping like a cherub by the time Rose came to his room. Soon after the morning's first light he found us sharing a bed and squirmed between us while we were half asleep. Then he clung to Rose, tried to push me away with his legs and, when this failed, kicked with his heels. I thought it better to leave the pair and expected his mood to improve after time alone with his mother.

At breakfast he said, "When is he going home?"

"This is Norman's home too now. And soon we'll move to a house with a garden where you can play with your new Daddy."

"I don't want to move and I don't want a new Daddy. I don't want him here."

His face had the scowl that would become so familiar.

"Norman's not going away. He wants to be your friend, but you're making it hard for him."

"Good."

And there was the smug smile that over the years replaced the scowl whenever Colin sensed he had said something hurtful.

His resentment expanded until he was waging a sullen war against me, caring little if Rose suffered as well. Occasionally he threw a tantrum, but for the most part he glowered to suck the joy out of us. Sensitive to Colin's disturbed early years, we chose not to smack him for being sullen. In any case, he punished himself by refusing to take part in activities that involved me or my relatives. As Christmas and his birthdays approached, my heart sank. No matter what the present from Croydon or Rose and me, Colin would avoid giving the satisfaction of seeing him pleased or excited. To overhear him with a friend and know that he valued his *Junior Chemistry Set,* or to see him having fun on his bike before he knew I was watching, was as much as we dared hope for.

I suggested to Rose that she did not mention a present came from me as well as her.

"It's giving in and anyway he'd see through it. Let's try another way. I'll buy him a set of encyclopaedias and you get something any boy would dream of having."

She bought the *Encyclopædia Britannica* for Colin's first birthday at Foxenearth, but made it appear to be a joint present from her and Marie and gave it while he was at his Nan's flat. While they were away, I cleared and decorated the basement and set up a trestle table onto which I screwed a large Scalextric track. I showed him how the cars worked, but he declined to have a go and left me in the basement. In the years that followed, he often used the Scalextric with his friends, but never when I was there and always with the door to the basement closed. Neighbours sometimes mentioned how a son raved about Colin's track, but the visitors never let on to Rose who had heard their excited shouts coming from below. We concluded that Colin made it a condition of racing that his friends never mentioned their use of the equipment to her or me.

If I happened to arrive home when Colin had friends visiting, he would either send them packing or leave with them. Any greeting from a child to me made the scowl on Colin's face more pronounced. This began well before adolescence when parents might expect some display of embarrassment at a parent's actual or imagined failings. Rose tried talking to Colin and he saw a child psychotherapist every week for over a year before he started secondary school. Perhaps he would have been worse without the therapy, but we saw no improvement and the therapist's ethics meant that she told us almost nothing about what happened behind her closed door.

Despite all the love Rose showed me, I have no illusions about the choice between Colin and me that she would have made with foreknowledge. She expected him to benefit from having a stepfather and by the time we knew this was not the case, only a sense of fairness stopped her ousting me after the efforts I had made to be a loving step-dad.

Rose and I very much wanted our own child and never used contraceptives after our wedding. At first, we assumed frequent lovemaking would do the trick. Then we paid attention to her cycle and on the weekends when she would be most fertile Colin went to his Nan's. We stopped making love for three weeks out of four and still there was no result other than what had always been so enjoyable could feel like a chore. After a year without any hint of pregnancy, Rose suggested a fertility specialist. My pride would not allow this because the fault, as I saw it then, rested with me. Not only had Rodney got her pregnant without any delay, but the difference between my appearance and that of my parents had long suggested that something was amiss in me. If my genes were ill-formed nothing was likely to come from medical investigations other than abject embarrassment.

Instead of sharing my fears, I avoided the fertility clinic by saying to Rose, "I've heard that couples who adopt sometimes find it leads to pregnancy. Would you consider adopting?"

"I would, but isn't having your own child important to you?"

"I haven't given up. It's just that if it does happen, I'd rather it was natural."

"Son or daughter?"

"No strong preference. How about you?"

"I already have a boy."

"A girl it is then."

We went back to lovemaking as the mood took us. Rose researched adoption and I read the literature that she obtained. What became clear was that having a spare bedroom in a tranquil location and a steady income was not enough. There would be visits to observe the family and questions.

"Rose, I've got cold feet about the adoption. The social workers assessing us would wonder what happened to Colin to make him so grouchy and rude and why he loathes me so much. And they're not going to put a child into a house with such an atmosphere."

"I'm glad you could tell me before we went any further. If they asked about Colin, I'd say it was due to what happened before you and I met. But I have other misgivings. How would he react to a kid in the house who happily called you Dad? I'm not sure it would be fair on a child to take the risk."

We not only dropped the idea of adopting but also agreed not to do anything out of the ordinary to encourage conception. If it happened, it happened. Decades later when we at last talked about my response to the idea of seeing a fertility specialist, Rose confirmed what I had suspected all along, that to protect my feelings she had not pressed for the consultation.

Before I give up the ghost, I have only a few duties. Completing my chapters, disseminating them along with Perry's, and what I owe to Winkie, the third Border Collie that Rose and I showered affection on. We had also loved our other two dogs, but from her first week at Foxenearth Winkie was special. One evening I found Rose full of silent tears. She was lying on the sofa with the newly-homed pup curled up asleep on her stomach under a tartan rug. I thought she was grieving for our second dog.

"I miss him too."

Rose hesitated, mouth widening without words. I knew then it was not about the ailing dog put down to spare further suffering. In any case, we had shared our grief for that animal.

"I'd rather know than not know," I said. Rose had often used these words to encourage me to speak.

"When you say that, sometimes what you end up hearing is hard to take."

"I still want to know."

"It's the weight of the puppy across my belly. It reminds me of being pregnant."

"Oh, is that it?" I tried to disguise shame, but sounded half-breathed.

"I'm sorry. I didn't mean…"

"It's alright."

I went to my study, closed the door and cried alone. Two days later when Rose was out, I enticed a sleepy Winkie onto my lap with slivers of ham, waited for him to fall asleep and covered him with the rug. The pup's weight and gentle movements were strangely satisfying and seemed informative. The bonds of motherhood and how they begin during pregnancy were clearer from these brief minutes of simulation.

Winkie's name comes from having one blue eye set in white fur and one dark pupil lost in the surrounding black patch. Gerald, my gardener since illness overtook me, has agreed to take Winkie. As I cannot provide enough exercise for her, he provides a daily walk. From tomorrow, he will keep her overnight so that she gets used to what will be her new home and the children there. Though I will miss Winkie at night and first thing in the morning, it would be selfish not to ease her transition by providing a second home for before she loses this one. And I am sure that the playfulness of Gerald's three children will make her adjustment easier.

If it were just me, I would leave Foxenearth to Gerald; both for Winkie's sake and as a thank you to the family for looking after her and being decent in other ways. However, Rose wanted to support her descendants and we agreed to pass on to them whatever remained when we had both gone provided that Colin was not a beneficiary. I suggested he was excluded and Rose did not think this spiteful.

Rose saw how hard I tried to overcome her son's hostility. Often I asked her, what can I do differently, but we both ran out of ideas. It was a struggle at times to remember that Colin was not born awkward; that his father's violence had damaged him. Through her voluntary work and courses, Rose met people, some with qualifications in psychology, psychiatry and family therapy. Given the chance, Rose would tell them about Colin's rejection of me. One of these people suggested the child psychotherapist and another, on hearing that Colin idealised Rodney, recommended telling the truth about the father. Rose discussed the idea with me. I expressed fears that it might be too late because we had never disparaged Rodney.

She planned to tell him during a school holiday while I was in Canberra for two weeks working with Australian counterparts. Rose took Colin out to places he chose over several days to build up rapport; he could treat her better when I was not around and my name was not mentioned. Then she showed him photographs of her first wedding that he had never seen. Colin asked what had led to the divorce and she spoke of Rodney's violence and infidelity.

"I lived in terror. It was bad enough he beat me, but then he started to hit you."

Colin changed in an instant from curious to defensive. "I don't believe it. Norman's put you up to this. He'd do anything to blacken the name of my dad."

"You trust your Nan, don't you? You could ask her. She was afraid for you just as I was."

"I won't ask her. She'd only tell me such lies because you and Norman made her."

Rose rang my hotel to discuss whether to involve Marie in trying to persuade Colin that Rodney had been a brute. Our conclusion was that doing so would risk disrupting the healthiest close relationship the child had with an adult because, provided we were not at his Nan's, Colin looked happy and behaved well.

Fortunately for our marriage, Marie could not see enough of her only grandchild. At least once a month she had him for a weekend. Our best lovemaking happened when he was away; not because we feared him overhearing or interrupting us, but because relaxing without him around worked like an aphrodisiac.

After our move to Lychinclay, Rose felt the trips to take and collect Colin from Marie's were worth it; he, his Nan and his parents all benefitted. During his teens, Colin acquired friends of his own age in Finchley and one got him interested in bootleg records. We heard from Marie that they visited markets where these were sold. Then she said Colin went to homes of dealers and collectors. We worried about the kind of people he might encounter and the implications of his burgeoning collection of illicit tapes and discs. It also seemed strange that he seldom listened to most of them more than once. His interest was in acquiring a copy from every concert by a band, almost regardless of the quality of the recording. We decided to say nothing. To question the suitability of his contacts would have stopped him talking to Marie about them, mentioning the legal position he placed us in would only have made him angrier, and to feign interest in his hobby would only have provoked scorn.

As Colin was nearing fourteen, Marie won a little over £70,000 on the pools. She asked her grandson during a visit what he wanted and phoned to tell us his answer. We guessed his request was awkward when Marie said she had sent him to the shops and wanted to speak to both of us. I left Rose in the hall and picked up the study extension.

"I couldn't believe it," Marie said. "Without a moment's hesitation, he asked to go to a boarding school. I said they were very expensive and he said it would mean a lot to him. I asked if he was unhappy at school, and he said, 'No, only at home.' I told him, 'A decision like this has to be made by your parents.' What do you think?"

I let Rose do the talking."

"It's too much money."

"All I need is a few thousand for a rainy day. The question is, what do you want? And Colin need never know I was prepared to pay."

"I need time to think."

That was not the case for me. Once off the phone, I spoke in favour of Colin going.

"I'm not ready to lose him yet."

"He's scraping by at his studies. Boarding school might be the making of him. And let's face it, he's determined to be unhappy here. Just think of the good it might do him not having to play Mr Grumpy every day."

"I can't bear the idea of not seeing him for months at a time."

"What if we find a school nearby, where you can visit him and he can come home some weekends?"

Rose agreed to visit possible schools and we took Colin to see Falkdene. As Rose had expressed reservations about boarding and I had kept quiet, he had no problems being enthusiastic about what he saw and heard from the staff. After the master accompanying us had sent Colin with a pupil to see the boathouse, Rose asked about weekends at home.

"Not really our style. A lot of our parents are overseas and even those in this country are often quite busy. Besides, classes are held on Saturday morning, followed by sport in the afternoon and recreation clubs on Sunday after lunch. Of course, if there was a special reason, like a wedding, we would understand."

"What about us visiting him?"

"May I speak frankly, Mrs Midlin?"

"Please do."

"I can see from Colin's impatience that he's striving to become his own person and you said boarding school was his idea. Boys like him prefer to take part in weekend activities with their friends rather than be absent, even for a visit. And he would be especially keen not to stand out for such a reason when joining a group who have known each other for years."

The master had spared our blushes. What he called impatience was Colin's body language communicating that he despised me and had no time for his mother when she expressed any qualms about boarding or displayed any regard for me.

The master went to fetch Colin. As soon as he was out of sight, Rose cried. She knew that Colin would be furious if denied Falkdene and sensed that she had lost him whatever we did. I soothed as best I could and said I would live with whatever decision she made.

When she asked Colin if he liked the school enough to attend, he said, "How soon can I start?"

When Rose continued to fear that Colin's absence would widen the gulf between them, I suggested that each vacation either she take Colin away for a week or I found work activities to take me away from home. Twice I stayed some days at a hotel near to my place of work to give the pair their seven days without me. He was not always gracious during these weeks with his mother. The worst incident, at the age of sixteen, involved a scene in a restaurant after Rose refused to order him a beer. He shouted at her, used bad language about me and stormed out. Apart from such incidents, Rose treasured what she correctly guessed would be the last significant contact with her son.

His plans to go with others from his class to Cambridge and read chemistry depended on good exam results that he did not achieve. UMIST offered him a place, but without masters to supervise his study and with the distractions of central Manchester he merely scraped along. His Nan saw more of him than Rose, though admittedly London was easier to get to and had other attractions, not least bootleg records. He bought stock in London to sell to his fellow students and acquired the kit to make unauthorised tapes of concerts in Manchester, which he sold copies of to southern dealers.

Despite his entrepreneurship, his visits to Lychinclay usually meant that he wanted money. His monthly allowance, which some affluent parents said was generous, was never enough. I suspect that he spent much on drink, drugs and summer holidays while most of his classmates worked. To be fair, I have no evidence that he took drugs. What roused my suspicions was Marie reporting for the first time that she found him moody and the articles he had written that she showed us.

During his three years at university his outlook and interests became increasingly New Age. Colin presented Nan with copies of amateurish periodicals that contained pieces by him about ley lines, crop circles, *Feng Shui*, astral travel, Primal Scream Therapy, Atlantis and the use of ciphers by alchemists. His writing was clear and conveyed his interest, but, just like the other articles in the magazines there was little evidence. He often did not bother to specify sources and when he did it was usually a book without a page reference.

After graduating, Colin followed an American drama student he had met in Manchester to the USA. He asked Rose to ship his recordings and equipment and lived in Seattle by making and trading bootleg copies. For a time we received news of him from his Nan, including that Colin had married another American woman, Clancy. His first direct communication with us came eleven months after this news. Clancy was pregnant and they had no medical insurance or money for doctors. A record company was suing him for copyright violation, his recordings and equipment were in an FBI warehouse and his lawyer had demanded up front what little savings the couple had.

I did not want to fund Colin on the basis of his word alone. I suggested Rose transfer £500 and visit Seattle before committing more money. Colin accepted the £500, but rejected the suggestion of her visiting for two weeks to help with the new baby. After the birth of their son,

Messiah, the breach of copyright trial stalled on a technicality. A second record company, which also had a case against him and had been waiting in the wings, offered to take no further action in exchange for the destruction of seized goods and a signed undertaking not to deal in recordings. Colin asked us for money to mount a legal challenge. Rose could not resist and sent £1000. He wrote to ask her for more money a few months later. She asked how the case was progressing and the chances of success. Colin did not reply for a year, by which time we knew from Marie he had undertaken not to deal in records.

We hoped he would get a regular job. Instead Colin and family moved to Lucet Fork, a remote community in Oregon. What I know about their new home comes from the Internet. The dilettante son of a wealthy family bought a large piece of land. After he tired of the few locals and their traditional values, he leased to anyone he liked, mostly people with an alternative lifestyle, five acres at a peppercorn rent. As the landlord had no particular beliefs, just a vague preference for the counterculture, there was no unifying philosophy. One web author who had lived in Lucet Fork said it was never a commune because the standards of living ranged from sumptuous to squalid and wealthier people exploited the poor. He gave the example of a man who expected two days' work cutting his firewood in return for a day's loan of his chainsaw.

Clancy bore two more children, Areda and Cayce. What little news we gleaned indicated that the family lived hand to mouth. When Marie died, Rose offered to provide airline tickets, yet Colin did not come to the funeral. Nor did he call or send as much as a card to his mother.

"He's got his own grief," said Rose.

Always she excused him, but she knew the nature of her son. Despite her generosity and Colin's decades of Aquarian beliefs, he neither forgave her nor accepted me. To punish Rose for marrying again, he kept her at a distance unless he wanted something. I discovered by chance an article by Colin on alchemists' ciphers on the Internet with his email address. My telling Rose this prompted the acquisition of our first home computer. But he sent little more information and contact remained sparse.

If it were not for Clancy sending a photograph every three or four years, we would not even have known what the children looked like. Rose posted presents for each child's birthday and Christmas. Nothing came back other than a homemade card from Clancy in a recycled envelope posted surface mail with a handwritten page that mentioned their thanks along with some news. Mostly we learned of educational achievements attained despite the bad weather that sometimes thwarted the school bus for weeks at a time. I suspected Colin deterred the children from sending their own thank-yous and Clancy from sharing news of how the family fared.

The aloofness and lack of gratitude reminded me of young Colin denying us any satisfaction for our gifts. His actions back then and later hurt me, but by far the bigger pain came from witnessing Rose's heartache and tears. From half way around the world, her son, even when he was twice the age at which she got pregnant, still jerked the sense of guilt that she carried for what Rodney had done to his son. I suppressed the urge to write saying, Colin you're torturing your mother. For all I knew, this might have encouraged his persecution of her. Besides, had Rose learned of such a letter she would not only have regarded it as interference but also as the kind of high-handedness that she had come to loath in her first marriage.

We had thought Colin had moved beyond asking for money until an email in February 1996.

Mum. Hope you have a good Christmas. Lucet Fork usually escapes flooding, but a landslide damned the river and we had over a foot of water in the house plus a lot of debris that we need to shift from where we grow food. The silt will improve fertility, but we can't do much until we clear the rocks and smashed trees. Any contributions would be appreciated. Colin

The Internet confirmed that Oregon had suffered flooding. We discussed how desperate the family might be and whether to ask how much they needed to make the house habitable and to be ready to cultivate in the spring. Rose, afraid that Colin would delay responding and disadvantage his family, sent £2000 without making further enquiries. Then, as ever, we waited.

Seven weeks later, I found Rose tearful over an email from Colin with no more than thirty words.

"At least he said thank you," I said.

"For all we know, he might have spent it on drugs."

"If it was drugs, he'd have asked for more."

"But why not say how the house is now or send a photograph?"

"We've never been able to understand his terseness."

"I want to see how they live."

"It might make things worse. Arrive unannounced and he won't like it. Say you want to come, he'll refuse. Try to snoop and an English woman would stick out a mile in the backwoods."

"What can I do?"

"A private detective?"

"That would be too sneaky."

"You're right. And if he ever suspected he would be even more ungracious."

I opened my arms for Rose to sob. Later she said she feared for his children. If he could be so cold towards her, what did that mean for them?

The next letter from Clancy spoke of the older children having left home. Rose's requests for their addresses went unanswered and she wondered if the kids had kept in touch. We speculated about them heading for a big city, maybe somewhere warmer and drier, and wondered what might happen to a young person from the backwoods drawn to the bright lights. I kept from Rose that I hoped Colin had been hurt by their rejection the way he had hurt his mother.

He did not come home when I emailed that Rose was in hospital. I emailed again offering tickets, hotel accommodation and spending money for Colin and any of his family. Nothing would have cheered Rose more and I was thinking of her need for support and family in the event that my cancer did not respond to last chance measures.

Then I emailed to say Rose had died, expressed my regrets at the loss of his mother, and said that the offer still stood; the funeral could wait if needed. Clancy answered the next day without explaining why Colin was not responding. She suggested not delaying the funeral as getting passports might take a while and offered her condolences without reference to Colin's sentiments. The estrangement between him and me was complete and his bitterness was matched by mine. To be honest, I was glad he was not at the funeral. By then it made no difference to Rose and I was too unhinged by grief to deal with her awkward and ungrateful son. She gave him so much and he took and took without returning the love that she kept for him despite his rejection and the cruel way he prevented her from ever holding her grandchildren.

And yet I see now that my anger towards Colin at the time of the funeral, while deserved, helped me to avoid reaching the full depth of my guilt. For I too had taken advantage of Rose's generous nature and never matched her readiness to acknowledge a failing, express appreciation and communicate feelings. Colin, like Perry, was damaged during his earliest years. As much as I want to make excuses for myself because of what Cuthbert Lodeley did to me, compared to Colin as an infant I got off lightly. It was only at school that tormentors got to me and until I was fourteen I had the two loving parents who had created me. The loss of my father was devastating, but he did not leave me feeling rejected or wondering where he had disappeared to.

I castigated Colin for reaching middle-age without making peace with his mother, yet I did not change my ways until retirement and then only with enormous support from Rose. What if, I ask myself, she and her son had lived alone for another decade? Would she not have untwisted the kinked green sapling before he hardened into the kind of dark knotted wood that we also see in Perry?

P Why link me to your dismal stepson? Neither of my parents was like Rodney and I was never so ungrateful to them as Colin was to you and Rose.

N Rodney was a monster. In that sense, your parents are completely different. They did the best they could, but infants need security and the war frayed your mother's nerves. Have you ever wondered what might have happened had you not had the respite of staying with the Kytes? Your mother might have put out your spark as she sought to protect you and then there would have been no Mr Vitriol, but also much less of a life for you.

P I don't see my home life as that unusual for a kid born around that time. It was school that did for me.

N Did school quell the urge to nurture as an adult? I think this has more to do with your early years. What did you nurture other than your grievances?

P I didn't have any urge to be a parent. Nor was I sentimental about animals. My parents didn't have pets. The Kytes had a smallholding. Their hens amused me, but I knew that the older birds got their heads chopped off. It didn't worry me. I loved Mrs Kyte's roast chicken and if she had killed one of the goats and served it, I would have tucked in.

N But do you see how it might be part of what made us respond in different ways?

P Not really. If I'd owned a pet or had children with Róisín, I would still have wanted revenge on people like the Owls and Knattmaw.

N Even if it risked being able to support a family?

P I supported my Mum. While I worried about her finding out or my losing work, it didn't stop me seeking revenge. And prisons are full of parents. This issue is more about Colin and you.

N You might be right, Perry.

P Can you see the resemblance between the hatchet job you've just written and the letters I sent.

N If people who know Colin read my account, they know who I was and that I am bitter about my stepson. They can speak to him or Clancy or the children to check facts. And if he has any correspondence that contradicts my claims, let him share it.

P But aren't you seeking justice like a vigilante without recourse to independent assessment? You expect others to think less of him and want that to be a punishment when you know Rose would never have approved.

N If she told me not to include it, I would. But you're playing games. You persuaded me to write by saying Colin did not honour Rose and that his children would assume he was screwed up by her and me. If I don't include this chapter, I will not publish the rest of my writing and the full decoding.
P I never suggested leaving it out. Please continue as you think fit.

I never talked about Colin with anyone except Rose. Before her, I belonged wholly to that class of men now known as nerds or geeks and formerly known as swots or boffins. Although some of this community are on the fringes of autism, my empathy was under-used rather than impaired. Only inhibition interfered with my expressions of sympathy; the sentiment was always there. I dwelt on linguistic and technical details and challenges because the work kept my demons at bay and I doubted my competence in other areas.

A superior's verbal recognition, and later receiving financial rewards, were important for shoring up my self-regard. Patriotism also helped steer my thoughts, because I knew that I made a difference to national security. Although I understood UK governments could be duplicitous – look at oppressed former inhabitants of Diego Garcia – and our main ally was disreputable in the company it kept and armed, the Russian threat was real. Stalin had risen to the top and become a tyrant who thought nothing of the wholesale murder of potential opponents; who could say what a future Soviet leader would do if he attained a similar unassailable position?

Outside home, the largely male world that I moved in favoured the stiff upper lip. David Stancher was my closest friend, yet apart from the occasional discussion about religion when we first met, we did not delve into deep matters. We told each other when we were chipper, but not when we felt depressed. If David ever had doubts about his marriage, child rearing, career or the like he never mentioned them to me. Nor did he hear of such issues from my lips. It was Rose who introduced me to the idea that adult intimacy could be far more than sexual. She also taught me that discussing trivialities with acquaintances and strangers was part of everyday life, no matter how odd I found it. And the small changes I made at work as a result of her influence were enough in that repressed masculine environment to help gain promotion.

But where did Perry direct his social energy?

The nearest he came to a real adult friend was Shelley. The poker school and other drinking companions were good for a laugh, but hardly confidants. He channelled most of his time into his new home, his wine cellar, his legitimate work and the pursuit of bullies.

P What's up with you tonight? You begin with an assumption of pathology. Let's say I never wrote a dodgy letter, but put all of that effort into collecting beer mats or coprolites. Who would bother to analyse my behaviour? Would ignoring all the bullying or turning the other cheek make me a more rounded person? Isn't there something sad about a man who accepts being a doormat?
N It's the way you campaigned outside the law.
P If I thought the law would have worked for me, I would have used it. But what do you think would have happened at Gatgash or afterwards if I'd gone to the Military Police?
N It would have depended on the integrity of those investigating. But if you operate outside the law, it's vengeance not justice.
P Revenge was the only possible form of redress and it became my hobby. Does that make me crazier than the millions who collect for the sake of collecting or for whom shopping is their main leisure activity?
N But you could have aimed much higher. You were born with great gifts.
P Easy for you to say that, Norman. You got to grammar school and did well enough at German for the Army to want to give you specialist training that became a ticket to a better life.
N I had the easier of two hard rides, but your intelligence is greater than mine. Once you became a contractor, you had every advantage. And then you became a consultant.
P But not so great an intelligence that you defer to my judgement. Think about what had happened before I went freelance. I chose celibacy after Róisín. Then all the

gains that I had made working in a great team were wiped out in a few months.

N Did you never find a computer team where you felt comfortable and might have got a job?

P But that would have meant giving up the chances to search scores of databases. By then, hunting was my passion. Nothing gave me greater pleasure than the feeling that the boot was on the other foot.

N So hurting others was more important than living your own life?

P I'd say humiliate rather than hurt. The Owls hurt me physically, but the pain that remained came from my humiliation. That was what I wanted to pay back. You're tired, Norman. You've written enough for today.

P I sometimes feel you end these conversations when they get uncomfortable.

N Just accept that I'm concerned for you. Sleep well.

Chapter 28: Perry ~ Ariadne

Mum and Dad were never paying guests in as much as a bed and breakfast. Going on holiday was what other families did with the exception of my fortnights with the Kytes. On the few occasions that we ate out it was nothing grander than a greasy spoon cafe. Offers to treat my parents to a restaurant were met with protests about wasting money and food that was foreign or at least too rich.

I also struggled to get Mum to stop for tea on the Sunday drives begun after Dad's death. We never went far because his car was slow and unreliable; there were limits to what loving maintenance could eke from a pre-war Austin. And as Mum was not one for walking – she rarely left the passenger seat – the trips lasted no more than two hours. After the accountant acquired for contract work suggested a new vehicle to reduce my tax, I bought a Ford Escort and took Mum far enough to warrant a break from driving. She would have refused refreshments had she not needed a toilet. It became clear that I was wasting my time pointing out delightful chintzy tea rooms in dainty villages as she would only visit chain establishments where we would sit at a Formica table overlooking a major road.

"How can you prefer this. Tea rooms are no more expensive and their cakes are fresher."

"It's modern here. You know the plumbing will work."

"I could ring up a tea room and check it has modern toilets."

"They would think you were odd talking about things like that. Besides, we don't have to walk so far here."

"I wouldn't mind dropping you off before finding somewhere to park."

Her lips pressing together prompted dropping the subject. The drives were for her and if she preferred a soulless roadside fast-food joint with pimply, disinterested and gauche staff, so be it.

I called Mum from the budget hotel used on my first consulting trip. She asked if the room was clean and the bed comfortable. Then she wanted to know whether the neighbours – as she called the other guests – were quiet and about the quality of the food. This set the pattern for such calls until a few months later when I mentioned the vile green bedspread with cigarette holes in a poky pub, all that was available in the Doncaster area due to a race meeting. She had me describe the rest of the decor and after that night sought a description of every bedroom used. These commentaries prolonged our telephone conversations because Mum had no idea of the swingeing rates hotels charged for every minute. Once we talked non-stop for almost an hour, far more than we had ever managed at home, because the hotel was a converted stately home with extensive grounds. She even had me open the window to hear the shrieks of parading peacocks.

I offered to take her there for a weekend, but she refused even when I said we could eat in cafés or have room service. Similarly, she rejected offers to fly or travel first class on a train for a day trip. When I showed her brochures of holiday cottages she objected to there being other rented units nearby. I found properties without neighbours and then she expressed reluctance to leave her home empty overnight.

"The house will be fine. You enjoy me driving you on Sunday afternoon. We could just go that bit further and see something different. I can afford it."

"You go gadding about if you want. I've got everything I need here. And who would look after the place when we're away?"

"What's there to look after? Ask next door to keep an eye out."

"It's not the same as being here to deter burglars."

"I could install an alarm. It would be useful during the day while you're out."

"That just tells burglars you've got something worth stealing."

She was irritated and I again dropped the subject. Not until she was sedated in hospital did she admit her real reasons.

"How come you would never let me take you anywhere to stay or for a meal?"

"I was always grateful that you offered, Perry. It still gives me a warm feeling to know you were so generous."

"But why not stay in a hotel for once?"

"They're not for the likes of me. I was in service. It doesn't feel right when other people do the waiting. Even the nurses here make me feel funny, especially the ones with posh voices. I always felt better when staff in a shop spoke more like me and called me dear rather than Madam."

"But why not stay in an isolated cottage?"

"Oh that's a childish thing."

"How do you mean?"

"Maurice told me when I was a tot about an uncle getting caught during a burglary and I asked what it was. He said burglars sneaked into your house and took anything they could sell. I got frightened about one coming to our place and Maurice gave reasons why they wouldn't come. First, we had nothing worth stealing. Second, they only robbed at night when someone had told them the place was unoccupied. I know it was silly, but what said back then to calm me as a tiny girl was almost enough to stop me going to Vaulting Ryego. And the more your Dad bought for us and the more goods I had under the bed, the scareder I was of not being there at night."

Sometimes a computing emergency meant there was no time to describe my accommodation over the phone. When I got back, Mum showed little interest in my hotel, as if she only cared while I was away. Our face-to-face conversations returned to their usual stunted patterns and yet I heard her more than once on the phone relaying what I had said about a hotel some nights earlier. She took pride in telling people about the features of the accommodation and the luxury rating.

I saw little advantage in five-star accommodation over four, and many three-star establishments were more than adequate, but as my staying at the best gave Mum pleasure I sought out an area's top hotel once clients had started to foot such bills without quibbling. She took particular delight in the complimentary soaps and lotions brought back. It was not just the sense of having something for nothing. After building up a stock for the cottage, she began to distribute the surplus to her friends and then mere acquaintances along with details of the hotel they came from and her son's achievements.

Had my competitors wanted insights into where I had been and where I was about to work they need only have sat near Mum at bingo. But Torquemada could not have extracted from her any knowledge of my inner life because she did not know. Eavesdropping had worked for me while she had Dad, but not for her. There was no one I confided in and the secrets I kept in my room were encoded.

Mum's health began to unravel the year after Payner went to prison. Many of her generation had such a fear of cancer and awkwardness about gynaecological issues that they preferred to ignore symptoms. By the time pain drove her to see her GP, his urgent referral to an oncologist was too late. By then the ovarian cancer had created an empire of malign colonies that ruled out anything other than palliative care. It took her four days to tell me what she had been told, but I blame myself more than her. Official and unofficial work had so preoccupied me that Mum's pained and worried expressions, tiredness and changed appetite had not registered. Had I paid attention and asked, she may not have shared her concerns any sooner. But if she had, perhaps the private consultations and tests that I would have insisted on could have improved the chances of a longer life. My lack of alertness to her symptoms provokes more guilt in me than anything else because her overprotection was a form of love that, had I returned it, might have made a difference.

Hospital conversations were hushed because of the other patients in the six bed ward and their visitors. I offered to pay for a private room, but Mum wanted the company and only resented the other women when they were too sick to talk or died. If I was the first visitor to arrive, I noticed how easily the patients, including Mum, chatted together. Then, when I tried to talk to her, the fluent family conversations coming from the other beds made our stiltedness all the more apparent.

We both pretended to be more open than we were; something achieved without discussing that she needed to compete with the other suffering women. Even facing extinction, Mum had her social standing to maintain and she led her fellow patients to think we had communicated over time much more than was the case. For my part, I was so desperate to make amends for former inattention that I sought out and grilled neighbours about their partners, children, grandchildren, pets, gardens and cars; anything to avoid one of those awkward silences at the bedside that suggested death, a topic she also avoided until medication loosened her tongue.

The nurses learned that my job involved travel and invited me to ignore visiting hours when I was only able to see Mum late in the evening. I arrived one night to find her in a drug-induced nap and assumed the stick-thin woman opposite was also asleep till I saw the look on the face of a nurse who went to take her pulse. The nurse drew the screens and then a succession of staff came and went. Next the screens around the other beds were drawn and a creaking gurney came and went interrupted by the sound of two men grunting. Mum woke and I explained the reasons for the drawn screens. When we could see the ward again, the bed was empty and had fresh linen.

Mum looked towards where the patient had been and said, "The thing I miss about church is knowing that as this life ends another one begins. She still believed and I'm sure it made her going easier."

"Why easier?"

"She had a visit from her rabbi yesterday and looked at peace afterwards."

"The hospital chaplain would see you, if you wanted. Or I could get another minister to visit. Or a medium."

"But it wouldn't work now. I no longer believe in the Upper Table or God."

"Is there anything that would make it easier for you?"

She closed her eyes and took a deep breath. "There is, Perry, but I don't know if I have the right to ask."

Remorse overcame anxiety. "I want you to say."

She pulled her sheet almost to her bottom lip and scrunched her eyes, which made her look childlike in the dimmed lights.

"I wish you were married and had kids."

She waited a few seconds before opening her eyes. To someone who did not know Mum, her voice might have sounded flat. I knew that tone masked strong feelings. My jollified reply was equally artful.

"There's still time for all that. In fact, I wasn't sure whether to tell you, but I'm seeing a girl at the moment. Her name's Róisín."

"The one you used to work with?"

I silently cursed myself for not using any of a thousand other names."

"No, that Róisín went into a convent. This one's a bit more down to earth, rather like you Mum."

"That's good to know, Perry."

Had she believed me, she would have asked for a visit from Róisín. But what I gave her was enough to patch a crack in her standing within the hospital. I understood; as a bachelor who never spoke of girlfriends, I was an embarrassment to myself.

Mum became so ill that the screens were left drawn around her. She struggled physically, but not emotionally, to ask me if she would die of the pneumonia that had set in.

"Pneumonia's always a serious condition for someone of your age, that's why the doctors keep checking on you."

I did not mention how much the strange noises coming from her windpipe distressed me. Was this a death rattle, a term I had only encountered in novels?

In sentences with curious gaps due to her difficulty breathing, Mum said, "It wouldn't be proper having a funeral without a minister. I don't want people to think I didn't have a respectable service."

"Do you want to see the chaplain?"

She weakly clutched my fingers in her clammy palm. "No. I wondered if death would make me religious again, but it hasn't. Once bitten, twice shy."

I said with tears welling, "I'd like to believe that you would communicate from the other side. That Dad is waiting for you and that both of you will be waiting for me."

"No, death is the end."

She closed her eyes from the exhaustion of speaking. I hoped that she was aware of only my touch. The rattle became fainter and more erratic. If I had called staff, they might have intervened to prolong her suffering when, as far as I was concerned, keeping her alive any longer would be selfish.

Bingo players and neighbours made up most of the thirty or so people at the Anglican funeral. I had considered contacting relatives in Watford, but feared their rejection would compound my grief. The minister provided surprising consolation. He was unfazed that Mum and I, apart from Dad's funeral, had not been to church for decades. His questions enabled him to eulogise as if she had been a personal friend for many years.

I took a fortnight off work and spent much time in the kitchen, Mum's dominion. Neighbours and her friends came by with cooked meals, but mostly I was alone. There was time for reflection on, among other things, what had led me to have morphine buried in my garden, the acquisition and selling-on of dozens of typewriters around the country, and boxes of file cards covered in exotic symbols. I had to admit that my life contained some odd features.

Despite sending so much anonymous mail, the inventory of targets had grown because I did not want to be like the army officers who had done nothing when others were humiliated. The cipher used to record the need for vengeance and my actions were alien to almost everyone else who knew me. Most other lads grew out of their obsessions or at least acquired a wife and children in addition to their bird-watching or collecting comics. But I was not prepared to risk moving on from celibacy or letting go of the quest for revenge.

One fact dominated the decision to continue hunting and hounding; if I did not act, people like Knattmaw would get off scot-free. I considered reducing the number of targets by only pursuing those most guilty of cruelty to me. But with both parents gone, my life felt empty and although work could be interesting, the greatest satisfaction came from locating my quarry, launching a letter or setting a trap. There was a kick in preparing each sting; contemplating the unfolding consequences for the target was the most rewarding use of my imagination. And on the way to an illicit assignment that alertness from dread tinged with excitement cloaked whatever else bothered or depressed me.

The vicar visited the cottage towards the end of my fortnight off work. He seemed like a decent chap and the invitation to talk at any time tempted me for a few days before turning to the old remedies of resolving computer security issues and visiting unpleasantness on those who mistreated others.

Not all staff welcome the consulting support their managers commission. Employees might agree that they lack know-how or the insights that a consultant acquires from working in many organisations, yet still resent the status of the visitors or their fees, be they known or imagined. As my rates climbed, so too did the number of salaried people who bad-mouthed or wanted to make me look foolish. On occasions, a decent employee warned that my work or character had been impugned.

Pointing out the security flaws in an organisation's equipment or software disgruntled the people who had supplied it and third party representatives from time to time sniped in meetings. Fortunately, my dislike of upsetting people meant that I never overstated a case and could always back up assertions. The organisations that had acquired the duff products were usually grateful, apart from individuals who had been lax in specifying or checking what was supplied. What I feared most was collusion between an employee and a supplier's representative when both held grudges. Word might spread and make it easier for my competitors to win future assignments. Such was my fear, I attended *gratis* many multi-party meetings to deter mutterings against me. But what was said when I was not present and who could be trusted?

These nagging questions led me to adapt a microcassette machine so that pushing the pause button made recording continue without the red light coming on. In meetings, I dictated the occasional note and looked for any signs of curiosity. Should anyone seem interested, I handed over the device and invited a trial recording. Once the novelty had faded, I waited until people were defensive, claimed my pager had alerted me to something urgent and left the room for a few minutes. My intention was to protect my reputation and earnings, but I also discovered personal abuse. For all the times I had heard people mock my height, there had been no habituation; the response was always one of deep anger.

Five months after my mother died, I was driving back from a particularly stormy meeting with a government department and a major corporation who had supplied a system so full of holes that the IT staff at the centre called it *The Colander*. My job had been to present the issues with security implications in such a way as to pressure the supplier to make good without seeking further payment. I had wanted to do this in writing only, but millions of pounds were riding on the firm being shamed into correcting the defects. As per usual with Whitehall, the contract poorly served the department. In particular, requests to amend the specification, although not the source of the design faults, provided the company with room for legal wriggling. A vice-president in a sharkskin suit had flown from California and had challenged me relentlessly until he knew that I could cite chapter and verse for every issue. For once, the recording of snatches of conversation lifted my spirits because the American had complimented the department on their choice of consultant while I was supposed to be making a call in another room.

After listening to the recording, I took the motorway and then an exit that led to Vaulting Ryego. I had done this before, perhaps once every six months from the time that my consulting began. The route I always took was not the quickest; it avoided sight of the barn that had once contained three dead people and a dog. After the town, I would drive to Raventulle. The house and outbuildings had grown more decrepit year by year. Weeds rampaged as the area of tended garden shrank. Pasture had swallowed up the orchard and not even a trace of the tree stumps remained. Cows, separated from Raventulle by a gateless fence, grazed in what had been the favourite play area of the Kyte sisters and their little friend. It felt as if someone had tried to uproot my memories.

On the day of the stormy meeting and illicitly recorded praise, there was a sign in the front garden. I longed for it to read, *For Sale*. The time had come to quit Rayners Lane and my heart leapt at the possibility of owning Raventulle. As soon as I saw that the estate agents' board proclaimed what I wished, I drove back to Vaulting Ryego.

Ariadne Morveseau saw me getting out of my car while she was tending the details of properties displayed in the window of Hoggson's, the area's oldest estate agent. She looked me up and down and noted the modest vehicle. As I gazed through the glass for Raventulle's details, I gave friendly smiles that her heavily made up blue eyes chose not to acknowledge.

She was in her mid-twenties and the sort of person who needs to register indifference, if not distaste, to boost self-esteem. When I entered the shop, no sales fulsomeness or welcome passed her lips. Ariadne did not see me as the sort of person who could afford even the least expensive of the properties listed. Although I hardly knew what to do with my earnings as a consultant, I never bothered with an expensive watch, jewellery or a flash car. I disliked drawing attention and big vehicles only made me look smaller. I loved the sleek lines of sports cars, but did not want the taunts they invited, such as *Big engine, small dick*. I also had witnessed the owner of a Lotus Elan set upon simply because some drinkers resented his good fortune. And not least, I liked to mislead people, to keep something hidden, possibly to use to my advantage. I have much enjoyed saying to myself, *you're not as clever as you think you are,* when someone has made wrong assumptions.

I had a tailor for suits, another for shirts, and wore handmade shoes, but my tastes were plain. There is no sharkskin in my wardrobe. Standing out too much could stoke professional envy and encourage more resentment of the fees paid to me. For work, I aped the sober attire of IBM staff – dark blue suits, white shirts and demure ties – and off duty clothes were also subdued. From my car and unstylish clobber, Ariadne probably took me for a clerk on a basic wage who was lucky enough to find an off-the-peg suit that fitted.

Her clothes looked expensive. That day it was a blue and white half-sleeved dress inspired by a sailor's jacket, which like much of her wardrobe made the most of her tall and buxom figure. She would have looked quite attractive were it not for the habitual scowl on her round face. I suspected that the blonde hair was not authentic but, like the rest of her, the coiffure suggested breeding. It did not surprise me when I learned her surname; the Morveseaus had prospered in the shire for two-hundred years and her father owned huge tracts of land and an agricultural contracting business to the north of the county.

Ariadne barely looked up from adding a property description to the display. "Can I help you?"

"I understand Raventulle is for sale. I'd like to see it."

The difference between our two accents did nothing to reassure her that I was moneyed.

"With a view to buying, Mr. ...?"

"Gray, Perry Gray. Yes, to buy. The price is well within my means. I'm not in a chain and I will not require a mortgage, just the sale of some investments. It all depends on the state of the property."

I handed her my business card. Not for the first time, someone seeing *Data Security Consultant* and the jumble of initials after my name responded with a different attitude. Only computing people knew that the affiliations signified little more than a membership fee.

"Would you like to look at it now?"

As she drove me in her Range Rover and during the tour of Raventulle, she questioned without shame. I described my work, how lucrative it was and the accountant who excelled in minimising tax.

The interior of the unoccupied house had hardly changed since the 1940s. Some of the Kyte's furniture remained. Every room and outbuilding brought back a surge of memories so good they came with regret for days gone forever that nothing will ever match. I had Ariadne fetch her torch and examined the room where the kiss that meant more to me than any other took place.

"Why are you so interested in the cellar, Mr Gray?" she shouted from the top of the stairs that she seemed reluctant to trust with her weight.

"For wine. It's my only vice."

Ariadne appeared to have no problem with this claim. What disconcerted her was my knowledge of building work, much of which I had acquired from Dad. By the time we arrived back at Hoggson's, I had gone from nonentity and nuisance to a valued potential customer.

I retired to the Assam Tea Rooms to estimate repair costs. When Ariadne saw these, her face fell.

"Tell the vendor that I'm not prepared to invest in a survey unless the price drops significantly. If the figures add up, he could have his money very soon."

No one likes having their commission squeezed, but she knew the property was uninhabitable and who would want to live there with building contractors coming and going for months on end? Hoggson's best customers were wealthy families moving to the area and they wanted homes that needed little work. As only developers more cut throat than me were interested in a building needing a major overhaul, the vendors dropped the price by fifteen per cent.

Salvageable fittings and furniture from the time of the Kytes went to restorers. An architect drew plans that included expanding the cellar, making safe the rickety outbuildings and adding a workshop with a greenhouse appended to its southern wall. To protect the property during frequent absences there would be an alarm system, CCTV, a tall gate and fences, retractable grills for windows and a steel door at the top of the stairs to the cellar. The latter would hold, among other things, a valuable wine collection. The architect recommended a builder who also acted as site manager and supervised the contractors. Although I visited from time to time, I left the work to the professionals and tradesmen until near completion.

The architect was puzzled that I wanted to move into a house where only the upstairs was carpeted and the decorators had painted the woodwork, but left the plaster bare on every untiled downstairs wall.

"Got to save money somewhere," I said.

He laughed. "So you can fill your humongous wine cellar?"

"It's my only vice."

After moving in, I took time off work, hung the curtains I had ordered and used them to enhance privacy while I cut channels in the walls and through the floorboards for cables to the cellar for additional power, telephone, CCTV and microphone links. I had a room for an office upstairs for my legitimate activities and devised a hidden room in the cellar behind what looked like a continuous wall straddled by a set of shelves. Silent fans, one impelling and one expelling, mounted on an outside wall behind large bushes above the concealed area provided ventilation. Had someone managed to break in or the police required me to open the steel door, it was most unlikely that they would have found the secret space.

Storekeepers and shoppers in Vaulting Ryego were curious about the refurbished house. I asked them to wait for the housewarming party after the conclusion of the decorating. On the day of the party, I did not want to draw attention to the cellar by constantly unlocking and locking it. Neither did I want people to access it when I was not there. My solution was pretending to have mislaid both keys for the steel door, a deception supported by buying last minute bottles from the wine shop in the Square.

One key I always wore around my neck or kept under my pillow and the other lay beneath a lavender bush, in the same row that hid what was left of the morphine brought from Rayners Lane.

The builder said, "I hope you find a key. Otherwise you'll need oxy-acetylene to get into your cellar. You really do take your wine seriously."

"It's my only vice."

"You make yourself sound like a monk who fancies a drop once in a while," said the architect.

I grinned. "The vows I've taken are a long way from saintly."

"And what would those be?" asked one of the women guests.

With the alcohol and the attention received, I considered for just a moment alluding to my commitment to settling scores.

Then my usual reserve kicked in. "I was in the Army Pay Corp when they were automating records. I saw where computers were going and promised myself I would have a slice of that."

Ariadne was not invited because I disliked her condescension. However, the way she had dealt with me was a minor offence because her slights had involved neither name-calling nor witnesses. She was not then on my list and in her favour she had helped to spread the word that I had a profitable business. Despite this being true long before I left Rayners Lane, the acquisition and lavish refurbishment of Raventulle made some local women take an interest in me. The friendliness of a few resulted in dates, which I enjoyed for as long as the woman appeared content with a platonic relationship and was not a gold digger.

As sophisticated listening devices became available to the public, I located a home-based dealer happy to supply for cash without knowing a customer's name. His sales to me included a microphone and transmitter hidden in a working calculator and a small suitcase fitted with a receiver, its own microphone and a voice-activated recorder that silently filled both sides of two cassettes. At some locations, I left the calculator on a meeting room table and the suitcase in my car. If there was no suitable parking space for wireless reception, I said that my car locks were defective and left the bag in an office to receive or set it to record what its own microphone picked up. Many miles of motoring sped by as I listened to what others had assumed were private comments.

Listening to a covert recording in the car one August evening, I had an *Oh fuck it* response, one of those moments when caution is thrown to the wind. Nye Swann, a systems analyst from the company that had provided a computing centre's primary software chatted to the manager of the office where I had left the suitcase. Nye, who had resented me pointing out a major security weakness in his firm's product, insinuated that in doing so I had questioned the purchasing manager's competence. That was bad enough, but then Nye called me an obnoxious dwarf. Anger made me race home to draft a letter. As soon as it was typed, I sped to post it sixty-five miles away in the city where Nye's company is based. After a bend taken too fast, my car slid where cows had deposited their effluent. I skidded, made things worse by braking hard and a reflector post dented the front bumper before the car stopped. Such was the shock, I raced though a gate to defecate behind a hedgerow; I was seconds away from soiling my pants. A mid-summer sun was sinking below a grey and pink streaked horizon. Cows approached, stood in a semi-circle a dozen yards away and emptied their bowels and bladders as if in sympathy. My gut squeezing panic came from the realisation that a more serious car accident could have resulted in exposure. Had the police found me unable to speak, they might have opened the letter in search of a name and address. The cassette player held the illicit tape and the equipment used to transmit and record it was still on the back seat, such had been the haste after hearing Nye's sneers.

I put the envelope and tape in the recording case, locked it, hid the key in the car manual and then drove with great care the remaining miles. After returning home, I thought hard about the risk to profession and income if caught bugging or sending anonymous letters. Yet I decided to continue, albeit with greater care, because only one thing gave more satisfaction than a letter intended to hit back; having proof that retaliation had caused someone who had dished out abuse to suffer.

But you may ask, why do I insist that I was not addicted? There were times, not many I admit, when I went a month or more without writing a letter or hunting for my prey; for example, when busy vacating Rayners Lane and adding finishing touches to Raventulle. I had no withdrawal symptoms then. True, I looked forward to restarting my hobby. But would you say a person who relishes the prospect of chocolate after giving it up for Lent or craves alcohol after an arctic expedition is addicted?

Is my enjoyment so different from the copper who gets a buzz from banging up villains, or the auditor who delights in sniffing out embezzlement? Such people would no doubt say they are performing a public duty.

But were it not for me, many bullies would have gone unpunished. And my sympathy for others humiliated in public is no less genuine because I derived satisfaction from making their persecutors wince.

In cases where I sought revenge for others, liveried vehicles were the easiest targets. I would tail the abuser and invent a piece of dangerous driving. Always I made sure that there were two letters sent from different towns reporting the same imagined or exaggerated incident. The letters arrived without phone numbers or email addresses and used the addresses of empty houses. That way, I figured, there was less chance of mail being returned as not known at this address, or at least the company's letter would be returned after a longer interval.

I never entered the home of an individual who had not directly bullied or humiliated me. That I reserved for the people whom I most hated because I needed a level of loathing that could only come from direct humiliation to overcome my fear of being caught housebreaking.

Wandering uninvited around the homes of others and discovering the letters, diaries and pursuits they would prefer were kept secret made me anxious about security at Rayners Lane. Mum welcomed my fitting better locks, window catches, and I attached a small safe to the floor and a wall of my bedroom, but I never convinced her to fit grills. She thought these, like an alarm, would attract burglars. And she would not replace the windows and external doors because Dad had fitted them.

After she made her final journey to hospital, I upgraded the cottage's security. Yet only at Raventulle did I feel confident because a detective or burglar with a day to search the house or a month to study the PC kept upstairs would have found nothing incriminating.

Raventulle provided a fresh start for me in another way. None of the locals knew how isolated I had been in London and many of them would have found it hard to imagine loneliness in such a crowded city. And while I had entertained some misgivings about advertising my income through buying and renovating the house, it was not a barrier to socialising with the majority. The town's tradespeople, such as the upmarket grocer and the woman who had made my curtains, treated me with deference and were pleased to attend the house-warming. Working class people greeted my arrival in a pub. If they had some reservations about another outsider depriving a local of a home, it was offset by me not being pushy, having a down-to-earth accent, providing help with computing problems, and responding generously to charity collections. I also soon became a valued member of quiz teams. In one I met my first Vaulting Ryego date and in another a fellow contestant facilitated my joining a group of local men who met each week for poker.

I liked the new life so much and so hated missing a poker session that I began to reject offers of work that previously I would have snapped up. Saying no to work led to larger fees being offered and more organisations suggesting tasks that could be done at home. Within a year of being more selective about assignments, my earnings were as high as ever despite being away for half as many nights.

One way I used increased leisure time was helping locals with their home computers. As well as dispensing advice over a pub table, I began to visit houses to service or mend. I charged modest fees for those I socialised with and accepted services in kind, such as helping to dig my garden, from those who were hard up. The income was unimportant, but providing free help that allowed access to other people's data might have roused suspicions. After requests for help grew, I asked people to bring their machines to Raventulle to allow me to make better use of time by doing other work while running tests. As soon as the owner of the machine had left it, I fixed the problem, copied their hard drive and rang to say their machine was ready for collection. The quicker they had it back, the less reason to suspect someone was sniffing through their files.

I devised programs that searched the copied hard drive for files with passwords or encryption and for key words such as *Dear, Yours, Perry, Gray, Raventulle* and nicknames that had been assigned to me. In about one computer in twelve, I found things of interest among all the dross; saucy photos, secrets that would have been scandalous if made public, gossip that had not yet reached my ears, and child pornography. A teacher had concealed, but not well enough for my level of skill, vile images. It took a few days to unscramble the files, by which time he had his laptop back. A picture of a local child suggested that he was an active abuser who created as well as consumed porn and some images from what might have been Morocco were sadistic. The teacher presented a dilemma. If I delayed reporting him he might abuse again. Had I moved too soon, he might have guessed who had tipped off the police. And if rumours started that I checked files, others would be less likely to trust me. The compromise was to wait a month before sending the police an anonymous warning.

Ariadne, who had all but ignored me after the sale went through, stopped me in the square with a rare smile to say her home computer was going slower and slower. It was galling that she thought she could ask a favour. However, my curiosity led me to invite her to bring the computer.

The machine needed little more than a defrag and getting rid of bloated and duplicated files to improve its performance. Ariadne collected her PC late the same day, by which time I had set my program to examine a copy of her hard drive. She was not interested in what had caused the slow down and her usual disdainfulness had supplanted the smile managed while seeking a favour.

I found that I featured in several of her letters and emails that she would have assumed were erased completely. Her gossip to people who were away from the town or had left it referred to me as an *upstart*, *pipsqueak*, and *a tiny and silly man*.

She also wrote, "Everything is miniaturised these days, even computer geeks. But not Perry Gray's income. However, no amount of money will make him acceptable to the people who really count around here."

According to her, my renovation of Raventulle was kitsch and she especially disliked the leaded diamond windows and using bricks rather than stone for my workshop. She speculated on whether my tastes were gay and passed on what she knew from a local woman, who was not identified, that I had shown no interest in making love.

The most consoling item in the correspondence was Ariadne admitting her computer illiteracy. She wrote that she had only managed to make the transfer at home from pen to keyboard with the help of a former boyfriend. Nothing suggested any of her relationships with men had lasted more than a few months and she had sent bitter emails to two who had ended with her. One former beau she accused of being ungracious, which was like Ms Pot complaining about the complexion of Mr Kettle.

On Sunday morning, I left a message for Ariadne about finding a screw and fearing her PC's cooling fan might come loose. I offered to come and fix this. When she called back, we agreed I would visit that evening her thatched cottage on the other side of the town. From the outside, it looked eighteenth-century if you ignored the electric lights and the glow of a television screen. Inside, much of the furniture matched the period, but no modern comforts were missing. The standard of decoration was impeccable.

"Do you own or rent?"

Her look suggested that she wanted to accuse me of impertinence, but she said, "Own, of course. Only a fool would rent around here."

She offered no refreshments. Once the music from *Antiques Road Show* started, she left me in the downstairs study to get on with my supposed job. I installed a virus that would make the viewable area of the screen shrink to the size of a postage stamp in six days' time. Then I secreted tiny voice-activated transmitters near to the phone in the study and another in her bedroom upstairs. On my way out, I mentioned the growing problems with computer viruses and recommended she get protection, confident that she would not.

As Raventulle was too far away for the transmissions from the bugs, I had placed a receiver connected to a recording device in the boot of my car. I made the engine groan a few times and went back to tell Ariadne that it would not start.

"I know what it is. I even have the part on order. I'll just leave the car here till it arrives."

She blinked annoyance that I again had interrupted her programme and was leaving a boring car outside her home. There was no offer of a lift to Raventulle. In a way, I preferred her rudeness; it's easier to act against people who lack redeeming moments.

I rented a car for the rest of the week. The next Saturday, a less haughty Ariadne left a message about her screen shrinking. I made a point of visiting unannounced the next evening just as *Antiques Road Show* was starting.

"I've come straight here from another job and I'm gasping. Would you mind making me a cup of tea?"

By the time she brought the tea without biscuits or smile, I was erasing the virus that had caused the screen to shrink. As soon as she was engrossed by the television programme, I retrieved the two bugs.

Listening to the humdrum parts of secret recordings for hours on end can be mind-bogglingly boring. I was fortunate to be able to do so while undertaking work that others paid large fees for. The tapes from Ariadne consisted largely of background noise, mostly Radio 2. She often used a cordless phone or a mobile so far from the bugs that only her louder exclamations were intelligible. But among the dross were snatches of conversation that revealed she had two lovers.

Selwyn Chuttick was a major landowner and married county councillor who was old enough to be Ariadne's father. I had wondered if his email messages to her were quite what they had seemed on the surface. The bug revealed arrangements for a further liaison at a hotel in a neighbouring county. Her other flame was a muscular, eighteen year-old, Jonathan Dunwich, son of a nouveau riche family that had come from London after the father had opened a plastics factory in the county. Gossips reported that Jonathan had recently left his public school with mediocre grades to work for his father while training to become a triathlon champion. Ariadne's conversation with the lad hinted at a dalliance that went back some years, perhaps to when he was underage.

I sent three letters, but used only two stamps.

Dear Mrs Chuttick, I find myself in a difficult position. I have great sympathy for you and feel driven to write because I have suffered as a married woman from infidelity. However, I have managed to conceal what so hurt me from the world at large. Please therefore forgive me for not identifying myself, but we do know each other.

At intervals, your husband meets Ariadne Morveseau of Vaulting Ryego in various hotels away from our county. They have been lovers for some time. I understand that Miss Morveseau met your husband through her work for Hoggson's Real Estate. They may think that they have been discreet, but, at least in my part of the world, their liaisons are common knowledge. They last met at the Imperial in Sandling Wells on May 28th. The room was booked in Ariadne's name.

It may be that you and your husband's views on such relationships are liberal. If that is so, I apologise for this intrusion.

If you decide to confront Mr Chuttick, my experience is that hiring a good private detective avoids the denial phase and leaves the injured party in a stronger position to secure all that she is entitled to.

May I also suggest you and your husband are screened for sexually transmitted diseases as Ariadne has more than one lover.

Best wishes
A supporter of fidelity in marriage

Dear Mr and Mrs Dunwich, Contained in the second envelope is information that relates to Jonathan. If you take the view that he is now an adult and free to make his own choices, then I suggest you do not open this but destroy it.
A Friend

Dear Mr and Mrs Dunwich, If it's any consolation, as a parent of two children who are both in their late teens, I too would have opened the second letter. I could not end my parental duties at some notional point of adulthood.

I have strived to treat equally my son and my daughter. This is relevant because it means the dim view I would take of an older man having a relationship with a teenage girl applies also to an older woman pursuing a youth.

Your son is having an affair with Ariadne Morveseau. She has other lovers, including a married man. This, of course, increases the risk of Jonathan contracting a sexually transmitted disease. If he does not know about the other lovers, he may not be taking precautions against HIV etc.

Worryingly, there is the possibility that her relationship began when your son was under sixteen. I cannot be sure of this in the way that I am sure of other details.

This must be anonymous because my family cannot risk offending the Morveseaus. You will appreciate that Ariadne's family has considerable commercial influence. I hope you are in position, once you have considered your options, not to feel inhibited by such constraints the way some are.

A Friend

The first suggestion of a palpable hit came with news that Jonathan had left to spend six months in Ohio with the North American distributor of his father's products. A week later, I found the Shoe and Anvil agog with news that a middle-aged woman had gone into Hoggson's and slapped Ariadne.

"What for?" I asked.

"I know why I'd slap another woman," said the barmaid.

"You reckon she was tickling trout that someone else had hooked?" said a leering male customer.

"Let's not jump to conclusions." I said. "People fall out about all sorts of things."

"Especially about a bit of poaching, though!" sneered another man.

"After the tickle comes the slap," said the barmaid.

I slept well that night. A few weeks later, gossips spoke of Ariadne leaving for a working holiday in New Zealand. I bought a case of Martinborough Pinot Noir to celebrate and opened the first bottle on hearing that a Hoggson's for sale sign had appeared outside her cottage.

Seven months after Ariadne flew south, her brother called me. "Sis' said you sorted out her PC. My laptop's frozen and the manufacturer says it will take two weeks to fix. I urgently need it sorted. Could you help?"

I read with interest his email correspondence with Ariadne. Mrs Chuttick had confronted Mr & Mrs Morveseau about their daughter's morals and the slapping was the talk of the county set just as much as the hoi polloi. Ariadne had asked about coming back to England and the brother advised her to wait five more months before raising this with her parents. He also suggested that she was more likely to continue to receive their financial support if she lived in London or somewhere at least equally distance from the shire.

Chapter 29: Norman ~ Arizona

N I want to ask you about the teacher's laptop.
P Each picture had a different password derived from its filename. I was so busy working out the algorithm that I overlooked the simple program on the laptop the teacher had used to generate the passwords until it was too late to save any time.
N It wasn't the technical aspects that I was thinking of. You waited a month before reporting him when he might have been abusing a child. What stopped you acting straight away?
P I thought I'd explained. I didn't have the laptop by the time I discovered the porn. If I'd told the police that I had a copy of the teacher's hard drive, they would've asked why and what I was doing searching it. So I had to report anonymously. And had I done that too soon, the teacher would've suspected me.
N You could have made an excuse to get the teacher to bring the laptop back to you. You invented one to plant bugs in Ariadne's house.
P Even if no one suspected me of copying personal files, once word spread that I'd reported the teacher, others with anything to hide would have stopped bringing their computers to me.
N So satisfying your curiosity about what people preferred to keep private was more important than the welfare of children?
P You don't know that any kid suffered because I delayed. And how about other locals with child porn on their computers; what chance of exposing them if they suspected me of alerting the police?
N Let's agree to disagree then.
P As you wish. But isn't it rich that I brought a sadistic child abuser to justice and end up hated like the Moors Murderers?

CARE provided me with an introduction to COBOL so that I had enough knowledge to say I was a programmer to the outside world. Although the course made me curious about computers and CARE had a monstrous mainframe, security restrictions meant that I did not see it during my first fourteen months. Then, instead of translating publications and technical documents obtained through espionage, I joined a team developing software to analyse Russian text. In-depth computer training was provided and colleagues acted as personal tutors. I went up a grade for my contribution to the project and a year later became the supervisor of a small team thanks to having both fluent Russian and the ability to write complex programs.

However, not having a degree was a barrier to further promotion until my boss, the son of a baronet, had a stroke. His replacement was a mathematical genius who, despite never going to university and working on his father's poultry farm, had corresponded with a Cambridge don about Boolean Logic. The don recruited him to the team at Bletchley Park struggling to understand a cipher machine known to Allied intelligence as *Tunny*. Unlike most other CARE managers before the 1980s, my new boss paid no heed to social origins, education or former military rank; what counted for him was ability and using it in a purposeful way.

He congratulated me on my self-taught Polish, but added, "Without knowing whether it was a priority language for us suggests a lack of strategic thinking. Reliable Poles in this country are not scarce compared to, say, Romanians and Bulgarians."

"Do you want me to learn one of those languages?"

"What I most would like you to study is a new approach to programming developed for the Pentagon. The only way to learn involves two months in the States. I was going to do the course myself until I took this job."

"What's so special about the approach?"

"One American said the language was as different as the English of a ten-year old is from the English of a college professor. The Pentagon has prevented it going commercial to prevent Soviet access. And to keep it secret, there's minimal documentation. Hence the length of the course. The people who complete it are the instruction manuals."

He mentioned an Institute run by a corporation for the Pentagon near a small town in the Sonoran Desert, outlined the course on offer and the importance of the UK acquiring its own expertise. His proposal flattered and excited me. When Captain Bligh had mentioned travel all he had in mind was attending the odd scientific conference in Europe. At the time that studying in America became a possibility, I had not travelled further than Padua.

"I'd love to go!"

He welcomed my enthusiasm and said the course began in three weeks' time. Only then did I remember that I had a loving wife and a difficult eight year-old stepson, but I did not admit to any hesitation.

Still buzzing when I arrived home, I blurted the news to Rose without thinking to apologise first or explain how the opportunity had swept me along. The tone of her questions made obvious her growing displeasure, which peaked after I admitted the voluntary nature of the assignment.

I had never seen her look so hurt by me. "You're the last person I expected to remind me of Rodney's high-handedness."

Instead of apologising for not anticipating her sensitivity to a unilateral decision, my heart hardened. Why did she have to frown and grill me rather than share my excitement? Lacking courage to express anger, I left her in the kitchen and lay on our bed with a book that remained unread. It became apparent that she was not going to come and make up. By the time she called to say dinner was ready, Colin was home from swimming club and neither of us wanted him to suspect there was tension between us. But after he went to bed, there was mostly silence.

We managed superficial civility in the days that followed. Our bedroom was the iciest place as we strained to avoid not just contact but also giving any warmth. My libido noted the falling temperature and hibernated. Colin detected the strain, looked pleased and grinned to witness us parting without a kiss in a flurry of March snow outside the airport. During my flights, the conclusion that the marriage was over – there was not even the pretext of staying together for the benefit of Colin – added to my resentment. A miserable life without Rose lay ahead. The chances of finding such a partner again were so remote that only a fool would think it possible. Perversely, I dwelt on the misery ahead rather than considering an apology to prevent the unhappiness, a state of mind that makes no more sense now than cutting off a finger to be rid of a splinter.

The Phoenix hotel reception rang to wake me at ten in the morning, by which time the room was baking hot. I wanted to go back to sleep, but not only was there a bus to catch, sweating had added to the dehydration of drinking airline brandy. Fierce sunlight had turned the space between the large window and curtains into a column of hot air that rose, hit the pelmet and convection-cooked the room. After four glasses of water and showering, the air-conditioning that I had switched on had hardly reduced the temperature. I put on a short-sleeved shirt with my thinnest trousers.

Glare from the pool and white stucco outside the dining room made clear the need for sunglasses. The only shop in the area was in the hotel foyer where pricing took full advantage of the concession's monopoly. When I hesitated over a pair, the proprietor offered to throw in a packet of postcards and five stamps that would get them to England. Not having enough cash, I offered a traveller's cheque. This could only be cashed at reception and queuing there twice, to get money and then to settle my bill, put me behind schedule. I was already agitated by the prospect of divorce and angry for not bringing the sunglasses bought in Padua for little more than sixpence.

To save time, I waited outside for the taxi I had ordered. By the time it arrived, my milky arms were tingling from the sun. We arrived at the bus station at the last moment, which meant lugging my case on board. At least one seat out of each pair was taken throughout the front of the vehicle and then everything was empty apart from a family at the very rear. They were a young couple with three under-fives sitting up half covered in blankets. The children – all rather beautiful – had jet-black hair, dark olive skins and large brown eyes that squinted far less than mine with sunglasses. They spoke Spanish and were well behaved despite their grinning excitement at being on the bus.

By the time I had manoeuvred the case half-way down the aisle, I was glad to have it with me because the air conditioning was creating goose pimples. I remained standing to take out a jacket. Just after I had fastened one of the locks, the bus lurched and the case crashed into the aisle. The nearest man, two rows ahead, turned his buzz-cut head. He was chubby, tall, in his late twenties and between a profusion of freckles the face was sunburnt. His skin, like my eyes, did not belong in such a climate. The ears and nose were peeling and the latter being rather bulbous gave him a clown-like quality.

"You OK back there?"

"I'm fine now," I said, wedging the case at an angle in the window seat. "Air conditioning's not something I'm used to."

Other passengers hearing my accent turned around. The man got up and sat across the aisle from me. We chatted about the unusually warm weather, my accent and then he asked how I was enjoying America.

"I only arrived last night. Where are you from?"

"Arizona born and bred. My folks came here in '33 from Kansas."

He said it the way an English peer might boast his family had lived in their castle since the reign of Richard the Lionheart.

I learned that he was single, lived with his parents and worked in their gas station. He was returning from a week's training with the National Guard. Something lumbering and gormless about him reminded me of a National Serviceman who, despite his height and weight, had attracted much bullying.

"How do the other soldiers treat you?"

"They gave me a hard time until we got some greasers in the unit. Now it's not so bad."

"What are greasers?"

"Mexicans. Makes you wonder why we bothered to kick Santa Ana's ass. Hell, if we're not careful the next thing you know the road signs will be in Spanish."

He had made no attempt to lower his voice and I hoped that the family at the back had not heard him. I was aware of English people who not only resented coloured migrants but also despised non-whites wherever they lived. This made me curious about how he felt about Mexicans who remained in their country.

"Do you visit Mexico?"

"Never. A guy in high school went and came back with crabs and anything people buy there falls apart. It's not for me. And all that Catholic stuff."

The religious angle took me by surprise. "But Kennedy was a Catholic."

"I can't say I miss him."

He too had spoken without thinking and looking embarrassed he asked, "Say, you're not a Catholic are you?"

"My parents raised me as a Protestant."

"Good for them."

He still looked uncomfortable and said, "Guess I'll leave you to enjoy the scenery."

Another man, older and plumper, came and sat alongside me twenty minutes later. Mosiah spoke about his two years with the US Air Force at Lakenheath servicing jet engines and how he missed the greenness, but not the wind, rain and sleet. I understood because the desiccated land we were travelling through appeared so alien to me. I mentioned that most of my army service had been in East Anglia.

"And what do you do now?"

"Computer engineering."

"So what brings you to Arizona?"

"Work."

"And where are you heading?"

After naming the town where I would be getting off, he mentioned the Institute and the corporation that ran it and asked, "Will you be there long?"

"A few weeks."

"I won't ask you anything else. I know it's hush-hush, but it's also the biggest employer for miles around. I've got relations who helped build it and others working there now."

Mosiah was a self-taught arborist who specialised in trees and plants for arid conditions and it was a pleasure to learn about what grew in the shimmering heat. After he got up to gather belongings for his stop, he chatted with others as he stood by his seat. Another passenger came to shake my hand and sit on the other aisle.

Seymour wore a dark suit, a white shirt with button down pockets, two-tone cowboy boots and a bolo tie that held my eye and not only because of its large silver-set turquoise stone. A Teddy boy had worn the last shoestring I had seen around a neck. It was another reminder that I was in a strange land.

"I hear you're going to the Institute to study. I know you ain't allowed to say much about it, but I just wanted you to know that people around here know it needs security clearance to go there and that means you're right welcome."

"Thank you. Do you live near the Institute?

"About fifty miles further on. I'm from Texas originally so fifty miles is near for me. Do you go to church?"

I suspected he wanted to invite me to a service and wondered if the singing would make it worth my while.

"I'm in the choir at a church called St Felix and St Pancras, near where I live."

He stiffened. "Is that a Roman Catholic Church?"

"Not since the time of Elizabeth the First."

He looked confused, but I did not elaborate.

Then in hushed tones, he said, "You know I sang in a Baptist choir with John Birch before the war."

It was my turn to be confused. The only John Birch I knew was an English musician famous for his organ recitals and choral work. Sorting out the misunderstanding convinced the Texan that I was a deeply religious Anglican; how else could I know who was responsible for the music at Chichester Cathedral when it was miles from where I lived?

Seymour said the John Birch he had known went to China as a missionary. "The Reds got hold of him in '45 and shot him. I do believe he was the first victim of the Cold War and a martyr to boot. That's why the leading anti-communist organisation here is called The John Birch Society. Do you have anything similar in England?"

"Not that I'm aware of."

"You should. Your Labour Party is full of Marxists. I also hear you have a growing coloured population, not to mention a lot of Jews in positions of power. What we have here is a lot of Jewish agitators stirring up the niggers. Sometimes I wonder if Hitler was right."

I was speechless and not just from my usual reluctance to dissent. For a moment, I wondered if the Cold War was worth the effort if our allies included such bigots.

As the bus was slowing down to stop in a dusty town, Seymour continued more quietly. "You'll find most of the local people who work at the Institute are Mormon. The best I can say about them is that, as far as I know, none of them is a bigamist. They may have some of the trappings of patriotic conservatives and call themselves Latter Day Saints of Jesus Christ, but they ain't truly American or Christian. The way some of them live is little better than collectives and what genuine Christian believes that Adam became a God? The Institute scientists, though, are mostly sound Protestants and regular Americans with the exception of a few Jews and Catholics."

"I was too jet lagged to read last night and there's something I need to study before I get to the Institute. Will you excuse me?"

"Sure. Good talking to you."

He sounded miffed with my excuse, all I could manage by way of an objection to his bigotry. The encounter was another reminder that a shared language did not mean a shared culture. Longing for what was familiar and soothing, my thoughts kept turning to Rose before realising again and again that she had provided no comfort from the time she had learned of the trip.

A gleaming black sedan with dazzling chrome and even colder air than the bus was waiting in the shade opposite the drug store that served as the town's bus station. A slim man, whom I took to be a Native American, drove back the way the bus had come. After a handful of shops and a few dozen adobe houses with cactus gardens, both sides of the highway were desert. The driver said that as the other students were expected the next day, one of the men running the course had invited me home for dinner that evening. The tutor would collect me from the accommodation block at six and bring me back before nine so that I could have an early night to help get over any jet lag.

Just after saying this, he turned onto a single lane that ran level and straight into a wide valley. With the speedometer touching seventy miles per hour despite the seal being barely wider than the wheels, I did not talk for fear of distracting him, curious though I was about Native

American culture. Ahead was a cluster of glints that turned out to be the windows of the Institute and vehicles parked under the lines of parkinsonia trees near the gate. In this arid land, cars, or at least these ones, water was used to keep cars clean and to grow shade for them.

As soon as the sedan doors opened, dry air rushed in and the sun penetrated clothing as if the fibres were transparent. Sweat hardly surfaced before being blotted by the parched breeze. Had a full bead formed and fallen to the ground, a sizzling sound would not have been surprising. The dominant noise came from the air conditioning mounted on the roof of the two-tier concrete central block. The other buildings, including the accommodation area and canteen, were single storey and had reddish walls that the driver said were made of rammed earth. My room was dark and cool. I turned the thermostat up, unpacked, set the alarm for 5.30 and lay on the bed with a spinning head that prevented sleep. I felt lost, trapped and a fraud. By local standards, I was an unreliable pinko who should not be allowed within a mile of the mesh perimeter. And if a day in Arizona left me so disoriented, how would I cope with two months? In theory, I could go beyond the gatehouse, but where after that? My meal that night might be the only time away from what felt more like an institution than an institute.

The course tutor was in his thirties and, although not ugly, had a round face that would have benefitted from a few character lines and more hair than a crew cut allowed. His accent struck me as bland for someone clearly from the Old South. And while he demonstrated the manners that Dixie is famous for, even holding open the car door for me and closing it, I had a hunch that the invitation had been his boss's idea. His house, just on the other side of the town and near the schools that served the area, was one of a number of recently built adobe-style homes with gardens of gravel, sand, desert plants and a swimming pool at the back. His wife had personality and warmth, as if she had somehow acquired the husband's share.

Four children aged between nine and fifteen joined us at the table. If only Colin could have smiled, obliged and yes-sirred a quarter as much as any one of them. They also asked intelligent questions when a gap appeared in the conversation of the adults. Yet even the eldest, a boy who excelled at physics, had a one-sided view of evolution – that of the family's church – and the thirteen year-old daughter believed a fragment of ancient wood found on Mount Ararat proved the story of Noah's Ark. The parents beamed their approval of theology before empiricism.

After the children had started homework, the couple said they had come to the Institute to escape the risks of drugs and violence in their native Atlanta. I suspected they also wanted to avoid exposing their kids to other ways of thinking and integrated schools. The modernity of their colour television and a refrigerator big enough to need four doors seemed at odds with their old-fashioned religion and attitudes.

The Native American collected me at nine. I established that he and his tribe, whose name meant Desert Dwellers, were from the area.

"What do you make of all the people who have come to live here?"

"I wish the tribes had united to develop immigration policies to keep out those not prepared to learn at least one of our languages before leaving Europe. But once the sand has sculpted the rock, the mesa will never be as big again. Right now we have no choice other than sharing the land. Perhaps after the water runs out the people of the desert will be left in peace again."

The sadness in his voice struck a chord. "I find being in the desert disorientating."

"I felt that way in school and college and it returns every time I go to Phoenix."

"Do any of the newcomers speak your language?"

"Missionaries, some of whom do good things, but they're selling not buying ideas."

The sense of intruding on his land added to the sense of discomfort that had come from keeping quiet while the couple had railed against trade unions, state funded medical services, the ecumenical movement and contraceptives for unmarried people. Yet they had said so much after mistaking my silence and flimsy smiles for consent. Although I had met Americans visiting CARE, that day in Arizona I understood how different the culture of their homeland could be from everyday English life. Just as alien as the cacti gardens were social views that reminded me far more of the repression of Victorian England than the rowdiness of the Wild West.

The insomnia that followed would have prompted in other circumstances a long and tender letter to Rose. Too piqued to apologise, I scribbled on a postcard of a saguaro cactus little more than confirmation of safe arrival. Then as I lay in the dark, it occurred to me that surviving the next two months would depend a great deal on the other tutor and fellow students.

A roly-poly man in his forties with a shaggy beard, gorilla-like black hair on his forearms and sprouting from the neck of his Hawaiian shirt knocked on my door in the middle of the afternoon.

"I'm Dan. The gatehouse guy said you were in here. Seems like we're the only trainees so far. I've just driven from New Mexico and I'm ready for a beer, but hate drinking alone."

We sat in the lounge sipping from the bottles he took from an insulated container and talked about the Institute, which he had visited before, and London, where he had studied for a year. He and his wife loved the sunshine and space of New Mexico, but missed the culture and cosmopolitanism of their native Chicago and other large cities they had lived in. Encouraged by his liberal outlook, I described my encounters with the National Guardsman and Texan.

"I'm sorry you met such bigots. Unfortunately their views are not a rarity around here. This is where Johnny Reb racism runs into California kookiness with a little Sonoran sorcery and desert madness thrown in. And I say that as the descendant of crazy people who roamed in the desert before they roamed everywhere else."

"You mean the ancient Israelites and the Diaspora?"

Dan was fascinated to learn about my parent's flirtation with British Israelism, which he had been unaware of, and their return to mainstream Anglicanism.

"So are you an Anglican?"

"I sing in an Anglican choir."

"Do you favour one form of Anglicanism over the others?"

"The theology is not so important to me. If the best local choir was in another church I would have gone there."

"What if the best choir was in a synagogue?"

"Why not? Provided circumcision was not a prerequisite."

He chuckled and said, "A lot of religious people wouldn't go to another church, let alone stray outside of Christianity."

"I guess I'm less religious then."

"Same here. Agnostic really. Ethel and I celebrated the holy days and used the rituals so our children knew something about Jewish culture. Now the kids have left home we don't bother so much."

I shared what the tutor's children had said at the dinner table about evolution and Noah's Ark and how strange it seemed when they were familiar with science.

"Many of the researchers here profess a form of a Christianity that would not have been out of place on the Mayflower. Nowhere else I've been have the majority of people with doctorates insisted on a literal Bible and dismissed any science that questions it. And the Texan was right about one thing, most of the ancillary staff here are Latter Day Saints. It tickles me the way the biblical literalists regard Mormons as gullible for believing in another improbable book."

Dan made me feel less like a solitary fish in the desert. Yet despite all but admitting to him that I had no faith, what most troubled me was still unmentionable. Some unwritten law dictated that discussing what had happened with Rose would be unmasculine and unfair to him.

He took the lead in greeting the arriving students traipsing past us. The first spoke of his pleasure at visiting Arizona because he so admired Barry Goldwater, another looked warily at our beer bottles, and a third asked if we knew anything about local churches and how to get to Sunday services. The men were clean shaven and short haired and most had ties. The women, six out of the total of fourteen, wore stockings and, with one exception, dowdy clothes. I felt fortunate to have spent the hour before others arrived with Dan.

At dinner, Dan avoided being drawn into politics or religion, choosing instead to joke about more neutral topics such as the rivalry between the branches of the government and armed forces represented. He became the life and soul of the class, not that he had much competition in terms of wit. Some no doubt thought he joked too often, but I welcomed any levity because the other tutor was as dull as the first. The pair knew their subject and worked hard to support individuals. What was missing was skill at teaching and passion. The course over-used rote learning when practical exercises such as writing mini-programs would have worked far better.

The women fussed over me partly out of American traditions of hospitality and partly from curiosity about England. Among their kindnesses were invitations, insistence even, to join tables in the canteen and offering to do my ironing when they found me in the laundry. Only the two women sponsored by the Navy had travelled outside North America and among the male students three had never been beyond the USA. Marcia, the nearest of the females to my age, was the most persistent of the students in asking me about England and spoke of how her dream of travelling around Europe had to be put on hold when she became pregnant. She was a freckled, flaming redhead, a good foot taller than me and although not as beautiful as Rose, she matched her in personality and warmth.

Nine of the group were teetotallers and the drinkers, rather than share the lounge with their disapproving looks, met on a Saturday night in Dan's room. He and another student, Wendell, were the only two who had come in their own cars and they took turns to collect money and fetch alcohol from the town. Then for a couple of hours we would drink, chat and listen to Dan's jazz tapes on his cassette radio. After a couple of drinks, Marcia played with double entendres, such as when the other woman drinker admired the way a saxophonist held a note and Marcia said it was always good when a man didn't tire too soon. It was a kind of flirting and if there was anything to it I reckoned she had her eye on

Wendell. Although not downright handsome, he was way ahead of Dan and me in the beauty stakes. In any case, it seemed innocent enough as Marcia often spoke about calls home and her two children.

On the fourth Saturday, Wendell brought back ingredients for margaritas that soon had everyone giggling. When a fourth glass was offered, Marcia said she needed fresh air and a cigarette first, picked up her handbag, stood and teetered. I jumped up to steady her as she wobbled on two-inch heels. She grabbed my arm and held on as she weaved past others and the furniture. I thought it better to escort her to where she could smoke leaning against a wall, but on exiting the building she tugged my arm to steer us towards the gatehouse. Perhaps she wanted to vomit away from where a teetotaller might spot the evidence?

After a cool spell, the weather had warmed up again. A lukewarm breeze carried the scent from night-flowering plants and sagebrush. Marcia let go as we neared the floodlit area around the gate and strode ahead to alert the guard, as we had been advised to do, that we would be following the path on the inside of the fence.

"I wouldn't want to meet that Dobermann in the dark," she said on her return.

"Are you sure you can manage in those shoes?"

"If I take your arm, I'll be just fine."

The effect of the gate lamps made the sand and gravel path almost invisible until our eyes adjusted to the light from the half moon.

At the first corner, she stopped, let go of my hand and said, "I need a Camel."

I was about to step upwind to avoid the smoke when she proffered her lighter, rummaged for cigarettes and placed one between her lips. I held a flame in front of her face wondering how many times I had witnessed film stars playing such a scene to communicate the passions stirring within them. It was the first time I had ever lit a cigarette.

She started to stroll and I fell into step alongside. Before long she confided how the night she celebrated graduating *cum laude* had changed her life.

"I felt so grown up and sophisticated that I let a boy go all the way for the first time and got pregnant. When I told

Jim, he disappeared for two days before proposing. After that, my parents rushed the wedding so that I left the county before the bump began to show. Jim's parents lived in New Jersey and owned properties there. They offered us a place near them and helped Jim get work touting pharmaceuticals to doctors. It shocked me how quickly he settled into the kind of life my parents, who had never gone to college, lived. I mean, he even said he was disappointed when we had a daughter. And it didn't matter that I had a better degree than him; my role was looking after the house and providing a son. The programming I'd taken as an option in college was my salvation because there was so much demand that I could work part-time from home. Anyway, our second child was a boy and when James Junior was five I hired a live-in maid and got a regular job working on computer-aided artillery. Jim didn't like it and as for this course, even though his mom jumped at the chance of look after her grandchildren, he's needled me about it for months."

Her fingernails dug into my flesh as she said *needled*, but she was too caught up in her feelings to have done this on purpose. At the third corner of the perimeter I lit another cigarette for her. Between drags, she pointed it towards constellations as she named them. After the litany of stars had calmed her down, she ground out the butt, apologised for sharing her domestic issues and walked on.

The tequila had caught up with me. I talked with growing emotion about Colin's antipathy. She squeezed my hand and kept hold of it. Before much longer, she heard about the friction with Rose over the trip and how I hated the way I had blamed Colin for what had happened.

"After all, he's only a child and a damaged one at that."

"My dad's a farmer and a good man most of the time. But two months of the wrong weather make him like a bear poked awake in January. He has his limits; we all do. Whatever the reason for Colin being ornery, he's still a force that will stretch the elastic too far. And here's time away from him to recuperate and you're tearing yourself apart over what the stress he created drove Rose and you to do. Go back refreshed and you'll find a way to reconnect with Rose."

"Will you go back refreshed?"

She laughed. "Finding solutions for others is always easier. Truth is, I decided two years ago the marriage is dead. He doesn't talk to me except to criticise and I don't know why I'm still taking the pill. But I won't do anything because he still cares about the children and they come first. After both have finished high school, that's when my new life will begin."

A coyote howled; it might have been miles away. The Dobermann responded as if he had never heard such a sound before and it presented some immediate threat. The ugly barking resonated with my unhappiness and made me shiver. Marcia slid her hand across my back and I reached for it. She gripped my fingers, swivelled her body so that she blocked my path, dropped her bag and hugged me. While she was drawing my face against her blouse just above her bosom, I put my other arm around her. She stroked my hair avoiding the balding area until, I think after she noticed my erection, she tipped my chin and brought her smoky mouth to my lips. I was beyond objecting to the smell and responded. For some minutes we continued to kiss and caress and then, taking my arm, she led the way to an area of light where a wall of the gatehouse obscured the view of the guard.

"Have you got a handkerchief," she asked.

I handed it to her and she wiped away the traces of lipstick on me before dabbing around her own mouth.

"Let me wash it. I know how to get the red out," she said and then giggled.

It was below her usual standard of double entendre, but some of my nervous excitement found an outlet in uncontrollable laughter that provoked the same in her.

After we had steadied our breath, she told the guard we had finished our walk, took my hand and led me in silence until we neared the lights of the accommodation block.

"Give me your room key. Tell the others I've gone to bed, have another drink and I'll be waiting for you."

Reading Perry's comments on guilt and addiction made me think of Marcia. She did not love her husband, but she had never cheated on him before and our affair was no small matter for someone who still had remnants of

Christian beliefs. My problem was being in love with Rose. Going to bed with another had a hollow quality to it despite the tenderness, confiding, enjoyment and the way Marcia never suggested that she wanted anything more than the time we had together at the Institute.

Not even the drinkers suspected our night-time assignations and Marcia and I did nothing in public that hinted at the affair. Yet the very act of concealment reinforced guilt and there were times after lovemaking that one of us started to cry and then we both wallowed in the self-reproach. As Perry said, recriminations can feed the very desire that produced them. No matter how much guilt Marcia and I felt post-climax, an hour or so later, or on the next night, the need for solace would lead us to make love again. We shed no tears the last time we shared a bed, as if we both knew that there would be punishment enough in not having the consolation of each other. I could not resist asking then something that had been on my mind since we first shared a narrow bed.

"Why me and not Wendell?"

"You really don't know?"

"What do you mean?"

"Wendell is not one for the ladies."

"I thought he was quite attentive to women."

"He's courteous and he's good company, but I was sure enough not to risk making a fool of myself with him."

"And would it have been Dan if I was not here, or one of the God-botherers?"

"Would it have been me if Raquel Welch had been on the course and made eyes at you?"

"Touché."

"But not a fundamentalist. Who needs their grief when I've got enough guilt of my own? You know, it would be better if we didn't keep in touch. I'm fond of you, but this can't go anywhere and you should not give up on Rose without fighting for your marriage."

"I'm dreading going home."

"I know the feeling. If it wasn't for my children, it's the last place I'd go."

I had two nights in Washington and a day at Langley learning from the CIA people who were using for code work what I had just studied. The city and North Virginia, while all novel, felt reassuringly familiar after the desert, as did talking with other cryptanalysts. And the importance of the briefings helped me to stop thinking so much about what might be waiting at home. I finished drafting a report – full of idiosyncratic shorthand and code words – about the course and CIA meetings during the first two hours of my return flight. The VC10 was less than half-full and after a meal with wine, I lay across three seats. Yet I could not sleep nor read for wondering about what awaited me at home. The drinks trolley reappeared and I sat with a brandy looking out of a window. How insignificant everything was compared to the textured grey Atlantic. How much easier it would be if the jet fell out of the sky. Rose and Colin would have a new start. All that made me want to live was how hurt my mother would be to lose another relative and knowing the contribution I could make at CARE after the course.

Towards the end of the flight, a man sitting ahead excitedly woke the woman with him and urged her to look out the window. Below were a skein of thirty or so long-necked white birds aimed at a green speck on the horizon that grew into a land mass. It felt like a blessing to see the sun shimmering on the flock and fertile ground after so much dreary water. The thought of swans mating for life came into my head and it was then I decided to admit the affair. If Rose was disgusted and wanted to end our relationship, so be it. What love she still had for me was uncertain and in my low state it seemed that the only possible return to being happy together was via honesty.

A puffy-eyed Rose waited at Heathrow without Colin.
"Have you been crying?"
"A lot. I'll explain when we get home. Colin's with his Nan for a few days." She hugged me, saying, "Don't ask until I can talk without having to look at the road. Tell me about America."

I assumed that Colin had played up to express his displeasure at my return and I was in no hurry to hear about this. It also seemed prudent to delay my confession until she had had finished driving. Instead I described what I had seen during two hours at the Smithsonian and the fowl flying high in formation. Rose looked ahead even at red lights. Her tone was pleasant and conciliatory. I was used to her drawing out a surprising level of detail, but there was something false about the minutiae she extracted about the museum and the skein.

At home, Rose said, "Have a shower and then I'll tell you all or as much as you want to know."

I checked the wardrobe and drawers in case Colin had taken to my clothes with scissors or paint. Nothing was amiss. I came downstairs damp-haired, wearing a bathrobe and carrying a silk scarf and her favourite perfume. Seeing the gifts prompted Rose to cry.

"I don't deserve them. I don't deserve you. Last week I slept with someone. Just the once. How much more do you want to know?"

I did not want to know. The benefit of shock is the tissue of disbelief holding together the shattered remains of an assumption; a tissue all too easily punctured by evidence and shredded by details. Then I wanted to hit Rose and to roughly force myself on her. Entertaining such vile ideas so disgusted me that I began to cry. Because I could not speak, I stood on the backyard's cold flagstones in bare feet, signalled that she should stay inside and closed the sliding door. Breathing deeply to calm down, I told myself that contemplating battery and rape was a momentary lapse, that passing thoughts, no matter how revolting, are not the same as the deeds.

I asked myself, When I'm so hurt by a much briefer liaison than my adultery, how will Rose respond to news of Marcia?

The guilt for my fling became overwhelming. Why had I betrayed marriage vows over and over again? The only consolation was Rose's remorse for her infidelity, which meant that she still loved me. I was shivering like a flame in a storm by the time I went inside. She sat on the sofa hugging her knees and with the look of a deer cornered by wolves.

"The only things I need to know are that you still love me and you won't contact him again."

Her gulping and facial contortions suggested that she struggled with my proposition. Does she love me? Is the man difficult to avoid? Can she not trust herself?

Eventually she said, "I'll always love you and I swear that from now on I'll be true, but I have to tell you one more thing. If I don't, then I'll feel that I took advantage of what you assumed. It wasn't a man. I've felt attracted to women before, but this was my first and last sexual encounter with one."

Little had prepared me for such a revelation. Such things happened, but I had never expected them to impinge on our marriage. All I could think to say to Rose was that I needed more time alone. Not able to face more of the cold outside, I lay on our bed with eyes closed. Memories of what we had shared on that mattress kept interrupting other thoughts. Did she promise fidelity because of her love for me, or following the guilt she felt, or because she was less attracted to women than men? There was an element of relief that the lover was female, that no other man's sperm could embarrass me by making her pregnant. Yet prejudice still suggested that I was better equipped for lovemaking than another woman. I noted with some discomfort that after learning the affair was lesbian the urge to penetrate Rose violently had disappeared. And although ending our marriage to escape the constant chafing of Colin had some attraction, Rose's love for me, and my love for her, made me want to rebuild our relationship.

The only question that remained was what might happen following my admission of infidelity? I wanted to avoid being a hypocrite, but what if confessing made her rethink her commitment? And why inflict more pain when there was no possibility of her learning about Marcia from another source? I was not a Puritan and least of all the sort who insists on truth regardless of the hurt it causes others. Rose did no wrong telling me what she did, but nothing guaranteed we would be a stronger pair or happier individuals because I offloaded my guilt. Along with her immediate hurt, Rose would wonder every time work took me away if I would stray again.

I returned downstairs. "I was wrong not to consult you about the trip. The way I behaved after telling you only made things worse. I'm so grateful you're still here for me. Let's open a bottle of wine and put on some records.

I'd prefer pretending the last three months never happened."

Keeping my affair secret altered our relationship in ways I had never considered, let alone intended, because Rose thought only she had been unfaithful. She put even more effort into taking care of household matters to make amends. I could not have done much with Colin, but I began to take for granted many other tasks she undertook until I seldom engaged in household chores other than gardening. Work provided excuses, but that is all they were. And when ideas from the women's liberation movement stirred Rose, I relied on her vestigial guilt to suppress any challenge to the status quo that suited me. Sometimes I fear that Rose does not speak now because after her death she learned what happened with Marcia and resents the deceit that took advantage of her confession. The atheist in me knows that this is not possible, but when reason lies exhausted in the early hours and less cogent faculties are awake and febrile, tears spill and I curse myself for the exploitation of her good nature that invited retaliation as barbed as Perry's .

The skills learned in Arizona raised my profile at CARE. I trained others, relying more on practical assignments than rote learning and worked with a range of experts to help them assess what the new computer language could do for their disciplines. Promotion made me a manager of managers. Then CARE got the go ahead to build its new complex on a former RAF airfield, a site that would provide better security and accommodate additional staff. I oversaw the installation of a new mainframe supplied by U-Comp and ensured all classified programs and data would run on it. It was one of the few relocation projects that went to plan and when some senior managers opted for redundancy rather than relocation packages, I went up another rung. The duties precluded hands-on work and what I did in its place could not contain troubling past events to the same extent. At the same time, the Machiavellian games at and near board level, which included pressure on me to take sides, added to my anxieties.

The U-Comp project manager for the relocation had said to contact her if ever I wanted to work elsewhere.

After the CARE Director got wind of my expression of interest, he took me to lunch and asked why. I spoke of my unease with conflict and a desire to get back to a hands-on role. The upshot was I retained my grade without being required to attend the number of meetings that usually went with it. My role was to be a hands-on manager of special projects with a team that never had more than six direct reports. After other senior managers realised I was not a competitor for promotion, they confided in me. This, when combined with my reluctance to speak against others except when national issues were at stake, greatly reduced the friction around me. Of course, I still experienced some sniping because no one can please everyone. However, unlike Perry, bullying and humiliation in the workplace had become rare events for me.

What I still feared was abuse from revellers on the streets of larger towns and cities. One incident stands out. Rose and I emerged from a choral festival in an overheated London hall. We were still carrying our coats when we passed a pair of well-dressed middle-aged men on a bench. The insistence of their slurred speech and jerky gestures made it clear they were drunk.

One shouted, "Blow me, if it isn't Snow White and Dopey,"

Rose's skin was pale from the winter. There was no bow in her hair, but she had a page boy cut. And her longish dress emphasised her small waist. The resemblance to the cartoon Snow White, once pointed out, seemed apt. By itself and in another context, someone with a smooth tongue might even have passed it off as a compliment.

We walked away without replying and said nothing to each other about the remark. Two days later, Rose greeted me at Foxenearth's front door with close-cropped ash blonde hair.

"What do you think?"

"It's stunning, but did you change it because you wanted to or because of what happened?"

"What did happen?"

She added to her pretence of the incident having nothing to do with the change of style and colour by using the hall's opposing mirrors to guide her right hand patting strands that needed no realigning.

"I like your hair now and the way it was. I'd hate to think this was to try and stop names aimed at me."

She hugged me, resting her chin not so much on my shoulder as tilting it into my back, where I can imagine it now. But because I do not hear her voice the illusion soon fades and is replaced by acrid tears. How I crave for her touch without use of memory, and the chance to watch and listen as she speaks.

"You've led a charmed life for a middle-aged husband." Her chin bounced on my flesh as she spoke. "The colour and length of my hair has hardly changed since we met. Don't you think it's about time I had something different?"

The mirrors showed her raising a cuff to wipe away a tear that had begun to roll from the corner of her eye. The other hand stroked my back. I was about to say something when the phone rang and she went to answer. It was Ed with news that he was at a hospital where Lily was about to undergo an emergency operation for a detached retina that had occurred without warning. In the following kerfuffle, Rose and I never returned to the topic of her changed hairstyle.

By the time I got to the hospital, the indications were that the procedure had succeeded. My mother was lying with her ears pinioned by sandbags to prevent head movement. She was grateful for the efforts to save the sight in her left eye, yet resented her dependence on others."

"If anyone deserves to put their feet up for a few weeks," I said, "It's you."

"It's not in my nature to rest. Apart from pregnancy and recovering from it, I've never spent more than eight hours at a time in a bed."

"Charity's a two-way street and heaven knows how many people you've looked after."

"What would you know about heaven? When were you last in church?"

I let pass the sharpest thing she had said to me in a long time because her distress at being immobilised was so great. Before long, her sharpness would have been preferable to the lack of response that followed. Visitors and staff had to work to get a mumbled reply. One nurse described her behaviour as passive aggressive and shocked me by asking if my mother had ever found comfort in religion.

I then prompted an Anglican hospital chaplain to visit. He reported feeling like an intruder. Lily had been polite without any smile, said next to nothing, and had closed her uninjured eye after he suggested saying the Lord's Prayer together. Her lips had not moved to say as much as amen and she had not answered when asked if she felt God was there for her.

Ed engaged Adele, a widow approaching my mother's age and a devout Anglican, to look after the house and my mother when she returned. The idea was for Lily not just to take it easy, but also to have a companion. Instead, she took offence on realising the new housekeeper was resident and not temporary. From the day Ed drove Lily home, she criticised food made by Adele and her standards of cleaning. A woman who could have become a bosom friend in other circumstances was resented and lambasted until after three weeks Adele's patience wore thin and she accused Lily of ingratitude and unchristian nitpicking. Ed found himself caught in a struggle between two queen bees. For weeks, I heard about and sometimes witnessed the growing tensions and heard tales, such as Lily rejecting Adele's wonderful oxtail soup as too salty. I agreed with Ed that sacking Adele would be unfair given she had held her tongue for so long before saying no more than was true.

Five weeks after the discharge from hospital, Adele rang Foxenearth at four in the morning."

"I'm sorry to disturb you, but I'm very concerned about Lily and Ed's away."

"What's happened?"

"She had a cold that turned to bronchitis and now her breathing is very erratic. I heard her fall on the way back from the toilet. She was only able to walk again with help, but she says I'm not to call a doctor. She won't let me turn on the radiator in her room or shut the window and it's freezing in there. I told her I think she's quite ill and she said I'm making a fuss about nothing and won't let me take her pulse or temperature. And of course, she's been losing weight for weeks because she won't eat most of what I prepare."

"Call an ambulance now. Tell her I insisted and that I'm on my way to see her in hospital."

Doctors and nurses struggled with advanced pneumonia, but to no avail other than buying enough time for Ed to reach Lily before she died.

"If only she'd come to us sooner," a nurse said, "Or seen a doctor about the bronchitis."

The needless loss of life enraged me and stirred guilt for not urging Ed to dismiss Adele. Wise after the event, I recognised that my mother had needed to be indulged. Would it have been so monstrous to put her needs first after she had spent a lifetime looking after others? To have let her continue to rule the roost that had been hers alone for decades? The reasons could have been explained to Adele and money offered to compensate for losing her position when she was not at fault.

But there was another element in my reaction. My mother's personality had deviated in a matter of weeks from its lifelong wholesome and generous nature. Her vision was healed, but she persisted in being blind to the possibility of a new friendship and then the seriousness of the breathing problems. Her fortitude and forbearance, which had always seemed like granite, had melted like wax and hastened the flames of her extinction. If a person as formidable as her capitulated following a loss of faith, what hope for me when I had never been as strong and had long dismissed any possibility of a god, let alone a caring one? Fear of a breakdown prompted my retreat into work to avoid acknowledging both the depth of loss and a loss confidence in my ability to endure adversity.

All of which, prompts reflection on Perry's reaction to the deaths of his parents. Although he wrote decades after their demise, I still find his mourning muted. As soon as I dictated that, Perry rattled the skull that he has made his home.

N What is it?
P You're assuming a lot about my grief.
N What would you add or amend?

P I've never stopped loving or grieving for my parents. They did so much for me, especially when you take into account their own rotten childhoods.

N Will you admit to mixed feelings? That love and anger towards a person can co-exist?

P To justify your claim than my mourning was muted?

N No, because love, even intense love, does not always displace other emotions.

P Is the way we feel about our parents that different?

N I see more parallels than differences. I stowed my grief for my mother by losing myself in codes and my garden. Then I had the chance to find my feelings again. I'm not sure that you did.

P Perhaps the lens of your own experience distorts your view of me?

N Inevitably. On the other hand, you spoke of harnessing our similarities when you asked me to write.

P I had hopes, Norm.

N Including the hope that I might continue your work and use my commentary to score a few more points against people you loath?

P Let's agree to disagree.

Chapter 30: Perry ~ Joan

Not long after I first met Ariadne, I walked around the square until I came to a firm of solicitors. The receptionist made an appointment after lunch with their conveyancing specialist, Eustace Troupe, a name remembered from childhood. Would he make the link to the lad who had stayed with the Kytes? While Gray is one of the UK's more common surnames, Perry had never made the list of the most popular names parents give to boys. In addition, any legal documents pertaining to me used Peregrine.

Eustace was eight years older than me. He had spent much of his youth at boarding schools. According to the Kyte girls, he wandered around Vaulting Ryego in the holidays, avoided by children of the well-to-do because of a resemblance to Billy Bunter and shunned by the ragamuffins for his posh accent.

"Everyone calls him Jumbo," said Lucy.

I wanted to know why.

She giggled. "Don't let the elephant troop trample you."

I laughed to hear him called Jumbo until others called me names at school. Then I felt sorry for Eustace. It was easy to imagine that his size also made him a target for bullies.

Mr Troupe had still not returned from lunch fifteen minutes after our scheduled appointment.

When I checked with the receptionist, she said, "He knows you're expected. I'm afraid his first appointment in the afternoon is always a bit risky. I only offered it to you because you said you wanted to see someone today."

As she sounded apologetic and I guessed she had said more than she should, I didn't press her for more information. Eustace collected me from the waiting area some minutes later carrying a mug of coffee and without offering an apology or refreshment. His breath smelt of beer and his clothes reeked of cigarette smoke. He was still very obese and his sad eyes suggested much ribbing at school and taunts in adult life about his girth. We reached his first floor office at the back via a corridor that wriggled from the landing around a windowless file room. It was as if he was banished to where others would see less of him. A tall tarnished trophy from an inter-university impromptu speech competition took pride of place on his room's mantelpiece. As he made small talk and then questioned me about the purchase I hoped to make, nothing suggested my names meant anything.

"What attracts you to Raventulle when it needs so much work?"

"I like the county, Vaulting Ryego in particular, and the house is in a wonderful position. And I've wanted to move from London for some time."

"Another refugee from the capital! When I was a boy, adults from outside the area were a rarity apart from Gypsies and seasonal Irish. One of the few exceptions was the family that lived at Raventulle for about ten years before they buggered off to South Africa to escape rationing. Rum sort of people. The chap moved here to maintain boilers at a factory, so I used to call him Mr Puff. In those days almost everyone was either Anglican or Methodist. He made it known he wouldn't bend his knees in any church and his wife was the same. They didn't even send their three girls. That didn't go down too well."

His babble smacked of what one might expect at the end of a boozy evening and, despite all the surface humour, sadness. Sometimes overweight people give the impression that they are happy on the inside, but he was too keen to appear nonchalant, not to mention the florid face that spoke of years of seeking solace in heavy drinking.

Pity for the man prompted a neutral response. "People took religion a lot more seriously then."

"Mr Puff, Kyte was his real name, was away for much of the war in Calcutta training natives to service engines. Then he came back with a chip on his shoulder, or so papa used to say. Puff's wife was a pretty thing. I used to call her Mrs Nooky because she had an affair while hubby was in India."

I had been lukewarm about his reminiscing until this snippet. "Who with?"

"Well, that's the joke." Eustace took a gulp of coffee, his giggles got in the way of swallowing and he spluttered. "It was the vicar, Reverend Randy I used to called him, who was old enough to be Nooky's father. Randy was an Air Raid Warden and used to tell his wife he was cycling around to check the blackout when he wanted to have his oats at Raventulle. Of course, everyone except Mrs Randy learned what was going on."

The idea of Mrs Kyte, who had been like a mother to me, having an affair was uncomfortable. Yet I pretended to find it amusing.

" Did Mr Kyte find out?"

"That's another bit of parish history. Mrs Kyte wasn't the only wife in the village who had a fling while her chap was serving elsewhere. And someone made it his business to write to the five cuckolds after they returned."

"Any idea who it was?"

"Probably some old cow jealous because no one offered to tup her."

"What did the police say?"

"None of the recipients wanted it made public."

The preciseness of the five when there had been no police investigation raised the possibility of Eustace sending the anonymous letters. If so, what had prompted his mischief making? And was he still sending such letters?

As Eustace had not connected me to my earlier stays in the town, there was a good chance no one else would. I told other locals that I hailed from London, which is not much more helpful than someone saying he is from Scotland when his burr has already given the game away. Some asked which part of London, to which I replied Harrow. And to the one who asked where in Harrow, I said Pinner. I would not have denied my previous stays in Vaulting Ryego, had someone asked; to do so could have raised doubts about my honesty. If people think you are furtive, so many things that would otherwise escape their notice can add to their suspicions.

Sharing childhood links to the town would not have stopped lifelong residents seeing me as an outsider. And had people like Ariadne been aware of the Hoggsons employing Mum as a domestic that would have been another reason to look down their noses. But just as important was the pleasure of concealing a secret and the sense of power derived from knowing something others do not.

The same sort of one-upmanship led to poker and determined with whom I played. Success in the game stems from noticing body language while remaining unread. I avoided cannier players who could spot tells at least as well as me and usually wanted to play for larger sums. Making money from cards was less important to me than winning the battle of wits and playing for small stakes reduced the chances of animosity.

The possibility of Eustace sending anonymous letters prompted me to invite him to my house warming in the hope of finding out more about him. Seeing people in the company of others who know them and especially when drink has flowed is often informative. He arrived in a dinner jacket and more than half-cut after some guests had called it a night. When the architect ribbed him about his attire, Eustace explained he had come from a Masonic dinner.

The grocer whispered, "You'll be glad your cellar keys are missing. Eustace likes to make up names for people. What he doesn't know is that he's been christened Mr Thirst. He'll drink anything, but watch him hoover up the sparkling wine first."

Eustace's loud attempts to amuse by challenging people to give him a topic for an impromptu speech meant that before long he was the only guest. I invited him to sit by the fire, which he did after touring the room to collect what was left of bottles of Champagne and Cava.

Splayed on my sofa, he said, "Through my father's mother, I'm a descendant of the Raventulles. This place was built by two spinster cousins of my greatgrandmother who were the last to carry the Raventulle name. Mad old bats. They left everything to support distressed gentlefolk. Had they not been so pious I might have inherited this place. Just as well that mama's family were better at holding onto their money. They were Hoggsons and while lacking blue blood they invested wisely."

A few roundabout questions established that Eustace was the grandson of the couple who had employed Mum.

I asked, "What do you remember of Vaulting Ryego during the war?"

"Pretty miserable. I spent all of my school holidays with mama's parents because she gadded about with the Auxiliary Air Transport and papa was on a cruiser."

I persisted despite the sadness in his voice. "What was the food like during the war when you were at your grandparents?"

"Fucking awful. Not much better than school. My grandparents were on every ruddy committee going and had bugger all domestics for most of the war. I barely saw either of them unless they had their meetings in the house. Some days I had to cook."

"Still, I expect with fields surrounding the town at least rabbit supplemented the meat ration."

He sneered. Was it the idea of eating rabbit or simply me that made him contemptuous?

I added, "In London people had to live on what they could buy with coupons. Round here you could always pick some vegetables and make a stew with a rabbit or two."

"I remember rabbit stew during rationing. Vile stuff it was. The real advantage of being in the country, if you had the right connections, was getting your hands on some proper game or a decent joint. Beef was hard to get, but farmers hid the odd pig or lamb from the Ministry. We left the rabbits to the peasants for the most part. Any more sparkling wine?"

I explained that my cellar keys had gone missing and he lumbered around gathering the still wine bottles – red, white, sweet, dry, plonk and vintage. He placed them all by his seat and simply reached for the nearest until all were empty.

I regretted discussing food. Rather than Eustace mentioning Mum and how much he had enjoyed her cooking, he had me doubting her story about the much-appreciated stew. Unsure how to take the matter further without arousing suspicions, I changed the subject.

"Did any of the Kytes ever return to Vaulting Ryego?"

"Not that I know of. Good riddance, if you ask me."

"Why do you say that?"

"They didn't fit in. Papa used to say Mr Puff didn't know his place. And then that hussy seducing Reverend Randy."

"It might have been the other way round. And Mrs Kyte wasn't the only woman who strayed during the war."

Eustace sneered again; his scrunched plump face seemed to say, I'm not sure you know your place. Or was it because he knew something that I didn't?

Joan Plasholl, who had arranged for Mum to stay with the Hoggsons, would have remembered me save for her Alzheimer's. I had no clear recollection of her because if she came to the cottage in Rayners Lane it must have been when I was too young to remember or fast asleep.

Not long after I moved into Raventulle, the almshouse warden joked in the pub about Miss Plasholl being away with the fairies.

"Unusual name," I said.

"They've lived around here for a while. Family used to own a smithy. Joan, that's Miss Plasholl, is the last of them, poor old bint."

"How do you mean?"

"Dementia. Doesn't know what year it is, let alone what day."

"So how does she manage in a cottage?"

"Other residents do her shopping and she still cooks. The funny thing is, even when she thinks it's before the war, she doesn't notice she's making tea with bags or that the bacon comes pre-packed."

"Does she wander?"

"She's got emphysema and by the time she's found her hat and coat and put them on she's too exhausted. If you catch her badly out of breath, she says she needs to lie down because she's got bronchitis."

"She sounds like a handful."

"Not really, as long as you don't contradict her. Last week a bloke came to replace her sash window cord and kept telling her the coronation was not happening next week. She got so bloody agitated that the woman next door rang me and I had to tell him to leave. And the sod still wants paying for the visit when the repair budget is already shot."

"I've replaced sash cords. Do you want me to do it as a favour?"

The warden left a newcomer unsupervised with a vulnerable woman when for all he knew I might have been a pervert or kleptomaniac. Several other things needed repairs and I visited Joan to fix them. She never remembered that my name was Perry – |I never avoided using Gray with her – yet was always welcoming.

Sometimes an older woman's face has proportions, character lines and shows a self-confidence that suggests that she once had great beauty and knew it. Joan had that look despite skin greyed and deep-wrinkled by decades of smoking. Perhaps part of the poise came from the dementia and thinking heads still turned to appreciate her.

She remembered Peregrine Gray and his parents. However, getting her to talk was not so much a trip down memory lane as the exploration of a labyrinth with many a turning. Whatever the topic, she would deviate and disliked any reminder that she had done so because what she spoke about absorbed her attention. It took time to collect and piece together what most interested me and even then others who had known the Plasholls provided some of the details.

Joan was born in 1902, the fourth and last child of Jacob Plasholl, a blacksmith. Her three brothers, fearing the

Great War would finish before they saw action, enlisted in the first week. The father could find no men to replace them after conscription and made Joan his assistant. The idea that she would do light duties was set aside as Jacob found his strength fading. After he died in 1917, Joan carried on the work with the help of Albert, a fourteen year old.

One brother vanished from a trench hit by a shell. Another died two days after a gas attack had damaged his lungs. Perhaps news of the second death killed the mother; she died eight days after hearing of it. Joan handed over the business in 1919 to the surviving brother, following his release from a centre treating soldiers for shell shock. She kept house while waiting for a few years of work and good food to restore his tranquillity. Two men proposed to her and one she wanted to marry. But he got tired of waiting for one of the surfeit of single women to catch her brother's eye, what Joan insisted must happen before she left home. The brother's bouts of drinking and the outbursts that followed them, resulting sometimes in broken crockery and furniture, became so notorious that not even the most desperate spinster in the area would have risked marrying him. Joan turned to cigarettes to cope with the strains of supporting such an unhappy man. The brother jumped from the church tower in 1937 after hearing that Albert had died fighting in the Spanish Civil War.

Finding the village too full of sad memories, Joan sold up and moved to London with ideas of opening a shop. Before she found premises, Britain was at war and Dad's manager could not believe his luck in recruiting a woman so experienced in metalworking. Come peacetime, she moved to assembling aircraft in Hatfield, which was a little nearer to Vaulting Ryego, a place she had begun to miss. On a visit to Vaulting Ryego, she learned that the tobacconist wanted to sell his shop. Joan was over fifty and finding factory work more tiring. She longed to escape its noise and looked forward to having time to chat with people. But the shop she bought also provided more time to smoke cigarettes; her hands were not so busy and buying a packet of ten a day to keep her habit under control was no longer an option. Within a year of moving back her consumption was up to forty a day.

The man who had bought the Plasholl forge went bankrupt and the property remained empty until a half-timbered hotel burned down. Within days, the pub transferred to the empty stone building that had withstood so many sparks. After the landlord acquired the freehold, the smithy became the Anvil and Shoe. Joan spent many a Saturday night in the lounge bar with people she had grown up with. One evening, Joan arrived and walked into the landlord's private area thinking it was still her home. After some confusion, she realised her mistake and apologised. It was around this time her business began to go awry. Tax went unpaid and stock missing. There were rumours of unscrupulous people buying cigarettes at pre-war prices. On a visit to her GP to complain about shortness of breath, Joan thought she was at a doctor's in wartime London. The GP, social services and others helped her to sell the shop and move into an almshouse cottage.

When Mum was most distraught during the war, Joan had helped. She deserved something from me in return, but I also loved the way she spoke about my parents as if they were still alive. On one occasion, I found her searching for her ration book. Taking Joan to the kitchen and pointing out the cupboards full of food would have bewildered and upset her. It was better to play along with the delusion as we looked for the book. She opened a drawer in her bedroom and found a large envelope stuffed with photographs, postcards and letters from her brothers at the front. The ration book was forgotten as she looked and read. Then she opened another envelope and among letters sent to her while she lived in London were two snaps of my father. In one he stood alone and rather awkwardly outside a workshop door with his left shoulder partly obscuring words that appeared to be *Authorised Entry Only*. In the other photo, he was in the same place and more relaxed with eight other workers, six of whom were women. Joan stood next to him with a big smile and good looks.

She spent a long time looking at the picture of Dad by himself and tears formed, which was strange when her eyes had remained dry while studying her brothers in uniform. I tried to get her to say more about Dad, but all she would say was that Mr Gray was a good foreman, a hard worker and a craftsman to his very fingertips.

I questioned her on other occasions about Mr Gray without success. Each time we start anew because Joan never recalled our earlier exchanges.

Then one day as I arrived, she said, "The doctor says I have to stay at home, because of bronchitis, but I'm worried about Mr Gray. He's got so much to do and I'm the only person who can help him."

"What do you do at work, Joan?"

"I can't tell you that. Careless talk costs lives."

After some minutes of other chitchat, I asked, "Can you give me any advice on working with Vitallium."

She jerked upright and looked pained. As I assumed that she blamed herself for careless talk, I quickly changed the topic and never brought it up again.

Another time I asked, "What makes Mr Gray such a good foreman?"

"He's always helpful and always a gentleman. I couldn't ask for better."

"And where's his wife now?"

"Maud took the baby to Vaulting Ryego. I didn't think she should go. It's not fair on Mr Gray when he's working so many hours to have to go home to an empty home. But what could I do? He was afraid she'd have a breakdown if she stayed. So I made enquiries. The Hoggsons were pleased to get a trained domestic, even if she did have a baby in tow."

"So Mrs Gray took the baby?"

"Yes, the poor mite. Tiny he is. I could hold Peregrine in one of these."

She lifted up her right hand far enough for a loose sleeve to slip back and reveal the flabby vestiges of muscles.

"So Gordon is good to you?"

"Oh, yes." |

She sealed her lower lip with her upper teeth, which prompted me to wonder whether Dad and Joan had been more than friends. When I tried to put the idea out of my mind, a picture of the vicar wearing bicycle clips and rogering Mrs Kyte popped into my head.

"It must be hard for Gordon with Maud away in the country?"

"He can't get away to visit; there's so much he has to do."

"He must get lonely. And you too, being away from your town. So you're both lonely."

She looked dreamy.

"So what do the two of you get up to?"

Her grey skin darkened. She was blushing.

"You can tell me. It won't go any further. Two hardworking, lonely people, one a good man and the other an attractive woman."

"But not attractive enough," she said.

"What makes you say that?"

She gasped to fill her lungs before saying, "The other day he was showing me how to set up a turret lathe. It was late and no one was around. Even if they were, no one else had permission to enter. His hand accidentally touched mine. He went to pull it back. I put my other hand on top. I had wanted to do that for so long. Then I kissed him on the cheek, but he started crying."

"Why did he cry?"

"He wanted to kiss me, but he couldn't let himself. It's such a shame. I really wanted him to kiss me."

It had been difficult enough to imagine my parents having sexual feelings for each other, but the idea of Dad perceived as snoggable by the then beautiful Joan had me teetering between giddiness and nervous laughter.

"Why won't he kiss you?"

"He says he received a spirit message that he was to marry Maud and he's terrified of offending God by being unfaithful. When I told him God died in the Great War as far as I was concerned, he said he'd pray for me."

The refusal to kiss was understandable, given the influence of the Newelms, but what of her interest in a chubby married man rather than some dashing bloke in uniform. Photographs from that period show her with a striking pale oval face and wavy fair hair. The only dark features are the lips and pencilled eyebrows. Few working women of that generation looked so attractive at forty. If she had wanted a male friend, there were plenty of airmen in or near Harrow.

"Why fancy Mr Gray rather than a man in uniform?"

"I won't get involved with someone who could get sent away to fight or come back like my brother."

After a fall led to a spell in hospital, Joan went to a nursing home. As far as I could tell from visiting, the modern premises were clean and not short of staff. But the only stimulation, if you can call it that, appeared to be rows of plastic- upholstered chairs facing a raised booming television set. None of the staff could work around Joan's disorientation and they were forever contradicting what she said. Each visit found her more upset and withdrawn until she died following a reaction to fly killer used in her room while she was elsewhere. It is thought she returned to lie down shortly after the spraying. Apart from the way Joan went – I fear she may have suffered like her gassed brother – I regarded her death as a mercy.

Chapter 31: Norman ~ Retirement

I noticed several floaters in my right eye in March 2001. An optometrist warned the spots might be a precursor for a detached retina and that experiencing flashes of light was a significant predictor for the condition. Two days after the examination, a wispy grey gauze appeared to hover over part of my vision. Then it resembled the cloud a drop of black ink might make in a glass of water. The next morning at work, golden dots of light danced for me like fairies in a breeze. These lasted much longer than flashes, so I did not act until lunchtime when a dark line began to obscure the bottom of the image registered by my right eye. I rang the optometrist who insisted that I immediately go to hospital.

As a colleague drove me, I told myself that at the worst I still would have one good eye, which would be enough for work or gardening. What was harder to cope with was the dread linked to the aftermath of my mother's operation. I closed both eyes and allowed the curious display provided by my peeling retina moving through shadows and patches of sun to distract me. Gaudy patterns – some vein-like and others more akin to Day-Glo bacteria – mutated.

Rose arrived at the hospital an hour or so after me. A team assembled to operate on me that evening. Much had changed since my mother's treatment. The anaesthetic was local and I spent no more than thirty minutes in the theatre. A bubble of gas applied to the eye held the repair in place and after resting face down for two hours with Rose holding my hand, I sat up to eat and then walked unaided to bed. When a nurse removed the dressing the next morning, a purple disc was imposed upon the world.

"That's the gas bubble," she said. "It will shrink until it disappears completely within a fortnight. Then most people find they have near normal sight again."

After my appointment with the eye surgeon after lunch, Rose drove me home. I went to read and found it uncomfortable, a condition that lasted for about a week. Unusually, no pressing technical issues rattled around my head and while I wallowed in a sea of slow time something stirred below. Rose, who had taken leave from work on my account wanted to know what had restricted my appetite and left me morose. I pretended it was the frustration of not being at CARE the first two times she asked. On the third occasion, I started to cry and acknowledged I was grieving for my mother.

"I think the grief is there not simply because you had the same condition as Lily. You hid from your feelings when she died. Until you work through them, the grief will find ways of coming out. Use this time to think about your mother and to say your goodbyes to her."

"How could I do that?"

"Don't rush back to work. Use some of your leave to extend your absence. Start by paying attention to your feelings, accepting that they exist and are appropriate. Talk about them. We could visit places that you associate with your family. If you won't do it for yourself, please do it for me."

"What's in it for you?"

She ruffled the nape of my neck. "I want to be married to a man who knows how to grieve."

Oh Rose, if only you could be here now you would have no doubts on that score.

We drove to Dover through rain so persistent that I stayed in the car outside the flats built where the Nutwands had lived. The small, Edwardian terraced houses that remained in the street made it easy to imagine how crowded the large family had been. I imagined what it had been like in bad weather when so many children could not leave the house to play in the street. Rose sat without talking while I wiped the mist from windows, gazed and remembered the one time my parents had taken me to what was then a bomb site.

A third of the Eflinwood houses, including my former street, had been replaced with equally small modern homes. Properties similar to the one rented by my parents existed in the less prosperous-looking corners of the village. The pit had struggled after railway engines switched from coal and was one of the first closures after the miners returned to work in 1985 without securing the future of their industry. Many of the colliery-built properties looked neglected although occupied, a dismal impression aggravated by the downpour. The peeling paint and missing pebble-dash spoke of a life on the margins for many of the mining families who had remained after coal production ceased. People who had persecuted me at school might be among the occupants, but I took no pleasure from the thought of them struggling to retain some sense of purpose and community.

Rose then drove to the churchyard where my father was interred near an enormous yew that had blocked the sun for years without providing his grave with shelter from rain. The characters on his tombstone lay under years of moss. I got soaked despite the umbrella held in one hand while wielding a trowel with the other to scrape until his details were legible. Then I planted five hellebores.

Ed had driven my mother four times a year to allow her to tend the grave. As I crouched in the rain and during the drive away from the church, I regretted avoiding these trips after starting at the print shop. My mother had got to the point where she would announce that she was going the next Sunday afternoon rather than invite me.

Rose had to pull over after a few miles to wipe from windows the condensation from my sodden clothes. When I rubbed my left sleeve against the glass next to it, the blurry images outside sharpening made me think of the operation on my mother's eye and how early on my evasion of grief had begun. I had limited the time spent with Ed after her funeral to avoid his grief and mine, even though I was his closest relative. He had been like a father to me, but with a light touch.

I recalled how he invited me to a pub to celebrate leaving the Army. It was a way of saying I was old enough to make my own decisions about alcohol and other things. We had sat in a quiet corner of the snug.

"My solicitor has been on at me to make a will," he said. "The house goes to Lily and if she pre-deceases me it will go to you."

"You're very generous." And I meant it, but at the same time I was uncomfortable with the reminder of death.

"You're the only family I've got and if I know anything about generosity, Lily taught me. There's one other thing I want to run past you. The solicitor said to think about funeral arrangements."

Despite my dislike of discussing death, I was curious to know what he meant. I knew from earlier conversations with Ed that he did not believe in God so much as value religion as a force for social stability in the same way he approved of the monarchy and censorship.

"How do you mean?"

"I like the idea of being buried near to Lily and she wants to be buried with Cedric. I contacted the church and they said the graveyard has been closed for years. The most they would allow is for Lily's ashes to be placed a foot under the earth on Cedric's plot. But Lily doesn't want to be cremated. The question is, do we tell her all this or not?"

I felt queasy talking about my mother being dead and wanted to end the discussion as soon as possible. "She'd only fret if she knew. And when she's gone it won't make any difference to her."

"Good," he said. "I'd prefer her not to worry."

Although I realised later that day that we had not decided whether to cremate and place the ashes with Dad or inter her in another graveyard alongside a plot for Ed, I did not return to these matters.

After the visit to Kent, Rose and I stayed in a hotel near to what had been Croydon Airport. The next morning brought sunshine. We went to where my mother had lived longer than anywhere else. The front door of Ed's old house had three bells, none of which I rang. I would have liked to have sat in the old kitchen and remembered my mother describing what was outside the window, but could not face explaining this to a stranger. After standing on the pavement for a few minutes, I walked alone around the block remembering people my mother had befriended and how they had swarmed to her funeral. My plodding pace evoked memories of unhappy adolescent hours spent wandering streets. I regretted how trying my awkwardness and angst must have been. I was no Colin because at times I showed affection, appreciation and wanted to please. Nevertheless, my darker moods must have tried her patience and been a burden for Ed.

Rose drove us to the church where my mother had worshipped more than any other. People had gathered to pray for a local man who had disappeared while visiting Afghanistan as an undercover reporter. Seated at the back, I recalled my mother's coffin entering and leaving the church and how throughout that day I had relied on Rose to prompt me and even to speak to people because I was so withdrawn.

A sculpted life-size figure suffered on a cross above the altar and some of those praying still found comfort in the depiction of agony. I reluctantly acknowledged that my mother's faith had benefitted me; she had drawn strength and kindness from the suffering of Jesus for over half a century and only in the last sliver of her life had God not made a difference.

The tears that had not come to me at the funeral began to well up. Rose, who had been sitting alongside me on the pew, saw them and said she would not speak unless I wanted her to. After some minutes I stood and we walked to a nearby park. Rose parked me on a bench and said she would fetch coffee to give me some time to myself. As soon as she was out of sight, I sobbed until two teenage boys approaching on bikes prompted an instinctive clamming response to the idea of males seeing me cry.

An hour later, Rose drove to Brandon Hill Cemetery to the south of Croydon. As we trudged through the acres of monuments to where Lily lay next to Ed, Rose noticed a smile on my face.

"What is it?"

"A remark my mother once made. During a radio programme about London running out of land for burials, someone suggested drilling twelve foot holes and putting coffins in upright."

"How can people rest in peace standing up?" she said.

I asked about people who wanted cremation. She thought for a moment and said it wasn't for her, she was more of a dust to dust person than ashes to ashes.

"Was she serious?"

"I thought so, but I was uneasy with the topic and changed it. I wish I hadn't avoided it because I'm not sure she wanted to be buried here."

This led me to tell Rose of the discussion with Ed about funeral arrangements, how my not following up had led to the adjoining plots at Brandon, while my mother had expected to be buried with Dad.

"I thought she'd chosen to be buried here." Rose looked and sounded perturbed.

"I'm sorry I didn't tell you. By the time she was dead, I knew it wasn't right, but I couldn't bring myself to upset Ed by saying I'd changed my mind. And then when he got ill, all he had to look forward to was being buried next to his sister. He didn't set out to compete with my father, but I don't think he loved Lily any less than him."

"It sounds like you're still unravelling emotional threads that got jumbled when you shut the door on them. It may be better to talk to a grief counsellor who doesn't know the people involved the way I do."

"It's hard enough talking to you. I couldn't say as much to anyone else."

"Then I'll do the best I can until perhaps you feel able to open up to a professional."

Rose encouraged me to sit for up to an hour at a time at Foxenearth with photographs of my mother and away from distractions. "Your mind will wander. When you realise this, accept it as part of grieving rather than blaming yourself and bring your attention back to Lily and whatever memories come up. Notice feelings and any urges to dodge them; both are part of dealing with loss."

After I had sat alone, Rose invited me to share my experiences. I spoke of how I missed my mother, the anger at her avoidable death, a sense of failure because I had not lifted her spirits or changed her attitude towards Adele, and my dread of dying and being forgotten as if I had never lived. Words often trickled and faltered and sometimes I fled the room or the house, as if I could leave the issues behind me. Once I was gone for five hours and only returned because Winkie was hungry and exhausted.

"You know how much you can take at a given moment," Rose said. "The important thing is that you keep coming back to talk."

Chapter 32: Perry ~ Mavis

Other residents of the almshouses knew me from my visits to Joan. Several used the benches overlooking the green in better weather and I sometimes sat down to chat. Complaints about the warden promising to fix things and nothing happening were frequent. I responded on occasions, especially to the pensioners better equipped to share local history.

A former teacher who had lived all her life in the town – as bright and sharp as a new pin despite being in her late eighties – spoke with feeling about World War II and what followed it. "The government took our men and gave us strangers. Some of the evacuees were little terrors. When it was safe again, the kids disappeared, but not all the men came back. Sometimes those that did, like my fiancé, couldn't settle. He joined the Foreign Legion. Nothing was the same after the war. Now the village is mostly strangers although I'll make an exception for you, Perry."

And a male chiropodist born in Bristol said, "The landowning families did well from the demand for housing, yet for all their profits they never made newcomers like me feel welcome. The memorials on the walls of the old church feature the same surnames over and over again. The Raventulles disappeared, but the other dynasties continue to dominate the area. We no longer have to tug our forelocks for them, but that doesn't mean they see us as equals."

He was a socialist, of course, but still right. The class warfare that continues is not just the work of Marxist agitators and woolly-thinking sociologists but also the fault of patricians and would-be patricians and all those who seldom miss an opportunity to find fault in others for being ordinary. Just to give one example, when locals who see themselves as the area's elite go out to drink, they favour the saloon bar of The Peacock. The barmaids there serve anyone, though you may find you wait longer than is fair. However, the reception for an outsider when not introduced by one of the regulars is chilly and especially if the intruder has the wrong accent. Ariadne was even more disdainful at The Peacock and Eustace was loath to acknowledge me there.

Even in the almshouses there were distinctions and one resident, Mavis Yewlett, a cousin of the baronet who owned Vaulting Hall, had never really spoken to me beyond a cursory greeting. She had been a governess in India until 1949, after which she taught at a girls' prep school in Surrey. For all her breeding, she had an exceedingly plain face and her branch of the family had lacked the wealth to attract a husband prepared to overlook such a large brow, prominent nose and horsey teeth. She was also gangling tall and not of a sweet disposition.

The warden mentioned in the pub that Mavis was partial to Madeira, which she could seldom afford, and lacked discretion after a few glasses. His own discretion left him towards the end that evening when he let slip that the wife of the baronet, who sat on the Almshouses Board, had pulled strings to get Mavis a place after her years of teaching in Devon. The bequest that had built the cottages specified they were for long-term residents of the town, which Mavis knew only as an occasional guest of the Thellows at the manor house.

I teased the warden. "So does Mavis have to wait as long for her repairs as the residents without connections?"

Perhaps he misheard on account of the noise of other drinkers because he interpreted this as an offer of help.

"Would you mind having a go at sorting out her radiators? She says they take forever to warm up."

I agreed, drawn by the idea of Mavis being indiscreet.

She followed me around her cottage during the bleeding of the radiators. At first, I thought she did not trust me with the many knick-knacks that littered the house, many of which would have been worth something to a collector. It became apparent that she was lonely and nosy to boot.

"What do you like doing Perry, when you're not working and helping out charity cases like me?"

Hearing Mavis describe herself in this way was odd, as there was nothing humble about her.

"Well, I've got my garden and I like a good wine."

"So do I. The wine I mean."

"What's your favourite tipple?"

"Well, if I had to choose one, Madeira."

"I have a bottle of Extra Reserve in my cellar. What if I brought it over this evening and we shared a glass or two."

"Mr Gray, you're on."

Mavis, who had changed into a long dark skirt and white blouse with pearl necklace, sat me by a display cabinet in the tiny front room that was as hot as the Indian plains in summer. The porcelain, glass and silver behind glass were exquisite, testaments to her refinement. Near the fireplace was a modern lamp that looked cheap and cheaper still when switched on. A revolving filter changed the glow from yellow to red to orange.

After her first glass, which was larger than one might have expected for a fortified wine in such a home, Mavis said, "I can't tell you what a relief it is to be warm again. If you fixed the radiators in fifteen minutes, why couldn't the warden? He's worse than useless. He puts in more hours at the pub than he does here."

This was encouraging, as she knew I drank with the warden. It also occurred to me that Mavis could act as a channel to reach others, including the village's inner circle, had I been the sort who spreads misinformation by word of mouth.

She sipped steadily through a second glass, pretended to be unsure about a third and then all sham hesitation disappeared. Only her growing loquaciousness and a slightly startled look suggested that alcohol might be at work.

What I was most interested in were the views that others had of me, but I tested the water with questions about people we had no great connection to. It was like turning a tap; gossip flowed.

I asked about Lowestoft, the only son of the Thellows. "So what do you make of your nephew's Aston Martin?"

"Boys and their toys!" she pooh-poohed. "Lowestoft hasn't got the brains of his father or the looks of his mother when she was that age. He's thirty-two years old and this is what he bought me for Christmas."

She pointed to the gaudy lamp.

"Why keep it?"

"I'd rather not give him any cause for offence. His parents look out for me and, who knows, I might just outlive them. Lowestoft is the heir, at least for the time being."

"How do you mean?"

"His parents might just disinherit him. He has a rather nasty inclination."

"I hope he hasn't been nasty to you."

"Certainly not. He knows my mettle and, in any case, it's trying to buy favours from servants at the manor as if they were floozies. There was a dreadful row a few months ago after his mother found out what he was up to. You can imagine how hard it is to get staff. A lot of the time they end up with colonials who only stay six months. Lowestoft offered an Australian gal money to go to bed with him, but she hit him so hard she broke his nose. Of course, this is just between you and me."

I joined her in laughing before saying, "I heard a horse had butted him."

"Would you want to tell people you got punched in the face by a gal for treating her like a strumpet?"

Mavis had cocked her head and stared at me, as if hinting there was more to the words than the obvious meaning. Whatever it was escaped me and I changed the subject to find out if she would be indiscreet about someone she knew I had been fond of.

"What did people say about Joan?"

Mavis giggled. "Some of them thought she was jolly odd working in the smithy and then never getting married. Kenneth's father used to say he wouldn't be surprised if Joan started smoking a pipe and wearing tweed trousers."

She looked down into the hand holding her chin, but any remorse about the jibe was lost in the smugness of her smile.

I made myself grin. "And what do locals make of me?"

Mavis stared for several seconds while I tried to hide my nervousness under a facade of looking bemused.

"You're a strange one, Perry Gray. But if you really want to know, I'll tell you."

It was my turn to hesitate, but before long I poured her another glass by way of assent.

"People are split. Some think you're queer and know it, and others think you don't know that you're queer. A few, like me say it's no one else's business."

She studied my reaction as I disguised the shock I felt.

"Queer, eh? I've only myself to blame for not getting married and not making my affairs public."

Mavis nodded. "Some wonder why you spent so much time with Joan."

"We were using each other. She wanted to hide that she was a lesbian, and I hoped my fascination with her, and of course with you now, would persuade people that I wasn't gay."

She chortled.

"Joan reminded me of my Mum who died of cancer not long before I moved here. The staff at the hospital where Mum died looked after her so well that I wanted to care for someone in my own way." Mavis nodded as if the second explanation was plausible. "Thanks for telling me what you did. I'd rather know than not know. Is there anything else going on behind my back?"

A glint in her eyes warned that she took a certain pleasure in what she was about to say.

"You have a nickname."

I dreaded that it was Tad.

"They call you Mr Thumbelina."

I struggled to conceal seething. "That's a new one on me. Where did that come from?"

"Hans Christian Anderson."

"I mean, who started to use it about me."

"I first heard it from Eustace Troupe. He's a second cousin once removed and he's made up names like that for as long as I can remember."

I had not known they were kin and I did not know to what extent the two were friends. I mentioned he was my solicitor, which was hardly true, as I had resisted his suggestion that he take over the work of my London solicitor.

Wanting to change the topic until I knew how the cousins got on with each other, I asked about a brass Indian statue with eight arms that stood on the hearth. The uppermost right hand held a trident, the tines of which were almost level with the mantelpiece. The brass reflected the lamp's changing colours in a way that hinted at the flames that had filled the fireplace before the installation of central heating.

Mavis said it was the goddess Durga and a gift for her work as a governess in a maharajah's palace. She spoke at length of how never before or since had so many servants waited on her, including a personal lady's maid and use of a chauffeur to take her in a Rolls-Royce to visit friends, or to the evenings when ladies attended a club for Europeans.

Then suffused by alcohol and nostalgia, she said, "Eustace is not a nice man. He's never forgiven me for keeping in touch with his ex- wife and the two children who wanted nothing more to do with him. He thinks you're queer and he hates them. I would be worried to have a solicitor who disliked me so much."

I did not disbelieve what she said. Such bigotry is common and the older the man the more likely that he has clung onto a rabid fear of gays.

But as I could not discount the possibility that Mavis had another agenda, it was more politic to say, "I'm sure Eustace is perfectly professional whoever he represents."

I left her with the bottle in the hope that she would drink herself stupid and completely forget our conversation. She made no reference to it at future meetings. I repeated that my interest in Joan was linked to Mum's terminal cancer, in case Mavis had forgotten, and made a point of telling her about any women that I had a date with.

While I have lost the loathing of homosexuals that I grew up with, I have no wish to be identified as one. Not only is it the wrong label for me, being gay also attracts abuse and even violence and I have had more than enough of those things already. But dispelling such rumours these days is difficult when people are more aware of bi-sexuality and know of gay celebrities who have tried to fool the public by being seen with opposite-sex partners or marrying. Only the most naive would now assume that a man having a girlfriend was proof that he was straight. Yet I told Mavis about the women I saw because she could be relied upon to spread the news and I had no other way advertising that I was heterosexual. We mostly chatted in the street, as she would have invited me inside only if I had offered to bring a bottle or to fix something. I offered neither in case another visit to her prompted the kind of curiosity and speculation that had followed my spending time with Joan.

Two years after our evening together, the police found Mavis dead in her front room in an advanced state of putrefaction. A coroner heard how the warden had ignored the concerns of residents who had not seen her for some days. The inquest concluded that she had fallen after drinking; her head had struck first the Durga's trident and then the tiled corner of the hearth. Decomposition had been more rapid due to the heating control being on constant and the radiators set to maximum.

As soon as I heard of Mr Thumbelina, it was almost certain that Eustace had started and spread the name. I could tolerate his condescension, but not mocking and encouraging others to do the same. But what if a tipsy Mavis was unreliable or had wanted to turn me against her cousin for her own reasons? There had to be proof before I lashed out.

Eustace had been rather sniffy that my London solicitor was both a woman and an Asian. I did not intend to risk my business interests and assets to a boozy chauvinist lawyer whose speciality was conveyancing, but his aspiration allowed a few liberties.

I took a bugging device disguised as a briefcase into The Peacock towards the end of Eustace's lunchtime. Without invitation from him or his friends, I left my case on their table, saying I needed to pee and would appreciate a quick word with Eustace afterwards.

I took my time in the gents before buying Eustace a drink and sitting him away from his cronies.

"Are you still interested in taking over from my London solicitor? It's not always convenient having to visit her."

He blinked and almost stammered, "I'd be delighted to help in any way that I can."

Having whetted his appetite, I whipped the meal away from him. "Good. My accountant will be helping me to select a replacement. He may want to ask you some questions about your experience with computing related contracts and investment portfolios."

I almost laughed to see the delight fading from his face as he all but stuttered, "Of course. That's a very sensible way of making the choice."

I started playing the cassette at home twenty minutes later.

"Gawd, Eustace," said Lowestoft, "Why can't the little prick make an appointment at your office?"

"Business is business and Mr Thumbelina's money, unlike his elevation, is substantial," said Eustace. "You know, if he's going to make a habit of coming here we'd best get a soapbox left by the urinal."

After the laughter had died down, the manager of Hoggson's Real Estate said, "I'm not sure we want to encourage queers to use the gents."

"I think he's more than queer," said Eustace. "It wouldn't surprise me if he was a kiddie fucker."

That vile speculation sealed this fate. I got my accountant to interview him over the phone and then rang Eustace to tell him the outcome.

"As a thank you for your time, come and share a Jeroboam with me. I've got this exceptionally stunning Champagne."

An hour before he was due, I turned the heating up and loaded the stove with three logs rather than the usual one. He took of his jacket before long. When he went to the toilet, I copied the details of one of his credit cards and put his keys in my pocket. On his return, I went to the laundry where I had left what was needed for making impressions. Then I asked about his Masonic Lodge and from there it was easy enough to find out when he would next be at a meeting.

At an Internet cafe in Hounslow, chosen because the young man looking after it spoke minimal English and was probably an illegal immigrant working for a pittance, I checked that the owner was not expected back. For a five pound note, the assistant allowed me to connect a portable drive to a PC in the most private corner. With information obtained from my legitimate work, where child pornography sometimes turned up, I used Eustace's credit card details to purchase ten disgusting images. I printed colour copies at home and burned the files onto a CD.

Eustace lived on the edge of the town in one half of the house his parents had left him. He had sub-divided after his divorce. His single status was common knowledge, or at least gossip, and townsfolk also knew that he had few visitors apart from a housekeeper who went in three mornings a week. His life outside work, apart from the Masons, revolved around pub drinking at lunch time and bottles at home in the evening.

Two nights before a December Masonic meeting, I went to Eustace's front door after midnight to check the keys made from the impressions. They worked. On the evening he was out, my intrusion was made much easier by lights left on and curtains already drawn. The first job was to secrete the pornography; being caught with it would have been much worse that simply being mistaken for a burglar. I inserted the prints inside an atlas on the top shelf and the CD into the back of a silver-framed photograph of Eustace aged circa twenty holding the trophy that was in his office. A search of the house revealed nothing more incriminating than two copies of Playboy, a staggering amount spent on booze and some attempts at self-pitying poetry. There was little personal correspondence and no personal computer. Nothing suggested he wrote anonymous letters, indulged in snooping or had a concealed room.

After I got home, I wrote to the police pointing out that I was the same person who had alerted them to a paedophile teacher in Vaulting Ryego.

... I recently was caught short during a lunch hour and popped into The Peacock to use the Gents. While seated there, I overheard a conversation. The one voice I recognised was Eustace Troupe. He invited whoever was with him to come to his place and see images of kids he had made prints of. He said, "If you like the porn you can borrow the disc to make your own." Then someone else came in and it went quiet. I waited for everyone to leave. By the time I left the pub, Eustace was getting into Selwyn Hoggson's car and waving goodbye to an Aston Martin that was leaving.

Despite the police finding the planted items and linking the credit card payment to a business owned by criminals in Spain, Eustace was not convicted. His barrister made much of the fact that the tip off was anonymous and that no one had ever seen Mr Hoggson's car outside The Peacock. He always parked in the square near his business and walked to the hotel. If the sighting of the car was a fiction, it was reasonable to query the veracity of the rest of the letter. And the police had found nothing incriminating in searches at his office or at the homes and offices of Hoggson and Lowestoft. And wasn't it too much of a coincidence that the only child pornography found, after a very extensive search of Mr Troupe's home, was exactly what the letter specified?

Nevertheless, mud sticks and even the people who wanted to believe that Eustace was innocent were less keen on a solicitor who could not ensure that his home was secure. Nor did the reputations of the other two implicated fully recover.

Seven weeks after the charges were dismissed, Eustace died from a heart attack. Some reading this may claim that by putting him through so much stress I was guilty of murder. Yet had I died because of the stress that came from others bullying and disparaging me, who would have suggested they stand trial for manslaughter?

What most annoyed me about the suggestions that I was gay was that one or more of the women I had gone out with had divulged that I was not interested in lovemaking. There were two chief suspects. One woman had resented me ending our relationship after she had declared her love for me. Another I dropped following her hints that generous gifts from me would lead to sexual favours. Following my evening with Mavis, I bugged both of these former girlfriends and also examined the hard drive of the gold digger. Nothing pertinent emerged. Despite what the media have alleged about Mr Vitriol being quick to attack and not caring who got hurt, I suspended my plans for retaliation until proof against one of these women emerged.

What I had wanted was a platonic friendship with someone who liked me, was easy on the eye, good company and trustworthy. I sometimes wished for more, but there is desire and desiring enough to crash through restraining barriers. It saddened me to give up some companions, but it was unfair to encourage hopes that would not be realised; be they for marriage, a child, or merely a sexual partner.

I could not explain what had happened at Gatgash or share my fear of a woman finding my manhood lacking. And most girlfriends, had I admitted to celibacy, would have had barrow loads of whys and wherefores that I would either have refused to answer or invented a barrow load of lies for.

Only one woman made me reconsider. But she was so attractive and had such a winning personality that I could not believe she would remain with me after she had fully recovered from a marriage that had ended badly. It seemed obvious that a tall Prince Charming would sweep her off her feet sooner or later.

Chapter 33: Norman ~ Crete

After returning to work with restored sight, I missed the amount of time that I had shared with Rose. Conversations with colleagues were devoid of what really mattered in life and I sensed that continuing to focus on feelings and discussing them would bring me further benefits. CARE sought voluntary redundancies at this time; the collapse of communism in Europe had led to a reduced budget. People of my generation could retire on an enhanced pension.

Rose looked at the redundancy package and asked a few questions before saying, "If it's what you want, go for it. I appreciate you consulting me, but it's your decision."

I applied and told myself that come retirement I would only consider other work if it did not get in the way of spending time with Rose. Towards the end of August 2001, a letter confirmed that my last day would be in October. Two days after September 11th, the director of CARE invited me to stay on and learn Arabic.

"You'd be better off with younger dogs to learn new tricks."

"Would you consider working on contract? There's a project assessing an emerging technology. If you took it over it would free someone else to learn Arabic."

I accepted on the understanding that I would work from home and limit my hours to forty a week. However, I let the cleverness of the technology and its potential for the Intelligence community seduce me. Instead of continuing the conversations with Rose, I was in my study morning through to evening, weekdays and weekends. The director, enthused by my report, authorised another contract for a project plan to implement the technology. As the work had the potential to make the country more secure, I let myself imagine that the benefits could only happen through my efforts. But by the time I had finished the plan, a new director was in post and she chose not to see my presentation. A thirty-something Deputy Director who attended in her place demonstrated with his opening question that he had not read anything relating to the technology. The young people with him were either equally ignorant or reluctant to appear better informed. My slides were for an audience that had studied the initial report and I could not think on my feet fast enough. Stifled yawns and glazed eyes conveyed that they found my floundering tedious. I felt for the first time that my age was a barrier to communicating both in terms of the ability to rise to the occasion and how they perceived me. Their routine thanks offered no consolation and there was no suggestion of a third contract for supporting documentation, which I had assumed would follow. All the way home, I compared my demoralisation to the high spirits enjoyed while driving from CARE on my last day as a salaried employee.

There was little to do after shredding and incinerating the paperwork accumulated during the project. Dealing with deferred personal correspondence took only a few hours and the weather limited what I could do in the garden. Rose was in a busy phase and not least because she had known of my hopes for a further contract. When I tried to read, pesky thoughts of failure got in the way. The streams from my unresolved past were no longer diverted by activity and sleep became more difficult. However, I did my best to conceal the growing unease in order not to spoil an approaching holiday in Crete that Rose had booked on hearing there would be no further contract.

Her company on the journey began to lift my spirits. We arrived on the island on Good Friday. It was warm, especially compared to the England we had left, and the scenery between the airport and hotel did not disappoint. A receptionist handed us an invitation to a free Easter Sunday lunch. The only letdown was finding the room had twin beds.

On the Saturday, we walked down a road that passed two hillside villages and along a stony beach that ended at a harbour with fishing boats. A taverna advertised *catch of the day* and we sat at an outside table in the shade of a wall. Skinny yet otherwise healthy looking cats whooshed around us, much to Rose's delight. Another English couple from our hotel joined us for coffee and explained how to get back by another route that was worth the steep climb because it was even more picturesque. Despite what should have been an easy pace, I was soon puffing and took off my hat in a bid to cool down.

While sitting on a low wall to catch my breath, I said, "Something reminds me of Arizona."

"But it's so green after the winter rain."

"Partly it's the intensity of the light. But also it's a sense of being out of place because I have no work to go back to. What's most different is you being here. How I wish you'd been with me in Arizona."

Then a pang of guilt made me clam up.

The English couple joined us that evening in the bar and we sat as a foursome in the dining room. She was a lecturer in English who had completed her doctoral thesis on Poe. He was a Reader in Anthropology recently returned from field work in the south of Sudan. They talked about their subjects in entertaining ways, asked questions about Rose's work in prisons, and where I thought information technology was leading society. They were such good company that Rose and I, forgetting we were old enough to be their parents, drank far too much, or so we realised the next morning when we woke muzzy-headed. In addition, my pate, nose and ears were red from having removed my hat without using sun block. Instead of breakfast, we drank a lot of water and went back to sleep.

By the time we went downstairs for lunch we were hungry. A waiter said the food would be ready in "thirty English minutes" and brought complimentary ouzos to where we sat on the terrace with a view of the azure sea. The Mediterranean appeared flat, but there must have been a swell for foam to lap the stony beach. The rising aroma of roasting meat was tantalising. Laughter and Greek chatter drew us to the balustrade. Below, staff in white jackets and check trousers stood in front a device that emitted faint smoke. Two men moved away at the same time to reveal three tiny lambs with heads attached rotating above a bed of charcoal. I gripped the marble slab that topped the balusters.

The next I knew, I was no longer in the sun. Rose looked anxious as I lay on a sofa near the reception desk. She took me to our room with the help of the manager who kept his hand under my armpit despite its trickle of sweat. I either slept or passed out again. When I awoke, Rose was talking to a man in his seventies who reeked of cigarettes and, when he bent to examine me, also of brandy. The fatty stain on the doctor's shirt suggested he had come from his own Easter feast.

As if I was too ill to understand, he said to Rose, "His temperature, pulse and blood pressure are normal. With so little hair he needs a hat more than most men for the sun. Also, he should avoid ouzo on an empty stomach. First eat some olives or better still cheese."

I dozed on the bed covered by a sheet while Rose read on the balcony with her chair angled so that she could keep an eye on me. When I stirred, she brought water and later ordered tea and sandwiches. I drank plenty, but lacked appetite despite no discomfort in my stomach other than a level of anxiety that had not stopped me eating on past occasions. Rose ignored my urgings to go to the restaurant for a proper meal and made do with the sandwiches rather than leave me.

My wandering attention made following my book difficult. At one point Rose, who was reading on her bed, asked what I was staring at because she saw my eyes looking up.

"I'm not sure. It's as if there was some vague form that hinted of light floating over the wall followed by a dark shape."

"Are your eyes playing up?"

"It stopped as soon as you spoke, so it must have been a day dream."

I pretended to start reading while wondering about the wraithlike light and darkness. The floating luminescence had been similar to the Will-o'-the-Wisp my father had taken me to see. Then for the first time I connected the flickering gas at the swamp that my father had claimed made him feel lucky and the exploding underground methane that had killed him. It troubled me that despite a secondary school teacher saying the two gases were the same I had not linked these two events before.

"Do you know you're rattling the dust jacket?" Rose asked.

Even after she had pointed this out it took effort to stop tapping the back of the book.

"Sorry. I'm finding it hard to read. Would you mind if I watched television?"

"I'm tired enough to sleep if you turn out the lights and keep the sound low."

I kept the TV on mute and rotated dozens of times through the dozens of channels, few of which were familiar, until drowsy. Yet by the time I had used the bathroom I was no longer sleepy and not having the comfort of Rose in my bed did not help. Perhaps I fell asleep at about two in the morning. Not long after four, I had a nightmare, the first in many years and as bad as the ones that had happened during my first week at Crail. As a torrent raced me towards Helgrund Foss, three struggling lambs overtook me, their frantic efforts to stay afloat speeding them on. Their pitiful bleating echoed as they fell to the netherworld. Just as I reached the lip of the abyss, I woke screaming.

Twice in our early years of marriage, I had screamed in my sleep. Rose had comforted me with hugs and not pressed me after I pretended not to know what lay behind the nightmares. But in Crete, she drew on her decades of experience with victims and prisoners living with their past horrors.

"Your dream might be a one-off, but sometimes old issues creep up on retired people. Do you know what the nightmare was about?"

Facing the monster after so many years of looking away felt dangerous; David at Crail had been the last to hear me speak about the near drowning. I had coped after that with a belief or hope that the fiendish events, if not agitated, would precipitate like sediment and remain covered by more recent memories.

"I'd rather not talk about it," I said to Rose, but already my unconscious seemed less of a deep lake and more like a geothermal area with a thin crust pockmarked by fumaroles and geysers.

"If it seems too threatening to speak, there's the risk that whatever caused this finds other outlets, such as more bad dreams. Talking will reduce its power over you. A doctor might give you pills that help with some of the symptoms, but only talking will tackle the cause. Am I making sense?"

I nodded.

"Did the dream have anything to with you fainting?"

Although the answer was in my mind immediately, it took time to say, "They both involved lambs to the slaughter."

"Ah!"

After a breathless pause, I said. "I don't know if I can say more than that now."

"You've made a start. Let's see what you can share later."

I had no appetite and was too afraid to fall asleep that night. The next morning, there were bruises on my arms from pinching myself to keep awake rather than experience another nightmare. After breakfasting on orange juice and coffee, I was too light headed to even pretend to read by the pool and stared through my sunglasses at a wall and whoever walked through my gaze. We ordered bread and cheese by the pool for lunch because I did not want to use the dining room. I ate very little. In the heat of the afternoon, I slept for a few hours in our room, something made easier by lovemaking and Rose's continued embrace. I was relieved to find sleep ended with no recollection of a bad dream.

As my stomach could not entertain the idea of hearty food, that evening I limited myself to gazpacho, or the Cretan version of it, and a slice of bread. When Rose also ate little and ordered no wine, it seemed that my memories had tainted the holiday she had been waiting for since I had applied for retirement. As we sat with coffee, the restaurant manager brought over an unlabelled corked bottle and two tumblers.

"I'm sorry your sunstroke meant missing the Easter meal. But we still have some of this left over from Sunday. It's Tsikoudia, like grappa only better, and made in the village below us."

He poured two large measures and left the bottle on the table. Rose looked doubtful. I took a sip and then finished my glass in two gulps. After that we sipped together. The spirit and guilt about spoiling her holiday helped me to speak back in our room about Helgrund Foss.

There were no more screams at night, but at times I woke up feeling anxious without recalling any dream.

What soon became clear was that while my appetite had returned in terms of quantity, I shunned meat and even swordfish because it looked too meaty. This was hardly a problem given the options available in Crete. When Rose asked about my new diet I said it was for my health. She was happy to provide vegetarian food on our return, but on our fifth evening back in England we went to Hungarian friends, a woman she had worked with in the past and her husband, for a meal arranged before we had left. They had prepared *Vadas Hús* because Rose and I had enjoyed it so much on an earlier occasion and I had not thought to advise them that I no longer ate meat. After the first course, I pretended that an upset stomach meant it was better to avoid the Hunter's Stew.

Rose, clear headed because it was her turn to drive, noticed I had no problem with two glasses of hearty wine, a second helping of dessert, the cheese board and a snifter of mulberry pálinka.

During our return journey to Foxenearth, she said, "What's going on? They must have spent hours preparing that stew and then you suddenly have an upset stomach that doesn't stop you enjoying everything else."

"I wish I had thought to tell them I've gone off meat."

"I don't understand when you're vegetarian only for the sake of your health. Would it have hurt to eat enough of the stew to be polite? After all, you had time to warn them. And if you're worried about your health, what about the dessert and all that full-fat cheese with Bath Olivers?"

Spoiling her evening on top of spoiling her holiday made me feel ashamed. "I have a confession. Since Easter Sunday the idea of eating meat revolts me. Even seeing raw meat upsets me. When I saw a butcher's window the other day, I turned around. I was too afraid to walk past it."

As we were driving on a deserted straight road, she turned her head to say, "Why not tell me before now?"

"Because I thought it would go away, not get stronger."

"Was the fear at the butcher's as great as your fear of lightning?"

"Yes, except there was a way of escaping. With lightning you never know that you're safe until the storm has passed."

"Phobias tend to grow through avoidance. Either the fear gets bigger or the range of triggers or both. I don't mind you being a vegetarian if you really want to be one, but not if you do it from fear."

"I have another phobia since the holiday."

"Go on."

"I was never comfortable with the swallet at the end of the valley, but I could walk past it provided I didn't look down. When I last took Winkie towards it, I couldn't get within a hundred yards. Just thinking about it now gives me the shivers."

"Most psychologists who specialise in phobias focus on reversing the symptoms, not getting you talking the way most therapies do."

"I would much rather it was you."

"I don't have their expertise."

"But I trust you."

"Not enough to tell me until I prompted."

"I won't hold anything else back."

"I need to see what I can find on desensitisation before agreeing. It's not something to go at blindly. In the meanwhile, it would help me as well as you if you talked more."

And so started another round of cafetière sessions followed by an hour of reflection. Rose also walked with me towards the swallet, making allowances for the level of the Lychinclay Stream and the anxiety in me that fluctuated with it. After many weeks, provided she was with me, I could look and listen to the draining water in any weather. Then she had me approach the swallet with Winkie before getting me to face it alone. I was never happy being in the area, but the desperate panic receded to something manageable.

Rose also worked to expand the range of foods I ate. To begin with, she added small amounts of clear meat stock to vegetable soups. Gradually, she increased the meaty flavour and then allowed tiny flakes of flesh. When I was comfortable with her usual recipe for *minestrone* she began to use sausage meat in spicy dishes, then mince, and then small cubes cooked until they were very tender. Next she let the flavour of the meat come to the fore. It was about this time she had me slice ham and other cooked meat in the kitchen, handle wrapped meat in the supermarket and then prepare a chicken for the oven. So successful was her reintroduction of meat that I almost forgot how extreme my loathing for it had been. One evening in a restaurant, I looked up half way through the steak I had ordered. Rose was smiling with a tear in an eye. Because my mouth was too full to speak, I raised a glass to her and sipped. Wine had never tasted better.

When my plate was empty, I took her hand and said, "I can't tell how much I appreciate the trouble you took restoring my appetite."

I know that I thanked her for other things, but the scene in the restaurant is the only one that stands out. And if the other occasions when I expressed gratitude are not distinct memories for me, why assume that Rose knew how appreciative I was?

Chapter 32: Perry ~ The Return

Almost twenty-five years ago, I arrived at a corporation headquarters where the foyer was in some disarray due to refurbishment. The manager who had invited me to discuss a possible contract had alerted reception that he would be delayed. A receptionist took me to a room to one side of the counter and invited me to help myself to the refreshments there. Missing ceiling tiles meant that a conversation taking place on a sofa in the foyer was audible. Two men from a supplier of photocopiers, one sales and one an engineer, were discussing how the vulnerabilities of the person they had come to see could be exploited to extract a higher price. It brought home the way visitors arriving together might be indiscreet, as if needing to use their last chance to be blunt about their host before yielding to politeness. This insight inspired some of the additions at Raventulle made after the builders had left.

A floodlight sits on top of the gatepost that houses the intercom. The same detector that triggers the beam after dusk also switches on the intercom microphone regardless of whether or not the lights come on. Another microphone and a detector sit alongside the front door. Sounds from both mikes feed to the hidden part of the cellar where, by flicking a switch, I can either listen directly or divert the signal to a sound-activated recorder. Sometimes the results were bizarre.

"Cripes! It's like Fort Knox. They must have something worth protecting."

The monitor displayed three male touring cyclists who had stopped to put on waterproof clothing.

"If I managed to break in I'd settle for a hot shower and stealing a change of underpants," said another.

"Count me out," said the third. "I don't want to appear in the Sunday papers as the accomplice of an underwear fetishist."

One Saturday afternoon five years ago, as I trawled a copy of a local's hard drive, the monitor showed a car pulling into the bay by the gate. Two plump mature women got out and studied the house.

A South African accent said, "Well, it's not just standing. Someone has lovingly restored it."

A similar voice asked, "Do you think they're from South Africa?"

"Why do you say that?"

"Look at the security. I wouldn't be surprised if a couple of *Boerboels* started barking at us."

After laughter, the buzzer rang.

"Hello."

"Sorry to trouble you, but we lived here until 1949 before emigrating. It's our first time back. Would it be possible to get closer to the house?"

I stared at the monitor and tried without success to work out if one of these women was Tilda. My heart pounded so much that I wanted time to calm down. I realised that for over fifty years I had been pretending I wanted no more to do with the Kytes, preferring to dwell on the memories before seeing them for the last time at the railway station. I had regarded their emigration as a betrayal until faced with the possibility of being with Tilda again.

To gain time to compose myself, I said, "You're welcome to look round, but right now I'm in the middle of something. Could you come back in fifteen minutes?"

They agreed and drove away. I closed the secret part of the cellar and left the door at the top of the stairs unlocked. I checked every room, got ready a plate of sandwiches and biscuits and left the gate open. By the time they returned, my breathing had settled. As soon as they drove through the gate, I opened the front door. Both women had the sort of large bosoms that would flop to their bellies without support. Given the amount of slap they wore, their cheap fleece jackets, sweatshirts and black polyester trousers seemed incongruous. One had a mauve rinse and the other blue. The heavy odour of cigarettes competed with freshly applied perfumes. Their type of hair colouring had become *passé*. Did they persist with it to hide the yellowing effect of smoke?

"Welcome back. I take it you're two of the Kyte sisters?"

The blue-haired one asked, "How did you know?"

That one of them might be Tilda made me want to say who I was, but if they chatted about this to someone in the village, my past would no longer be a secret. Then again, if they guessed my identity and spoke to locals, what would people make of my concealment over years?

"I'm Perry Gray."

They looked at each other open-mouthed before coming forward to hug and kiss me. We all had tears.

"But I can't tell who you are."

"I'm Lucy and this is Grace," said the woman with the mauve rinse.

"And where's Tilda?"

Their faces turned sombre as both waited for the other to speak.

"She died in 1981."

I do not recall which sister said this. The next thing I remember is showing them the outbuildings and every room inside with the exception of my secret chamber. Unlike me, they soon forgot Tilda and ate without restraint when we sat down for tea.

After they had learned that Maud and Gordon were dead, I asked about their parents.

Lucy said, "Mum died from a melanoma eleven years ago. We persuaded Dad to move in with me. He was very low and hardly left the property for three months. Then he said he was going to look for butterflies and didn't come back. Police found his net and rucksack three metres from the edge of a cliff and him at the bottom. It was probably suicide."

I expressed sympathy and apologised for bringing up the subject of their parents.

"No, no," said Grace. "We've never avoided talking about Mum and Dad."

Encouraged by this, I asked, "What happened to Tilda?"

Again the strained faces waiting for the other to respond until Lucy spoke in a flat voice. "Tilda became political at university. We thought she would grow out of it, but she never did. Dad lost business and people shunned us, especially following her arrest at a demonstration. She went to prison. After that she was more radical than ever. In '68 she went to Zambia and from there to Mozambique when it became independent. She was killed there by a letter bomb. The blast blinded her and caused an infection. They didn't have much in the way of medical treatment where she was and she was in no state to travel over rough roads."

"But who would want to hurt her?"

Bitterness tinged Lucy's answer. "There was no sender's name, but everyone assumes it was from an agent of the government in Pretoria that she was fighting. You have to understand, there was a war going on. I lost a son in Angola. Only his family remembers him now, but in the new South Africa there are buildings and streets named after Tilda."

"It's very hard, Perry." Grace said. "She was probably right about blacks having the vote, but she betrayed her family. I was luckier than Lucy. I married, moved from Cape Town and did not let on that I was related. And I didn't lose a son. I still don't say I'm a Kyte because those who read about Tilda now know that her family disowned her."

Lucy added with bitterness, "We can't win either way."

They turned the talk to when I had stayed with them at Raventulle. Tilda was curiously absent from their recollections and tight lips appeared when I brought her escapades into the conversation. On a second tour, Grace videoed Raventulle inside and out while Lucy took stills. They did not expect to come to England again unless events in South Africa took a turn for the worse. That Christmas, both sent cards. I did not respond and nothing else came from them.

Even before the sisters had left I was angry, in particular at their lack of remorse for not supporting Tilda. To make their life easier, the family would have preferred their youngest not to ripple the waters of apartheid. I swallowed my bile while they were at Raventulle and they thought that only the news of their sister's death upset me. I realised later that in keeping quiet I had done what they had wanted Tilda to do.

I did not sympathise with Tilda's involvement in revolution because the manifestoes and fervour of the far left, or the National Front for that matter, are too similar to the religion that duped my parents. What I identified with was Tilda's opposition to the humiliation visited on the majority within her new country. How easy it would have been to follow her father's example, forget about the social injustices resented in England and live high on the hog as one of the ruling caste in Cape Town.

The couple and their older daughters, who had been so kind to me, had no trouble grasping the privileges of a cruel and divisive system based on colour of skin. Only Tilda had the courage to reject siding with the oppressors. I noted with a degree of discomfort that an anonymous correspondent had killed her.

The morning after Lucy and Grace had visited, I awoke with a severe hangover, a rare event. Yet I made myself retrace the journey taken with Tilda on our last walk in 1949. After lunch, I searched the web for photographs of her. The sisters had withheld that Tilda had been a member of the South African Communist Party and had spent a year in London between Zambia and Mozambique. I made copies of three images. In one, Tilda is six or seven. I reckon other people had been in the original, possibly even me. Another print shows Tilda well into adolescence and far from flat chested, which somehow shocked me. The third was taken nine weeks before the letter bomb. The web caption read: Tilda and Ruth. Tilda wears a camouflage-patterned shirt and lovingly holds a contented toddler.

Lucy and Grace had never mentioned their niece, Ruth Kyte Nkosi. Tilda marrying a Zulu, even one with a doctorate from Leipzig, and having his child would have been intolerable for her family. Dr Ambrose Nkosi provoked envy in me for his years with Tilda and his towering good looks. However, humble his origins, he had become a person of influence. Ruth had followed Ambrose both in obtaining a PhD and joining the South

African diplomatic service. I fantasised about Ruth being posted to London and inviting her to Raventulle. But what did I have to offer? Only a reminder of the family that had disowned her mother, loathed Ruth's father, and did not want people to know that they were related to a mixed-race child.

I blutacked prints of the three pictures above my desk in the cellar. After some months, I threw away two and framed the oldest and least clear, the one of the Tilda I most wanted to remember. She looks back at me and I think about how different my life might have been with her remaining in England to protect, share affection and give me courage.

I regretted that Tilda had not sought me out when she was in London. But if she had, by then politics would have divided us. Had she asked what I did for justice and I had told her, she would have urged me to forego personal grudges and nit-picking letters in favour of a wider political struggle.

For a time after the sisters' visit, I toyed with planting morphine or child pornography on those who champion white supremacy in my country. It would have been a kind of remembrance of Tilda. But without experiencing humiliation directly from racists, I did not have enough anger to prompt me to take such risks against them, no matter how vile I thought they were.

Chapter 33: Norman ~ Lunch at the Tate

David Stancher's promotions at the Metropolitan Police led him to a position that included liaising with government security agencies that meant he knew what CARE did and learned of their plan to move from London without me telling him. I did mention during a phone call that Rose and I had looked at properties within twenty miles of the new complex without finding anything suitable.

"I suspect we'll either end up renting until a house with a large garden that's within our budget comes along."

Without telling me, the Stanchers spent a weekend in the area exploring further afield than Rose and I had. When they were our guests for dinner, Felicity described driving through the Lychinclay Valley the previous Sunday and seeing the estate agent's sign outside Foxenearth. Then she produced a local paper with details of the property.

"For some reason," David said, "The prices at the upper end of the valley are almost double those at the lower, but it's not that much further from where you'll be working."

Because they enthused about Foxenearth's large and well kept garden, the quaintness of the village and the wooded hilltops. Rose and I said we would visit the next day.

I remember David that evening for another reason. He drank until the wine he had brought and the bottle I provided were empty. Felicity refused alcohol as she was driving and Rose and I both stopped after two glasses because we wanted an early start in order to visit the valley before collecting Colin from Finchley at the time agreed with Marie. Had it been someone other than David drinking, I would not have given much thought to the quantity. Many friends of our age then drank more on a Saturday evening and some did so without a substantial meal.

Had David's Christian outlook changed? He had told me at Crail that some Baptists regarded all alcohol as sinful and others tolerated occasional drinking in moderation. While his family were not teetotal, David in khaki had never sipped more than two halves of mild during the course of an evening.

The next time just the two of us met for lunch in London, I asked about his faith. He was as devout as ever and no more liberal in his theology. Rose suspected that the drinking culture of the police and the stresses of work had combined to change his habits. We had no great concerns for him because he did not drink most days and did nothing he would regret while under the influence. If anything, he was mellower and more fun when he drank heartily.

Lower Lychinclay turning out to be a frost pocket made us no less fond of the Stanchers who, after all, had merely alerted us to a possibility. I owed David much from my time in the Army and Rose had developed a warm relationship with Felicity. We were pleased that they drove to our housewarming party and continued to be regular visitors.

During a meal at their house, Rose explained how our new village had long been poorer than Upper Lychinclay. "After the improvements to the road at the turn of the century, speculators built houses, including Foxenearth, for people who could not afford the better climate up the road. And with mechanisation reducing the number of farm workers in the valley, landowners sold former tied cottages. Wealthier newcomers tended to buy the ones in Upper Lychinclay and several former tenants from the uplands had to move down the road, including new council homes built in a shaded corner of Lower Lychinclay. The split between the ends of the valley can be awkward. People want you to take sides, or at least tolerate them saying catty things about the residents at the other end."

"How do you manage that?" David looked at me.

"I hide behind Rose's skirts."

Everyone laughed, but it was not far from the truth.

"What's your strategy, Rose?" Felicity asked.

"I try to see the positive side. If they're complaining at least they're talking to me. If I can, I steer the conversation in another direction. And there are a few people at both ends that almost everyone thinks well of. I sometimes mention one of them as a way of saying *thou generaliseth too much.*"

Perry paints a somewhat dismal portrait of snobbery in The Peacock, but at least he had the choice of five pubs in the town. Our end of the valley has just the Cul-de-Sac. I usually find pub chatter of little interest but, because Rose wanted us to be a part of the community, we went to get to know the regulars. Mostly we attended when alerted of a special occasion marked there, such as an engagement, wetting the baby's head, and fundraising evenings. But it took time to be accepted with many Lychinclay people being standoffish and inward-looking. And when we did get to know them, conversations all too often drifted to what absent residents were reputed to have done. Many ascribed the foibles of others to their location in the valley, social origins, gender, sexual inclinations, religious or political views, or source of income. For all my talent at assuming, I passed as one of the less prejudiced drinkers.

Rose won acceptance for us in our village with her easy chat and willingness to be a good neighbour. Upper Lychinclay, where people tended to speak more crisply and were likelier to attend a church, was a tougher nut to crack for someone not prepared to disown her London accent or conceal her agnosticism. She did not flaunt her views, but neither did she mislead people the way I did. If asked why she did not attend church with me, she explained that she no longer believed. And even when people looked at me as if to say, what a cross you have to bear with an infidel wife, she never hinted at my closet atheism.

Some people assumed that Colin was irreligious because of Rose. In fact, he was interested in religions all through secondary school. However, he loathed Anglicanism because he thought I took it seriously. Unlike his mother who would come to hear the choir perform a new piece, he refused every invitation to hear me sing whatever the venue.

Until I retired, I used the excuse of work to avoid being drawn into other parish activities. Even the drinks after choir practice were not important to me, but Rose enjoyed socialising with the choristers and often joined for an hour or so when she came to collect me. She could break the ice for both of us and stimulate those already merry to more laughter without drinking alcohol. Yet such talents were not enough to make her acceptable to everyone in Upper Lychinclay.

Her beauty attracted men there who were interested in an affair. She told me their chat up lines and propositions, though never in a boastful way. Nor was she judgmental about most of the men being married. What she most resented were those who sought to bed her, but would have avoided her socially.

After a local landowner had invited her to a hotel in Wales, she said to me, "Some men don't know which century it is. They still think they can sleep with a woman one day and pretend not to know her the next. If I had a daughter, I'd tell her that when Lord Muck doesn't want you at his table because his friends are there, don't bother with his bedroom."

The Lychinclay Anglicans were more fractious than other congregations that I have known. For our first three years in the Valley, most considered the vicar too much of a fundamentalist. His successor was too high for the likes of many of the Low Church persuasion. Our bishops' reputations have been similarly divisive with the exception of the one opposed by the overwhelming majority of both camps for being too intellectual, a hanging crime in this neck of the woods. Into sparks created by the friction between Evangelicals and Anglo-Catholics seeped two volatile vapours. The first to sear the nostrils was the suggestion that a priest did not need a male appendage. Before the dust from this flare-up had settled, in rushed something even more explosive: where priests may park said appendages.

To unbelievers like Rose and me, these debates made no more sense than arguing whether a million or a billion angels fit on the point of a needle. Both pro- and anti-zealots assumed that I would fall off the fence on their side if pushed hard enough. Some went so far as to seek my support for their cause through invitations to homes never before opened to me.

I would say, "I've never studied theology or felt the need to. I just don't have a view other than hoping that a decision is reached soon and everyone can live with it."

This dissembling only inflamed the passions of the more argumentative. Often they responded to my attempts at neutrality as if it was the religious equivalent of playing hard to get.

The only issue in the Lychinclay Valley more contentious than ordaining women or openly homosexual priests was foxhunting. Blood sports divide both the top and bottom dwellers, but the majority of Lowerites opposed hunting, compared to a minority of Upperites. Hunts occasionally had destroyed fields and gardens in Lower Lychinclay until 1958 when the trampling of a crop of Brussels sprouts helped persuade key lower valley farmers to forbid entry to riders. Needless to say, as well as protecting property this cocked a snook at the folks up the hill and added to the tetchiness between the two communities.

A few managed to keep talking to parties from all sides and worked to promote harmony. Rose's best local friends were mostly from among the peacemakers. To communicate with both factions was no small achievement when so many relished the bickering and the deriding of anyone not in their camp as stupid, ill-informed or insensitive. Reputations in Lychinclay often suffered from the death of a thousand small cuts. Is there that much difference between Perry's malicious letters and the repeated insinuations and accusations people share about another who is not present?

Because of these communal tensions and the devastating frosts, Rose and I talked of leaving the area after Colin had started university. However, we did not want to re-graft ourselves onto the stock of a city or a suburb. If we had moved, it would have been to another rural setting and we concluded that the perfect village did not exist. At both ends of the valley, Rose had found good friends and there were many others who were neither bumpkin nor snob. The most tangible benefit of moving would have been an improved climate but, despite the surfeit of icy mornings, we had come to love our garden and its seasons.

Vaulting Ryego is different in many ways from Lychinclay. It is one settlement and one climate rather than two, has uniformly good farmland, a bigger population than the whole of the valley, and had more to do with neighbouring towns even before commuters took up residence. Yet still Perry found it inward looking and full of divisions. Despite the many new arrivals, his accent was alien both to those who spoke the shire dialect and the English of the upper classes. He noted and resented the social distinctions of his new location from the time he made enquiries at Hoggson's Estate Agents, but the snobbery did not deter his move or make him want to leave because Raventulle meant too much to him.

We know little of his relationships with neighbours in Rayners Lane. Some were dead, others had moved and the few that the reporters had traced said little more than recalling him to be a loner or a mummy's boy. If they drew attention to his helpfulness or said other favourable things, the media did not share such comments, perhaps because they were too busy making Perry into a monster. No neighbours in Rayners Lane have come forward with a letter from Mr Vitriol. Was it simply caution on his part? Perhaps those living near his parents' house never offended him. Or perhaps he put vengeful brickbats for locals to one side in deference to his parents. Another possibility is that he felt accepted by people like the Ovesians and Pritchards. And unlike many other children in the area then, he was not an outsider in terms of his origins.

Many families in Harrow during Perry's childhood had come from much further afield than his parents. A significant Welsh community lived there along with the English people who had come from way north of Watford, and Jewish families from Eastern and Central Europe via the East End. Perry's accent would not have been that different from the majority of other youngsters born in Harrow. His classmates mocked him for many things, but there is no suggestion that anyone mocked the way he spoke before the fencing class.

The sense of difference and disdain that he encountered in Vaulting Ryego served to add fuel to his rage and, by the time he had moved there, he was not one to sit and suffer. In other circumstances, say had he been radicalised at university, he might have become a class warrior screeching Marx and scratching Mercedes before emerging as a middle-of-the road councillor or a Labour MP happily pocketing consultancy fees from major companies.

P Are you trying to rile me?
N No. I think you may well have responded to university by intellectualising and finding another outlet for your hurt and anger. And while you attacked people from all classes, the well-to-do appear in your writing a disproportionate number of times. I don't find class prejudice, as distinct from seeking a fairer society, is any more acceptable than other prejudices.
P Have you stopped to consider that that the upper classes are more likely to wield power or that some of them are prone to thinking they are better by birth or education or because they inherited wealth? I've had no issues with many individuals from elite backgrounds who have left me in peace. But I resent condescension, including what you just wrote about me.
N I'm sorry that you saw that way. Let me explain. Had I gone to university from school, I may well have got involved in left wing causes. Some might think my conservatism inherited; I don't. First the Army and then CARE kept my politics in check, or at least my mouth shut. Even in retirement, I never told my fellow Rotarians that I disagreed with much of their outlook. I just wasn't committed enough to my views to be prepared to argue about them. Nor did I want to be thought of as oddball. But studying for a degree might have radicalised me. If education did this to others from our generation, why not to you or me had we gone to university?
P We'll never know. But I can tell you that you were wrong about Harrow. I sent letters to people there and added bullies from school to my list.
N Did you make any distinction between the offences of adults and children? Are they both equally guilty in your eyes?
P The same insult is more painful to a child than an adult. So why should the tariff be any less just because the mouth that spouted it was younger?

N That sounds harsh, Perry. In your heart of hearts, can you really justify it?
P If those children had any heart, they would not have bullied. Why should I
make allowances? In any case, young bullies will continue to persecute, given the opportunity, until someone smacks them down. And heaven help underlings when a child thug grows to occupy a position of power. Why would they stop? Where would any change of heart come from?

I invited David to lunch in Pimlico at the Tate, one of his favourite restaurants, to thank him for recommending me to Ann. After catching up with news of families, gardens and people we both knew, he asked what need the police had for a decoder. I trusted him as a friend completely, not to mention that he had passed every vetting for access to state secrets. And by the time he enquired, our bottle of claret was almost empty. My discretion was limited to lowering my voice, stopping when the waiter approached, and, after saying Perry's name once, referring to him as Dolly.

Describing and discussing what I had decoded took long enough for us to drink a second bottle. David expressed regrets about Ann Grove's behaviour when I had visited her and said he suspected Catchpole's vanity was behind the attempt to enlist me in deleting parts of the decoding. The unreserved support plus the wine going to my head prompted me to mention the presence that Perry had assumed in my mind and Rose's take on this.

David's face grew long. "I know you don't hold with religion, but I recommend an exorcism. There are ministers who could help to set you free. I know men who have been delivered from a lifetime of homosexual depravity by the casting out of evil spirits. I bitterly regret mentioning your name to Ann."

Despite knowing that David's theology was old fashioned, I was stunned by the suggestion of exorcism, both for me and homosexuals. At the same time, Perry became very vocal. Although I knew that ecclesiastical mumbo-jumbo could make no difference to his presence, he felt threatened by the possibility. An odd sensation grew from the mismatch between Perry's panicky thoughts and the lack of anxiety symptoms in my body.

A braver person would have told David his ideas belonged to the Dark Ages. Instead, I said that, far from blaming him, I was grateful for the decoding work. The only regret was causing him to worry by sharing how Perry had assisted me.

"The thing that you think has helped your work is an evil spirit that seeks to continue the wickedness of Dolly. It may well be the same devil that possessed him."

"He did nasty things. He was twisted, but I don't need demons to explain the way he was. He disturbed people because he was disturbed. And while Dolly hurt many, not one of them has a physical wound that came directly from him. A lot of people who commit assault on a regular basis don't get half the vilification."

"That doesn't mean Dolly and whatever has got into you isn't Satan's tool. I guess if you can't see it, all I can do is pray for you and ask others to do the same. But please be very careful. If you ever sense that this spirit is getting more powerful, call me and I'll bring a minister."

The glut of wine combined with my distaste for David's need to bring the devil into what I saw as an all too human story. I spoke a little too loudly while forgetting to use the alternative name.

"When I first read about Mr Vitriol, I thought he was pure evil. The more I got to know Perry, the more I came to see his actions as little different from the media that whipped up the furore. Reporters routinely snoop and disclose if not invent tittle-tattle that serves no public interest. What Perry did was despicable, but compared to much journalism his prying and slandering were a mere cottage workshop. You and I know hacks invade privacy on an industrial scale, fib to the millions and routinely blight lives to add to a mogul's profits. Perry hurt hundreds, but for each victim the audience, those who knew of his allegations, was small."

David looked surprised at first. He had seldom heard me say as much. Then he appeared deflated, resentful and distant; not the conclusion to the meal that I had wanted. I would have walked with him to Victoria Station in other circumstances. Instead, I said that I needed fresh air after the wine and would go along the Thames. On the bottom step of the Tate, we shook hands. Then for the first time, rather than let go he used his grip to pull me towards him and hugged.

At one point, I turned to watch him striding away. Though others probably would not have noticed, his walk was not as steady as it should have been. I thought, David you're like me; age is reducing the capacity for alcohol.

Rose picked me up five hours later from Upper Lychinclay. As she drove and I was telling her about the sad end to the lunch, Ann Grove rang. A friend in the Metropolitan Police had just called to say that David was dead. A cyclist had run into him as he had crossed a road near Victoria Station. A head injury led to death before an ambulance got him to hospital. The Met knew from David's wife that he had lunched with me and the officer who had alerted Ann had mentioned this. The Chief Superintendent who took no prisoners was crying and saying how much support David had given her as a mentor.

After the shock, I also cried. I blamed myself for ordering a second bottle, not matching my friend glass for glass, not predicting his reaction to Perry as a muse, and for not accompanying him to the station.

The cyclist's solicitor sought a second post mortem. By the time details of David's funeral arrived, Rose was in hospital. In any case, I could not bring myself to speak with Felicity and dreaded looking into her eyes in case she recognised my sense of guilt and thought it deserved. I wrote apologising for our absence, mentioning my cancer and Rose's illness. Although I was concerned about Rose at the time, I had never considered the risk of her dying. I regret this and the cowardice that led me to avoid Felicity to the point of not informing her of Rose's funeral. It seems only fair that I lost the friendship and support that Felicity would have offered me as a widower.

Chapter 34: Perry ~ Last Words

I have not recorded the events that shaped me and where they led to steer other victims of bullying towards covert retaliation. Telling folk what to do is not what I am about, but should victims become aware that they have more choices, well and good. And if abusers understand that bitter memories can provoke retaliation, which may be immediate or years in coming, perhaps some will hesitate. Bullies should also consider that the more people they pick on, the harder it will be to identify who has struck back. And take note that a few, like me, will hit back on behalf of others humiliated for no good reason or harried for minor failings.

Every target either bullied me or encouraged others to mock. Had someone limited their cruel remarks to a private diary, they would not have joined my list. I am a *don't tread on me* libertarian who believes in letting people get on with their lives so long as they do not disturb the peace of others.

The choices I made were sometimes flawed. I do not blame myself at the age of ten for selecting an inferior education, but after leaving secondary school I should have known better and avoided National Service. Instead, my desire to avoid harridans in typing pools and create a breathing space from Mum, blinded me to what the Army was capable of doing. Enough former servicemen had shared stories about the harshness of basic training, brutish NCOs and officers who looked the other way.

The problem with escaping the heat of the frying pan is that you do not think about where you are leaping. I regret those *Oh fuck it* moments when an urge to relieve tension dispelled common sense. The need to reduce symptoms of discomfort can feel very compelling. Who hasn't scratched an itch till it bleeds despite knowing that the itch will remain? Pressures and emotions at times led me to make poor choices that added to the dangers ahead, as if the path was not already fraught enough. The example *par excellence* was my response to Knattmaw when he appeared on television. Had I resisted the urge to act quickly, he did not have to be at the root of my downfall.

I used to feel safe in any part of Raventulle. The last weeks have been different. To buy time, I told people that I would be away. My car is in the garage. At night, I move around without lights. In the daytime, I avoid the front windows. I run fan heaters non-stop and have cold showers in case steam from the boiler arouses suspicion.

To stop me unthinkingly answering my landline, I disconnected all the extensions bar the one to the answer phone, which has its receiver clamped by an elastic band. An unruly patch of the garden has caught my eye from time to time and set me walking towards the back door to tend it. Then the missing key – around my neck rather than in the door – reminds me that my gardening days are over. I am about to deadhead myself and there will be no re-flowering. If there is no news of a Ryego Forest murder suspect on the six o'clock news, I will not see the dawn.

Without my curtains drawn together, the lights of passing vehicles have disrupted sleep. Some solace came from drafting in my head much of what I have written on these pages. I have also found release during the long nights through planning my exit. There will be no histrionics and nothing bloody or painful. Apart from the posturing Catchpole and Knattmaw and his ilk, I respect police officers and have no wish to make their duties following a suicide more onerous than they need to be. I cannot imagine how a person volunteers for a job with so many unpleasant facets – dealing with vomiting drinkers, the mentally ill roaming the streets and having to tell parents that a child is dead or assaulted by a pervert.

After I have finished writing, I will fetch my last bottle of 1990 Penfold's Grange Shiraz and leave my hidden den exposed, but lock the steel door. I will open the wine to let it breathe. Come twilight I will dig up a lavender bush to retrieve a container with a collection of sedatives taken from a house visited while the owner was out.

I will write a letter to Chief Superintendent Ann Grove in plain English and enclose a device to open the gate, the house and cellar keys, and the alarm code. She will learn that I am Mr Vitallium and where to find my corpse.

Preparing good food is always soothing and I will eat well tonight. Then I will walk to the nearest post box and take a last look at the lights of Vaulting Ryego and the stars above. If anyone wants to speak with me, I will say, "Catch up with you later."

When I have eaten, washed up, emptied the fridge of perishables and taken all the rubbish out, I will finish the remaining Shiraz before raising a globe of thirty-year old Armagnac to the Tilda who kissed me in the cellar. I will disconnect the answer phone and place all the receivers and my mobile in the garage to prevent any chance of my using them. It is not a lack of will I fear so much as some confused state from the overdose prompting a call for help.

After turning off the heaters, I will place a plastic sheet over the sofa and the kilim in front of it to catch any leaks that emerge before the removal of my body. As I am squeamish about needles, I will use only a cocktail of pills starting with an anti-emetic. There are ample stolen sedatives, provided I swallow enough of them before passing out. Water will help to wash them down continuously until I pass out or the pills are exhausted. Mixing different drugs, not to mention the alcohol, is pharmacological over-engineering to prevent the possibility of failure.

What will the police make of me when this writing is decoded? I hope the better ones will sympathise with my pursuit of wrongdoers. Crime fiction and some news reports suggest that cops cut corners in their pursuit of criminals, especially when frustrated by legal niceties. And most of the public, or at least the ones I have drunk with, are prepared to give the benefit of the doubt to an officer accused of over-zealousness. Even when the police shoot and kill the wrong man, most law abiding citizens want lessons learned, but quietly accept that the odd stray bullet entering a criminal's body has a deterrent effect. And many regard a villain roughed up in the back of a police van as just desserts. Every year, the justice system admits that some prisoners served long sentences after wrongful conviction, yet still the mob complain about the police fighting crime with one hand tied behind their backs and a namby-pamby court system. I hope that the public will extend this sort of latitude to my quest for justice.

I accept that had I reported what happened at Gatgash, even years later, an honest copper might have investigated thoroughly. But if Knattmaw made himself at home in the police, who knows what sort of officer might have led the enquiry? A court might have convicted the corporals, but it is more likely that the conspirators at the Fort would have closed ranks, claimed to know nothing about the boiler-house and insisted that the demotion of the Owls happened for other reasons. And Maddan is no longer alive; all that remains are his notes, which might even suggest that my anal wound was self-inflicted.

Why should a victim seeking justice have to go through an embarrassing process with an uncertain outcome? Like my persecutors, I lacked restraint when pursuing them. The difference is, their attacks were unprovoked while mine responded to situations where the law was unlikely to help victims.

If I was found to have given another person a fatal dose of poison, the charge would be murder. For a dose that posed a threat to life, I would face trial for attempted murder. If unpleasant symptoms resulted without risk to life, the charge would be grievous bodily harm. Even if the dose was minute and doctors found no toxic reaction, once my administration was proven, I would be charged with administering a noxious substance and quite rightly.

Bullying is also toxic. One small dose is seldom fatal, but may contribute to physical and mental deterioration. Continued harassment gnaws away at the quality of an individual's existence. When society tackles so many other evils, why is it that bullying persists in almost every area of life? We have major initiatives against racism, burglary, guns and knives, but when did the police last campaign to encourage the public to report name-calling?

But the issue goes much wider than the police. Our government invests little in understanding the causes of bullying and seeking to eliminate it. If society responds at all, it is usually reacting at the point where a more serious crime has happened or someone has been driven to suicide.

I covertly harassed my tormentors because no legitimate practical redress was open to me. To avoid the reprisals creating more innocent victims, I did not act on hearsay alone. What my sly form of justice lacked was a deterrent effect, a defect publication of this account could remedy. I have considered delaying death a day or so to type it up and post it online, but time is short and this way at least one other person will have to pay it close attention in order for it to be decoded.

Until three weeks ago, my will benefitted an anti-bullying charity. Knowing that what the papers will call *Mr Vitriol's bequest* would embarrass the organisation, I visited my London solicitor. Now the beneficiaries are my relatives in Watford. If one declines his or her share, the amount going to the others will be greater. I have never contacted them, but it was easy enough to find their names and addresses. Surely, no one will blame them for being my beneficiaries when we never met?

And at this stage, a bequest is the only amends I can offer for the distance that Mum felt was necessary to create between her relatives in Watford and her new found respectability.

Chapter 35: Norman ~ Conclusion

I have been checking for the last two days my earlier chapters and how it sits between Perry's text. While I was content with my commentary and comparisons, he was often agitated. He is far less composed than when he took his own life and begs me not to dispose of myself so soon because he wishes to linger. If Rose's voice was urging me to live, I would heed her.

Rather than helping with the proofreading, Perry sought to slant my text towards his bitter view of the world and would not desist when reminded that I undertook to write to certain standards and not merely to scribe his outpourings. He sulks and it is a shame that we will not exit this world together on better terms.

All that remains is to record some thoughts prompted by three characters on television last night. First, a chat show host interviewed two young women from Watford. They appeared to have spent hours in a beauty salon getting ready for the camera, so much so that every vestige of natural beauty was hidden under bouffant hair, layers of slap and that goldfish skin that masquerades as a tan.

"So what was it like to discover that you were related to Mr Vitriol?"

The girls turned their false eyelashes towards each other before speaking at the same time. Both raised their voices to deter the other. The older looking, perhaps twenty-two, spoke louder and silenced the younger, who then looked peeved.

The dominant one said, "Well it's weird, really. We didn't even know he existed. I mean, like, we knew about Mr Vitriol, but we never knew *nuffink* about Perry Gray. And what he did was, like, well out of order."

"But you will take a share of the money that he left?"

That took the wind out of her sails.

The other niece spoke. "Why shouldn't we? It's not like we did anything wrong."

"But the money could be used to compensate your relative's victims."

The older one said, "Show me a company that pays out when it doesn't have to. Why should we be any different?"

"Sometimes companies are shamed into making payments," said the interviewer. "Do you feel any shame in accepting the money?"

The girls frowned until the younger said, "We aren't doing anything illegal. And what about the money we're getting for this show. Are you ashamed to be paying us?"

"But your agent insisted on fees and we wanted the public to have the chance to hear answers to questions many of them have been asking."

The host persisted with four more minutes of questions. The interviewees, who no longer had any trace of a smile, said nothing new. It hardly seems credible that major crises in the world go unreported while such non-news fills the screen.

The vacuous interviewees were followed by an advert for a new series starting later in the evening called *Sex and the Noughties Woman*. The face and then the voice of Ariadne Morveseau filled much of the trailer. She had forgone all pretence of being naturally blonde and appeared with platinum hair. After the police version of Perry's coded document appeared on the web, a reporter had unearthed her in Devon. She brazened it out with the help of a publicist who kept her away from television and radio – they had to make do with amateur videos of her – and ensured that anything printed was more public relations than independent journalism. It would appear she has given up on winning back her parents. The image cultivated was of a woman comfortable with modern sexual mores whom others had targeted because she had done things that many men do without attracting such attention. Then came the softest of interviews on a chat show. Ariadne acknowledged, while complaining about double standards, a five-month affair with Councillor Chuttick and a briefer one with Jonathon Dunwich. Mr Vitriol's unfavourable portrayal of her stemmed, she claimed, from his infatuation and her refusal to go out with him. If he half of what he wrote about her is true, the latter is improbable. Perry was no masochist, so why would he want the company of someone who disliked him from the outset?

However, the reviews of the chat show appearance were unanimous; Ariadne looked good for a forty year-old and spoke up for women. No one discussed whether her version of events was less credible than Perry's.

I was curious enough about Ariadne to watch *Sex and the Noughties Woman*. It appeared she had undergone voice coaching because the cut-glass accent heard earlier was less pronounced and she sounded husky. Her introductory piece presented her views on *flings*, which were no less liberal than her exposure of cleavage and made no pretence at rational argument.

"If God had wanted us to be prudes he wouldn't have made sex so enjoyable," pretty well represents the standard.

She introduced a female guest who had directed a pornography video for heterosexual women and a man whose chief claim to fame was the extent to which his body had patterns created by branding and scarification. There were short prurient films on ways of rating the strength of female orgasms, vibrators and related devices that another person can control remotely, and polyandry. The clips were divided by shallow chatter. Before the frequent commercial breaks, Ariadne offered a weak gag, such as, "At least if you have only one man in the house, you know who has peed on the toilet seat."

The last part began with a film about two women in their thirties. They commented on their experiences of giving up same sex relationships and becoming traditional spouses. They then joined Ariadne and the two other guests in a debate, using the word in its loosest sense, on why some women who had no hang-ups about having a lesbian partner become exclusively heterosexual. Ariadne lost the plot and started talking about what she called *predatory women* being good for marriage because it kept wives from taking their husbands for granted. The former lesbians blinked their astonishment at the way the subject had changed. By the time they had recovered, Ariadne was promoting a philosophy that boils down to, *If men are sexually greedy, women have the right to act in the same way.* Then the audience clapped, credits ran and raunchy music played.

With a publicist and her willingness to titillate, Ariadne will continue to make a living through media appearances. She need never return to selling real estate for at least as long as her looks last. In one way, I envy her. She may be a tinselly star on that low ceiling populated by minor celebrities, but she is recorded. As channels proliferate and audiences and budgets shrink, repeats of her cheap blether will fill screens for years to come and will be available to researchers long after she is dead.

I lack her brassy courage in facing the world via video. Thank goodness no one revealed to the media that I had transcribed Perry. Confronted by a television camera, my awkwardness would have overtaken that of the Watford pair. I could have filmed myself at home talking about Perry and deleted the more gauche moments with the editing software on my PC, but vanity prevented this. In any case, my looks would only distract and writing is my stronger suit.

Ariadne unwittingly sparked one welcome idea. Rose shone on video camera, as she did everywhere. I realise now that writing alone cannot do her justice. By editing some of the home videos in which she features and adding them to the disc that will hold the chapters by Perry and me, people who never met her will have more sense of how special she was. Preparing the video will not take long because, soon after the funeral I compiled a DVD with footage of Rose. I have seen it often enough to know where to find the best moments.

We know about monarchs, generals and politicians from the past because they made key decisions and rallying calls. And characters like Perry feature in the collective memory because of their freakishness. But history overlooks a woman like Rose with her myriad small acts of kindness in much the same way that I failed to appreciate her until it was too late to say thank you for all that she had done for me.

Neither book nor video can capture the frequency or cumulative significance of her giving. Yet the five minutes of clips will show the warmth in Rose's face, how her eyes are full of intelligence, and the grace of her movement. People will hear the voice and laughter and wonder, as I often did, what she ever saw in me. Looks aside, I was not a bad man. Yet the gap that existed between the richness of her humanity and my selfishness is at least as vast as the divide between my standards and Perry's.

Perry was so right and so wrong. The problems of bullying persist and repeated small hurts are very damaging to well-being. However, his responses are unacceptable and his thoughts on justice flawed. He avoided direct violence, but should have known from his own experience how very painful words can be. His attempt to justify injuries to relatives of his targets by citing the iniquity of collateral bomb damage or police brutality is sophism.

Perry rants that he is no sophist. Sorry, Perry. This is my final piece and I alone will write it. You did not always use the further opportunities that I offered you to expand your views. Now I have no plans to debate further.

He calls me ungrateful and threatens to make the rest of my life a misery.

Do your worst, Perry, but be quick. I only have this chapter to finish, an hour to make discs, and letters to post.

I still am grateful for some of his ideas and the times he helped me. I would prefer to die with him as my friend, but not if it means censoring. His stimulus to write meant that I needed fewer painkillers and had a head clear enough with which to think. And the levels of energy that emerged came as a surprise. But I will not surrender the last words to him.

My preference is to die in the manner of my choosing at home; not in an ambulance, a hospital or hospice. Death has accompanied me all through my life. The fear of lightning existed before I could talk and by the time I could it was a reminder of how fragile people are. After my parents related what had happened to the Nutwands, I often thought about how easily I could have been in my grandparent's house when the flying bomb fell. For the first fourteen years, the idea of heaven and reunion with loved ones took away some of death's sting. Then the accident that killed my father shattered religious illusions.

Following his funeral, I continued to think of his metaphor of life as a walk up a mountain until one slips. Yet without a god, there could be no angels to catch the falling and carry them to heaven. At Gatgash, fingernails were all that saved me. Until I met Rose, it still felt that one foot always trod on the crumbling brink. Then she held my hand and encouraged me to look away from the drop. That is the way life is; if you are lucky sometimes the views to the more solid side are pleasant or demands on our attention help us to forget the few inches that separate us from annihilation.

On life's trail, beasts stumble over the edge through clumsiness, plummet from illness or exhaustion, collapse from old age or fall to predators. For a human being with an intact brain and no blinkering beliefs, there is another way to go. I choose to leap a month or so before the void rises up to meet me. Like Perry was before his second coming, I am prepared.

Just before I start swallowing pills, I will put on the compilation video. Images of Rose and her voice will be with me as I begin to feel woozy and as I slip into unconsciousness. She will continue to smile, laugh and joke after I am dead.

Acknowledgements

Thanks to those who encouraged my writing through an earlier novel. Without your support I would not have attempted this book.

I owe much to tutors on two courses in London that dealt with writing novels, Neil Fergusson at The City Lit and Alison Burns and Emily Pedder at City University. Students on these courses also taught me much and provided great feedback.

Writers' Block, a self-facilitating writing group has also provided support, ideas and critique.

Ian Conrich proved invaluable for spotting my inconsistencies and made a number of suggestions that helped improve the novel.

The advice often given is not to share what you are writing with those closest to you because it will be unhelpful. My partner, Sue Crofton, proves that there are delightful exceptions. She has seen my work at early stages and been prepared to proofread several drafts and offer comments.

Thanks to the British Library and the National Army Museum and Imperial War Museum for use of their facilities. Many accounts and anecdotes posted on the Internet by former National Servicemen were very helpful.

The majority of National Serviceman appear to report good experiences. I am pleased for those who can look back with fondness at days of camaraderie and firm but fair NCOs and officers. As well as this being better for recruits, units with such leadership are less likely to be involved in war crimes and conspiracies to cover up acts that shame the UK and its armed forces.

Lightning Source UK Ltd.
Milton Keynes UK
UKOW051716070712

195629UK00001B/21/P

9 781781 765012